THE
SERPENT SEA

THE
SERPENT SEA

MARTHA WELLS

NIGHT SHADE BOOKS
NEW YORK

Cover art by Steve Argyle
Cover design by Claudia Noble

Edited by Janna Silverstein

Printed in China

To Janna Silverstein

CHAPTER ONE

Moon had been consort to Jade, sister queen of the Indigo Cloud Court, for eleven days and nobody had tried to kill him yet. He thought it was going well so far.

On the twelfth day, the dawn sun was just breaking through the clouds when he walked out onto the deck of the *Valendera*. The air was damp and pleasantly cool, filled with the scent of the dense green forest the ship flew over. It was early enough that sleeping bodies still crowded the deck, most of them buried under blankets or piled up against the baskets and bags that held all the court's belongings. A few people stirred somewhere toward the bow, where the look-outs were posted. On the central mast, the fan-shaped sails were still closed. Their companion ship, the *Indala*, floated a short distance off the starboard side, pacing them.

Moon heard someone stumble up the narrow stairs from below decks. Then Chime climbed out of the hatch and squinted at the dawn light. He said, "Oh good. Another nice day to spend on this flying torture device."

Moon had been having variations on this conversation for days. Raksura weren't meant to live on flying boats—that had been very well established by everybody—but there was no other way to move the court to the new colony.

Indigo Cloud had been in decline for a long time before Moon had arrived, with outbreaks of disease, attacks by predators, and the Fell influence that had caused fewer warrior births. When the Fell attack had forced them to finally abandon the old colony, there hadn't been enough warriors to move the court in the normal way. Everyone knew they had been lucky to convince a Golden Islander trading family to let them pay for the use of the two flying boats. But while the *Valendera* was over two hundred paces long and the *Indala* only a little smaller, there just wasn't enough room to do much of anything but sleep or sit. The situation was the worst for the wingless Arbora, who were used to spending their days hunting, tending their gardens, or in carving, weaving, or working metal. When the Aeriat were sick of the cramped quarters, they could always go flying.

Moon said, "Do you need me to say anything or do you just want me to stand here?"

"Yes, yes, I know, I know." Chime rubbed his eyes and glared at the lightening sky. Moon and Chime were both Aeriat Raksura, but Chime was a warrior and Moon was a consort. In their groundling forms there wasn't much difference between them; they were both tall and lean, both had the dark bronze skin common to many Raksura. Moon had dark hair and green eyes, and was used to blending in with real groundlings. Chime had fluffy, straw-colored hair, and had never had to live outside the close-knit court, though he had his own unique problem to deal with. Chime added, "I just can't wait until we get to the Reaches. I've read all the old histories, but actually seeing it . . . Stone says we're nearly there."

Stone had been saying they were nearly there for three days, but Stone's idea of "nearly" was different than anyone else's. Moon just lifted a brow. Chime sighed, and said, "Yes, I know."

They stood there a moment while Chime continued to grumble and Moon just enjoyed the predawn quiet. All everyone wanted to talk about, when they weren't complaining about the conditions on the boats, was how excited they were to be going to the new colony. Courts didn't move very often; Stone was the only one who could remember the last time Indigo Cloud had moved, turns and turns before any of the others had been born. But Moon had never looked at any place with the idea of living there forever. It was daunting, and he couldn't even pretend to share everyone's enthusiasm.

Moon felt something watching him, something not friendly. He looked toward the *Indala* and saw River, Drift, and two other warriors crouched along the railing, staring at him and Chime. They were all in Raksuran form, River's green scales catching the morning light and reflecting their blue undersheen. River twitched his mane of spines and frills, a not-quite-deliberate challenge.

Now that Moon was Jade's consort, River's place as the lover of Pearl, the reigning queen, was safe. But it didn't mean they were friends now.

Instead of hissing, Moon yawned, stretched extravagantly, and tried to look like a tempting target. A fight with a half-Fell half-Raksuran queen had left him with broken bones, but Raksura healed fast, and he was mostly recovered now. Though he was still a little stiff, especially in the mornings. A couple of days ago the mentors had all agreed that he was well enough to be up and around, and had given him his clothes back. The dark shirt and pants he had borrowed when he had first arrived at the colony were a little the worse for wear but cleaned of dirt and dried blood. Since then he had shifted a few times, and had done some easy flying around the boats, but nothing more strenuous yet. Beating River senseless and throwing him off the *Indala* would be a good test to see just how healthy Moon was.

But River didn't take the bait, just lashed his tail in contempt and looked away.

"What are they looking at?" Chime said, but he faced toward the *Valendera*'s bow, and hadn't noticed River and his cronies. Halfway down the deck, Bone, the chief of the Arbora's hunter caste, and several other Arbora stood at the railing and stared down at something. Chime picked his way across the deck, stepping around the sleeping bodies. Any diversion being welcome, Moon followed him.

All the Arbora were shorter than the Aeriat and more heavily built in their groundling forms. Bone, despite the age revealed by his white hair and the ashy cast to his bronze-brown skin, was still heavily muscled and strong. He had a ridge of old scar tissue circling his neck, where something with big teeth had nearly bitten his head off.

Moon leaned on the railing next to him. All the Arbora tasted the air, their expressions intent. "What is it?"

Bone nudged him with an elbow and pointed. "There."

They had been flying over increasingly dense forest for several days, the trees rising and falling in waves of vivid green fifty or so paces below the wooden hulls of the ships. Now a big shallow lake was just coming into view over the gently waving tops of the plume trees. A large herd of furry grasseaters grazed there, eating the reeds and flowering plants that grew in the water. Moon's stomach growled; they had been able to hunt sporadically along the way, but for most of the trip they had been living off dwindling stores of salted meat, dried fruit, and wilting roots. And it felt like forever since he had been able to hunt.

The hard line of Bone's mouth quirked in a smile. "I think everyone could do with a little fresh meat."

One of the other Arbora snorted at the depth of that understatement.

Moon caught hold of the railing and slung himself up to crouch on it. He said, "Tell the others." He leapt away from the boat, shifted to Raksuran form in midair and caught the wind.

☾

Moon flew a long slow circle over the lake, playing the cool morning wind against his wings, to stretch his muscles and make certain he was well enough to stoop and dive. He didn't want to be the first to fall on the herd, meaning to leave it to one of the others.

He had been a child the last time he had lived with his own people, so young he hadn't known what they were called or where they came from. And this was the first time in his travels through the Three Worlds that he had even lived with other shifters. He hadn't known anything about Raksura, and he hadn't known he was a consort, the only fertile male Aeriat, born to be mated to a queen and to produce royal clutches and infertile warriors for the court. He had a great deal of experience trying to fit into various groundling tribes and settlements, just in search of a place to live. But trying to fit into a group where he actually belonged, and had an important role, was . . . still daunting. He nursed a lingering fear that he was somehow going to wreck it and get thrown out of the court. It wasn't that odd a notion; he had gotten thrown out of a lot of places for various reasons.

By the time Moon had circled the lake twice, the decision had evidently been made to stop for a full-scale hunt. The two boats slowed to a crawl, then dropped lines. Arbora climbed down to tie them off to tall plume trees. All the Aeriat took the opportunity to jump off the boats and fly over the lake.

Aeriat didn't normally hunt for themselves unless they were traveling away from the colony; that was left to the Arbora hunters. Judging by everyone's enthusiastic response, this definitely counted as traveling away from the colony. They circled above the lake, their scales in shades of blue, green, gold, brown, and copper-red. They all had retractable claws on hands and feet, long tails with a spade shape on the end, and manes of spines and frills down their backs. Moon was the only one here with black scales, the color that marked him as a consort, though he had a faint undersheen of bronze that caught the morning light.

The Arbora's shifted forms looked much like the Aeriat, except they didn't have wings. They climbed down from the boats on rope ladders so they could butcher the kills on the grassy shore above the lake. Normally this was a task reserved for the hunters, but Moon could see Arbora who were members of the other three castes joining in; teachers, soldiers, even a couple of young mentors, Heart and Merit, leapt enthusiastically into the job. Just another sign that the long trip and confined quarters had worn on everyone.

Another group of Arbora went after some of the grasseaters that had retreated into the trees, and the younger ones dug through the shallows for clusters of edible roots. It was just as well all the work could be done on the ground; early on in the journey, Niran, the groundling whose family owned both flying ships, had put his foot down about butchering kills on the ships' decks. Moon could see his point; nearly all the woodwork, from planks to railings to masts, was now scored with claw marks, and would need to be sanded down eventually.

Three warriors wheeled and dove on the herd, and the hunt was on. Moon found Chime, still a novice at hunting, and made sure he managed his first kill successfully. Then Moon took a small buck for himself. Like all the Aeriat, they dragged the carcasses off into the reeds to eat immediately; the second kill would be for the colony. They met Song, a young female warrior with coppery scales, already there eating her kill. "This was a fantastic idea," she said between bites.

After he finished eating, Moon left Chime with Song and swam out into the lake to wash the blood off his scales, then took a second kill to haul back for the Arbora. After he dragged the carcass up onto a sandbar to bleed it, he scanned the sky to see where the others were. Most of the Aeriat were finished, though Chime and a few others still circled above the lake looking for prey. The herd had all moved off now, either further down the shore or into the trees.

A flash of vivid blue made him glance up, but it wasn't Chime coming in for another pass. Jade cupped her wings and dropped down toward the sandbar.

She was the sister queen of the Indigo Cloud Court, and like all Raksuran queens, she had no groundling form. She could shift only between her winged form and a wingless shape that looked more like an Arbora. Her scales were blue, with a silver-gray web pattern. Behind her head, the frills and spines formed an elaborate mane, reaching all the way down her back to her tail.

She landed neatly, her claws digging into the sand. Folding her wings, she picked her way through the lilies toward Moon. He shifted for her, though he was still standing in the water and it soaked his pants to the knees. His groundling skin was more sensitive and he liked to feel her scales against it.

She caught him around the waist, and he relaxed against her. Her teeth grazed his neck in affectionate greeting, and she asked, "Did you have any trouble flying?"

"No, my shoulder's fine." He was a little sore, but it was the welcome ache of unused muscles finally being pushed to work. He nuzzled her neck. "My back's fine, too."

"I'm tempted to find out for myself." Jade's growl had a warm tone to it. She rubbed her cheek against his. "But we can't afford the time."

The grassy bank was very tempting, but she was right; they had to get the ships moving again. They hadn't had much chance to be together onboard, between the crowding and Moon recovering from his broken wing. But now that Indigo Cloud had adopted a fledgling queen and two consorts from the destroyed Sky Copper court, it wasn't quite so urgent that Jade get a clutch immediately.

Song, Root, and Chime banked down to circle overhead, and called to them that it was time to leave.

☾

Later that afternoon, Moon woke when a strong cool gust cut across the flat roof of the *Valendera*'s steering cabin. It carried the clean scent of rain, but with a bitter undertone that meant thunder and lightning, and the force of it made the wooden craft creak and rattle.

Moon pushed up on one elbow for a better taste of the air. At the moment that was harder than it sounded. He was nestled between Jade and Chime, with Song, Root, and a few other warriors curled up around them. Jade had an arm and her tail wrapped around Moon's waist and he was warm and comfortable from the sun-warmed wood and the heat of friendly bodies. He had to wriggle to sit up enough to look out over the wooden boat's stern. What he saw made him wince. *That's a problem.*

In the distance, just above the forest's green horizon, a dark mass of storm built, reaching out toward them with gray streaks of cloud. On their journey so far, they had gone through a few days with rain, but no high winds or lightning. It looked like their luck was over.

Jade stirred sleepily, disturbed by his movement. Sounding reluctant to wake, she murmured, "What is it?" After the indulgence of the hunt this morning, most of the court were spending the day napping. Many had fed to the point where they wouldn't need to eat again for two or three days.

Moon squeezed Jade's wrist. "There's a storm to the north."

"What?" She sat up, shouldered the others over enough that Root and another young male warrior rolled right off the cabin roof. She spotted the storm and frowned, then slapped her hand on the planks, making a loud hollow thump. "Niran! Come out here, please."

Niran's voice came from somewhere below. "What now?" He sounded angry, but that was normal for Niran. He was the only groundling aboard, a grandson of the Golden Islander family who had traded them the use of the two flying boats. It had been Niran's grandfather, Delin, who had wanted to help them. Niran had distrusted the Raksura intensely, but had volunteered to stay and try to protect the valuable ships when the Fell had forced Delin and the other Islanders to flee. Forced proximity and shared danger had made Niran trust them, but it hadn't made his personality any less prickly.

Niran came out of the cabin, a figure as short as the Arbora, but slim and with golden skin and eyes. His long straight white hair was tied back with a patterned scarf and starting to look dingy. It was hard to bathe on the boat, especially for those who couldn't just fly down for a swim in a pond. He was dressed in a heavy robe, borrowed from one of the

Arbora, and clutched a pottery mug. "What is it now?" he demanded again.

"There's a storm coming," Jade told him, and pointed.

Niran squinted in that direction. Groundling eyes weren't as keen as Raksuran and he probably couldn't see the cloud formation. "Oh for the love of the Ancestors, that's all we need," he muttered, turned, and stamped back inside the cabin.

"The boats can't outrun it, I suppose," Jade said, still frowning.

"I doubt it," Moon told her. The power to keep the ships aloft and moving came from the tiny fragment of sky-island, kept in the ship's steering apparatus, that let them ride the lines of force that stretched across the Three Worlds. Their progress was steady, but not very fast, and a storm-wind would tear the sails apart. Moon sat up all the way and nudged Chime over. "I think we'll have to stop and winch them down to the ground."

Chime twitched awake and sat up, blinking. "Winch what to the— Oh." He stared uneasily at the approaching clouds. "That's not good. What do we do?"

"Don't panic," Jade said. The others were blearily awake now, looking into the wind. She prodded Song with her foot. "Song, go and find Pearl."

Song nodded and pushed to her feet. She shifted and jumped off the cabin roof, to land on the railing and leap again, taking flight toward the *Indala*. Pearl was the reigning queen, and Jade's mother, and while the situation between them was better than it had been, there were still ripples of tension. Since Moon had caused one big wave of tension by becoming Jade's consort and not Pearl's, it was a relief that Pearl had decided to spend much of her time on the other ship.

"I wasn't panicking," Chime said with dignity. He drew his legs up, wrapped his arms around his knees. "I just never liked storms, even in the colony. Do you know what happens if lightning hits you?"

Jade didn't bother to answer that. Most of the Raksura, especially the Arbora, would be used to weathering storms safe inside a colony, not in the air on a fragile flying boat. Moon wasn't happy about it either. Thunderstorms made him edgy. The day after his family had been killed, he had been caught in one, huddled high in the branches of a too-small tree. The Tath had still been hunting him so he couldn't chance climbing any lower, and the storm had grown in intensity all day, as if it meant to tear the whole forest apart.

At least he wasn't going to have to face this one alone.

Niran came out of the cabin again, dressed now in the clothes Islanders usually wore on their boats: white pants cropped at the knee and a loose shirt belted at the waist. He held a copper spyglass up to one eye, twisting the lenses to focus on the storm. He said, "We need to find a place to shelter, and we'll have to lower both ships to the ground and tie them off— Wait, what's that?"

A dark shape flew toward them out of the gray clouds. Moon squinted to identify it. "That's Stone."

Stone was the line-grandfather, the only other adult consort in the Indigo Cloud Court, the oldest person Moon had ever met, as far as he knew. Queens and consorts grew larger and stronger as they grew older, so Stone's shifted form was nearly four times Moon's size.

Consorts were already the fastest flyers among Raksura, so fast only queens could keep up with them. Stone's approach was at nearly full speed, and he reached the ship in only a few moments. He cupped his wings to slow down at almost the last instant, then dropped down onto the stern deck. The ship dipped under his weight and Niran grabbed the railing to steady himself, cursing in the Islander language.

Stone shifted to his groundling form, and the boat righted. He caught hold of the edge of the cabin roof and slung himself up onto it, as the last two warriors scrambled away and jumped down to make room for him. He sat down on the planks, a tall lean man, his face lined and weathered, dressed in a gray shirt and pants. Everything about him had faded to gray, his hair, his skin, something that happened to the groundling forms of the oldest Raksura. The only spot of color was in his blue eyes, though the right one was dimmed and clouded. He jerked his chin toward the streaked sky. "You noticed?"

"Yes." Jade settled her spines, which had bristled involuntarily at Stone's rapid approach. "Niran says we'll need to stop and lower both boats to the ground."

"If we can find the ground," Chime put in. "The forest has been getting deeper and there aren't that many breaks in the canopy."

"If we don't lower the ships, the high winds will surely tear them apart," Niran added, apparently braced for an argument.

Stone conceded that with a nod, but said, "We're nearly to the new colony. We should make it before the storm reaches us."

Startled, Chime said, "What? Really?"

Jade gave Stone a hard stare. "Are you certain?"

Stone shrugged. "Sure."

Annoyed, Jade tapped her claws on the roof. "Were you going to share this information with anyone else?"

"Eventually." Stone looked toward the bow and the endless sweep of the forest, as if gauging the distance. "I wasn't sure until today. We've been making better time than I thought we would."

Jade looked down at Niran. "Well?"

Niran set his jaw, but after a moment he said, "Very well. If you want to risk it." Then he added grudgingly, "Chime is right. The forest beneath us seems too thick for a good landing spot. We'd have to search for a clearing anyway."

Jade disentangled herself from Moon and pushed to her feet. She shook her frills out and shifted to her winged form. Moon rolled onto his back, just admiring her. She smiled down at him. "I'd better let Pearl know we're nearly there, too."

Jade leapt straight up, snapped her wings out to catch the air, then glided over to the *Indala*.

"I'll find Flower," Chime said, and threw a nervous look back at the distant clouds. He shifted to jump down to the deck.

Moon stretched out, taking advantage of having the roof nearly to himself, basking in the sun before the clouds covered it. Stone still sat on the edge, looking out over the mist-wreathed forest, his expression preoccupied. "So what's this place like?" Moon asked him.

"A tree."

Moon swore under his breath. He had gotten that much from everybody else. They were all very enthusiastic about it, but nobody had been able to say how much work they were going to have to do to make it habitable. "Fine, don't tell me."

Stone snorted. "I just told you. A tree."

Moon rolled onto his stomach, pillowed his head on his arms, and pretended to go to sleep, one of the only effective ways of dealing with Stone when he was in such a mood. He had been hoping for something not much different from the ruin where the court had lived before, except more defensible. He had lived in trees, and they weren't comfortable. And he had seen how fast the Arbora could build temporary shelters, but they would have no time to do that before the rain hit.

He heard the wood creak as Stone moved around and stretched out on the other half of the roof. Then Stone said, "It's a mountain-tree, the place our court originally came from."

Moon opened his eyes a slit to see Stone lying on his back with one arm flung over his eyes. *A mountain-tree.* Moon turned the words over, searching for familiarity, hoping it stirred his memory. For all he knew, he had lived in one as a child, but he didn't remember it. "I don't know what that is."

Stone's voice was dry. "You will before nightfall."

☾

Moon was standing on the deck when Flower told Jade and Pearl, "I don't need to augur to know we need to get to shelter." She waved a hand toward the approaching storm. She was small even for an Arbora, her white-blonde hair wild as usual, and after the long journey her loose red smock was even more ragged. She was the oldest Arbora in the court, and age had leached the color from her skin so she looked far more delicate than she actually was. She was also the chief of the mentor caste, the Arbora who were shamen, augurs, and healers. "We'll have to go below the tree canopy anyway, so Stone's right: we might as well try to reach the new colony."

Pearl's tail lashed, though whether she was angry at the storm or angry at Flower, or just angry in general, it was hard to tell. Her scales were brilliant gold, the webbed pattern overlaying them a deep blue. The frilled mane behind her head was bigger than Jade's, and there were more frills on the tips of her folded wings and on the end of her tail. A head taller than any of the Aeriat, she wore only jewelry, a broad necklace with gold chains and polished blue stones. She said, "I could have gotten that advice from a fledgling."

Jade's spines twitched with the effort to keep silent, but she had been trying hard to get along with Pearl. Moon hoped she could last until they reached the colony. Flower, who was better at dealing with Pearl, said dryly, "Then next time, ask a fledgling."

That had been in the late afternoon, and it was the edge of twilight now. Thunder rumbled continuously, the sky dark gray with clouds and the cool wind heavily scented with rain. The Arbora and Aeriat crowded around on the deck, waiting with nervous impatience, most of them in groundling form to conserve their strength. Moon, by virtue of being a consort, had a place along the railing. He stood next to Chime and Knell, who was leader of the Arbora caste of soldiers.

Knell scratched his shoulder through his shirt, grimacing. He had been wounded in the Fell attack on the colony, the attack that had killed many of the other soldiers, and had new claw scars all down his chest. He said, "I hope Blossom knows what she's doing."

Blossom was the teacher who steered the *Indala*, on Niran's instructions. Chime stirred uneasily, but said, "She's done fine so far."

"She hasn't had to do anything so far." Knell threw him a sour look. "Except go forward and stop."

Knell was Chime's clutchmate, along with Bell, the new leader of the teacher caste. Neither looked much like Chime, Knell and Bell both having dark hair in their groundling forms and being more brown than bronze, though they were both tall for Arbora. It wasn't unusual for Arbora clutches to produce one or two Aeriat warriors, something that the mentors attributed to generations of Arbora breeding with queens and consorts. It was unusual that Chime had been born an Arbora mentor, not an Aeriat warrior.

Sometime a turn or so ago, long before Moon had come to the court, Chime had shifted and turned into a warrior. Flower and the other mentors believed it was because of the pressure on the colony from disease and warfare, and the lack of warrior births. Unlike Arbora, warriors were infertile, and could also travel longer distances to find food. Chime had been horrified by the change, and from what Moon could tell, still wasn't that reconciled to it.

"All right," Chime said to Knell, annoyed. "Both boats will crash and we'll all die. Are you happy now?"

"We'd better do it soon then, before the storm kills us," Knell told him.

Suddenly I see the resemblance, Moon thought, carefully not smiling. Knell was right about the storm, though. Moon could already feel the presence of lightning somewhere nearby, as a tingle on his skin.

From the forest below, Stone flew up through a gap in the canopy, his wings knocking aside branches and leaves. He shot up past them, circled back, then dove back down through the gap.

From the bow, Jade shouted back to Niran. "We need to follow him down!"

Niran, standing in front of the steering cabin, looked horrified. Thunder rumbled again, reminding everyone that they didn't have a choice.

The *Valendera* went first. It carefully maneuvered down through the narrow gap in the canopy, while Arbora hung off the sides to give directions to Niran. The ship sank past layers of branches that scraped at the hull and the railings, and scattered leaves and twigs across the deck. Finally they moved down into green shadows, as the wind died away to a cool, damp, sweet-scented breeze. The lower branches of the trees grew lush flowers in blues and purples that wound down the dark gray trunks. There was far more room under the canopy than Moon had expected, a vast green space. The flying boats could sail around down here easily. Niran eased the *Valendera* forward, gliding between the trunks, leaving room for the *Indala* to follow it down.

Moon leaned over the railing and tried to see the ground, but it was hundreds of paces down, lost in the shadows. Not far below the ship he could see platforms covered with greenery standing out from the trees and completely encircling the trunks, connecting the trees to each other in a web, many more than large enough for the *Valendera* to set down on. They looked like tethered chunks of sky-island, covered with grass and flowers, dripping with vines, most supporting glades of smaller trees. But as the ship drifted closer to one, he saw the platforms were thick branches that had grown together and intertwined in broad swathes, catching windblown dirt and seeds until they built up into solid ground.

Everyone was quiet, just taking it in. "These are mountain-trees," Chime said softly, as he leaned out over the rail. "The platforms are the suspended forest. I read about this a long time ago, but I never thought I'd see it."

Once the *Indala* had safely lowered down to join them, Niran came out of the cabin to look up at the tree canopy critically. "We should be safe enough if we can tie off somewhere down here."

Knell nodded, looking up. "We're going to get wet, though." High overhead, the heavy wind bent the treetops and rushed through the leaves as rain fell in fitful gusts.

Stone caused a mild sensation by climbing down through the upper branches and dropping down onto the deck. Arbora and Aeriat scrambled out of his way, and the ship rocked under his weight before he shifted back to groundling. The rainwater that had already collected on his scales splashed down onto the boards to form a pool around him, and his hair and clothes were soaked. Not seeming to notice, he pointed off between the giant trees. "That way."

Niran turned to him, frowning. "Is it far? If the wind rises too much, we could still be driven into a tree."

"It's not far, and it's better shelter than this," Stone told him. "If you think it's getting too dangerous, we can stop."

Niran looked up at the treetops again to gauge the strength of the wind. He didn't look entirely happy, but he nodded. "Very well."

Stone headed toward the bow, where Jade and Pearl waited. Niran threw a thoughtful look at Moon. "It surprises me that he listens to my objections."

Stone was used to taking advice from the Arbora, and he had traveled further and dealt with more different peoples than anyone else in the court, even Moon. It had been Stone's idea to go to the Yellow Sea to trade with the Islanders for the use of their boats. But Moon only said, "He likes groundlings."

With a skeptical shake of his head, Niran went back to the steering cabin.

As the *Valendera* began to move again, Moon left the railing and followed Stone toward the bow, making his way through the Arbora and Aeriat. They crowded along the railings, clung to the mast, perched on every available space that gave a view. The fear of being caught in the storm had given way to excitement and anticipation, and uneasiness, since not everyone was as sure of their situation as Stone. Moon couldn't imagine the confidence it took to bring these people all this way, to live in a new place that only you had seen. Not that they had anywhere to go back to if they didn't like it, but still.

Jade stood against the railing in the bow with Flower. Pearl was there with River, Drift, Vine, Floret, and some other warriors. River flicked a resentful look at Moon, but even he was too preoccupied to provoke a fight.

Moon stepped up to the railing next to Jade, and she absently put an arm around his waist. He leaned against her, trying not to feel self-conscious in front of Pearl.

It grew darker, the green-tinted sunlight muted as clouds closed in high above the treetops. The drizzle turned into a light rain that pattered on the deck. The platforms of the suspended forest grew wider and more extensive. Many of them overlapped, or were connected by broad branches, with ponds or streams. Waterfalls fell from holes in some of the mountain-sized trees. Moon wondered if the water was drawn up from the forest floor through the roots. It was like a whole multi-layered second forest hanging between the tree canopy and the ground, somewhere far below.

Then the trunks of the mountain-trees fell away, though the canopy overhead seemed even thicker. Moon realized they were sailing toward a shadowy shape directly ahead, a single great tree.

Jade looked back at Stone. There was tension in her voice as she asked, "Is that it?"

He nodded. There were nervous murmurs from the others, a shiver of movement that reverberated back through the crowded deck.

The multiple layers of branches reached up like giants' arms, and the trunk was enormous, wider around than the base of the ruined step pyramid that had formed the old Indigo Cloud colony. From the lower part of the trunk, greenery platforms extended out, multiple levels of them, some more than five hundred paces across. A waterfall fell out of a knothole nearly big enough to sail the *Valendera* through, plunged down to collect in a pool on one of the platforms, then fell to the next, and the next, until it disappeared into the shadows below.

The platforms held only flowers, mossy grass, and stands of smaller trees, but many showed signs of once being worked into beds for crops, with the remnants of raised areas for planting and dry ponds and channels that must have been for irrigation.

Everyone was silent. Then Pearl twitched and settled her spines. She said, "Stone, lead us in."

The warriors moved back, and Stone took two long steps forward, caught hold of the railing, and vaulted it. He shifted in midair, his big form momentarily blotting out the view of the tree as he snapped his wings out.

Pearl hissed a command and went over the railing. The warriors followed, and Vine paused to pick up Flower. Moon leapt after Jade.

They flew through the light rain, and Stone led the way toward the huge knothole, which was more than big enough for him to comfortably land in. He moved further in, around the edge of the pool, and shifted to groundling. Moon landed beside him, folded his wings, and turned to look around. Jade and the others landed, and Vine set Flower on her feet. Chime and a few other Aeriat caught up with them a moment later.

In the cavernous space, folds of the trunk formed multiple nooks and chambers, extending back into the interior until the green-gray light failed. The pool, partly choked with weeds and moss, wound back away into the depths. The water fell over the edge of the opening, the sound as it struck the pond below so faint it was lost in the rain. Lush green vines wound over the walls, but Moon could see carvings in the smooth wood: serpentine shapes, claws, a pointed wingtip, like the images on the metal vessels and jewelry the Arbora made.

Stone walked beside the pool toward the back of the chamber. No one seemed to want to break the silence. Moon glanced back and saw River touch Pearl's arm, pointing to something on the floor. He looked down and saw small squares set into the wood, something with a faint shine like mother of pearl, white shading to green and pink, glittering in the dim light. They were set all along the rim of the pool, scattered over the floor.

There was a doorway ahead, round and ringed with carvings. Stone stepped through, Jade and Pearl followed him, and the others trailed after.

Moon paused to taste the air, but there was nothing but the musky-sweet scent of the tree itself, and the earthy smells of dirt and dead leaves and water. Whether he liked it or not, this would be their permanent home, he reminded himself. He took a deep breath, told himself to stop worrying, and followed the others.

Light shone ahead in the entry passage, and he found a disk set into the wall, a curving, graceful shell-shape, like something that would wash up on a beach. It glowed now with the soft, heatless light of magic. Flower must be renewing the spells on them as she went by. It was enough to show that the passage narrowed to only a few paces across and wound through several switchbacks, probably for defense. Major kethel, the largest breed of Fell, couldn't get through here at all without shifting to groundling form. Even minor dakti, the smallest Fell, would have to come through a few at a time; an attempt to swarm would probably leave them jammed up in one of these tight turns, and the whole passage could be easily blocked or defended from the inside. And if there were multiple exits, hidden in the folds of the trunk, it would be near impossible to trap the inhabitants inside. *And that canopy, nothing could dive through that without knowing where the openings are.*

Right at the point where Moon was wondering if the whole place was a maze, the passage widened out again and he heard water falling.

He stepped out into another cavernous chamber. Two glowing shells were already lit and Flower was just touching a third, its light blooming to catch reflections off walls so smooth they seemed lacquered. Two open stairways spiraled up the far wall, with slim pillars widely spaced along the steps. They criss-crossed and led up to balconies, higher levels with round doorways. Directly across from the entrance, just below the first cross of the stairways, there was an opening with water falling out of it, streaming down the wall to a pool in the floor. There wasn't any open channel leading away, but this could be the source for the water flow in the outer knothole.

The others moved around, staring, exclaiming softly. Stone said, "This is the opening hall, for gathering, for greeting."

Jade turned to take it in. "The court must have been huge."

Chime went to the nearest stair and ran his hand down one slim pillar, marveling at it. "Did they carve it all out?"

"No." Stone stood in the center, his face tilted up to the central well. "The Arbora made it grow like this."

Everyone looked around again, as if trying to picture it. Flower shook her head, regretful, awed. "There's much we've forgotten."

Moon moved to Stone's side and looked up. The well wound up through the tree in a big spiral to vanish into darkness. It was like the central well of the step pyramid that had held the last colony, only much larger and far more impressive. He wondered if the slight resemblance was why the Raksura had chosen the ruin.

Stone nodded toward a stair spiraling down the wall. "That leads down to the nurseries and the teachers' bowers. We should be able to fit most of the court in there, at least for tonight."

"One section of bowers big enough to fit all of us?" Chime muttered. "I don't know whether it means our court is too small or this one was too big."

"A little of both, maybe," Floret said, looking up at the well.

"This was our court." Stone's voice was quiet, but everyone went suddenly still. "You're all descended from the Raksura who lived here."

Except me, Moon thought. He had found Indigo Cloud intimidating enough when it had been installed at the small colony. Trying to imagine this place populated with hundreds of Raksura made his nerves twitch.

Thunder rumbled outside, and Moon flinched, then settled his spines to hide it.

"We need to get the others in, and tie off the boats," Jade said to Pearl.

Pearl flicked her spines in acknowledgement, but for once she seemed more excited than annoyed. She turned to the warriors. "Go back and tell Knell and Bone to choose a group of soldiers and hunters as guards and scouts, and have the rest of the Aeriat fly them over. We need to make certain there's nothing dangerous before we bring in the clutches and the rest of the Arbora."

Everyone scrambled to obey.

CHAPTER TWO

M oon helped fly the first group of Arbora, including Bone, Knell, forty or so other hunters and soldiers, and the two young mentors, Heart and Merit, from the boats to the tree's knothole entrance. With all the warriors joining in, it didn't take long, though the steadily increasing rain drumming on their wings and the deepening gloom under the canopy reminded them that time was limited. The other Arbora still stuck on the boats weren't happy with the delay, but they had to make certain the tree was safe.

Once they were assembled in the greeting hall, Pearl told them, "The Aeriat will search upwards, the Arbora will go down. Move quickly, make certain there's nothing dangerous here. You can stop and gawk at it all later." She jerked her head at Knell. "You stay here with the soldiers and make certain this level is safe."

Flower turned to Merit and Heart, both bouncing with barely restrained excitement. "One of you go with Chime, and light the lamps for the Aeriat. The other stay here with Knell and light the rest of this hall and the passages around it."

"I've never done shells before." Merit looked anxious. "Just moss and wood."

"You'll learn as you go," Chime said firmly, and caught Merit around the waist. He sprang up after the warriors who were already climbing the central well.

Moon hissed to himself in frustration, torn between wanting to join the warriors who were heading upward, and wanting to be a good consort. Stone had already disappeared and was unavailable to give advice; possibly he was making his own search or getting reacquainted with the place. Not wanting to admit to insecurity, even to himself, Moon followed Jade, Flower, and the Arbora exploring party down the stairway that led below the greeting hall, to the section Stone had said they should make their camp for the night.

They followed the curving stairs down into another large, central chamber with a high domed roof and round doorways leading away. Only a little light from above fell down the stairwell. The room was a dark pit, even to Raksuran eyes. But the only scent was of must and leaf rot, and the space felt empty. Moon ran his hands over the wall as high as he could reach, feeling for light shells. *Groundlings would have brought a candlelamp or a torch,* he thought, frustrated. The hunters went down the steps, spread out along the wall in the dark, searching, until someone said, "Here's one!"

After a moment, a shell further down the steps started to glow, revealing Flower standing on tip-toes to reach it. Jade and the hunters turned to look around the room.

The light crept up the wall onto carvings of trees that curved up across the ceiling. It was a forest, picked out in detail, with plumes, spirals, fern trees, many others Moon couldn't name. Their branches entwined overhead, and their roots came down to frame the round doorways that led off to different rooms, as if you were standing in an enclosed and protected glade. The hunters murmured in appreciation, and Bone said in a hushed voice, "If every part of this place is as beautiful . . ."

Flower nodded, amusement and awe mingled in her expression. "If this is just the teachers' gathering hall, I can't wait to see the queens' level."

"We'll see it later." Jade stepped over the edge of the stairs to drop down to the floor. "We need to find all the approaches to this section, make certain we can guard it tonight." She turned to Bone. "And there have to be more passages outside, and a better place to land the boats and unload them."

"We'll find it," he told her. He turned for the nearest doorway and made an abrupt gesture. The other hunters scattered, and Flower hurried after them to light the shells. Moon and Jade followed more slowly, lingering to look. The other doorways led into an interconnected, multi-leveled maze of rooms, smaller stairways winding up, with balconies extending out over the wells. Without the sound of moving water it was too silent, haunted, much of it lost in darkness. Moon tried to shake off his uneasiness as he followed Jade through the empty place.

In one of the first rooms, they found something hanging from the ceiling, a big wooden thing like half a nutshell, only it was nearly ten paces across. It swayed gently when Jade pushed at it. "It's a bed," she said, sounding startled. "Stone's right—I think they grew this. Or made the tree grow it."

Moon felt the thick rope supporting one end of the bed, and realized it wasn't rope but a heavy vine. It joined the wood seamlessly, with no knots. The basket beds made for the old colony were obviously an attempt to duplicate this.

As they wandered through the level, they found more beds hanging from the ceiling or extending out from the walls. There were also shallow metal basins set into the smooth wood floors. Flower scratched experimentally at one, and said they were probably for the stones that mentors spelled to give off heat. She added, "I hope it means they had a forge, somewhere lower down."

"Did they bring the anvils?" Moon asked, remembering there had been some concern about that at the old colony.

"I left with Stone before they settled all that," she told him, looking around distractedly. "Niran thought they would plummet right through the ship's hull, and he may have been right."

Moon kept finding bits of debris, things left behind that hinted at the life once lived here. A spill of beads in the dust, each carved like a tiny flower; a curved wooden comb, some of the tines missing; a scrap of faded fabric caught on a carving; a white-glazed bowl, set aside and forgotten on a ledge.

Finally one of the hunters called Jade to come and look at another entrance on a lower level. It was a large round doorway closed by a heavy wooden panel that slid into place and sealed with bolts. After some tugging and pushing, they had got the panel open, and found the doorway sat just above a big branch nearly forty paces across, that lay nearly atop one of the old garden platforms. The Arbora thought it would be a good spot to secure the two boats, and would make it easier to unload them.

Moon followed them out the doorway into the rain and picked his way across the big muddy expanse. It felt like solid ground, barely trembling in the wind, and was covered with rambling root vines, probably all that was left of the crop that had once been planted here. He watched as, with careful maneuvering and a lot of shouted instructions, Niran and Blossom brought the two ships close in to the massive trunk. Arbora scrambled under Niran's direction to cast ropes over the huge branch at both ships' bow and stern.

As the Arbora finished fastening the ships into place, Pearl and some of the Aeriat flew out of the knothole entrance above them and spiraled down to land nearby. To Jade, Pearl said, "The upper levels are empty."

Chime came over to Moon, squelching in the mud, his tail twitching with excitement. "It's the best colony we could ever have," he said. "There's so much room!"

Bone came out to report that he and Flower and the other hunters had ventured nearly down to the roots, to the bottom of the habitable areas, and found no sign of anything big enough to threaten them. "There's a lot of dirt and beetles, and tiny treelings that eat beetles, but that's all," Bone finished, the rain dripping off his spines. "The roots and the ground may be a different story, but the doors down there are sealed, and we didn't want to chance opening them without more help."

Lightning cracked somewhere overhead, and everyone ducked and winced. Jade said, "Even if there's a Ghobin colony down there, we still need shelter now."

Pearl didn't look at her, but she told Bone, "Call back the searchers and tell them to start unloading the boats. Have everyone keep to the teachers' level for tonight. We'll worry about the rest of the place tomorrow."

Everyone scattered to obey. The Arbora started to climb off the boats, all carrying loads of baskets and bags. Tired of feeling useless, Moon jumped up to the *Valendera's* railing to help. Rill, a teacher who was organizing the activity on the deck, called to the cluster of Arbora around her, "Take these first! We're bringing in the food stores and the bedding now, we'll worry about the rest later!"

Moon took the basket someone handed him, and flew it back to the doorway. He landed to carry it into the foyer, and was directed up the passage to a larger chamber where they were putting everything until they could decide what to do with it. He thought it was too small for even the goods stored on the two ships' decks, but he knew how quick the Arbora could be to arrange and organize, so he decided to keep his mouth shut and let them handle it.

As he came back down the passage, a group of teachers carefully carried in the clutches and fledglings. Moon passed Bell carrying the Sky Copper clutch. The little queen Frost was in one arm and Thorn, the consort, was in the other. The smaller consort Bitter was wrapped tightly around Bell's neck, and from Bell's expression it wasn't comfortable. As they passed, Frost informed Moon, "This place is dark and wet and it smells funny!"

It was hard to argue with that. Moon said, "It'll be fine." *Just keep telling yourself that,* he thought.

But in the rush to unload the *Valendera* and *Indala,* Moon forgot his misgivings. Once the rest of the Aeriat returned, it was easier for them to move things from the decks down onto the platform, where the Arbora could then carry them into the tree. The wind was rising, but the two ships had been as well fastened to the giant branch as they could manage, their sails tightly folded. They vibrated, but did not show any sign of movement that might cause damage.

As Moon lifted a cask off the deck, a warrior with gold scales passed him, carrying a basket. He glanced up in time to see her face. "Balm?"

She was Jade's clutchmate. She had been staying on the *Indala* and while Moon had asked after her, he hadn't managed to see her during the trip. Startled, she hesitated, as if about to speak. But the wind gusted and knocked a smaller warrior off the railing right toward Moon. He dropped the cask in time to catch the warrior, but when he set him back on his feet, Balm had already moved away. Moon collected the cask, giving up for the moment. It wasn't as if he knew what he was going to say to her, anyway.

They had gotten everything off the open decks of both ships, and moved part of the contents of the *Valendera*'s hold, when the rain suddenly increased from an annoyance to a drenching torrent. The wind was still rising, hard enough to stir the branches of the lesser trees, and it was getting darker as night drew in.

A gust knocked another Aeriat off the railing and the smaller Arbora were getting stuck in the mud. Moon thought it was time to halt for the night. The last thing they needed was for an Arbora to get swept off the platform or an Aeriat to be slammed into the trunk. He caught Song, and told her to pass the word to the others to go inside. Then he shooed a last few Arbora off the *Indala* and braved the wind to fly over to the *Valendera*'s deck.

Arbora ran around helping Niran close and fasten down the hatches so the ship wouldn't fill with water. Moon found Bead pulling down the last of the waterproofed awnings and helped her bundle it up. "We need to get inside. It's too rough out here," he told her.

She nodded distractedly, water streaming off her head frills. She trembled with exhaustion. "We've got everything off the decks, all the food stores. I think everything else can stay for now."

"Good." Moon saw Floret and Root perched on the branch, and waved them down. As they dropped down onto the deck, he handed the bundled awning to Root and handed Bead to Floret, telling them, "Make sure she gets inside. Tell the others we're done for tonight."

Floret scooped up Bead and leapt back to the branch. Root said, "You know, consorts aren't supposed to do things like this, not unless they're line-grandfathers like Stone."

Moon, about to turn away, paused and stared down at him.

Root stepped back, saying defensively, "That's what I always heard."

Moon lifted his spines. "Get in the tree."

Root got.

Moon stalked across the deck, caught a last few Arbora and Aeriat and sent them after the others. The problem was that Root might well be right. But for most of Moon's life, traveling from groundling cities to settlements to camps, joining in for community work was one of the best ways to be accepted. For smaller settlements, it was sometimes required for travelers who wanted to stay for even a few days. And he found it hard to believe that a real consort raised in a court would just stand around and do nothing while everyone else worked frantically. *You could ask Stone or Jade or Flower,* he told himself. *But they might answer you.* And it might be the wrong answer. He had no idea what he would do if Jade told him to just sit to one side and watch. *Besides die of boredom and frustration.* No, it was better to keep pretending he just didn't know any better, at least for now. Hopefully he could keep it up for a long time.

Moon found Blossom and Niran in the bow, arguing. Or at least he thought they were arguing; the rain was so heavy now they might just be shouting to hear each other. He got their attention by lifting and spreading his wings, shielding them from the downpour. Blossom turned to him and waved a hand in exasperation. "Niran thinks he should stay out here tonight!"

Moon should have seen that one coming. Stubbornness in the face of implacable odds was Niran's specialty, and he was determined to bring both ships home intact to his family, whether it killed him or not. Moon would rather get Niran home intact to his family. He said, "Niran, we don't know this place at all. Something could climb up here, crack this boat like a nut, and eat you."

His clothes dripping and his white hair plastered to his scalp, Niran shook his head. "I've spent many nights in strange places aboard these ships . . ."

"Yes, with your people. Not alone." Moon had seen how the Islanders had reacted when the Fell had threatened them. They had been more than willing to abandon the ships to save the crews. "You're telling me your grandfather and sister would think this was a good idea?"

Niran just set his jaw and didn't try to answer that. "If the wind grows worse . . ."

"You won't be able to do anything," Blossom insisted. "If something happens to the ships, we can always give you their value, or fix them. We can probably fix them."

Moon considered just grabbing both of them and dragging them inside, but Niran seemed to be swayed by Blossom's argument. Water streaming down his face, he grudgingly assented, "Very well."

Niran and Blossom still wanted to check over both ships, but finally they admitted both were as secure as possible. Moon picked Niran up and jumped down from the railing to land on the grassy platform, now awash in mud. He set Niran down as Blossom swung down the side of the ship after them and landed with a splash.

They squelched through the mud, Niran staggering in the wind, and made their way toward the circle of light that marked the doorway. Blossom scrambled through, and Moon gave Niran a boost, then climbed in after him.

Niran sat down on the floor with a gasp of relief, and Moon resisted the urge to shake the water out of his spines. The foyer was still crowded with wet, muddy Raksura; no one had shifted to groundling, since that would just transfer the mud to their clothing. Others were carrying the last of the baskets and bundles away down the passage.

"That's everyone!" Bone called out. He and two other hunters put their shoulders to the heavy door, sliding it closed and shutting out the rain and wind.

Blossom took Niran's arm and helped him up. "Come on, let's find Bead and Spice. They were supposed to make up a bower for us."

"A what?" Niran said, wringing his shirt out as he followed her.

Someone handed Moon one of the pieces of scrap cloth being passed around, and he used it to scrape the mud off his feet and claws. As he finished, he glanced up in time to see Balm slip unobtrusively down a passage. He tossed the cloth back onto the pile and followed her.

He caught up with her just past the foyer, where the passage divided into three directions, all heading up into different parts of the teacher's level. "Balm, where are you going?"

She stopped, her spines twitching uneasily. "To find somewhere to sleep." Three young warriors slid past, carefully not looking at her, and Balm hissed. "I'm tired of feeling like I did something wrong."

Balm hadn't done anything wrong, except be unlucky enough to be used by the Fell to spy on the colony. Fell could influence groundlings, cause them to believe anything the Fell told them, and to do things they would never do in their right minds. They could use this power to a lesser extent on Raksura, but it didn't work as well. The Fell had been able to make Balm tell them about the court's plans, but she had had no memory of it, no awareness of what she was doing. Moon had seen enough groundlings in this same state to know it wasn't her fault. But it had put Balm at a severe disadvantage in the maneuvering for dominance between Pearl's faction of warriors and Jade's. He said, "Then stop acting like it. Don't let them treat you like this." Jade's influence could only protect Balm so far. River and his cronies couldn't attack Balm outright; now that Pearl was taking more interest in the court, the last thing River wanted was to make her angry enough to intervene. But they could make Balm's life a misery, and know that they were hurting Jade by proxy. And Balm just didn't deserve it. "You belong with Jade."

Balm hesitated, obviously torn. But she said, "I'll . . . think about it," and turned away.

Moon hesitated, half-tempted to follow, but he didn't know what else to say to persuade her. He turned to the passage to the teachers' hall.

As he walked through the bowers this time, they were anything but haunted and silent. Flower and the other mentors had been renewing the spells on every light-shell they could find. The warm light caught red and yellow highlights in the wood, chased the shadows away, threw the wall carvings into high relief. Arbora and Aeriat were everywhere, cleaning dirt and debris out of the bower beds, hanging wet clothes off the stairwell balconies, pulling bedding out of baskets. Their voices echoed through the rooms. They were excited to finally be here, relieved to be free of the cramped quarters on the boats.

Moon wanted to check on Bitter, Frost, and Thorn, and see the other clutches, so he followed the sound of squeaking and chattering. He had been the one to find the three Sky Copper fledglings in the Dwei hive, where the Fell had been keeping them as part of their plan to make more Raksuran crossbreeds. He wasn't sure if the clutch had gotten so attached to him because of the rescue or because he was the first Raksura they had seen after their colony had been destroyed. Whatever the reason, Frost persisted in telling everyone that they were Moon's clutch now.

There had been no question that Indigo Cloud would adopt them; at the moment the court had no other royal fledglings. If Moon and Jade didn't produce any fledgling queens of their own, Frost could end up as reigning queen of the court. Moon knew that wasn't anyone's preference, but it was a relief to have the option available. And it would be twenty or thirty turns at least before Frost would be old enough to even be considered a sister queen, which gave him and Jade plenty of time to have their own clutches.

He found a round doorway with the lintel carved with baby Arbora and Aeriat tumbling in play, and stepped through into a big, low-ceilinged chamber.

At the moment, it was a chaotic mess, with Arbora children and a few warrior fledglings, all overexcited and shifting at random, as the teachers tried to calm them and put them to bed in nests of blankets and cushions. It was even more obvious here that there had been far more Arbora births than Aeriat. Hopefully things would even out, now that the court was in this new colony and free of the Fell influence that had haunted it for so many turns.

Circling the chamber as he looked for the Sky Copper royals, Moon passed a maze of smaller rooms opening off the main area, and several shallow fountain pools, now dry. The place had been meant to house far more children than Indigo Cloud could boast.

"Moon," Bark called, a little desperately. Her arms were full with a crying Arbora toddler. She nodded down toward her feet, where Bitter, in Raksuran form, tried to hold onto Bark and two very young and squirming Arbora. "Could you—"

Moon crouched down, untangled Bitter's claws from Bark's skirt and coaxed him to let go of the toddlers. "Bitter, if you want to hold them, you have to shift otherwise you could scratch them." From what Moon had seen, Arbora at that age shifted randomly back and forth, but their claws and spines were still soft; Bitter's had already hardened, and he was still learning how to handle them.

Bitter looked up at him with big eyes, then reluctantly shifted. As a groundling he was a thin little boy, with dark bronze skin and a thatch of dark hair, dressed in a shirt that was too big for him.

Moon sat Bitter down on the nearest cushion, put one of the Arbora in his lap and the other next to him. Now that they weren't being accidentally prodded by Bitter's claws, they settled comfortably against him and shifted back to groundling.

"Thank you," Bark said in relief. The baby she held settled down too, and sniffled and hooked claws into her shoulder. Bark nodded toward a bundle of blankets nearby. Frost and Thorn were curled up asleep there, Frost in her wingless form and Thorn as a groundling. He clutched her tail in one hand. "Those two went right to sleep, but Bitter's been upset about the storm. Haven't you, sweet baby?"

Bitter looked up at her and nodded solemnly, keeping a firm grip on the Arbora. Moon suspected it wasn't the storm. Any upheaval had to be frightening for him. Bitter, Frost, and Thorn had seen their entire court killed, the queens and consorts, the other children in the nurseries, the Arbora who had taken care of them, everyone they had ever known.

Something similar had happened to Moon. He just didn't remember it. He told Bitter, "I won't be far away. Jade and I are just out there in the central hall. All right?"

Bitter nodded solemnly again, and allowed himself to be tucked into a nest with the Arbora babies.

Moon left the nurseries. Bitter obviously remembered what had happened to his court, all too clearly. Moon's earliest memory was of living in the forest with Sorrow and the others, so he must have been even younger than Bitter when his court had been destroyed.

Just down the passage, he found Chime, Flower, and Rill in the teachers' hall, all in groundling form, unpacking baskets and laying out bedding. Root and Song were already there, vigorously drying off their scales. With the glowing shells casting light on the carved forest, surrounded by the noise and scents of the rest of the court, the hall was much more welcoming.

Moon's scales were dry enough now, and he shifted to groundling and stretched, trying to ease his sore shoulder. Chime looked up, still flushed with excitement, and told him, "Jade's staying in here tonight, and Pearl is near the stairs on the level below with some more warriors. That way if anything tries to get in, it'll run into one of us first. One of them. You know what I mean."

"Good." Even if nothing else had taken up residence in the tree, there was always the chance their presence would attract predators.

Flower carried a basket over to the heating basin and dumped out a load of small, flat river rocks. She sat beside the basin and held out her hands. After a moment, heat started to rise. She sat back with a sigh and tucked her skirts under her feet. "That's better."

Rill nodded, pulling out more blankets to hand to Song and Root. "It'll get the damp out of the air." She glanced around and pointed to one of the baskets. "Moon, those are some things from Jade's bower, and we put yours in there too."

As far as Moon knew, he didn't have any things except the clothes he was wearing. Everything he had owned had been left behind in the Cordans' camp. He went to open the basket.

On top were heavy quilted blankets and bed cushions, in shades of dark blues and sea greens, with patterns picked out in gold. He lifted those out and set them aside, figuring that was what they would be sleeping on tonight. Next there were a few rolled leather wraps. Peeking inside one, he saw it held jewelry, silver strands wound with polished green stones and deep-water pearls. Jade had used all the jewelry she had been wearing on their trip to the east to pay for supplies and to give to Selis in return for helping them. Apparently there was plenty more where that came from. He was beginning to realize that the Raksura didn't measure wealth in gems or even the sturdy, colorful fabrics the Arbora made. He wasn't sure what they did measure wealth in. "That's a lot of jewelry."

Flower sounded wry. "It's nothing to what Stone's collected over the years."

"I only hope we found it all." Rill, unpacking a copper-chased kettle, made a helpless gesture. "He had it hidden all over the colony. After everything that happened—"

"Don't worry about it, not tonight." Chime took the kettle away from her and set it on the warming stones.

Looking for more bedding, Moon pushed the leather rolls aside. The fur blanket beneath, the long soft hair dyed to the purple haze of twilight, looked familiar. He pulled it out to find it was bundled around a belt with a sheathed knife, the dark soft leather tooled with red in a serpentine pattern, with round buckles of red gold. These were the consort's gifts Jade had left at the bower he had been using in the teachers' hall at the old colony. The knife's hilt was carved horn, the blade was a tooth, sharp as glass but as strong as fine metal. He hadn't accepted them at the time, having no idea what he would be getting into and mostly certain that he hadn't wanted to get into anything. Now . . . *Now it's different,* he reminded himself. And he still really wanted that knife.

He left it and the belt on top of Jade's jewelry and added the blanket to their nest of bedding. Suddenly self-conscious, he looked around to make sure no one was watching him, especially Stone. Then he realized he hadn't seen him since they arrived. "Where's Stone?"

Flower, carefully unwrapping a cake of pressed tea, said, "He went up to look around the queens' level. That was a while ago," she added, frowning.

Chime dropped a last cushion onto a pile of bedding and glanced up, worried. "You think something's wrong?"

"No, not wrong, just . . ." Flower hesitated. "This place was his home, a long time ago."

She was right; this had to be strange for Stone. Moon put the lid back on the basket and said, "I'll find him."

He took the stairs up to the greeting hall, where the soldiers had spread their bedding out around a hearth basin near the fountain. Merit was still with them, looking small next to the bigger Arbora. Merit waved, but the soldiers just stared at Moon with wary curiosity.

He shifted and jumped to climb straight up the wall, finding plenty of handholds built into the carving, rough from where generations of Raksura had hooked their claws. He followed the spiral well up and up, climbing past open balconies and galleries.

Somewhere far below, he heard a voice raised in song that echoed up through the passages of the tree. Moon winced. *Please, not tonight.* He hoped they were too weary for a full chorus.

The court had sung once aboard the flying boats, one night when they had been passing over a grass plain. It had been a dirge for the dead members of the court, and for the colony ruined by the Fell. The mingled voices had been so low and deep, so heavy with pain and loss, the deck of the *Valendera* had trembled like a sounding board.

Moon had slipped away from Jade's side, retreating to the deck cabin. The door was partly open, and he ducked his head inside. Light came from glowing moss stuffed into the glass candlelamps, and Niran sat on the bed, which folded out from one of the benches along the wall. He said, "You might as well come in. Everyone else does."

Knowing Niran, Moon took that for the invitation it was. He stepped in and sat cross-legged on the deck. For a normal voyage, Niran would have quarters below deck, but all those rooms were stuffed with supplies and Arbora. The waist-high wooden pillar in the center of the cabin held the fragment of flying island that kept the boat aloft, and let it travel the streams of force that crossed the Three Worlds. There were also a couple of clay water jars, and baskets of supplies, one with a pottery bowl and cup stacked atop it. Niran had a few bundles of paper next to him on the blankets, and a wooden writing tablet in his lap. He said, dryly, "I'm keeping a record of our travels, for my grandfather. He would never forgive me if I didn't."

Moon settled his back against the wall to support his sore shoulder. "It'll help him get over missing this trip."

"Hopefully." Niran nodded toward the door. "You don't participate in the . . . concert?"

Moon hesitated, debating several different excuses, then settled for, "I don't know how." Not counting the court's stupid rules and customs, everything else about being Raksuran he had either learned from Sorrow or figured out for himself. The singing was alien, and it made him deeply uneasy. In its own way, it was as disturbing as the queen's connection to every member of her court, the connection that let her keep you from shifting, or draw you in and make you feel like you were sharing a heart. It was too much like the Fell's power to influence and cloud the minds of groundlings. Jade hadn't shown any evidence of that ability yet, but that might be because she wasn't the reigning queen. Moon wasn't looking forward to the time when she did.

Niran lifted his brows and made a note. "I forget sometimes that you have only recently joined them."

Moon had wondered if anybody else would ever forget it. *And you're worse than all of them,* he told himself now. He hadn't even tried to sing, just run off to hide with the only available groundling.

Climbing the wall of the mountain-tree, he pushed the uncomfortable thoughts away. They were all here now, and it was time for new beginnings.

The greeting hall was far below him when the ceiling finally curved up to form a wide circular gallery. He climbed up onto it and found it opened into another hall.

A few wall-shells glowed, enough to chase away some of the shadows. More round doorways led off into other chambers, and there was a dry fountain against the wall, the basin below it empty and stained with moss at the bottom. The carving above it made him hiss in appreciation.

It was a queen, a queen bigger even than Stone's shifted form, her outspread wings stretched across the walls to circle the entire hall, finally meeting tip to tip. Her carved scales glinted faintly in the dim light, and as Moon moved closer he saw they were set with polished sunstones.

High above her head there was another open gallery. The rooms off this level had to be the bowers and halls for the reigning queen and her sisters, and he was guessing that the level directly above was for the consorts.

The gallery was a little high, but Moon crouched and made the leap up, caught the ridged edge, and swung up onto the floor.

The open space was ringed with doorways into a series of interconnected rooms. Moon shifted back to groundling, and wandered through the empty spaces, finding bower beds, heating basins, and dry fountain-pools, easily deep and wide enough for swimming. He found a couple of small stairways that led to the queens' chambers just below, and then another one that seemed to wind down a long way, probably to join the main stairs in the central well. There was an opening to the outside somewhere, because the air moved with the rush of wind, damp and fresh. With the place cleaned and swept, with warming stones and running fountains, furs, and rich fabrics, it would be ridiculously comfortable. Moon couldn't imagine being born into this kind of luxury.

In a room against the outer trunk, he finally found Stone. He stood at a big round opening to the outside, looking out into the rainy gloom. The opening had a heavy wooden sliding door, like the one they had found on the lower entrance. Stone must have opened it, dislodging the dirt and rotting leaves now scattered across the floor.

Moon stepped up beside him. A giant branch blocked the view directly overhead, but the doorway looked down on the platforms far below, now sodden under the pouring rain. In the failing light, he could just make out the old irrigation channels and ponds filling up, making a ghost outline of the gardens that had once been there.

Stone didn't look around. His expression was, as usual, hard to read. He said, "It feels . . . wrong. It's too quiet."

The rain was a rushing din, but that wasn't the kind of noise he meant. Moon said, "It's not quiet downstairs." He leaned against the wall beside the opening. The air smelled rich with the rain, the dark earth, and loam. "Were you here when they built . . . grew this place?"

His eyes still on the drowning gardens, Stone's brow furrowed. "I'm not that old."

Thunder rumbled, not quite close enough to make Moon twitch. "But you lived here."

"For a while. I was a boy when Indigo and Cloud led the court away." From his expression, it was hard to tell if it was a good memory or a bad one. "I was too young and stupid to see it as anything but an adventure."

Then these rooms had been filled with light and life, when there had been so many Raksura here they had had to leave for more open territory. It had to be strange to see it like this, dark and empty, scented of nothing but must and stale water. Moon had never gone back to a place he had lived before, unless he counted the Cordans' camp, and he hadn't felt anything there except impatience.

Still lost in memory, Stone added, "No one ever thought I'd get a queen, but Azure picked me out of the lot."

Moon frowned at him. "Why didn't they think you'd get a queen?"

Stone tapped his cheek, below his clouded right eye. He said, dryly, "I wasn't born perfect."

Moon had always thought that was a fighting injury, like the rest of Stone's scars. He knew consorts often went to other courts; Stone had been trying to get one from Star Aster when he had found Moon. But he supposed another court wouldn't want an imperfect consort either. "What do consorts do, when they can't get a queen?"

Stone thought about it for a long moment. "It depends on the court. Here . . . it wouldn't have been so bad. All the benefits of being a consort, and none of the responsibilities."

Moon was still working out what he felt about the benefits and responsibilities of being a consort. Before Jade, he would have been more than happy with the less complicated life of a warrior; all he had ever wanted was a place to live. Finding a place to live without having to hide what he was had been a completely unexpected turn of luck. But he could imagine how someone raised with the idea that the point of his life was to be a queen's mate and to make clutches would see things differently. "That could seem . . . pointless."

Stone didn't look away from the ruined gardens. "It depends what you make of it."

Thunder crashed, near enough to send a tremble through the wood underfoot, and Moon flinched back from the flash.

Stone glanced at him, lifting a brow. Moon was prepared for some sort of remark, but all Stone did was drop a hand on the back of Moon's neck and shake him—affectionately, not hard enough to rattle his teeth. "Let's go."

Stone shoved the door into place, slid the bolts home, and they made their way down again. They took the long stairways through the silent spaces, since Stone didn't seem to want to shift. The light-shells had been sporadically lit, giving glimpses of balcony-bowers hanging out over circular wells, dry fountains and pools, and carvings of Aeriat, Arbora, strange plants and animals mixed in with the more familiar. Much of it was inlaid with polished shell or glittering stones, or clear crystal. The singing had died away. Most of the court must have settled into sleep.

When they reached the greeting hall they found Knell sitting at the hearth with the other soldiers. He nodded to Stone. "The hunters are at the stair just below the teachers' bowers, with Pearl and some warriors. Jade's just below us, outside the nurseries."

Stone looked around the hall thoughtfully. "I'll come back up later and sleep here."

Moon saw the flicker of relief cross Knell's face. This was the only entrance they had found so far that wasn't sealed, and if anything was going to object to their presence, it would probably choose to enter that way. Stone would be a big deterrent.

They took the stairs down to the teachers' hall. Vine, Floret, and Sand had joined the others there, all in groundling form, and settled into a pile of bedding on the other side of the chamber. Root, demonstrating a youthful lack of nerves, was already curled up asleep.

Sand had always been in Jade's camp, but Moon had thought Vine and Floret were closer to Pearl. Either they had changed their allegiance or they were just here to help guard this side of the nurseries and the Arbora's bowers. It made him a little edgy not to know.

Moon sat down on one side of the hearth. Stone took the other and settled into place with a groan. Flower dipped cups of tea out of the steaming pot for them, asking Stone, "Are you all right?"

He gave her a sour look. "I'm old."

Flower smiled. "We'd noticed."

Jade came in from the passage, and Chime asked her, "Are we settled for now?"

"Finally." Jade shook out her head frills and shifted to Arbora. "Everyone is convinced that we need daylight to finish exploring, and we need rest before we make plans and argue about where to put everything."

Song said, "Your consort got your bed ready."

Lifting his cup, Moon froze, self-conscious. He had made the sleeping place without even thinking about it. When he and Jade had flown to the east together, they had quickly got into the habit of taking turns, one finding and preparing a place to sleep and the other hunting for food. Aboard the flying ship, he had been recovering from his injuries and staying in a cabin with the mentors and Chime, who had been taking care of him. He realized he had no idea how to live with Jade inside a colony, and he kept running into subtleties of Raksuran behavior that he had no idea how to react to. He knew the others were staring at him, and made himself take a sip of tea as if nothing was wrong.

Jade tilted her head to study Song thoughtfully. Song's eyes widened and she said, "I was just teasing!"

"Hmm," Jade commented. She went over to the baskets and opened one to dig through it.

Chime gave Song an exasperated look, then turned to the others, obviously changing the subject. "How much food do we have left?"

"Enough for several days, plus the fresh meat from the hunt this morning," Rill answered. "We still have about half the dried meat, because the Aeriat were refusing to eat it. We're getting low on dried fruit, sava flour, dried sava, and roots."

Stone said, "There are a lot of plants in this area that we can eat. Since no one's been eating them for who knows how many turns, there should be plenty around."

Jade sat down next to Moon, then leaned over to put something on the floor in front of him. It gleamed red-gold against the wood, catching the light: it was the bracelet that Stone had taken to Star Aster, the token to be given to the new consort. Moon picked it up. Having seen more of the Arbora's artwork, he could tell now that the fluid serpentine shapes etched into the band were two entwined Raksura. He looked up to see Jade watching him, the scales on her brow faintly creased with worry.

Moon put the bracelet on, just under the knobby bone in his wrist. Jade pulled his head down and her teeth grazed the skin behind his ear in a gentle nip.

Flower cleared her throat and smiled faintly. "At least there should be plenty of game around here, too."

Stone set his cup down. "We'll need to reestablish our territory. I should be able to find the old boundaries."

Jade glanced up. "Our territory? I wouldn't think we'd need to worry . . ." She eyed Stone more sharply. "Unless there's another court in this area?"

"There are several. This is the home forest, where our bloodlines were first born. There used to be colonies everywhere through here. Too many." Stone shrugged. "Now there's plenty of room."

CHAPTER THREE

Moon woke buried in blankets, with Jade warm beside him. His inner sense of the sun told him it was still some time before dawn, and the storm had calmed to the point where the wind was barely audible. He pulled a fold of fabric down, just enough to get a good taste of the air.

Nothing had changed since last night. The others in the hall breathed deeply in sleep, except for some of the warriors on the far side of the room. From the soft noises, they were enjoying each other's company under the blankets. *Good idea,* he thought, and flipped the blanket back up to settle down again and nuzzle Jade's neck.

She slid an arm across his waist, curling around him. Nipping his ear, she whispered, "When we know we're settled here for good, we'll start a clutch."

He nodded against her cheek. He was looking forward to babies in the nurseries that had actually come from him and Jade. But first they had to make certain this place was as secure as it seemed, and that the court could find enough food in the surrounding forest. More things to consider when you were choosing a permanent place to live. He said, "We need to make a consort for Frost." Since Jade had taken Moon as consort, Frost had been demanding that they get a consort for her, occasionally remembering to request queens for Thorn and Bitter.

Jade hissed, ruefully amused. "I never realized what fledgling queens were like. I'm starting to feel a little sympathy for Pearl and Amber, when I was that age."

Moon didn't have any trouble imagining Jade as an imperious little fledgling, making Pearl's life difficult, but he wasn't going to say so. There was something else he was reluctant to bring up, but he had to know about the awkward moment last night. "What did it mean when I made a bed for you?"

This time Jade sounded more annoyed than amused. "It's an old custom. It means you want to sleep with me. Song was being a little idiot."

"I do want to sleep with you," he pointed out, emphasizing it by nuzzling her collarbone.

"Consorts have their own bowers." Jade's tone was teasing. She pulled him more firmly against her. "So they can be guarded and chaperoned."

This was the first time Moon had heard about the guarding and chaperoning part. Though it made sense, with everyone being careful to inform him that consorts his age—normal consorts his age—were supposed to be shy delicate creatures who seldom ventured out of their colonies. "So you're telling me that Stone and I are going to sleep up there above the queens' level? Because it's about thirty turns too late to chaperone me."

She tugged at the tie of his pants, her claws carefully sheathed. "When Thorn and Bitter get past the fledgling stage, they'll come out of the nurseries and they'll need bowers. As well as any other consorts we happen to produce."

"I don't know how that's going to happen, if I'm sleeping up there with Stone—"

Jade growled, and rolled on top of him, and that was the end of that conversation.

☾

Moon drowsed for a while, and woke when Jade climbed over him to get out of their nest. He shook himself free of the blankets, stretching extravagantly.

Chime and Rill sat by the hearth basin, blearily waiting for the water kettle to boil. Flower was nowhere to be seen.

Jade, who was waking the warriors by the simple method of kicking various piles of blankets, told Moon, "I'm going to take a look around, make sure everything's all right."

"I'll come with you." Moon climbed out of the blankets and pulled his clothes back on. They left while the others were still stumbling around.

Moon and Jade made a circuit of the perimeter of their new home, going first up to the greeting hall, where Knell and the soldiers said all was well. Looking around, it took Moon a moment to find Stone. He was still asleep, but in his winged form, curled around the pillars of the stairs, his black scales blending into the carving. "How does he do that?" Moon asked Jade, as they went back down to the teachers' hall. "Sleep in his other form." Moon could do it for short periods of time, but it didn't give him much real rest. He hadn't seen any of the others do it either.

Jade shook her head. "I don't know. It's just one of the things that come with age."

They walked the outer passages and found many of the Arbora already up and moving, scrubbing dirt and moss out of the bowers or the dry pools, or sorting through baskets and bags of belongings. As they passed a doorway into an unused room, Moon felt a gritty crunch underfoot and looked down. The floor was covered with broken pottery shards. He stopped to scrape the remnants off; fortunately none was sharp enough to penetrate the thick extra layers of skin on his groundling feet. Jade glanced back and said, "I hope they didn't break anything important."

Moon leaned into the room. More broken pottery was strewn across the floor, pieces with the same blue glaze as the tall jars stacked near the doorway. Several wooden bins, covered with delicately incised images of flowering grasses, stood against the far wall, and the lids had all been smashed. But dust had collected on the splintered debris. He stepped into the room to look into the bins, but they were all empty, except for mold. "This wasn't one of us. It's old."

"I suppose they were broken when the old court left." Jade dismissed it, turning away.

They moved on and took the next stairs down to the level below. At the bottom, they met Pearl, trailed by River, Drift, Coil, and a few other Aeriat, all in groundling form. Pearl flicked her spines at Jade and said, "Where's Stone? We have decisions to make."

Jade flicked her spines back. "He's in the greeting hall, still asleep."

The other warriors avoided Moon's gaze, but River gave him a look of pure contempt. Pretending to ignore him, Moon folded his arms, so the sleeve of his shirt tugged up, revealing the gold bracelet. River looked away, seething.

Pearl said, "Then come with me." And as if she couldn't bear to leave the encounter on a mostly neutral note, jerked her head toward Moon and added, "Leave that." She started up the stairs and her obedient warriors trailed behind.

Jade hissed at her retreating back, then turned to Moon. "Go on," he told her, before she could speak. During the Fell attack, Pearl had had no choice about including Jade in governing the court, or what had been left of the court. If she was continuing that now, without Stone or Flower or anyone else to cajole her, it had to be a good thing.

Jade hesitated, lashing her tail. "I suppose I'd better." She caught his shirt, pulled him close, and rubbed her cheek against his. "I'll tell you what we talk about."

Jade stepped back, jumped up to catch the wall of the stairwell, and Moon went to look for something to do. Pearl's attitude didn't bite as much as it might have. A real consort would probably have been bitterly offended at the slight.

Of course, it probably wasn't good that he didn't think of himself as a real consort.

He followed the sounds of activity to the passage outside and the platform where the flying boats were anchored. The door stood open, and he shifted to make the jump from it down to the wet grass. The sunlight falling through the canopy was bright and tinged with green, and the air was fresh from the rain, heavy with the intriguing scents of the damp forest. A few Arbora were unloading the last supplies from the *Indala*'s hold, while others tramped around in the mud of the platform, digging and looking for roots among the trailing vines. Niran, Blossom, and Chime stood on the *Valendera*'s deck, talking and looking up at the mast. Both boats seemed to have come through the storm with no serious damage, which must have been a relief to Niran.

Moon saw Flower standing knee-deep in the muddy grass, the only Arbora out here in groundling form, and went over to her. "They're having a meeting in the greeting hall."

She nodded absently. "I know. I've already had my say with Pearl. I think we should all live in the teachers' levels for now. It'll do everyone good to be all jumbled together."

At the old colony, the Aeriat had lived slightly apart from the Arbora, and the hunters and soldiers had had separate bowers from the teachers and the small group of mentors. And the tree's living quarters seemed to be designed for that same system. Moon flexed his claws and prodded thoughtfully at a root buried in the grass. "That's not normal, is it?"

"No, but in thriving courts, living by caste doesn't seem to create problems." Leaning down to pull up the root, Flower added, "At the old colony, it just caused more trouble. We'd all been moving apart, separating into factions, losing our sense of each other."

Moon had seen some of that, when one of the hunters had told him he should be sleeping in the upper levels with the Aeriat instead of down in the teachers' bowers. Since by that point Moon had been ordered out of the court by both Arbora and Aeriat, he hadn't seen much difference between them. And he had liked Petal, who had been the leader of the teachers before Bell. She had been one of the small group who had made Moon feel welcome in the court. As Flower paused and crouched to examine the leaves of a vine, Moon said, "Everybody was jumbled together on the boats."

"Being jumbled together in comfort may be more productive." Flower looked up at him, but from her expression her thoughts were on something else. "We'll have to see what happens. It's been turns and turns since this court was out from under Fell influence."

The same could be said for Moon, though he hadn't realized it until lately. It still wasn't something he wanted to think about too closely.

Chime glided down from the *Valendera*'s deck and landed beside them. He said, "Everything came through the storm fine. I don't think we'll have to do much work before we send the boats back."

The plan was to loan Niran a crew of Arbora and Aeriat to help him sail the ships back to the Golden Isles, then the Aeriat could fly the Arbora back to the colony. It would be a long flight, but it was the only way to get the ships back. "Who's going with him?" Moon asked.

"We haven't gotten to that part yet." Chime scratched his head frills. "Blossom knows the most about how to steer the boats, and Bead knows the second most, but they'll need more Aeriat." He looked down, the tip of his tail twitching uneasily. "I'm thinking of going myself."

"You are?" Taken aback, Moon stared at him. "Why?" Chime had never spent a night away from the old colony before the trip to the Golden Isles, and he hadn't given the impression that he particularly liked to travel.

Chime shrugged. "I thought I'd do something useful."

Flower eyed him thoughtfully, and he seemed determined to avoid her gaze. Moon reminded himself Chime wouldn't be leaving permanently.

Strike, one of the younger hunters, bounded out of the doorway and landed in the mud with a loud squelch. He hurried over, saying, "Flower, Knell has some things he wants to show you, down in the lower levels."

Moon and Chime hadn't seen anything below this level, so they followed Flower back inside and down the stairwell. Strike led the way off the stairs into a wide high-ceilinged foyer, but Chime stopped to stare at the carving along the curving wall. "What happened here?"

Moon paused to look, as Flower and Strike continued down the passage. The carving covered most of the wall, a detailed depiction of a seascape, with tall rocky islands rising above ocean waves. But it was covered with holes, as if someone had struck at it with a knife or a chisel. Moon touched one of the gouges and felt rough tool marks and splinters. "Somebody pried out whatever was in here." There must have been inlaid stones, like the carvings in the Aeriat levels.

"What a waste." Chime brushed chips away from a section, distressed. "They broke through all the writing here."

Bead wandered in through another doorway, and saw them examining the carving. She said, "I noticed that too. Whoever carved it must have wanted to take the inlay with her when the court left. I'm going to fix it when I have a chance. Spice has some nice chips of amethyst that I could polish up and fit in there."

Moon touched an undamaged corner that depicted two warriors crouched on a branch, overlooking the scene. "They never show anybody in groundling form." He had noticed that particularly in the upper levels yesterday.

"Not often," Bead admitted, absently brushing more splinters out of the chiseled lines. "It's traditional that queens and consorts are only depicted in their winged forms. You can show warriors in groundling form, but they get all spine-ruffled about it. Arbora sometimes show each other in groundling form, but it's not common."

Chime was still occupied by the broken carving. He picked at one of the gaps with a claw. "It's like they bashed it out with a rock."

"They must have been in a hurry." Bead seemed to have too much on her mind to give the mystery much attention. "Oh, we found a forge down here, a big one, all lined with metal and stone. Pottery ovens, too. We should be able to get it all going again as soon as we unpack our tools."

Chime turned away from the carving, distracted. "Are there more workrooms?"

Bead pointed toward a passage. "Huge ones, down that way."

As they headed in that direction, Moon asked Chime, "How are you going to find metal in this forest?"

"There are rock outcrops scattered all over the forest floor, some of them with veins of ore. The old records have maps to the ones on our territory. And we can trade with other courts. Once we find the other courts." Chime's brow furrowed. "If they want to trade with us."

Moon followed Chime down the stairs, finding three levels of large airy chambers, all facing into another central well. The walls were covered with carvings here too, a whole landscape of Raksura, Arbora and Aeriat, queens and consorts, woven in with unfamiliar symbols, plants, animals. Suspended over the well was a wooden ball studded with the white light-shells, in all different shapes and sizes. "This is more room than we ever had before," Chime said, sounding overcome, his eyes on the glyphs carved above the round doorways. "For weaving, carving, pottery, metalwork . . ." He moved toward one of the rooms, pausing on the threshold.

Moon stepped past him. Merit was inside, along with a few hunters and teachers. It was a big room, winding far back into the tree, the walls lined with shelves. They stretched up to the curving ceiling, the material a richly-colored green and white stone, like polished agate. "What's this for?" Moon asked.

Chime turned abruptly and walked out to the well, stepped over the edge and fell out of sight.

Merit watched him go, his face set in a sympathetic wince. He told Moon, "It's the mentors' libraries."

And a too-pointed reminder that Chime wasn't a mentor anymore. Moon went out to the well and jumped down to the next level, then the next. He found Chime at the bottom, in a central chamber not nearly as grand, sitting beside a large dry pool filled with turns' worth of dead moss. More doorways led off this level, and from the comments of the Arbora who were exploring them, these were storerooms.

Moon sat down beside Chime, curling his tail out of the way. Chime slumped over, his spines drooping in dejection. After a moment, he said, "We don't have nearly enough books to fill those shelves. We must have lost so much."

Moon said, "Maybe they just left a lot of extra room." But he was thinking about the ruined books he had found on the flying island back in the east. Moving a court as large as this one had been, there must have been so many things that had had to be left behind, or let fall to the wayside.

Chime snorted in bitter disbelief. "Not that it's any of my business. That's for the mentors to worry about."

Moon didn't know what to say to that. Chime wasn't a mentor anymore, and there was nothing anyone could do about it. He watched the Arbora go in and out of doorways across the chamber, exclaiming over the things they were finding, making plans. "What did you do? Besides being a mentor."

It was probably the wrong question, but maybe Chime needed to talk about it. Moon was beginning to understand how important their crafts were to the Arbora. There was no pressing need for weapons or any other metalwork, or new crockery, or for Bead to fix the damaged carving. But they were anxious to get the forge running, and had been just as pleased at finding pottery ovens as they had been at finding the herd of grasseaters at the lake. And nobody had turned the inside of this tree into a living work of art unless they wanted to, unless they wanted it as much as Moon wanted to fly.

Chime rubbed his eyes. "I painted. The leather cases for keeping paper, and for holding books together. You harden the leather with a paste, then decorate it." He took a sharp breath. "I know it doesn't sound like much—"

"Why can't you still do it? It's not like you need to be a shaman to paint." Just because Chime had lost one ability, Moon didn't see the use of giving up everything.

Chime sighed, frustrated. "I've been afraid to try. What if I can't anymore, like I can't heal or augur or anything? At the Dwei hive, when Heart wasn't strong enough to put you into a healing sleep, I tried. I thought maybe I just had to be desperate to make it work now. But it didn't. And you could have died."

Moon shook his head. "You should try to paint. Then you'd know."

Chime grimaced at the thought and looked away. "Yes, that's the point of not trying."

There wasn't an answer for that, either.

A voice above them said, "Moon? Chime?" It was Strike again, hanging one-handed from the edge of the balcony above. "Flower wants you to come see something. I'm supposed to go get the queens and Stone."

That didn't sound good. "What is it?" Moon asked, pushing to his feet.

Strike waved his free hand. "Nobody knows—that's the problem!"

☾

Before hurrying up to the greeting hall, Strike pointed them back to the passage that led in toward the center of the trunk, and they found the way by following the trail of lit shells.

Flower and Knell stood in a junction of two passages, and at first Moon thought the dark, irregular blot on the wall was a shadow. But as they drew closer he saw it was something smudged on the wood itself. It stretched all the way up to the curving ceiling, and down to the smooth floor. The scent was like rot, like wood left in water until it softened and fell apart.

"What is it?" Chime demanded, and stepped close to peer at it. "A fungus?"

"That's what we're trying to figure out," Knell said, giving him a thoughtful glance. "The hunters saw it last night, when they came through here to make certain there was no danger, but they thought it was just moss. Today I saw there were spots of it all down these inner passages."

Flower had made a small stone glow with light, and held it close to the dark splotch, studying it intently. "Moon, have you ever heard groundlings speak of anything like this? A blight that kills trees?"

"Kills trees?" Moon stepped forward, startled. He had thought this was a curiosity, not a threat. "This tree?"

"That's what I'm afraid of." Flower beckoned him closer.

"Look. This isn't a growth on the wood, it's the wood itself."

Moon leaned close. She was right. The dark spongy substance still showed the grain. He touched it, pushing gently, and his claw sunk through. "I've never seen anything like it." The Hassi had had a problem with fungus in their orchards on top of the link-trees, but it had been a mushroom-like growth that made the fruit turn sour, nothing like this.

Chime stepped down the wall, and picked cautiously at the damaged wood. It flaked away under his touch. "It doesn't look like blight. It looks like the wood is just dying, for no reason."

"I was afraid you'd say that." Flower stepped back, her face etched with worry. "Because that's what it looks like to me, too."

Knell grimaced and shook his head in denial. "But this tree must be hundreds and hundreds of turns old. How can . . ."

Moon wasn't sure how Knell meant to finish that sentence. Maybe *How can our luck be this bad?* that Indigo Cloud had come back to this place just as the ancient tree was finally failing.

He heard movement behind him and caught Jade's distinctive scent, then Stone's. He glanced up just as Stone came around the curve of the passage.

Stone's reaction answered one question. Moon had just had time to form a slight suspicion that Stone might have known about this when he had brought the court here, that he had meant this to be only a temporary resting place, not a permanent home, and he just hadn't bothered to inform anyone of his plans. But Stone was in groundling form, and as he stopped in the passage, his expression of shock was easy to read. Moon found himself wishing his suspicion had been right. At least then there might have been a plan for what to do next.

Stone put one hand on the wall. "This is heartwood."

Jade stepped past him, and worriedly looked up at the blight spread across the curve of the ceiling. "What's heartwood?"

He grimaced. "It's the core of the tree. It can't die, because it doesn't grow, it doesn't change."

"Then what is this?" Flower pointed to the blight.

Stone abruptly turned away, back up the passage. There was a startled moment of hesitation, then they all scrambled to follow.

They passed Pearl and River out in the stairwell and Knell skittered to a halt to explain. Stone tore past out into the big hall with the Arbora workrooms. He jumped down into the well, shifted into his winged form in mid-air, then caught the lip of a gallery and climbed rapidly straight down the wall. Moon leapt after him, the others following.

He thought Stone was going all the way down to the roots, so was caught unprepared when Stone suddenly whipped over a balcony three levels down. Moon caught a pillar with his tail to stop himself, and swung up and onto the balcony.

Stone took a passage toward the interior, flowing down it like a dark cloud. His tail whipped back and forth, and Moon hung back to avoid being struck.

Then Stone stopped abruptly in front of a large hollow in the wall. Moon slid to a halt and backed up hastily, out of tail range, just in case Stone hadn't wanted to be followed. But Stone shifted to groundling, and stepped forward into the hollow.

Now that the bulk of Stone's other form wasn't blocking the way, Moon saw there was a plaque at the back of the hollow, large enough to be covering a doorway, with a carving of intertwined branches with leaves and fruit. "The bolts are broken," Stone said, and touched the carving.

As the others caught up, Moon shifted to groundling and stepped forward to look. Broken pieces from the side of the plaque lay on the floor near the wall, as if they had been kicked out of the way. He hissed under his breath, the realization making him cold. *Like the carving in the stairwell. Like the broken bins and jars.* He looked at Stone, whose face was still with suppressed fury. *Someone's been here before us.*

From behind them, Pearl said harshly, "Stone, what is this? What's wrong?"

"I don't know yet." Stone shoved at the plaque, and with a raw creak it swung open, revealing a dark opening. It released the strong scent of stale air laced with a faint sweetness. Stone snarled and stepped inside. "Flower, make a light!"

Flower hurried forward, lifting the spelled rock she had used to examine the rotting wall. Moon moved aside for her, and she slipped through the doorway after Stone.

The light revealed an oval chamber, the walls rough and unworked, just dark, warm wood. There were no light-shells mounted anywhere either, as if no one was meant to be in here. Then Moon looked down at the floor. It was covered with white tendrils, like the exposed roots of a plant. The resemblance to something that lay in wait on the ground to whip up and grab unsuspecting passers-by made Moon jerk back, and he bumped into Jade.

She took his shoulders and moved him aside, and said quietly, "Stone, talk to us. What is it?"

Stone hissed, passing a hand over his face. "Someone's been in here and taken the seed. It should be there, in the cradle."

Moon craned his neck to look. In the center of the tendrils was an empty space, round, not much bigger than a melon. The tendrils around it were cut and had turned dark with rot. Stone continued, "The seed is what changes an ordinary mountain-tree into a colony tree, that lets the Arbora shape the tree and change it. Without it, the tree is rotting from the inside out."

For a stretched moment the room was silent. *He said something was wrong,* Moon thought. Up in the consorts' bowers yesterday, Stone had been uneasy. Not because of old memories, or seeing the place in this empty state after so long away. Because the tree itself must have felt different, wrong.

Flower groaned under her breath. River twitched uneasily and looked at Pearl, who stood like a statue. Then Jade let out her breath in a low hiss. She said, "Can you tell how long it's been gone?"

Stone scrubbed a hand through his hair in frustration. "No. I'm not a mentor."

Everyone looked at Flower, who lifted a hand helplessly. "I'll have to look through our histories. I've never even seen a mountain-tree before, and I can't augur the past."

"They wouldn't have taken it with them?" Jade persisted. "The court, Indigo and Cloud, when they left?"

"No." Stone sounded certain about that. "There's no other use for it, and it has to stay with the colony tree, or the tree dies." He looked at her, his gaze sharp. "It can't have been missing long. I came here two turns ago, to make sure nothing had happened, that the tree was still livable. It didn't feel wrong then. And I think the blight would be worse if the seed had been gone for turns and turns."

"It could be worse." Chime sounded sick. "We haven't had a chance to look at the roots yet."

Everyone stared at him, and River growled.

"What did the seed look like?" Moon asked. Everyone turned to him, and he clarified, "Is it covered with jewels or metal? Is there any reason to steal it besides making another colony tree?" He was wondering if other Raksura had taken it, though that didn't make much sense. Why take a seed to make a colony tree when there was a perfectly good colony tree, uninhabited and ready to occupy, right here?

"No, it looks like a seed," Stone said. "Like it's made of wood."

"It must be a powerful artifact, though." Flower bit her lip as she leaned down to touch one of the cut tendrils. "There are many magics something like that might be used for."

Moon stirred uneasily. Like the way the Golden Islanders used the rock from inside flying islands to make their boats fly. That wasn't a pleasant thought. If someone had stolen the thing for magic, it could have been cut to pieces, destroyed, anything.

"Maybe they stole other things." Chime turned to the others. "We saw a carving that was damaged where the inlay had been pried out. Whoever did this must have passed that way."

Jade nodded, her expression grim. "We've seen other things broken, in ways that didn't make sense. As if someone was searching."

Moon added, "They didn't get as far up as the Aeriat levels. The stones are still in the carvings there." The inlay was all up and down the main stairwell; the intruders couldn't have missed it.

Stone's eyes narrowed. "If they left other signs they were here—"

Pearl snarled suddenly, furious, and the sound echoed off the walls. Everyone but Stone twitched, and even he barred his teeth. Her voice a growl, she said, "These thieves left a trail! Find it!"

☾

The trail might be old, but last night the hunters had been looking for predator scat and traces of recent occupation, not signs that intruders had searched the tree within the past couple of turns. Now that they knew what they were looking for, it wasn't hard to find.

There wasn't enough dirt or moss on most of the floors to show tracks, but on the level below, off a main stairwell, two hunters reported finding a room with more smashed storage jars. Others found several more carvings, on passage walls and the pillars supporting a lower stairwell, where inlaid stones had been pried out. "They were in a hurry," Moon told Jade as they climbed down the well in the Arbora levels. "They could have checked every carving in the tree for inlay, but they didn't."

"It's as if they knew exactly what they wanted, and didn't waste any time once they found it," she agreed grimly, and swung down onto the next balcony.

The trail led to a level far below the Arbora's workrooms and the storerooms. This part of the tree had smaller passages and wells, narrower stairs woven through and around thick folds of wood. The floors were lumpy and the walls had been left rough and undecorated. Moon and Jade followed a passage toward the tree's outer trunk, and found Knell and a group of soldiers and hunters there.

As Stone and Pearl arrived, Knell said, "All the doors down here are sealed from the inside, so the hunters assumed no one had used them since the court left." He ran his thumb along the seam where the door met the wall. "But the other doors have a thick crust here, hard as rock, from turns of wind and rain forcing dirt through the cracks from the outside." He glanced up. "This one doesn't."

Pearl hissed. "Open it."

"Wait." Stone frowned at the door. "Let the Aeriat scout it from the outside first."

Jade regarded him doubtfully. "You don't think whatever took the seed is still out there?"

"I don't know what I think." Stone's voice was dry. "I just know I'm against the idea of opening any convenient passages to the ground at the moment."

"Very well." Pearl sounded as if it was an effort not to growl. Her spines twitched with impatience. "Hurry."

☾

With Stone, Chime, Vine, Root, and a few other Aeriat, Moon went up to the knothole entrance to take flight, making a cautious spiral down the outside of the tree.

They dropped past more platforms, through the spray of the waterfall. Some of the overgrown foliage was still flattened from the rain, but Moon spotted berry bushes, yellow vines that might be whiteroot, and tall slender nut-trees. They dropped further, until the sun was dimmed to a deep green twilight. The ground was thick with fern trees, their fronds spreading like giant parasols. The mountain-tree's roots were huge, great ridges of wood sloping down from the massive wall of the trunk and running out and away. Moon didn't sense any large animal movement, and the air tasted of the musk of small treelings. A whole tribe of green-furred ones fled shrieking as Stone dropped down to perch on a root.

The run-off of the tree's cascade formed a shallow marsh. Much of it was choked with weeds and lilies, but there were flat rocks arranged in a way that looked deliberate, and a lot of white objects that from this distance looked like flowers.

Moon landed on the upper ridge of another root, as Chime and the others lighted around him. He crouched for a closer look at the marshy water below and saw the white objects weren't flowers; they were the elaborate spiraled shells of snails, some as big as his head, with blue and green speckled bodies. Chime climbed down beside him, and said, "They must have cultivated these for food. I don't think we need any more lights, but we could use the shells for jewelry."

Moon gave him a look. "Because you all need more jewelry."

From above them, Vine called out, "I think the door is through here!"

Moon glanced up. Vine had landed higher on the root, where the ridge sloped up toward the bulk of the tree, looming over them like a giant cliff. He leaned down to peer into a cave-like opening in the living wood.

Moon hopped up to join him; the others scrambled to follow. The opening extended back into the tree, festooned with vines and stained with moss. He tasted the air, but there was no predator scent, and he couldn't sense any movement. He looked back at Stone, who climbed up the broad root, then shifted to groundling. He brushed past Moon to walk into the cave.

Moon swung inside and dropped down beside Stone. Only dim light made it this deep into the crevice, but Moon could see that a path had been formed in the wood, leading in toward the trunk. The path was heavily coated with dead fern fronds and beetle husks and seemed to dead-end in a flat wall of rough wood. Then he saw the steps cut into the wall, and the round shape of the door, about ten paces up.

Stone stopped so suddenly Moon brushed his shoulder. Stone looked down at a hollow in the side of the path. Leaf mold had piled up in it, washed there by rain. He knelt suddenly and dug through the detritus. Moon realized the mold covered a huddle of yellowed bones, still wrapped in disintegrating cloth and leather.

"What is it?" Vine asked from behind them.

"Bones. Looks like one of them didn't make it far." Moon crouched down for a closer look as Stone dug out the body, which had fallen or been shoved into the hollow.

Moon asked him, "It's not there?" He didn't think there was much hope that the seed had been left behind. It wouldn't be that easy.

"No." Stone stood, his jaw set in frustration.

Chime slipped past Vine and Stone and crouched down to poke at the remains. Root and the others crowded around to see.

Moon picked up the skull, but without flesh there wasn't anything to tell him what species it was. In shape it didn't seem much different from his own groundling form, but it could have bare skin, fur, scales, feathers.

Still digging through the leaf mold, Chime pulled out a handful of small metal disks, badly tarnished. "I think those are buttons. There's some thick leather down here, maybe a belt . . . There's more than one here. There's too many bones, and this." He held up another part of a skull, this one with the jaw sheared off.

Moon heard a thump and twitched around, then realized it had come from the sealed door. Root bounced up to the doorway and knocked on it. After a moment it creaked, cracked, and then slid open, releasing a shower of dead bug shells. "We found groundlings!" Root reported.

Stone growled, irritated. "Groundlings that have been dead a turn."

The others spilled out of the doorway, and Jade landed beside Stone. She looked down at the bones, frowning in dissatisfaction. "Well, at least we know it was groundlings, and that they came here about a turn or so ago."

"This door doesn't open from outside, and it was still sealed with a bar," Knell said as he climbed down the wall. "They must have had help, someone who could fly up to the knothole, to get inside, and then let the others in down here."

"One of us?" Song wondered. "A Raksura?"

"Or something else that could fly or climb." Moon put the skull back on the pile of bones and stood. "It doesn't have to be a Raksura."

"Or they got some solitary to do it for them—" Root began, then twitched his spines in confusion. "Oh, sorry, Moon."

Moon controlled his annoyance. Even during a crisis this serious, nobody forgot who had been a feral solitary.

Chime flicked his tail at Root. "The question is, how do we track them?"

Knell edged past Stone to examine at the groundling bones. "It's been too long. We can't track them."

"We should search anyway," Jade said, and looked up to where Pearl sat crouched in the doorway. "If they left their dead behind, they might have left other traces, some sign of where they came from."

From Pearl's expression and the angle of her spines, she had already gone from righteously angry to depressed. Moon didn't think that was a particularly good sign. One of the problems at the old colony had been Pearl's growing apathy; necessity, and being away from the Fell's influence, had shaken her out of it. Now would be a terrible time for her to slip backward.

The moment stretched to an uncomfortable point. Then Pearl settled her spines, and said, "Go and search. Maybe they were careless."

Moon felt the others' relief. Their chances of finding something didn't matter; the important thing was that their reigning queen wasn't giving up. Or at least if she was, she was managing to hide it.

Jade acted as if she hadn't noticed the lapse, and told Knell, "Send someone for Bone. We need all the hunters."

CHAPTER FOUR

They started the search through the strange twilight world of the mountain-tree's roots, finding their way through the hanging moss and vines, the forests of fern trees, and the marshes. The teachers and the rest of the Aeriat had been told to keep searching the inside of the tree and up into the branches, on the chance that some trace of the thieves had been left inside.

Moon searched the ground with the hunters, but he didn't hold out much hope. Unless the groundlings had camped for a long period while trying to find a way into the tree, the damp and time would have wiped out any sign of them. And if they did find old evidence of a camp, it wasn't as though there would still be tracks to follow.

But there just wasn't anything else they could do at the moment.

Casting over the ground in a stand of reeds, he passed a clearing where Jade, Stone, and Flower were talking. He heard Jade ask Stone, "Does it have to be that seed? Can we get another?"

Stone didn't sound hopeful. "I don't know. Maybe."

Flower wasn't as discouraged. "I told Heart and Merit and the others to unpack the court's library. The answer should be somewhere there. I'm going to join them now."

Moon continued through the reeds, working his way further out. *If we could get another seed . . .* It was a hope to hold onto, at least.

As the roots spread further away from the mountain-tree, they grew smaller, only as big around as the trunks of the big fern trees. Some roots arched up off the ground, forming fantastic shapes, supporting curtains of moss and vines.

Then Bramble, one of the hunters, slipped out of the brush and made a faint clicking noise, beckoning Moon. Startled, Moon ducked under the foliage to follow her. He had been so convinced they wouldn't find anything.

They came to a tall thatch of big green flowers with brilliantly red centers. Bramble crouched in its cover and pointed.

Not far past the flowers was a shallow pond, barely more than a widened section of stream. It was home to a collection of snails with dark brown shells. And there was something crouched over the pool, watching the snails.

It was a groundling, but of a kind Moon had never seen before. Its legs and arms were skinny as sticks, lightly furred, and its torso was narrow and flat, and seemed to be all ribs; its stomach and bowels must be tiny, and he couldn't tell where it kept its sex organs. The head was squarish, eyes and mouth round, the nose just a slit. It had vines draped around its body, or maybe they were growing on its skin; it seemed to wear them like clothes.

Moon would have been half-inclined to think it was just a big treeling, but it had a bag slung over one shoulder, made of braided grasses, and a couple of sharpened sticks lay beside it on the rocks. Moon also thought a treeling would have noticed them by now. He looked inquiringly at Bramble, who shrugged to show she had no idea either.

It didn't look at all like the dead groundling, but if it lived here it might know something about the theft. Moon eased forward, and made a clicking noise in his throat.

The groundling glanced absently around, saw him, and froze. Then it shrieked, bounced up, and splashed across the pool to dodge off between the ferns.

"Go get the others," Moon told Bramble, and lunged after it.

He caught up with it in two bounds, landed on top of the curve of a root as it ran beneath. He could have caught it, but he was afraid if he dropped on it his weight would crush it like a bundle of sticks.

It ran through another stand of trees and he jumped to the ground to follow. Several hunters caught up with Moon just as he reached the end of the copse and slid to a halt. He had found a village.

Big round structures, huts made of woven sticks, hung from the undersides of the tallest roots, connected by elaborate webs of vine rope. There were dozens of them, strung all back through this part of the roots, as far as Moon could see. More of the strange groundlings gathered on the ground below. They sat on grass mats, weaving vines or sorting through piles of vegetation. They stared in blank surprise at Moon and the hunters. Some leapt to their feet or called out, but none made threatening gestures.

Chime dropped down next to Moon, and a moment later Stone walked out of the trees. Stone was still in his groundling form, which was probably a good thing, since they didn't want to terrify these people.

"These aren't anything like the dead groundlings we found," Chime said, studying the strangers. "The ribs were too big."

Stone eyed the nervous groundlings. "These are Kek. They're native to this forest, like we are."

Jade landed beside Moon and folded her wings. Song came up behind them, while Root and Vine perched on the fern tree branches overhead. The hunters gathered around, their spines pricked with curiosity. Jade said, "These people live under the roots?"

Stone said, "They're good for the tree. They help keep the soil around it healthy. We didn't have any Kek when the court left. They were dying out in this part of the forest." He stepped forward, holding out empty hands.

One of the Kek came toward them as the others gathered nervously behind it. It looked old, as far as Moon could tell. Its body was thin even by Kek standards, and it had lots of white stringy things hanging off it in odd places. It was wearing a necklace of small shells, and carried a staff with tattered leaves attached to the end.

Stone added, "They don't have any reason to take the seed. But they might have seen who did."

☾

With Jade and Chime, Moon sat down on the spongy carpet of moss that covered the ground and listened to Stone talk to the Kek. The Aeriat and the hunters gathered behind them, perched in the fern trees, and the other Kek, reassured by Stone's overtures, came out to gather around their leader. Some tiny Kek, the young of the tribe, peered at them from the safety of the hanging huts.

Fortunately Stone could speak a pidgin version of the Kek language, which he had learned when he was a boy, who knew how many turns ago. The old leader, whose name was something that sounded like "Kof," could speak a pidgin version of Raksuran, but not Altanic or Kedaic or anything else Moon recognized. With gestures and a lot of fumbling for words, Stone drew out their story.

These Kek had left the roots of their original colony tree when their population became too large for comfort, splitting off from the main tribe. When applied to for help, the Raksura there had given them directions to this colony tree, long abandoned, and they had traveled across the ground in search of it, finally reaching it about twenty turns ago.

"They know a lot about us," Chime said hopefully, "Maybe they took the seed for safe-keeping or something and they'll give it back when we ask."

To that optimistic suggestion, Stone replied, "Shut up."

Moon nudged Chime with his shoulder in sympathy. But he didn't think there was much hope that the Kek had taken the seed. If the Kek knew a lot about colony trees and depended on their roots as a place to live, they would know better than to do anything that might hurt one. He couldn't see these delicate creatures breaking bins and jars searching for treasure, or knocking inlay out of carvings. They didn't even wear wooden beads; everything they had was made from plants, with flowers or snail and insect shells for ornaments.

And when Stone asked about strange groundlings coming here recently, Kof shook his staff in assent.

It had been when the warm rain season ended and the cool rain season started with the second growth of the moss-flowers, which Stone identified as being a little more than a turn ago. When he asked if the groundlings had come on foot, Kof had waved vaguely.

"They must have come on foot. They couldn't get a wagon through here," Moon put in.

"They might have had a flying boat, like the Islanders," Jade said. "That would have been more of a clue to where they came from."

Stone coaxed out more information. Apparently Kof hadn't seen them himself. The Kek who had approached them to talk had been attacked, and three killed. The village had feared they were being invaded, and all had fled to a safer position on the far side of the tree. But the scouts who had stayed behind had seen the groundlings enter through one of the doorways in the roots.

"How did they open it?" Jade asked, overriding several people trying to ask the same question, including Moon and Chime. Some of the Kek jerked back in alarm.

Stone paused to hiss for quiet. Kof lifted his hands. "Do not know. Door opened."

"What then?" Stone asked.

After a time, the scouts had seen the strange groundlings leave through the same door. Not long after that the groundlings had left the area, a process which Kof described with vague waving motions. When the Kek had ventured to investigate, they had found the door closed again.

"That doesn't tell us much more than we already knew," Jade said, tapping her claws impatiently. "What did the groundlings look like? Did they have skin or fur?"

Stone translated the question, but Kof scratched his chin tendrils thoughtfully, not seeming to understand. Moon shifted to groundling, which caused a stir among the Kek. Apparently it had been a long time since they had seen a Raksura shift. He leaned forward beside Stone, and pushed his sleeve up and held out his arm. "Skin like this, like we have, or something else?" Stone held out his arm too, dull gray next to Moon's dark bronze.

Kof reached out and touched Stone's arm, then Moon's; it was like being gently brushed with sticks. Kof turned and spent a few moments consulting the other Kek, some of whom had presumably seen the groundlings. Then he spoke to Stone again, who translated, "At least some of them had bare skin like our groundling forms. They didn't see many of them closely, so the others might have been different." He added to Kof, "But your scouts didn't kill any? Up in the root passage near the doorway?"

Kof replied with an emphatic negative. The strange groundlings were strong, and had metal weapons, and the Kek knew they couldn't survive a battle. They had hoped only for the strangers to leave, and once the strangers had, they hoped they never came back.

"Tell him they won't come back," Jade said, propping her chin on her hand, disappointed. "They got what they wanted."

☾

They left the Kek, who were happy to have the colony tree inhabited again, even though Stone had told them it might not be permanent. When they got back to the greeting hall, Stone went up to lie on the floor of the queens' level and growl at anyone who came near him. Pearl disappeared, probably to barricade herself in a bower with River and her other favorites. Bone went down to report the conversation to Flower and the other mentors, who were trying to find information about the seed in the court's library.

Moon ended up standing in the teachers' hall with Jade, Chime, and a dispirited collection of Aeriat and Arbora. "What do we do?" Bell asked, glancing uncertainly at Rill.

"We were going to clean out the rest of the bowers on this level, and start working on the gardens, but . . ."

"The flying boats need repairs before we send them back," Blossom added, then made an exasperated gesture. "I mean, even if we have to use them again, they still need work."

"And we still have to eat." Bead shrugged wearily.

Jade twitched her spines in half-hearted agreement. "Whatever happens, we'll be staying here for a time. The hunters will search for game, with the warriors to make scouting flights and guard them. The others can keep making the bowers comfortable, and start the repairs to the flying boats."

Everyone seemed relieved to have a decision made; even if they didn't know what to do in the long run, at least they knew what to do now.

As the group dispersed, Moon caught Chime's frustrated expression. He nudged him with an elbow. "Go help Flower and the others."

Chime hesitated. "You think I should?"

"That's more important right now." From the way the others were talking, all the hunters and most of the warriors were going out to hunt. They didn't need Chime, and the mentors could probably use all the help they could get.

After a moment of indecision, Chime nodded. He seemed relieved to have something to do that he felt confident about. "You're right. I'll go help with the books."

As Chime left, Jade said, "I'll go down and help them as well. I don't know as much about the library as a mentor, but the last few turns I haven't done much more than study."

Moon realized he had been assuming that he was going on the hunt. "Uh, do you mind if I go hunting?"

She tilted her head, giving him a sideways look. "Would it matter if I did?"

A little stung, Moon said stiffly, "Yes." Then he hesitated and found himself adding more honestly, "Probably."

Jade sighed, but it was wry. She said, "Go on."

Moon went.

☾

The hunt turned out to be almost interesting enough to distract Moon from worrying about their immediate future. With a group of Aeriat, he scouted the suspended forest, finding that grasseaters lived on the platforms of the mountain-trees. After a consultation with Bone, they decided to focus their attention on a herd of jumping grasseaters that looked like the eastern bando-hoppers, except with dull green fur, horns, and much meaner dispositions.

The colony tree's platforms weren't connected to those of the surrounding trees, though the Arbora had found the remnants of wooden bridges, long since collapsed. The Aeriat flew the hunters over to a platform near the bando-hopper-like creatures, and the hunters took it from there, finding their way from tree to tree, leaping or swinging down to the lower platforms, crossing branches, or climbing the swathes of greenery to the higher levels.

In a clearing on one of the platforms, perched on a dead hopper, Moon watched the end of the hunt. They still needed to identify the big predators in the area, and the Aeriat would have a lot more scouting to do, but he could believe that this suspended forest was the place the Arbora had been meant to live. The green-tinged sunlight was bright, the place sang with birdsong, the breeze, over the blood and dead hopper, was laced with the scents of a hundred different flowers. As Bone dragged another carcass into the clearing, Moon said, "This is a good place."

"Well." Bone straightened up and shook blood out of his head frills. "It would have been." He sounded resigned.

Moon didn't think it was time for resignation yet. "We fought off a Fell flight that had crossbreed mentors," he pointed out.

Bone sighed. "If we had something to fight, I wouldn't worry."

When the hunters called a halt, Moon helped transport the carcasses back to the colony. They had enough fresh meat for the whole court for a few days, and the Arbora could dry some to store. The hunters took over the skinning and butchering, and Moon flew to one of the platforms to stand under a small waterfall, rinsing his scales off. He had fond memories of the hot water baths at the old colony, heated by rocks that the mentors spelled to give off warmth. They could have much the same set-up here, once they cleaned out the moss and figured out how to get the water to flow back into the pools throughout the tree. If they were here long enough.

To dry his wings, he flew over to the platform where the flying boats were docked and landed on the *Valendera*'s deck. A group of Arbora worked on the ship under Niran's direction and Blossom's watchful eye, sanding away claw marks, patching holes, and winding new ropes. The news had already spread, and Moon found Niran unexpectedly sympathetic. "It's similar to the loss of a ship's sustainer," he said, leaning on the railing. "The rock that forms flying islands is hard to obtain for those who have no means to reach it. Instead of trying to purchase it, some try to steal it." He shook his head. "But we know where to get more, and we don't live in our ships."

Blossom leaned on the railing beside him, her spines and frills drooping with depression. "I don't know what we're going to do. We were all counting on living here."

"Can't you find another place to live in this forest?" Niran asked. It was something Moon had been wondering himself. "Are there other deserted colonies?"

Blossom's expression was bleak. "There must be, but all of them would be claimed by their original courts. Just like this tree still belonged to us, even though we hadn't been back here in generations. If we take someone else's colony and territory, even if it's unused, it leaves us vulnerable to challenges by other courts. We'd have to leave the Reaches completely. That's a long trip, when we don't know where we're going."

Moon had no answers. There were more than enough Arbora working and he didn't want to just stand here and watch. He jumped over the side, flew back up to the knothole entrance, and took the winding passage into the greeting hall. Several soldiers were still there on guard, a considerably more glum group than they had been that morning. One looked up, a dark green Arbora with a heavy build, and Moon recognized him. It was Grain, one of the soldiers who had ordered Moon out of the old colony on his first day there.

If Grain remembered the incident, Moon couldn't tell; he looked just as depressed as Blossom. He told Moon, "They're all down in the big room below the teachers' level, reading."

Moon twitched his tail in acknowledgement and headed for the stairs. "Big room below the teachers' level" actually took in a lot of territory, but he found them in the room they had been using to sort the unloaded supplies from the ships. It was round, with several passages leading away or up into the bowers, and the domed ceiling was a carving of the sky, with the sun's rays stretching out to give way to stars, then the half-moon. Light-shells ringed the room, set just below the rim of the carving.

All the mentors and several teachers sat around on the floor, reading from loosely bound books or piles of loose parchment. Jade sat near Flower and Merit and Chime, paging through a thick book.

Moon shifted to groundling, because everybody else was, and Jade was in her Arbora form. He went to sit next to her, and she put an arm around his waist to tug him against her side. He leaned against her, and rubbed his against hers. She said, "Was it a good hunt?"

"It was great," he said absently, distracted by the book. The paper was a thick, soft parchment, the binding a silvery cord as thin as wire, the covers a soft blue reptile hide. The writing was absolutely incomprehensible. It looked like a solid block of serpentine scrawl, ornamented in places with colored inks. He hoped he was looking at some sort of decorative embellishment, until Jade turned the page and hope sank. He snuck a look at the books and papers that Flower and Chime and the others were examining. No, this was actually the writing.

He could read Altanic and Kedaic well, and pick out words in several other common groundling languages, but this was a complete mystery. He assumed this was written Raksuran, but he couldn't even tell where one character ended and another began. He had had the vague idea that there might be a book about consorts, something that would give him some idea of how to behave, what was expected of him, or at least a better frame of reference. That was out; there probably was something like that, but it wasn't going to be written in Altanic.

He hesitated, but asked, "Did you find anything yet?" If they asked him to help, he wasn't sure what he was going to say. He would have to admit it eventually and ask someone to teach him, but he would rather not do it just yet. He didn't want to give River and his cronies anymore ammunition to use against him just now, not with the court so unsettled.

"I think we finally found where we need to be looking," Jade said, her voice dry. "That's an improvement."

Chime stirred, rubbing the back of his neck. "We started with the oldest records first, but those all seemed to be from the time Indigo and Cloud led the court away."

Flower nodded, not looking up from her book. "It looks like the paper they used started to fall apart, and they had to re-copy most of the old volumes. They were in too much of a hurry to bind most of it. So we can't go by age of the cover to tell the date. We just have to read until something indicates it."

From what Moon could tell, she had continued to read the entire time she was speaking. Being a mentor was apparently even more complicated than it had seemed at first glance.

Merit turned a page, yawning. "At least we found out that when the court originally left, there was no mention of anything being wrong with the tree."

"Stone already said that," Heart pointed out.

Merit shrugged. "I know, but at least if he hadn't been here to tell us we would have found it out anyway."

Heart frowned at him. "Could you make less sense? I almost understood that."

"Argue later, read now," Flower said, a growl in her voice.

Moon waited until they were all deeply engrossed in the books again, then slipped away.

He stopped at the nurseries to visit the kids, trying to forget the court's troubles while the Sky Copper royals played mock-fight with some of the young fledgling warriors, and the baby Arbora climbed on him.

Spring came to sit next to Moon, and said, without preamble, "Copper says we can't stay here." She was a gawky, half-sized warrior; she and her clutchmate Snow were the oldest warrior fledglings, the only survivors of the old sister-queen Amber's last clutch.

Moon eyed her over the head of the Arbora toddler who had clamped herself to his chest. It was either Pebble or Speckle, he couldn't tell them apart yet; even their scent was identical. "Who's Copper?"

Snow, who was shy, edged up behind Spring and supplied, "He thinks he's smart, because Flower says he'll be a mentor when he grows up."

Moon ruffled Pebble or Speckle's head frills, trying to think how much to say. The little queen Frost had switched sides at some point in the mock-battle and had pinned Thorn to the floor; she stopped to listen, and so did the rest of the combatants. Bitter, perched on Frost's back, watched Moon with wide eyes. Three teachers, busy feeding baby Arbora, also looked over this way, worried and curious.

Moon let out his breath, resigned to being the bearer of this news. "We don't know yet. But we might."

He was braced to have to explain the theft of the seed, and just hoped he could do it in a way that wouldn't make them all feel that the tree might be invaded at any moment. But Frost just said, "On the flying boats?"

Moon admitted this would probably be the case. Then Thorn flung the distracted Frost off him, Bitter pounced, and the game resumed.

Snow bounded off to join the other fledglings, but Spring said, "They don't understand."

Moon thought Frost, Bitter, and Thorn probably did understand, but compared to what they had been through, moving again just wasn't a daunting prospect. The others were still unsettled by the Fell attack, and most seemed to be just pretending it hadn't happened. Spring was old enough to realize all the implications of their situation, and maybe starting to feel the weight of the responsibility she would have soon, as a female warrior from a queen's clutch. He tried, "We survived the Fell, we'll survive this."

It worked better on Spring than it had on Bone. She sat up a little straighter and said, "We will."

☾

Later Moon went back to the teachers' hall, but found that in a frenzy of organization, the Arbora had moved everyone into newly-cleaned bowers. He found the one Jade had been moved into, a good-sized room on the far side of the nurseries, with a balcony looking out onto the stairwell and an intricately carved ceiling. Furs and cushions had been arranged on the floor for seating areas, there were warming stones in the hearth basin, and the blankets were piled into the big hanging bed. Moon found his fur blanket on top and took that as a good sign that he was living here too. He slung himself up into the bed for a nap.

Jade woke him sometime later, climbing atop him for sex before he had a chance to ask how things were going with the books. Afterward, she fell asleep, and he lay there stroking the frills along her back, thinking of how much he wanted to live here with her. He would live anywhere with her, but here was his first choice.

He drifted off again, and next time woke to Merit knocking on the bottom of the bed. "Jade? Flower says she found something."

☾

They gathered in the teachers' hall, under the branches of the carved glade. Stone had reappeared, aborting the argument about who would go and get him. Vine brought Pearl, River, Drift, and a few other Aeriat back from wherever they had been. Chime, Bone, Knell, and Bell were here, but none of the others had been summoned. Everyone seemed to intend to wait until they had a coherent plan before calling everyone else together to hear it. Though given the speed with which news spread among the Arbora, calling a meeting of the entire court probably wouldn't be necessary.

While everyone found a place and sat down, Flower settled in the center of the group. She had a roll of paper in her lap, its painted leather case lying nearby. "We found a mentor's journal that speaks of the seeds. Unfortunately it doesn't speak of what to do when a colony tree loses its seed. I suspect we may be the first court to ever have this problem, at least as far as our ancestors knew."

Jade snorted in bitter amusement. "Why does that not surprise me." Moon had been thinking the same thing.

Pearl spared her a glare, and prompted Flower, "Then what does it say?"

"It says how the seeds are made." Flower tapped the roll of paper in her lap. "They're taken from the heart of a mountain-thorn, a very rare plant that grows only in these western Reaches. This tree was seeded from a mountain-thorn about four to five days of warriors' flight from here, which is occupied by the court of Emerald Twilight. Or it used to be occupied by it, when this was written."

"They're still there." Stone's expression was at its most opaque. He didn't seem to find this news as encouraging as everyone else did. "I saw their scouts when I was here two turns ago. They're the oldest court in this reach, and the largest."

Jade leaned forward, her expression intent. "So we can ask them for another seed?"

Flower nodded. "I think it's our best hope. Of course we don't know if there are any to spare, but we can certainly ask."

Everyone looked at Pearl. She twitched her tail angrily. "I suppose it'll have to be a formal embassy." She said this as if it was a terrible thing to contemplate.

Moon looked at Jade, whose expression was more disgruntled than grim. No one else seemed taken aback by the idea of a formal embassy either. Apparently Pearl just didn't like other Raksura. *At least it's not just me,* he thought.

"We'll have to go begging to them," Pearl added, her tail flick turning into a full-out lash. Her warriors sidled away a little, out of immediate hitting range.

Jade told her, "I'll go. If you go, it will look like begging."

Pearl eyed her angrily. "You've never greeted another queen before, not as an embassy. You never even went to Wind Sun."

Jade bristled. "I would have, if I'd been given the chance." She looked away for a moment, clearly gathering her patience. "It's a good time for me to learn."

Pearl was obviously torn between not wanting to give Jade an important responsibility, and hating the idea of going herself. She finally said, "Fine, then. You'll leave tomorrow."

Moon felt the tension in Jade's body relax, and he took a breath of relief himself. They had a plan, a chance, or at least a way to get more information, and Pearl wasn't going to be difficult about it. Or no more difficult than she normally was, anyway.

Then Stone cleared his throat. Pearl regarded him steadily for a moment. "What?"

He said, "Indigo Cloud doesn't have an alliance with Emerald Twilight."

Pearl dismissed it. "We'll offer alliance. They have no reason not to accept."

Moon managed to keep his expression blank. Emerald Twilight had no reason not to accept because Pearl hadn't been here to antagonize them, the way she had Wind Sun, the court that had refused to help fight the Fell.

Stone scratched his neck, and added thoughtfully, "We almost went to war with Emerald Twilight, before Indigo Cloud left the Reaches."

There was a startled murmur from everyone. "War?" Flower repeated, incredulous.

"Are you serious?" Jade demanded.

Pearl lifted her spines. "Was it something you did? Just tell us."

Stone glared at her. "I was barely ten turns old." Under Jade and Pearl's concentrated stares, he admitted, "Indigo stole Cloud from a daughter queen at Emerald Twilight. I forget her name."

"Stole?" It was Moon's turn to stare. "What . . . how . . . That can happen?"

"We can only hope," River put in, nastily. Drift snickered.

Moon met River's gaze in deliberate challenge. "Do you need another beating?"

"Quiet, both of you," Pearl snapped. She turned back to Stone. "Was Cloud taken?"

"Yes. The daughter queen took him when he was too young, and after a few turns, it wasn't working out. There was no clutch yet." Stone shrugged. "At least that's our side of the story. I have no idea if that's actually true or not."

Bone shook his head, affronted. "Is this even in the histories?"

Flower groaned and rubbed her eyes. "I've never seen it there. And I'm fairly certain I'd remember."

This sounded serious. Nobody seemed to think that maybe Emerald Twilight would have forgotten the incident by now. Moon wasn't even sure what they meant by "stolen." *Kidnapped, carried off? Like the Fell did with the Arbora?* He didn't need anything new to worry about.

Jade tapped her claws on the floor, impatient. "How did it happen?"

Stone said, "This was when Indigo was still a sister queen—when her mother Cerise was still alive—and she was visiting Emerald Twilight. She saw Cloud and just . . . grabbed him. Half the queens in the Reaches got together to settle it to prevent a war, and by that time Indigo had talked Cloud into accepting her and repudiating his first queen. The other queens talked Emerald Twilight into letting it go." He spread his hands. "It was a successful match. Indigo succeeded as reigning queen, the court renamed itself after her and Cloud, and they led us to a new colony when this one started to fail. They had eight clutches. But I have no idea how Emerald Twilight sees it."

Everyone was silent as they digested that. Bell and Knell exchanged an uneasy glance. Bone growled under his breath, sounding disgruntled.

Chime cleared his throat. He said tentatively, "Maybe this would be a good time to revisit the discussion about changing the court's name?"

Everyone ignored him. Jade asked Stone, "If we had to search for another colony, where would we go?"

Stone's expression wasn't encouraging. "If we stay in the Reaches, we'd have to find an unclaimed territory and build one ourselves. That means no solid shelter for the rain seasons, no prepared ground for gardens."

Her voice quiet, Flower said, "I'm afraid to think how many of the wounded and the aged wouldn't survive that."

Chime hunched his shoulders, as if shuddering at the thought. "We've had too many illnesses in the last twenty turns. I know it was the Fell influence on the old colony, but if we have another outbreak of lung disease . . ."

Moon could imagine it all too readily. He had seen enough failing groundling camps to know what could happen. A fire, a flood, a bad crop year, a disease that took too many for the group to recover. Small settlements were vulnerable, especially when forced to migrate.

Stone didn't acknowledge their comments, and just continued, "If we go back outside or into the Fringes . . . I'd have to scout for a ruin to settle in."

"And hope you could find one before this tree collapses on us," Knell said.

Pearl told Jade, "We'll try Emerald Twilight first. You'll just have to go anyway and hope that . . . Just hope."

Jade nodded, for once in complete accord with Pearl. "I will."

The talk turned to who would go, and exactly what a formal embassy should consist of. Apparently five warriors was the right number for a formal greeting, and everyone thought that the addition of Stone and Flower would show how serious their errand was. Also, Jade admitted, it might make Emerald Twilight think twice if they were inclined to be difficult and refuse the greeting. It was a much more serious breach of etiquette to ignore a line-grandfather and an elderly Arbora mentor.

"It takes away their choice to refuse," Pearl explained, still cranky even though she wasn't going. "Be aware that that alone may make them angry."

It was a good point, but Moon didn't think it mattered. If the other court was inclined to be angry, everything they did or didn't do was just going to make it worse. He was going to say so, when Pearl added, "And you'll need a consort with you. Moon will have to go along." Her tone made it clear she didn't enjoy this prospect at all.

Startled, Moon looked at the others, expecting an argument. Instead, everyone just nodded agreement. Some of it was reluctant agreement, but no one protested. Jade said, "But is he recovered well enough for a long flight?"

Flower said, "He should be. He's young, and his injuries healed well. And I'll be there if he has any trouble."

It wasn't his injury that Moon was worried about. "Are we sure that's a good idea?" He wanted to go, to see the mountain-thorn if for no other reason, but the etiquette of the formal visit sounded fraught with complication. There were so many nuances he didn't understand, even here. He didn't think he was ready for a big busy court yet. "Stone's already going."

Flower explained, "Stone is a line-grandfather. And they'll expect Jade, as a sister queen, to bring her own consort. A sister queen and a consort are essential for a first-time meeting with a court of Emerald Twilight's stature."

With a grim expression, Knell said, "And when they ask what court he's from, what are you going to say?"

And here was yet another nuance Moon didn't understand. As far as he knew, he was from this court. "What do you mean?"

Jade answered, "It's going to be a formal embassy. If we introduce you, we have to give your lineage."

"Oh." That was going to be awkward. He didn't want to have to explain himself or prove that he wasn't a crazy solitary every time they met someone new. "Can't we just make one up?"

Jade gave him an exasperated look. "No."

He thought it was the best solution. "You could say I came from Sky Copper." The only survivors of the destroyed court were Frost, Thorn, and Bitter, and they could probably be coached to confirm the story if it was ever necessary.

Stone looked intrigued at the suggestion, but Jade said, "Moon, no."

There was an uneasy silence.

Stone said, "So it's going to be, 'This is Moon, we won't say where he came from so you can assume he's a feral solitary.'"

Jade gave him a sour look. "How about, 'and this is Stone, our cranky line-grandfather that we dragged along so he could start fights with everyone.'"

Grimly determined, Pearl told Moon, "You'll have to tell them the truth. Just don't embarrass us."

Moon suppressed an irritated hiss. "I've walked into strange camps and settlements all my life. I know how to act." But even as he said it, he knew he would probably eat those words.

☾

Later, Moon and Jade sat outside on the edge of the knothole, watching the fall of night under the mountain-trees. The light had turned a deep green-gold, gradually fading as the sun set somewhere past the trees. A little flurry of tiny yellow flying things played in the spray of the waterfall. When one strayed close enough, Moon realized they were flying frogs, something he hadn't seen before. On one of the platforms about a hundred paces below, a group of Arbora still explored the beds of the old gardens, searching for buried roots. A few young warriors flew around under the upper branches, looping and diving in play.

Her voice tight, Jade said, "I hope we can stay here."

It had to be what everyone was thinking tonight. Stone hadn't promised them anything, and this place had been more than any of them had expected. Moon leaned against her shoulder and said, "That was good, when you got Pearl to send you to Emerald Twilight instead of going herself."

Jade's spines rippled in a shrug. "It's not as if she wanted to go. She hates talking to other queens." She added, "I think we'll take Vine with us. Pearl trusts him, and taking him will make us look more united to the rest of the court."

Moon thought it was a little late for that. No one in the court with any sense could possibly have missed the tension between the two queens. But he didn't have any real objection to Vine. "What about Balm? She's done this before." Balm had gone to Wind Sun with Vine in an unsuccessful attempt to ask the other court for help.

"I want her to come. We need a female warrior to speak for us when we arrive. Floret's the only other one who's spoken to other courts before, and she's close to Pearl." Jade stirred uneasily. "But I've tried to talk to Balm, and it didn't go well. It was hard on the boats. There was nowhere private, and she wouldn't fly off anywhere with me."

It might be that Balm just didn't want to talk about what the Fell had done to her, not yet. Moon could understand that at a bone-deep level. "Tell her you need her help. Tell her it's her duty."

"It'll make her feel guilty."

"She already feels guilty." It might as well be used for a good purpose.

Jade thought about it a moment more, then nodded. "It can't hurt to ask. I'll go find her."

Jade went inside, and Moon sat there a while longer, watching the light fail. He was about to go in when a green warrior swooped down from above, cupping his wings to land on a narrow ledge just below the lip of the knothole. It was River.

Moon leaned back and propped himself on his arms, deliberately casual. "Here for that beating?" He really hoped so.

Sounding amused, River said, "You should be afraid of this trip, solitary. This will be a big court, with lots of consorts to spare."

Moon didn't show his sudden sense of unease. "So."

River climbed a little closer, gripping the bark with his claws. "Jade's never been near an adult consort she wasn't related to. All the ones at the courts near us were taken already, or too young. Why do you think she settled for you?"

Moon shoved forward and shifted in a blur of movement. But River fell backward off the ledge and twisted into a dive through the spray of the waterfall.

Moon stopped, trying to settle his spines. Chasing River was no good. It wasn't as if he could kill him when he caught him. It would upset the others too much.

The words stung because they were true. By the time Jade had grown to adulthood, Pearl had driven off the consorts who had been born to Amber, her sister queen, sending them to other courts. The other consorts had died of illness, or been killed in fighting off attacks on the colony.

Stone had said Azure had chosen him out of the lot, but Jade hadn't had a choice. It had been Moon or nobody, and the court had been reluctant to move without a consort for her.

He knew Jade wanted him now, but his position in Indigo Cloud had been far more secure when he was the only available consort in flying distance. He knew queens could take more than one consort, and have warrior and Arbora lovers, but that wouldn't affect his place in the court. And he had thought that as long as he was with Jade, he could handle it. He hadn't counted on the members of the court who weren't happy with an ex-feral solitary as first consort having the opportunity to pressure Jade to replace him.

Moon turned and went back to the passage, taking it through to the greeting hall, snarling under his breath. Now he had yet another reason to be uneasy about this trip.

CHAPTER FIVE

They left at dawn the next morning, flying under the canopy through the suspended forest. Traveling as fast as they could, Moon and Jade could have made the trip in three days rather than five. Stone could fly much faster than that, even carrying Flower, but all three kept to the warriors' pace. Everyone agreed that showing up at a strange court, especially one that had no reason to be friendly, without the warriors necessary for the formal greeting would waste more time than it would save. It would give Emerald Twilight's queens an excuse to delay speaking to them, or to refuse to see them at all. Moon had already gotten the idea that Raksuran courts saw no inherent reason to be nice to each other; this was just more proof that alliances between courts, let alone friendly relationships, had to be carefully managed.

The warriors they brought were Chime, Balm, Vine, Floret, and Song. Chime had spent little time outside the colony compared to the others, but after flying to the Golden Isles and chasing kethel across desert plains to a Dwei Hive, he wasn't much daunted by a trip to visit another court. Vine and Floret were Pearl's choices. Vine had visited other courts before, and he was easier to deal with than many of the warriors she might have picked. Moon didn't know Floret well. In groundling form, she had the copper skin and red-brown hair that was common in Indigo Cloud to both Aeriat and Arbora, and she seemed to get along with the others. Song was young, but Jade trusted her and she had visited Sky Copper when it was Indigo Cloud's closest ally. Moon had always thought her groundling form looked enough like Balm's for the two to be related; they both had warm, dark skin and curling, honey-colored hair.

Moon wasn't sure how Jade's talk with Balm had gone, but Balm had shown up in the greeting hall before dawn, ready to leave. She was tense and quiet whenever they landed to rest, but at least Chime and Song were treating her as they always had, as if nothing had ever happened. Hopefully that would help her feel more at ease.

Just before dawn, when they were nearly ready to leave, Moon had gone down to the nurseries to see Bitter, Thorn, and Frost. Most of the younger kids were still asleep or just stirring, so Bark had shooed them into one of the smaller rooms off the main area so they could talk without disturbing the others. Moon had told them he was going to be away for a while, and why. Considering how unconcerned they had been about the possibility of leaving the colony tree, he thought they would take it well. He was wrong.

Thorn huddled in a bristling unhappy heap, refusing to shift to groundling, and Bitter just stared at Moon with big hopeless eyes. Frost threw an actual fit, flared her wings, and snarled that he had no right to go and railed against Jade for taking him.

"Frost, stop." Moon had seen groundlings spank their young before and had no idea how that would work with a Raksuran fledgling queen. But he was ready to give it a try.

That must have shown in his expression, because Frost stopped in mid-word, eyed him a moment, and settled into a sulk. She said, "We don't want you to go. Who'll take care of us?"

"Bell and Bark and the other Arbora." Moon hadn't been taking care of them anyway, not the way the teachers were, with all the real work of feeding, bathing, and making them behave. On the boat, while his back and shoulder healed, he hadn't been able to do much of anything except watch them play.

"They can't fight like you can," Thorn said, his voice deeper and raspy in his other form.

"Pearl will be here." Pearl might be moody and pessimistic, but she could rip a Fell ruler apart like a straw doll and wouldn't hesitate when it came to physically defending the court.

Bitter leaned over to Thorn and whispered inaudibly. Thorn translated, "Bitter says we want you."

That one went right to the heart and Moon winced. He wasn't even sure why they felt that way about him. He had barely gotten them out of the Dwei hive before Ranea had caught him. It had been Jade and Pearl who had saved them all. But he had been the first Raksura they had seen since the destruction of Sky Copper, the death of everyone they knew, the end of their world. "I have to go. But when I come back, I'll teach you all how to hunt."

Bitter blinked. Thorn's spines flicked and the two exchanged a look. Frost's eyes narrowed suspiciously. She said, "Bitter can't fly yet. He's too small."

Sorrow had started teaching Moon to hunt when he was barely big enough to leap from branch to branch, a precaution that had allowed him to survive after she was killed. "He can still learn."

Frost had considered that, consulted with the two consorts, then finally agreed, grudgingly. "All right. But don't be away long."

Moon managed not to let her maneuver him into any promises as to how soon he would be back.

⟪

The scenery made the journey pass quickly. The variety of grasseaters and predators living on the platforms of the mountain-trees seemed endless; Moon saw tree frogs nearly as big as he was, mottled gray-green to blend into the bark, clinging to the broad branches and thoughtfully watching the Raksura fly past. And the trees themselves often took on fantastic shapes. They passed one that was covered with giant gray nodules, each as big around as the *Valendera*, and another that was hung with curtains of moss, thousands of paces long, draped like fabric. They had no difficulty finding the way; Raksura always knew which direction was south, an ability which Chime had described as a natural pull toward the heart point of the Three Worlds.

Moon's bad shoulder was sore after the first full day of flying, but the discomfort lessened every day, and he could feel the muscles stretching and getting strong again. He thought he was healing faster flying than he would have just sitting around the colony.

They stopped to rest and sleep on the platforms or the wide branches of the mountain-trees. As Moon had noticed when they crossed the grass plains together, Stone's presence seemed to drive off predators, even when he was in his groundling form, and he had the same effect here.

They slept one night in a hollowed out space on a branch, and Moon woke to hear the dry rustle of something big slithering away. He sat up, out of the warm pile of the others, to see the dark outlines of Song keeping watch at the top of the hollow and Stone sitting next to her. Song crouched down a little, but hadn't hissed an alarm. Stone must have heard Moon move, because he shook his head slightly, telling him it was all right.

From where he was huddled behind Moon, Chime whispered nervously, "What is it?"

"Nothing," Moon whispered back, and lay down again.

They had eaten heavily before they left the colony, but long days of flying made them hungry, so they stopped briefly to hunt as they went along. On the fourth day, Moon sat out the hunt with Stone, Jade, and Flower, watching from an upper branch as the warriors stalked a big wooly gras-seater on one of the platforms below. Stone had said they were close enough to Emerald Twilight that scouts might be watching. It brought home the fact that Jade might not care much about Moon's unconsortlike behavior, but another court would.

Jade had told him as much as she could about what to expect, but Moon could make all kinds of mistakes, most without even knowing he was making them. *This could go very badly wrong, and it could be my fault.* It wasn't a pleasant thought.

☾

On the afternoon of the fifth day, they flew into an open area under the forest canopy, and got their first glimpse of Emerald Twilight's mountain-thorn.

Thorn-covered branches as big around as the flying boats wound out and up to form a giant globe. The branches were wreathed with vines and flowers, and so large the smaller trees of the suspended forest had taken root on many of them. A trio of warriors flew across the clearing, banking close enough to see the newcomers, but not to bar their path.

Fortunately Stone seemed to know how to approach the colony. He flew unerringly toward a big wreath of vines that turned out to be marking a sizable gap in the thorns. Stone slowed further, and they followed him through the green tunnel.

Once inside they could see the central trunk of the thorn, bristling with branches and platforms, some formed naturally on the nested branches but many others constructed. There was a big one, near the center of the trunk, that had to mark the main entrance. More warriors flew around in this interior space, and Arbora were out on the platforms, working in the gardens or stopping to watch the visitors' arrival. This court was obviously much larger than Indigo Cloud.

They landed on the big platform, and Stone set Flower down. Moon folded his wings and managed to shift to groundling in time with the others. Only Jade stayed in her winged form. The arch of thornvines and leaves high overhead dappled the sunlight, and the air was scented with flowers. There was a narrow waterfall in the carved trunk, the flow controlled by small platforms somehow fixed at intervals down the tree's wall, each forming a little pond stocked with flowering water plants.

Chime leaned over to whisper to Moon, "We should do that in our tree. If we can stay in our tree, I mean."

Moon nodded, feeling overwhelmed. Again. The others were trying to look as if none of this was the least bit impressive, though Stone was the only one who managed it convincingly. Jade kept her expression blank, but Moon could read the tension in her shoulders and spines.

Arbora stood on the surrounding platforms, and Aeriat perched up in the branches, all watching them. Before it got more uncomfortable, a warrior dropped down from an upper balcony, cupping her wings to land lightly. She shifted to groundling, turning into a tall slim woman with dark bronze skin, and dark hair that was just beginning to lighten with age. Her sleeveless tunic and skirt were silky blue, trimmed with tiny silver-gray pearls.

Moon was suddenly glad they had taken the time to bathe in a stream and change clothes this morning. The warriors were dressed in the fine weaving of the Arbora, shirts over loose trousers, in soft blues and greens, dark rich browns, and Flower wore a dark blue robe. Moon's clothes were black, except for the sash over his knife belt, which was shot through with red. Jade wore a belt, pectoral, bracelets, and armbands of silver with dark blue stones and deep-water pearls. Stone looked like he always did, having made absolutely no concession to their hosts but then, as a line-grandfather, he didn't have to.

Looking around at the Emerald Twilight Arbora and warriors, Moon suspected they were still going to seem poor compared to these people, but at least they were clean. The warrior said, "I'm Willow, of Emerald Twilight."

It was normal for female warriors to greet strangers, and it had to be a good sign that one had come forward so readily. If Emerald Twilight had really wanted to be rude, the warriors could have simply ignored them. *At least they're open to visitors,* Moon thought. Maybe this wouldn't be too difficult.

Balm stepped forward to answer her. "I'm Balm, of Indigo Cloud. Our sister queen has come to greet your queen."

"Indigo Cloud?" Willow lifted her brows, startled. There was a stir from the watching Arbora and Aeriat, a wary flutter.

Damn it, Moon thought, biting his lip to control his expression. It didn't appear Emerald Twilight had forgotten Indigo Cloud, even after all these turns.

"Yes." Balm, with commendable self-possession, managed to look as if she thought the reaction was surprise due to hearing that a new court had arrived in the Reaches. "We've recently returned to our old colony, some five days flight from here."

"Oh." Willow hesitated, then seemed to decide that pretending ignorance of any past history between the courts was best for the moment. "Come into our greeting hall."

They followed her across the platform, through an arbor and a short tunnel into the trunk. The hall was a round high-ceilinged cavern, but it wasn't as impressive in size as the one at Indigo Cloud; the central well only went up six levels, with balconies looking down. It was softly lit and vines grew all around the balcony railings, the flowers purple, white, and blue. There was a shallow pool in the center, the bottom inlaid with polished white stones. It took Moon a moment to realize where the light was coming from. It wasn't the stones or shells or moss, it was the flowers.

On this level, three tall archways led off into the depths of the trunk. A queen walked out of the center one, still in her winged form, her light blue scales webbed with gold. Trailed by several warriors, she crossed toward them to stand in front of Jade. The two queens stared at each other for a moment and Moon found himself holding his breath. Then both shifted to Arbora.

Behind him, Moon heard Chime sigh with relief. Being acknowledged by a sister queen was the second big obstacle and it seemed they might get past it.

The new queen said, "Tempest, sister queen of Emerald Twilight."

"Jade, sister queen of Indigo Cloud." She inclined her head toward Stone and Flower. "Our line-grandfather, Stone. And Flower, who is a mentor, and our elder of Arbora."

"We're honored." Then Tempest looked at Moon. He kept his expression neutral, though he felt a flush creep up the back of his neck. Her glance seemed critical, which made it harder to bear. He had never seen another adult consort except for Stone, who was apparently not the best example, so he had no idea if he looked like he was supposed to or not.

Jade and Flower had explained that young consorts were only introduced to courts that were friends or allies. Since they had brought him, it was a sign that Indigo Cloud wanted to be friends, but the formalities would have to be gotten through first. Flower had also indicated that Emerald Twilight might possibly attempt to thwart that process by trying to skip the formalities, just to put Indigo Cloud in a weaker position. One way to do that was to try to provoke them to introduce Moon before it was time. It was all just as hideously complicated as he had feared. He knew he was going to fumble the etiquette at some point. He just wanted to get it over with.

He had been lucky when he had been brought to Indigo Cloud by Stone. There was no etiquette for solitaries, even if they were consorts.

After a moment that stretched Moon's nerves even further, Tempest gave in, and turned deliberately back to Jade. "We were aware another court had arrived in the Reaches. Our scouts reported that you came here in a strange way." She managed to convey the fact that she was bringing up a delicate subject. She had to mean the flying boats.

Jade said, easily, "We had wounded, and the wind-ships were the best way to move them. We fought the Fell at our old colony. We defeated them, but . . ." She flicked her spines in a slight shrug. "It was impossible to remain there."

Tempest tilted her head, suddenly genuinely interested. "The Fell attacked you?"

"We're a small court. Our colony was vulnerable." Jade's face tightened, as if it cost her something to make that admission to another queen. "They destroyed our closest ally, Sky Copper, a small court in the grass plains to the east. Then they attacked us." She hesitated, exchanged a glance with Flower, then continued, "This Fell flight had a scheme for interbreeding with Raksura. Apparently they had been carrying it out for some time."

The Emerald Twilight warriors stared, openly appalled. Tempest dropped her formal pose, leaned forward, and said in shock, "How? I mean— Is that even possible?"

Jade tilted her head to Flower, who said dryly, "It caught us by surprise, too."

Tempest and the others listened intently as Flower told the brief version of the story, of the Fell attack on the colony, the crossbreed mentor-dakti and their powers, the pursuit to the Dwei hive, and the crossbreed queen, Ranea. Flower left out any mention of how Moon had actually come to Indigo Cloud, and said only that the Fell poison had come from a groundling tribe in the far east. She did say that he had been badly wounded by the Fell after freeing the Arbora captives. Moon saw Tempest glance at him again, this time with a trace of sympathy. She was probably thinking, *So that's what's wrong with him.*

Then Flower pressed a hand to her lower back and winced. Jade said, in mild reproach, "We've come a long way."

Tempest flicked her spines in annoyance. Moon thought they had just scored a point, either because Tempest had been lured into a breach of etiquette by keeping them standing out here, or that she had treated them like people by engaging in a real conversation, and now had to either continue it or be deliberately rude. Whichever it was, Tempest said, not too grudgingly, "Come into our queens' hall. The others can wait over here, and be comfortable."

That was what they had been hoping for. Tempest led Jade, Flower, and Stone on through the big archway, and Willow took Moon and the others over to the side of the hall, furnished with cushions and a little metal brazier shaped like a berryvine leaf. They dropped their packs and took seats, and Willow retreated a short distance, politely out of earshot.

Aeriat and a few Arbora, all mostly in groundling form, wandered through the hall, or appeared briefly on the balconies above to snatch curious glances. Moon felt the pressure of their stares, and forced himself not to twitch nervously. He had always hated being stared at; in most of the places he had traveled, being singled out for curiosity was never a good thing.

"The warriors aren't coming to talk to us," Floret said. She folded her arms and looked uncomfortable. "They did when we visited at Sky Copper."

"Yes, but we'd known them for turns and turns," Balm told her. She sounded more like her old self. Being out of the colony and having something important to do was obviously good for her. "We've just met these people."

Song looked around, trying to be casual about it. "So you don't think we'll be invited to eat with the Arbora?"

"Be patient." The taller Vine dropped an arm around Floret's neck. "They haven't even gotten through the queens' greeting yet. It's going to be a while."

Then Balm murmured, "What's this? The queens should all be inside." Moon turned to look.

Another queen glided down from an upper balcony to land in the hall. Her scales were silver-gray, with a web-tracery of brilliant green. Moon expected to see her turn down one of the passages, but instead she furled her wings and started toward them.

Her pace was deliberate and she lashed her tail lazily. Sounding bewildered, Song whispered, "What is she doing?" Vine and Chime shushed her. The queen had the attention of the whole hall, everyone staring. At least the Raksura who lived here seemed to be just as taken aback by this as they were. Willow actually looked alarmed.

The queen came closer, focusing on Moon and ignoring the others. She stopped only a pace away, her gaze a threat and a challenge. Moon's shoulders tensed, his back itching to lift spines he didn't have at the moment. Then she said, "What a pretty thing. I'm surprised your queen leaves you unguarded."

Moon pushed to his feet, the movement slow and deliberate. She was a little shorter than him, which meant she was younger than Jade. He said, "Maybe she thought this was a civilized place." Behind him he heard a startled snort, possibly from Floret.

Surprised, the queen lifted her spines sharply. He realized she had expected him to be too intimidated to respond. Compared to Pearl, she just wasn't that intimidating. She snarled, "This is a civilized place. But if you're foolish enough to challenge me, don't think I'll spare you."

Behind him, the others stood now. They had the attention of the entire nervously silent hall. It occurred to Moon belatedly that he should have ignored the queen. He hadn't been introduced yet and no one from Emerald Twilight was supposed to be talking to him, so the breach of etiquette would have been all on her side. It was too late now. He tilted his head. "If you want to fight, then attack me." As a queen she could keep him from shifting, or at least try to, but if she fell on him while he was trapped in groundling form he doubted it would reflect well on Emerald Twilight.

She leaned toward him and hissed in fury. "If I thought you were serious—"

A dark shape dropped from an upper balcony, and landed lightly on the floor just a few paces away. The queen flinched back from Moon, and the others twitched away, startled. Song shifted to her winged form, then shifted back when Balm hissed at her. Moon didn't move. The newcomer was another consort.

He was nearly half a head taller than Moon, his shoulders broader. His black scales gleamed in the soft light with a faint red undersheen, and his eyes were a dark, deep brown. He dropped his spines and folded his half-furled wings, his hard gaze never leaving the young queen. Then he shifted to groundling.

He had even, handsome features, dark bronze skin, and was lean but strongly built. He was dressed in dark clothes and wore a gold band around his upper arm, over the silken material of his shirt, that was studded with polished red stones. Small gold hoops pierced his ears, all the way up the curves. He tilted his head at the queen and said, dryly, "Ash. What are you doing?"

She flared her spines. "Since when do you greet unwanted guests?"

He didn't respond to that obvious attempt at distraction. "Must I speak to your mother of this?"

Ash hesitated, half-snarling, then turned abruptly away and strode out of the greeting hall toward the outer platform.

The consort turned to Moon, eyeing him thoughtfully. Then he stepped closer. It should have been threatening, but Moon had to still the impulse to lean toward him. There was something about him, that ability to draw you in, the same power that Pearl had. With the consort it was easier to resist, and Moon couldn't tell if he was doing it consciously or not. He touched Moon under the chin, a light pressure that made Moon lift his head slightly. It was a challenge, but Moon didn't growl, didn't twitch away. He might still know little about how Raksura behaved, but he knew this wasn't that kind of challenge.

Then the consort said, "You're feral."

Behind Moon, there was a startled stir, and somebody hissed, offended. Apparently it was fine for Indigo Cloud to say it, but no one else was allowed. Chime started to say, "He isn't. He's—"

The consort flicked a look at them, and they all went still. *I wish I could do that,* Moon thought, not taking his eyes off the other man. The way he had said it had been a statement of fact, not an accusation. And it seemed to mean something else besides the usual insult. Moon replied, "A little."

There was a brief glint in the other consort's eyes, possibly amusement, but it was hard to tell. He let Moon go and stepped back. "But you're taken?"

Consorts couldn't tell, couldn't scent the marker that queens left on the consorts they took for their own. Moon said, "By Jade, sister queen of Indigo Cloud. I'm Moon."

"She must be brave." He considered a moment, watching Moon intently. "Will you come sit with me?"

It might be a bad mistake. This was a game Moon didn't understand and he had already made a serious error, just sitting here. But he didn't want this man to walk away without him. "Yes."

The warriors exchanged glances, worried and confused, as if they would like to object but knew better. Chime stared urgently at Balm, and she stepped forward and said, "What do we tell his queen when she asks where he is?"

"Say he is with Shadow, first consort to Ice, the reigning queen." Shadow shifted and leapt straight up to cling to the wall high above. Moon shifted and leapt after him.

They climbed all the way up to the fourth level, then Shadow slung himself up onto a balcony and shifted back to groundling. Moon followed, shifting as they started down the passage. Unlike the Indigo Cloud tree, the walls here weren't solid wood, but were made of dark brown vines, woven together. It left gaps for air to pass through, and Moon could catch glimpses of the rooms and passages to either side. He could also hear movement, the slight rustling of wings and spines, pacing them. There was a faint chance Shadow could be walking him into an ambush, but if so, the ambushers weren't doing a good job of concealing their presence.

As they walked, Shadow asked, "Why did you leave your birthcourt?"

That was an easy question, at least. "I didn't. They all died, when I was too young to remember."

Shadow's brow creased in a wince, but he didn't offer sympathy. "How did you survive at that age?"

"There were others at first, a female warrior and four younger Arbora. Later they were killed, too." He didn't add that he had thought the warrior was his mother and the others his siblings, until Stone had told him that was impossible.

The passage wound around, then opened into a larger hall. It was an irregular shape, with sections curving off out of sight, lit by more of the spelled flowers. It took Moon a moment to realize those were bowers suspended from the ceiling, formed of large globes or half-shells of woven vines. They dripped rich fabrics in jewel-like colors, reds, golds, shimmering in the light. Seating cushions and furs were scattered on the floor below them. The place smelled of jasmine and Moon heard water running, somewhere out of sight.

A dark shape climbed across the ceiling, then clung with its claws to the vines and hung upside down to watch them pass: another consort. Faces peered out of some of the bowers, some of them shifted to Raksura before climbing out. The back of Moon's neck itched with nerves. Everyone he saw was male, and when they shifted they had black scales. All consorts, and from the movement he could hear, there were a lot of them.

Moon had felt self-conscious plenty of times, but these were Raksura. They would be able to smell the sweat breaking out all over his body.

Shadow led the way through the confusing space toward the outer wall of the trunk, ignoring the curious stares. A doorway there let in green-tinted sunlight, and they went through and out to a broad open balcony.

It was protected by the arch of thorn vines and partly enclosed by the spreading canopies of smaller trees growing in the big branch just below. In a shallow pool lined with polished stone, tiny water-lizards skittered across and away at their approach.

Dark gray furs were spread near the pool. Shadow gestured for Moon to sit and settled across from him. Moon sat on the fur, trying to look calm, or at least neutral. From here he had a good view of the sculpture above the pool, where the whole side of the trunk had been turned into an elaborate carving. It was made up of small figures of Raksura, Aeriat and Arbora. They were all different, all picked out in delicate detail. Beneath the figures were rows of twisty writing, the same language he had seen in the mentors' books.

Watching him, Shadow said, "You have never seen this design before?"

"No. What does it say?"

He knew immediately it was a mistake. Shadow flicked a thoughtful sideways glance at him. "It's a myth, of how the Raksura came to be."

Intensely self-conscious, Moon managed not to twitch. He should have been able to read that for himself, obviously, even if he hadn't recognized the carving. *Idiot.*

Shadow continued, "It explains that in the beginning, the Aeriat were shifters so that they might hide among groundlings and deceive them."

"To kill them," Moon said. "I've heard that part before." *Just don't ask me where,* he thought. He wondered if the myth mentioned the connection between the Aeriat and the Fell or if it ignored that aspect, but he wasn't going to ask.

Shadow nodded. "And that the Aeriat came to these forest Reaches, to the mountain-trees, where they met another tribe of shifters, the Arbora. That in joining with them they changed their ways, and both became stronger."

Moon had heard that part too, but not quite phrased that way. "It happened here? In this forest?"

"That is what the legends say."

A few other consorts drifted out onto the balcony, all in groundling form, watching curiously. Shadow glanced at them and apparently his expression made it clear that they weren't invited to get any closer; they kept their distance. They were all younger than Moon, with strong slender builds, dark hair, slightly pointed features. Two of them bore a strong resemblance to Shadow, with darker skin and broader shoulders. They all wore dark silky clothes, in deep blues or black, all wore jewelry, gold or silvery metals. Moon felt even more dirty and awkward than he had before, if that was possible. He was starting to get an inkling of the difference between what he was supposed to be and what he actually was, and it wasn't pleasant. Shadow turned back to him, and asked, "What was your birthcourt called?"

"I don't know." It was clear Shadow probably wouldn't have taken any interest in Moon at all, except that he was curious to meet a solitary. "It was somewhere to the east."

A young consort carried out a lacquered tray and set it between Moon and Shadow. It held two delicate green glazed cups, and a kettle ornamented with writhing serpentine forms. He poured out tea, then sat back, as if planning to stay. Shadow regarded him, lifting a brow. The younger consort held out for a moment, then stood and retreated with a reproachful hiss. Shadow picked up a cup and handed it to Moon. As if the interruption hadn't occurred, he said, "The other consorts at Indigo Cloud did not object to you?"

"Uh, no. Not really." Moon waited until Shadow had lifted his own cup before he tasted the light yellow tea. Admitting that there were no other consorts except Stone and the fledglings would just suggest that Indigo Cloud was desperate and hadn't had a choice. It was true, but Moon didn't want to suggest it. "The line-grandfather found me and brought me to the court."

Shadow turned his cup, as if admiring the glaze on the pottery. "So. Does Indigo Cloud visit only to make an alliance?"

This was the tricky part. Moon felt free to give information about himself, but he wasn't sure if he should say anything about their mission yet. It didn't help that he was fairly sure his dilemma was crystal clear to Shadow. Moon struggled for a moment, but he felt any attempt he made to avoid answering the question would be clumsy and probably unintentionally offensive. Feeling like he was jumping off a cliff without shifting, he said, "No. We need help. When we got to the Indigo Cloud colony tree, the seed was missing."

"The seed?" Startled, Shadow listened as Moon took a lesson from Flower and told the story as briefly as possible, telling him about the damage to the tree, the dead groundlings near the outer door, and what little the Kek had seen. Shadow finally shook his head, saying, "These groundlings must have come from some distance. If they were native to these Reaches we, or the Kek, would have heard of them before. But then how did they know where the tree was, or that the seed was even there?"

"That's what we thought. Our mentor thinks they wanted it for groundling magic."

Shadow frowned as he thought it over. "It seems the only explanation."

There was a faint commotion from the door into the consorts' bowers, then Stone strolled out, as casually as if he had just happened to be in the area. The young consorts watched him warily as he crossed the balcony and took a seat near Moon and Shadow. Shadow greeted his arrival with a somewhat ironic nod. If he had said, *You're here and I can't do anything about it, so I might as well accept it,* it couldn't have been any clearer. He said, "Are they talking yet?"

Stone regarded Shadow thoughtfully. "They're getting there."

"I told him about the seed," Moon said, figuring if it was the wrong choice, they might as well get the consequences over with.

Apparently it wasn't, because Stone just grunted an acknowledgment.

Shadow said, "I was just realizing how little I know about the seeds. No one has needed to create a new colony tree for uncounted turns, so there has been little reason to speak about them."

Stone nodded. "Got any extras?"

"I'm sure we must have."

❨

They went further down inside the mountain-thorn's trunk, a level or so below the consorts' bowers, toward a chamber where Stone said the queens were gathered. Shadow stopped at the intersection of the passage that led to it, saying, "Go on. I must speak to Ice first."

He took another doorway, and Moon and Stone started down the passage. Moon asked, low-voiced, "Is he going to help us?"

Stone shrugged. "He's going to tell his queen what we told him. It all depends on her." He added, apparently serious, "When we left you in the greeting hall, I thought this might happen."

Moon threw him an exasperated look. "You did not."

The way opened into a big round chamber and, like the upper passages, the walls were closely woven branches, allowing air and light to pass through. The floor was made of squares of different woods, all smoothed and polished to show the grain. It didn't seem elaborate enough for this court, until Moon glanced up. Between the two wells that opened into the domed roof hung a giant circular sculpture of queens in midair battle. It wasn't a particularly good omen for this encounter.

There were seating cushions scattered in the center of the room, and Jade, Flower, and the sister queen Tempest sat there, with three other queens. All four Emerald Twilight queens had consorts with them, all about Moon's age, and from even a cursory glance he could tell that like the consorts up in the bowers, they were all better dressed and prettier than he was. At least Ash wasn't present, which would save some embarrassment.

As Moon and Stone stepped out of the passage, all the queens and consorts turned to look. Moon froze for a heartbeat, pinned by those concentrated stares.

Jade touched an empty cushion next to her. Stone put a hand on Moon's lower back and gave him a little push forward. Moon forced himself to move at an even pace, to walk to Jade and sit down. "Where were you?" she whispered.

Settling next to Flower, Stone answered for him. "He got in a fight with a daughter queen then ran off with the reigning queen's consort."

Jade stared at Stone. "What?"

Flower leaned around Stone to frown at Moon. "Where was this?"

Moon threw a glare at Stone. "I saw Shadow and he said—"

But Tempest cleared her throat, making it obvious they were being rude. Jade turned back to face her and the other queens, her jaw tense as if she suppressed a hiss. Moon sat back on the cushion and tried to hide his impatience.

Tempest formally introduced the other queens and consorts. Three of the other consorts had been born in different courts, Sky Cinnabar and Sunset Water. The way this was presented made it clear they represented very important alliances. Then it was Jade's turn. She introduced Stone, and then said, "My consort, Moon of Indigo Cloud."

There was a short expectant silence. Then one of the other queens tilted her head inquiringly. "Of a different bloodline within Indigo Cloud?"

Oh, here we go, Moon thought, gritting his teeth. They had to know the answer already, either from someone who had seen the confrontation with Ash in the greeting hall or who had heard him talking to Shadow in the bowers. If Flower's sardonic expression was any indication, she thought so, too. Stone just looked bored.

Jade didn't betray any irritation by so much as a single spine twitch. She said, "No. He's the only survivor of a court that was destroyed almost forty turns ago."

There was another silence, this one far more uncomfortable. There weren't many replies the other queens could make without calling Jade a liar, or calling Moon a liar and Jade a fool for believing him. Tempest flicked her tail and gave the queen who had spoken a look of reproof. Moon couldn't tell if the reproof was for being rude or for presenting Jade with the opportunity to be rude back.

Then a faint sound from above made everyone look up. Someone was climbing down the wall, and Moon didn't need anyone to tell him that this was Ice, the reigning queen.

She was easily twice Pearl's size, and her scales looked pale, barely tinted with yellow, but reflected warm gold as the light struck them. She was so old she had started to lose her color. Her frills had grown long and wispy, like frayed silk. When she partly extended her wings to balance, Moon could see the bones outlined through the near-translucent skin. She had to be much older than Shadow, who was mature but hadn't begun to show noticeable gray on his groundling skin. Moon wondered how many consorts she had outlived.

She reached the floor, then Shadow half-dropped, half-glided down after her. He shifted to groundling and they both moved to join the other queens. Ice sat down on the cushions that waited for her, Shadow taking a seat beside her.

If Tempest was supposed to make the formal introduction of Jade, Ice didn't wait for it. She said, "Jade, sister queen of Indigo Cloud. You have a lovely young consort. May he come closer?"

Moon thought he was plenty close enough and had a moment to hope that this was another attempt to trick them into violating etiquette, that it was expected that Jade would refuse. Then Jade turned her head toward him, said in a breathless whisper, "Go on. Just sit in front of her, two paces away."

Apparently she was serious. Moon managed to get up without fumbling or tripping over the cushion. He crossed over to Ice, his spine prickling with tension, and sank to the floor in front of her. His hand made a sweaty mark on the polished wood.

Ice regarded him. Her eyes were dark, with a faint rim of blue, and her gaze seemed to go right through him. She wore jeweled sheaths on her claws, the gems tiny sparks of blue and green. She said, "You remember nothing of your birthcourt?"

Shadow must have told her everything. At least Moon didn't have to repeat the story in front of the other queens. He cleared his throat. "No."

Her brows arched. "Not what it was called, not the queen's name?"

Moon found her size daunting. He had to force himself not to lean back away from her. "Nothing."

"Hmm." She didn't sound doubtful, just thoughtful. "And after so long alone, it was not difficult for you to . . . adjust, to living within a court?"

He should lie and say no, it wasn't difficult at all. But her eyes were sharp, a wise old predator's eyes, and he knew she wouldn't believe him. He said, "Yes, it's been . . . very strange."

Ice smiled in dry acknowledgement. "I can imagine." She lifted her hand, and the jewels on her claws glinted as she made a gesture of dismissal. "Go back to your queen."

Relieved, Moon pushed to his feet and went to take his seat behind Jade again. He ignored the look Stone tried to give him. Jade touched his knee lightly, a reassurance.

Ice turned her attention to Jade. "This new knowledge of the Fell, and what they are capable of, is of import. I agree that it should be known as widely as possible and will send messengers to all the courts we are allied with." Almost as an afterthought, she added, "Shadow has told me of the theft from your colony tree. Your mentor may speak to ours."

Jade inclined her head to Ice. "I thank you."

As Ice turned away to speak to Tempest, Jade gave Flower a meaningful glance. Flower got to her feet, murmuring, "Wish me luck."

Moon felt a knot of tension evaporate from his spine. *They're going to help.* They could get the seed and be gone by tonight.

CHAPTER SIX

The sister queens made more pointed conversation, but mercifully none of it was about Moon's lack of bloodline. They also talked about other courts in the Reaches, a subject which Moon found fascinating. Stone apparently didn't think so, and after a while exercised his right as a line-grandfather to just get up and wander off without a word to anyone. Moon found himself trying to calculate how many turns it would be before he could get away with that.

Ice finally claimed to be fatigued so they could all escape, and an Arbora came to show them to the guest chambers.

Moon and Jade were in a passage that spiraled down away from the hall, when Jade asked, "What did Stone mean when he said you got into a fight with a queen?"

Their Arbora guide, in groundling form with dark curly hair and an amber-colored dress, politely quickened her steps to get out of earshot. Moon slid a sideways look at Jade. Her spines were still under rigid control from speaking to the other queens, but the scales on her brow were furrowed. He said, reluctantly, "There wasn't a fight. A daughter queen called Ash said something to me in the greeting hall. I said something back. Then Shadow came and sent her away, and asked me to come to the consorts' bowers with him."

Jade hissed through her teeth. Feeling the hiss was aimed at him as well as Ash, he said, "I know, I should have ignored her."

She was quiet for a long moment, then said, "Well. Maybe nothing will come of it."

The guest quarters were lower down in the colony, big round chambers hanging around the outer ring of the mountain-thorn. Jade and Moon climbed steps that wound up through doorways in the curved walls woven through with faintly glowing vines and moss. The Arbora led them to a room with a tile-lined pool set into the center of the floor. Four hanging bower beds were stuffed with blankets and the wood beneath them spread with striped grasseater hides.

The warriors were already there, sitting near the edge of the pool. They all looked bored and worried, and Chime even jumped to his feet when he saw them. "Well?" he demanded.

Jade quelled him with a look and he sat down with a thump. She turned to the Arbora and thanked her formally, then waited for her to leave before she turned back to the others.

"How did it go?" Balm asked, too anxious to wait longer.

As Jade took a seat on the furs, she asked, "Are we alone here?" Moon settled next to her and glanced around. The woven walls didn't provide much of a sound barrier; he could see through the gaps to the walkway.

Vine jerked his chin toward the far side of the chamber. "There's a group visiting from a court further west, but they're down at the other end."

Jade kept her voice low. "Ice acknowledged us, and Flower went to speak to their mentors. We should know soon."

Floret and Vine exchanged a look. There was definitely an undercurrent there, but Moon couldn't tell if they thought Jade had done too well, or not well enough. Balm nodded thoughtfully, and Chime slumped in relief. Song blurted, "So we just wait?"

"Yes." Balm gave her a stern look. "We wait." Song subsided reluctantly.

It should have been a good time to nap, but everyone seemed too tense to settle down. Moon shifted and jumped up to the top of the chamber, and wrapped his tail around a strong vine to hang upside down. It was a position that helped him relax.

The others aimlessly wandered the chamber or pretended to rest. Jade and Balm had drawn together to talk quietly, which was probably a good sign. If they could get back their old relationship, from before the Fell had changed everything, it would be a relief for Moon.

Chime shifted and climbed up to join him, clinging with his claws to the vines. He whispered, "Does Jade know about that queen, in the greeting hall?"

"Yes." Moon looked at him over the edge of his wing. "Why?"

"Nothing. If—" Chime shrugged and settled his spines. "I guess that's going to be all right, then. We talked to some of their warriors. I can't believe how big this court is."

Chime had never been to another court before either, and wanted to talk about it. Fortunately he didn't really need a response from Moon, who just listened and made thoughtful noises occasionally.

Sometime later they heard someone coming up the steps to the chamber, and everyone tensed in expectation, thinking it was Flower returning. But it was only another Arbora, come to tell them there was to be a formal dinner later in the day and that they were invited to attend. This seemed to please Vine and Floret and Song, at least, but it just made Moon more impatient. *Does it really take that long to say "yes" and hand over a seed?* Maybe it did, but if there was some lengthy process the mentors had to go through to get the seed ready, it seemed like Flower could have sent a message to tell them so.

Finally, they heard someone on the walkway again, and this time it was Flower and Stone.

As they came up the steps Moon dropped to the floor again and shifted back to groundling. He didn't think the news was good. Flower's expression was tense and thoughtful, and Stone didn't look relieved. The others gathered anxiously around, and Jade pushed to her feet. "Well?"

Flower took a deep breath. "They can't give us a seed."

Moon hissed a frustrated breath and glanced at Jade. Her spines lifted and she asked dangerously, "Can't or won't?"

Stone answered, "Can't." With a weary groan, he sat down on one of the furs. "Their mentors thought that a new seed wouldn't work on a mountain-tree that had already been implanted."

Flower added, "Our tree would keep dying and the seed would be wasted. They're looking back through their lore on the seeds to make certain."

Her voice tight, Jade said, "So they can't help us."

"I didn't say that." Flower hesitated, as if not certain how much she wanted to explain. "They had a suggestion. This court has a number of mentors, with several elders. They think we can all augur for the location of our seed."

Augur for it? Caught between disappointment and hope, Moon glanced at Stone, who just shrugged slightly. Moon took that to mean that Stone had no idea if this was possible and wasn't going to give an opinion on it. Jade asked Flower, "And what do you think?"

Flower spread her hands. "I've never done anything like that before, but I think we have to try. We don't have any other path to take at the moment."

Vine said, "But what if whoever took the seed destroyed it?" Song nodded anxiously.

Flower betrayed some exasperation. "Then the augury won't work."

Watching Flower intently, Chime said, "Do they really think it's still somewhere around here, and we can just go and get it?"

"They have no idea." Flower's voice was wry. "But we don't know why the groundlings took it, and anything could be possible." She looked around at them all. "They aren't certain, but they think a colony tree would only be able to last two or three turns without its seed. It will rot from the inside out."

And it's already been gone a turn, at least. Moon folded his arms, trying to contain his impatience. They had to try this. The groundlings had been traveling on the forest floor, and that had to be dangerous. They might have been killed, the seed left to lie forgotten in the moss somewhere. *If it hasn't been eaten by a grasseater.* If it hadn't ... How far could groundlings on foot travel in a turn, through hard country? *Not nearly as far as we can.*

"Of course you'll have to try," Jade said. "But will it be hard on you?"

"Yes," Flower admitted. "But it's not something I can leave to others."

Jade nodded, acknowledging the necessity. "We'll wait for word from you."

As Flower left, Chime looked after her, his expression miserable. Then he shifted and jumped up to the ceiling of the chamber, and curled himself into a tight ball among the vines.

Floret snorted derisively. "What's that about?"

"He wants to help," Moon said it deliberately, keeping his tone just short of threat. He wasn't in the mood to hear any garbage from the warriors, about Chime or anything else. "He can't."

Floret twitched uncomfortably. To her credit, she said, "I forgot."

Song sighed. "I want to help too, but there's nothing we can do but wait."

"No." Jade tapped her claws impatiently. "We have to go to this stupid dinner."

☾

Moon had never been to a formal meal in a court before. Usually eating meant either tearing apart a kill outside, or sitting around with everyone talking while they passed around food. This was a little different.

It was held in a well that wound up around the central trunk of the mountain-thorn, its walls ringed with wide platforms and crossed at intervals by bridges for the Arbora. The light emanated from living cascades of blue and purple flowers, growing from vines woven through the branches that supported the structure. Moon and Jade shared a balcony with Tempest, her three sister queens, and their consorts, everyone sitting on furs and cushions covered with rich fabrics. The younger unattached queens and consorts were confined to separate platforms across the chamber.

Ice and Shadow sat on another platform with the leaders of their Arbora. Stone had vanished again at some point on the way to the well. Most of the court, including Balm and Chime and the others, were seated on the platforms below. From what Moon could hear, it was a lot more lively down there. The only ones not present were Flower and the Emerald Twilight mentors.

Earlier, Moon had asked Jade why Emerald Twilight was putting itself out to entertain them. She had said, "They probably don't get many sister queens and consorts as visitors. Usually it's young daughter queens, or warriors acting as messengers or bringing Arbora to trade crafts."

It explained Shadow's curiosity about Moon. As reigning queen, Ice probably never left the colony, which meant Shadow never left either. He probably got few opportunities to talk to consorts he didn't already live with.

Before the food was brought, the queens sat to one side of the platform to talk, with the consorts taking the other. On their side, Jade and Tempest and the others made pointedly polite and occasionally cutting remarks at each other until it was apparent that no one was going to be lured into an embarrassing outburst.

On the other side, the consorts stared at Moon, and he stared back. These were the consorts taken by the sister queens, the ones with important bloodlines who represented important alliances. Finally, one said, "They said you threatened Ash in the greeting hall."

None of the queens had mentioned the incident. Moon was starting to suspect that if one of them brought it up, Jade might have to do something about it, like fight Ash. Which would be a stupid waste of a fight, considering how easily Shadow had dealt with it. He corrected, "She threatened me."

"And you offered to fight her," another consort said, his derision obvious. "That was foolish. What if she was hot-headed enough to accept?"

Moon looked away, knowing his expression was sardonic. "Then maybe next time she'd think twice."

"You'd fight a queen?"

"If I had to."

"They claimed he fought Fell." This was said with deliberately provoking skepticism.

Moon turned his head just enough to eye the speaker. Apparently he was being asked to prove it. The trick was to do that without disrupting the dinner.

He was still young enough that his wounds had healed without scars. All except one. He pulled his shirt down his right shoulder and twisted around. At least two of them gasped.

Only the very top of the red ridge of scar tissue was visible, where it curved up along his shoulder blade. It marked the spot where Ranea had broken his wing joint in his other form. It hadn't made an open wound, but when he had shifted to groundling, it had transformed into broken bones and this ridge of damaged skin. Flower had said it would probably fade a little over time, but it didn't hurt often now and it wasn't where he could see it, so it didn't much concern him.

He pulled his shirt back up and turned around. They were all staring, this time with shock rather than disdain.

After that, the consorts talked to each other, but not to Moon.

Jade had said Indigo Cloud had had consorts fight to defend the colony, but Emerald Twilight was too secure to need defending. Moon had proved he was different from them. Too different. *You are your own worst enemy,* he told himself. Not that that was a new revelation; it was just that he was starting to notice it more.

Emerald Twilight warriors started to bring food, and the consorts got up to join the queens. Moon took his place next to Jade and settled on her cushion. She leaned against him, her scales a welcome warmth. Her voice pitched low, she asked, "Are you all right?"

"Yes." He had thought he had his expression under control, but maybe not. "Do I look upset?"

"You look angry."

That was funny, because all he felt was weary resignation. He looked away and she didn't press the point.

The warriors who were probably clutchmates or lovers of the queens and consorts were invited to stay and eat with them, and the conversation became more cordial, but that was a mixed blessing. Moon had already been stared at enough. Now he had the warriors sneaking curious glances at him.

At least the food was good. There was meat, raw and fresh, cut into small pieces so you didn't have to shift to chew it, and piles of cut and peeled fruit. There were also various roots, some raw and some spiced and baked in coals to soften them and bring out the flavor. There wasn't any flatbread like the Arbora in Indigo Cloud made, but there was a pressed seedcake that was almost as good.

It had been a long, anxious day, and once Moon had a full stomach, it was hard to stay awake. He tried to find a position where he could lean against Jade's shoulder and doze off without falling over, when she said, "Was that true, what you told Ice? That you don't remember anything about your birthcourt?"

She kept her voice low. The others were still occupied in talking or eating. "You thought I was lying?" He had to admit, he did lie a lot. Turns and turns of lying his way into groundling settlements, lying about what he had done and where he had been and how he had gotten from here to there so fast, had made it second nature.

"It occurred to me," she said, her voice a little wry. "Well?"

"No." His earliest memory was of sleeping in the bole of a tree, warmly tucked in with the four young Arbora. *Leaf, Bliss, Light, and Fern.* He hadn't let himself think their names in a long time. "I don't remember anything. I told Shadow that, too."

"Hmm." Using her claws with delicate precision, Jade picked a pit out of a piece of fruit. "Maybe Ice just wanted a close look at you, then."

"Why?"

"She might have thought she could recognize what court you came from. Sometimes queens and consorts from the same bloodlines have a strong resemblance to each other."

He looked at her closely, trying to see it, but she just looked like Jade. "You don't look like Pearl."

"To another queen, I do." She straightened, frowning. "What's this?"

Moon pushed himself upright to see someone glide over from the platform where the unattached queens had been seated. Moon recognized the gray and green pattern of her scales and cursed under his breath. It was Ash.

By the time she landed all the queens were alert, the consorts and warriors startled and a little wary. Tempest's spines twitched in agitation.

Ash stopped in front of Jade, spines aggressively lifted. "I'm Ash."

Jade regarded her steadily. "And why should I care?"

Ash bared her teeth. "I spoke to your consort in the greeting hall. I said I thought he was a pretty thing and was surprised that you left him unprotected among us. But then I found out you were desperate enough to take a solitary."

Moon didn't move, though he dearly wanted to jump right off the platform, whether he could shift or not. The greeting hall had seemed private compared to this, with the queens and consorts staring and the sound dying away above and below as the rest of the court gradually realized something awkward was happening.

With unstudied calm, Jade sipped tea and set the cup aside, her extended claws clicking against the pottery. "Your bitter envy of my fortunate choice of consort is your shame, not mine."

Ash snarled. "Your consort offered to fight me. If you aren't afraid—"

Jade shoved to her feet and shifted to her winged form in a blur of motion. Moon rolled away and landed in a crouch, braced to shift and leap. Jade halted barely a pace from Ash, spines flared. Ash jerked back in reflex, but all Jade did was say, "I accept your challenge."

Ash growled, but it was unconvincing; she had given ground by flinching away. Trying to make up for it, she looked at Moon and said, "When I win, maybe I'll take you."

Moon bared his teeth. "If you win, I'll eat your guts."

Ash stared at him, incredulous. Jade said, with deceptive mildness, "That's not an idle threat." She flicked her spines. "Do you mean to fight me now or at some undetermined point in the future?"

Tempest's deep-voiced snarl cut across Ash's reply. "Settle this outside."

For a long frozen moment, the two queens didn't move. Jade stood like a statue, a coiled threat. Ash was breathing hard and, Moon realized suddenly, struggling to keep her spines flared. Maybe she hadn't realized Jade was older. *Or used to facing down Pearl,* he thought.

Then Ash stepped back, spines quivering. She said, "Outside, then."

Jade eyed her, then turned deliberately and stepped to the edge of the platform. Collecting Moon with a glance, she jumped off into the well.

Moon shifted and jumped after her. Three platforms down she dropped onto the balcony where Chime, Balm, and the others sat. Moon didn't stop, spiraling down toward the bottom of the well. At least Ash had waited until they were finished eating.

Jade must have only spoken briefly to the warriors, because she landed just a moment after Moon. She started immediately for the archway that led out of the well. The tilt of her spines said she was furious, and he was starting to feel a burning resentment of his own. *This is not my fault.*

Moon followed her into a wide foyer, where several passages met. Jade stopped beside a fountain that cascaded down carved rocks into a flower-strewn pool. She faced him and said, flatly, "You offered to fight her." The growl grew in her voice. "What were you thinking?"

He knew he should shift to groundling; it was dangerous to argue like this. But he cocked his head, deliberately provoking. "I was thinking I was offering to fight her."

"Queens don't fight consorts."

"That's hard to believe."

Her eyes narrowed, conveying cold threat. "When I fight her, don't interfere."

Resentment turned into fury, and he flared his spines. "If she leaves a scratch on you, I'll rip her apart."

He could tell it was taking a good deal of her control not to just slap him in the head. "Moon—"

"You knew what I was when you brought me here." He hissed in pure frustration. "I'm not like them. I never will be."

Jade's tail lashed, but his words seem to strike home. She regarded him steadily, and the growl had left her voice when she said, "You can pretend to be like them while we're here."

Stricken, Moon looked away. That was . . . not an unreasonable request. He just didn't know why he couldn't grant it. *You provoked Ash, and you've walked into enough strange places to know better.* But he had spent so many turns trying to fit in to whatever group he was with, trying to conform to expectations he barely understood. It was as if he had used up all his patience for it, and had none left for his own people. "I can't pretend anymore."

Jade shook her head, her tail still twitching. But she sounded resigned. "Ash is young."

He faced her again. "So are you."

Jade tilted her head in irony. "I'm bigger. I'm stronger. And I've fought in earnest. She hasn't."

A warrior landed on the floor of the well and shifted to groundling as she walked through the arch. It was Willow, who had welcomed them in the greeting hall. She stopped a few paces away and addressed Jade. "Tempest wanted me to speak to you."

Jade's mouth set in a grim line. "Go on."

"This wasn't planned." Willow twitched, uncomfortable. "Ash is the youngest daughter queen in the court, and rash with it. She was goaded by her sisters and their warriors, who are just as foolish as she is."

Jade's spines twitched uneasily. This had to be a generous admission of fault on Tempest's part, even if it was being made through her warrior. Apparently it required an admission in return, because Jade said, "My consort is accustomed to defending himself. He didn't realize she meant to make a childish insult, not a real threat."

Moon looked down, resisting the urge to dig at the floor with his claws. He had realized it; he just hadn't cared.

Willow hesitated, then added, "I know Tempest would rather this challenge not take place."

Jade inclined her head. "Tell her if Ash doesn't appear, I won't pursue her. If she does appear . . . I won't kill her."

Relief flickered in Willow's expression. "I'll tell Tempest. Thank you."

☾

They went through the colony's greeting hall, outside to the open platform they had landed on when they had first arrived. Stone waited there in groundling form, his opaque expression somehow conveying a deep disgust with all of them, but especially Moon.

There was no one else on the platform, and only a few warriors in flight, circling near the outer barrier of thorns. Jade walked forward, crouched, and took to the air; hard flaps of her wings carried her out away from the colony's platforms. She banked before the thorn barrier and began to circle. The patrolling warriors stayed well away from her.

Moon shifted to groundling, folded his arms, and tried not to tense his shoulders. Stone was silent in a way that seemed to speak volumes. Moon wanted to say something, like *I didn't mean for this to happen.* Saying it to Stone would be useless; he should have said it to Jade. He had helped Ash do something terribly stupid. A real consort would have ignored her or deflected her attention and never let it get to this point.

Self-consciously he looked for Ash, trying to see if she was perched somewhere on the vines or branches, but she wasn't here yet. *Maybe she won't come.*

On a broad balcony built out onto a curving branch above and to one side of the greeting hall entrance, Tempest stood under the shadows of the vines.

After a moment, a subdued group with two queens and several warriors walked out of the greeting hall entrance and moved to the opposite side of the platform from Moon and Stone. The two queens must be unattached, because they were Ash's age or younger, and they hadn't been among those introduced by Tempest. The warriors were in groundling form, all young and pretty, wearing color-ful clothes and an excess of jewelry. He wondered if these were the rash companions that Willow had mentioned. So far they were the only spectators. Keeping his voice low, he asked Stone, "Why aren't the Arbora coming out?"

Stone said, with a tinge of irony, "They have more sense. The court won't want to make more of this than it has to."

Moon heard a rustle overhead and looked up in time to see Ash shoot out of an opening high in the curve of the mountain-thorn. He twitched and managed not to shift, watching her arc toward Jade.

Jade waited until almost the last instant, then twisted in midair and fell out of Ash's path. Ash banked smoothly back toward her and the two circled each other. They might have been talking but they were too far away for Moon to hear.

This went on long enough for Moon's already tense nerves to tighten past bearing. He kept hoping Ash would change her mind, but the way she steadily gained height wasn't a good sign. Jade had to see it, but she wasn't trying to counter. Then Ash suddenly twisted to fall on Jade.

The two queens met in a furious flurry of wings and tails, plunging down toward the ground far below. Moon set his jaw, though his whole body shook with the instinct to leap into the air and join the fight.

The flurry stopped, with Jade on Ash's back. Jade's wings shot out and cupped to slow their descent. Ash flapped weakly and Jade released her, and watched as she glided down toward the lower branches of the colony.

Three warriors jumped off the platform to spiral down after her. The others stood there, not looking at each other, clearly uncomfortable and guilty. Jade flew leisurely toward the balcony where Tempest waited. It was empty now, the other queen having already vanished inside.

Stone just grunted, and said, "Come back in."

There wasn't anything else to do. Moon followed him.

☾

They returned to their guest quarters. The warriors were there now, sitting near the pool. This time it was Song who jumped to her feet and demanded, "What happened?"

"Jade won," Stone said succinctly, taking a seat on the furs.

"We knew that would happen. But what . . ." Song took in Moon's expression, and subsided. "I don't really need to know the details."

Moon went to the far side of the chamber, where the wall curved around. There was an opening in the woven barrier, a small shelf that extended through the outer wall under an arbor of vines. It looked down onto a broad garden platform with fruit trees. Only a few Arbora worked on it now, climbing the trees at the far end to pick fruit. Moon sat down on the shelf, hoping no one came after him.

The breeze was cool with the approach of evening, thick with the scent of the white flowers on the sapling trees. He wondered what they would do if Frost grew up to be headstrong and overly aggressive, starting fights with every other young queen in reach. He concluded glumly that Indigo Cloud would probably be lucky to get to the point where that was the worst thing they had to worry about. After a time, he heard someone come up the steps from the walkway.

He heard Jade's voice as she spoke to the others, too low to catch the words. Then she picked her way over toward the back of the chamber, toward Moon. She ducked under the arbor of vines and settled next to him. He slid a look at her, saw she was in her Arbora form, apparently unhurt.

She said, "I spoke with Ice and Tempest and Shadow. We came to the conclusion that Ash is hotheaded even for a queen, and she would probably have gotten in a fight sooner or later. They expressed relief that the fight was with a queen who had the self-control not to hurt her badly, and that the consort she chose to harass was not one who was so sheltered as to be terrified by her. You weren't terrified by her, were you?"

Moon eyed her. He couldn't see much resemblance to Pearl, but this was one of the times when he could tell that Jade was descended from Stone. "No."

Jade flicked away a stray flower petal. "I didn't think so."

So that seemed to be the end of it. It had all been mostly Moon's fault but he had avoided any of the consequences, by virtue of being a consort. Except that all of Emerald Twilight thought he was a crazy savage, but he was used to that. "What does our court think about me?"

Jade's brows lifted at the unexpected question. She didn't answer immediately, thinking it over. "The teachers and hunters like you. They've spent more time with you, they know you better. And they know what they owe you after you went into the Dwei hive after Heart and the others. The soldiers don't like you, but then . . ."

Moon had figured that. "They blame me for bringing the Fell."

Jade pressed her lips together. "They'll get over it." Her tone suggested that they had better. "In the meantime, Knell will keep them from starting any trouble."

That was a surprise. "Why? He told Stone he didn't think I should be with the court."

Jade gave him a dry look. "That was before you started showing interest in Chime. Chime is his clutchmate, and since he changed, he hasn't had any status among the Aeriat. So becoming the favorite of a consort wasn't something anyone expected for him."

Moon had realized Chime's lot in the court had improved by association with him. But he didn't think Chime had calculated it. He thought Chime had just been drawn to someone who was also different, who was a misfit. "That must make it hard for Knell."

"Knell can handle it. When Chime changed, it was a shock, but it finally convinced everyone who still had their heads buried in the dirt that something was wrong. All the doubters finally admitted that we needed to move to another colony. If a few of the others had changed too, it would probably have made it easier on Chime. He wouldn't have stood out quite so much. But that won't happen now."

"Now that the court is away from the old colony, maybe Chime will change back." If that happened, Moon was certain Chime would miss flying, but Chime had also made it clear that he would rather be an Arbora than a warrior.

"Flower didn't think so." Jade frowned absently. "It was strange enough that it happened once. But we'll have to wait and see. We're away from the Fell influence, we have plenty of food at the colony, and more room than we can fill."

Moon looked out over the terrace. "If we can stay there."

She nodded, resigned. "If we can stay."

☾

Outside the walls of thorn, the dark of evening settled over the forest. Jade had gone back in some time ago, but Moon stayed, still wanting to avoid conversation with the others until the thrilling excitement of Jade fighting another queen over him had worn off.

He was going to have to get better at dealing with the pressure of others' personalities. He had lived in crowded places before, but he had always been an outsider. With the Raksura he was still an outsider, but everything he did and said mattered so much more. He watched two warriors fly past the outer edge of the platform, the reflected light from the colony glinting off their scales. *You have to get better at this,* he told himself.

When the night insects sang in chorus and a light rain began to patter the leaves, he went back inside.

Stone was the only one sitting up. He was beside the hearth basin, nursing a cup of tea. No one had gone up into the bower beds; they were all dozing on the floor. Jade was curled up on a fur, but not asleep. She patted the spot next to her and Moon picked his way through the prone if not sleeping bodies.

He lay down beside her and she tugged him back against her chest and nuzzled his neck. His clothes were damp and the fabric cold with the night air. Her body heat was a welcome warmth that sank right through him. *You have to get better at this,* he thought again. Because he couldn't leave these people. *Your people.*

Chime sat up on one elbow and said softly, "Maybe we should send someone to see if she's all right."

Jade sighed, her breath warm in Moon's hair. "That's . . . not a bad suggestion. Stone, do you know where—"

Stone lifted his head, suddenly alert. "Here she comes."

Moon sat up as Jade uncoiled from around him. He could hear it now, too: Flower, with two other Arbora, approaching along the walkway. The others stopped at the stairs up to the guest chamber, spoke quietly for a moment, then Flower came up the steps alone.

They were all on their feet by the time she reached the doorway. She looked terrible. There were dark smudges of exhaustion under her eyes, and her skin was so pale it looked nearly translucent. Vine was closest, and caught her hand to help her. He guided her to the nearest cushion. Flower sat down heavily, saying in irritation, "I'm fine, I'm fine."

Jade sat in front of her as they all gathered around. "Tell us."

"We saw the way to our stolen seed." Flower rubbed her temple with the heel of her hand. "It's good we came here. I couldn't have done this alone, and the others at home are too young to be much help." She took a roll of paper out of her robe and spread it on the fur. "It's vague, but it should get us near enough for me to augur the rest of the way myself."

Stone leaned over and studied it intently. Moon sat forward to see over his shoulder. It was a map, drawn in bold strokes, with scribbled writing in Raksuran, all in different hands and inks. Several of the Emerald Twilight mentors must have contributed. Stone said, "To the west, past the Reaches." He tapped a section. "This is water?"

Flower nodded. "We saw a lake, or an inland sea. It's at least a day of warrior's flight over water, southwest." She blinked, and swayed.

"Rest," Jade told her. "We know enough now to make plans." At Jade's nod, Vine scooped Flower up despite her exhausted protest.

Chime and Song hurried to make a bed near the hearth basin, piling up furs and cushions. Vine set Flower down in it and she grumbled, "I just need to lie down for a bit." She curled up in the cushions and was asleep immediately.

Jade took the map from Stone and turned it so she could read it. The others gathered around again, watching her. Song said, "What should we do?"

Floret nudged the paper. "Take it back to ask Pearl."

"That's a waste of time," Jade spoke with quiet authority, looking around at them all. "We need to get there as soon as we can. We'll leave at dawn."

Vine exchanged an opaque look with Floret. He said, "Pearl isn't going to like it."

"She's not going to like it whatever we do," Moon said. He didn't think he was exaggerating there. "But we have to go after the seed. We don't know that the groundlings aren't still traveling with it. This spell showed where it is now, not where it's going to be five days from now if we go back to the tree so Pearl can tell us to go find it."

"It's not our only choice," Floret said, though it was clear she was uncomfortable defying Jade. "Pearl might not want us to find it. She might think it was a better idea for Stone to go outside the Reaches and look for another ruin to turn into a colony."

Moon said, "Pearl didn't want to move when the old colony was surrounded by Fell and Stone actually knew where to go. You think she wants to move now?"

"Back east, to another place we can't defend, while we're so weak?" Chime added. "What if other Fell hear what happened and come looking for us?"

Floret hissed, more in dismay than threat. "Stone hasn't said he doesn't know where we should go."

Stone snorted. "If Stone had a better suggestion Stone would have made it before now."

Jade fixed Floret with a gaze hard enough to make her twitch uneasily. "Are you saying this because it's your opinion, or because it's the opposite of what I want and what you think you should say to support Pearl?"

Floret glanced at Vine for support, but he said nothing. After a tense moment, she admitted reluctantly, "I don't want to have to move again. That's my opinion."

Jade said, "That's my opinion, too. We'll go after the seed while we have the chance." She waited a moment for more objections, but no one else spoke up. She added, "Song and Floret will go back to tell Pearl where we've gone."

Moon flicked a wary look at Vine and Floret, and he wasn't the only one. Vine didn't react, but Floret's mouth set in a cynical line. Chime was the least experienced next to Song. He should have been sent back, not Floret. But Jade trusted him more.

Jade ignored the byplay, picking up the map. "And we should draw a copy of this for you to take to Pearl. If we don't return, she can send others after us."

"I'll copy it." Chime reached for the map and got to his feet. "Flower has paper and ink in her bag."

As Chime carried the map away, Moon watched Floret and Vine. Jade lifted a brow at them, and said, "You have something to say?"

Floret started to speak but Vine said, "No." Floret stared at him and he told her in exasperation, "I know what Pearl is going to say. But when she calms down, she'll realize this was right. The groundlings could move the seed, and Emerald Twilight might not be willing to help Flower augur it again. If we all went back to let her make the decision, she'd be angry about that, too."

Floret grimaced, and then let her breath out in resignation. "You're probably right. But you're not the one who has to tell her."

CHAPTER SEVEN

At dawn, Song and Floret left to carry the news to the colony tree, and Moon and the others flew west, following the mentors' directions.

It took them seven days to reach the edge of the forest, pushing the warriors as hard as they could. Jade and Moon took turns carrying Flower, which let Stone fly ahead to scout their route and find game so they could stay well fed, while Balm and Vine left markers in the treetops so whoever Pearl sent could follow them. It was Jade's opinion that Pearl was bound to send someone, since she wouldn't trust them to do this right. Moon just hoped they wouldn't need the help.

It wasn't as easy as flying over open country, and they had two days of rain, but food was plentiful and finding shelter in the suspended forest was never difficult. The long flights left them all exhausted but, as Moon had discovered on the other lengthy journeys he had taken with Raksura, it left no one with the energy to argue. When they stopped to eat and rest, Stone talked about his travels, and Chime told stories from the mentors' histories. Flower must have had stories too, but she was always too tired to talk. Moon knew from experience that being carried wasn't easy or comfortable, even for Arbora.

They all avoided the subject of what they would do if their quest failed.

Before they had left Emerald Twilight, Flower and one of the other court's mentors had shown them a mountain-thorn seed. It was a dead one, separated from the husk and used only to show young Raksura what they looked like, but Flower had explained that their seed would be very similar. It was about the size of a melon, a light brown color, with a hard ribbed shell like a nut.

Moon had lifted it, feeling the light weight. He could tell this one was dead; it felt empty on the inside, the rind dried away to nothing. He said, "How long can our seed stay disconnected from the tree before it dies?"

Chime and the other warriors had stared at him in horror. Apparently none of them had thought of that. Always more practical, Jade answered calmly, "I asked Stone that and he said he didn't know."

The Emerald Twilight mentor, a withered gray-white Arbora who looked older than the mountain-thorn, took the seed back from Moon and said ruefully, "No one knows. This has never happened before."

The mentors had also been able to tell Flower the things that might need to be done to the seed to get it to attach to the tree again, once they found it. If they found it. It was all just speculation, since in the annals of seed-lore, this was a unique problem. But Flower had had Chime copy it all down, and sent it back to the court with Song and Floret.

Late afternoon of the seventh day, the forest ended abruptly, giving way to a field of lush green grass dotted with white and gold flowers, and then a vast blue body of water, stretching forever.

Moon landed on the shore and folded his wings. A light breeze came off the water, but he couldn't smell salt. A short strip of sandy beach dropped away abruptly into the shallows, which were thick with reeds, cattails, and blue and purple lilies, their pads a good couple of paces across. Insects hummed and frogs sang. He stepped down to where the waves lapped the sand and crouched, scooping up a handful of water to make certain. It tasted fresh, so this could be anything from a large lake to a sweetwater sea. He stood and looked up and down the shore. The land curved out in a great arc, and there was no sign of any groundling inhabitants.

The others landed a little further up the bank, and Jade set Flower on her feet. Stone circled twice overheard, then dropped down to light near the others and shift to groundling. Moon joined the group, the grass releasing a sweet fragrance as his claws pressed it down.

Stone stretched, then winced and rubbed his neck. "I'll scout for the island, the rest of you wait here."

That was the only option. Flying over water was always problematic. Raksura could only go so far without rest and food, and they couldn't get real rest without stopping to shift to groundling. And it was one thing to fly out over the shallow Yellow Sea, knowing the direction of the islands and that they lay less than a day's flight for a warrior. It was another to fly out over an unknown body of water. But Stone had easily three times the range of even a young consort like Moon.

"You mean to start right away?" Jade looked out over the water. "You should rest and leave in the morning."

Stone gave her a glare that Moon knew well. "I'm not wasting most of a day."

"You should at least eat," Moon told him. "It's a bigger waste if you fall out of the sky and drown."

This had the effect of transferring the glare to Moon. And Stone must be in a worse mood than it seemed, because he growled, a low rumble of threat.

Everyone twitched in nervous reaction, except for Moon, who was unimpressed, Jade, whose expression turned sardonic, and Flower, who yawned.

Stone was usually acerbic, but he didn't growl often, especially in his groundling form. He had done a good job of hiding his impatience so far, but it was clear he hadn't forgotten that it was his doing the court had come back to the colony tree. Moon figured that if someone was going to get slapped unconscious, it might as well be him. He said, "Good, let's fight. That'll save time too."

Stone controlled a hiss, his jaw set. Then he flung his arms in the air. "Fine! Then get off your asses and hunt!"

As Stone stomped away, Chime, Balm, and Vine scattered toward the forest. "Hah," Flower commented, and started back up the bank, wading through the tall grass.

Jade gave Moon a look, lifting a brow. He turned to stare out over the sea to avoid her gaze. Up to this point, the journey had been fairly straightforward. Now if the map was wrong, if they couldn't find the island, they would have to turn around and go back to Indigo Cloud. And then figure out where to look for a new colony.

They made a camp on one of the broad lower branches of a small mountain-tree at the edge of the forest, only about a hundred or so paces above the ground. Jade kept watch over Flower and Stone while they napped, and Balm and Vine went hunting. Chime dug in the shallows, looking for roots, and found some sand melons and big white clams, while Moon wandered along the shore and made sure nothing tried to eat him.

Balm and Vine came back shortly with two hoppers out of a herd further back in the forest, one for Stone and one for the rest of them to share. After they had cleaned up in the lake, Balm flew back up to the tree to talk to Jade. Vine stayed on the beach, and Moon took the opportunity to ask him, "Why are you so anxious to help Jade now?"

"Do I look anxious?" Vine said, cleaning his claws in the grass at the water's edge.

Moon didn't react to the attempt at a joke, and Vine said, reluctantly, "I'm older than River, I'm bigger than River, and he doesn't like me. And I'm not thrilled about having to defer to him. And that's how it's going to be, until Pearl gets tired of him." He shrugged his spines. "It's different for Floret. No male warrior is going to order the female warriors around. They're too big, and they stick together."

It had the ring of truth. Moon said, "So you think you'll do better with Jade?"

Vine correctly interpreted the undertone of that question. "I think I don't have to put up with River telling me what to do. Jade's always been close to Balm; she was never interested in male warriors. And now you're here, I'm guessing no male warrior is going to have much chance with her."

Vine had that part right. Moon still didn't entirely trust him, though his motives made sense.

After they ate, Stone said only, "Don't wait up," before he shifted and set off across the water.

They watched from the branch, through the screen of leaves, until Stone's outline dwindled in the distance. Moon let out his breath, frustrated. He couldn't just sit here and wait.

It was a good day for flying, the bright blue sky clear except for a few high clouds. He turned to Jade. "We could scout along the shoreline, maybe find some sign that groundlings were here."

It was a relief that Jade didn't ask why they should bother, or what good it would do if they did find evidence of groundlings, because Moon couldn't answer either one of those questions. She looked at the warriors inquiringly. "Well? Scout or rest?"

"I'll scout," Balm said, sitting forward. She looked anxious for something to do as well.

Chime nodded. Vine said, "I'll go with Balm."

"No." Jade looked down the shoreline. She was in her Arbora form, and her shorter mane of spines trembled as she tasted the air. "I'll go with Balm. Vine will stay here with Flower."

Vine gasped at the unfairness. "Why me?"

Jade twitched her tail, but she sounded more amused than angry. "Because I said so."

It's a test, Moon thought. Another test. Jade must have also noticed that Vine seemed to be changing his allegiance from Pearl to her. It would be good if he did; Jade could use another male warrior, especially an experienced adult like Vine.

Vine grumbled and made it clear he was being ill-used, but didn't make any real protest. Jade and Balm set off to the south, and Moon and Chime headed north.

☾

Moon flew along the curve of the shore, maintaining an easy pace so Chime could keep up with him. The fields between the forest and the beach were thick with grass and flowers, empty except for an occasional herd of grasseaters. Big and slow-moving, their backs were protected by a heavy green shell, so that only their little heads and stumpy feet were visible. Not a very good prospect for prey if they had to stay here much longer.

Moon wanted to get a good look at the shoreline, though he wasn't certain what he was looking for. *A groundling town with a harbor would be nice, a place where people who came across the sea to explore the forest might land their boats.*

To his surprise, it wasn't long before he found it, or what was left of it.

First he spotted stone pilings standing in the shallow water, making a rough square shape. He tilted his wings, gliding downward for a closer view. It looked like the remains of a dock or a platform that had been built out from the shore. If there were any remnants left on the land, they were hidden under the grass.

The further they went, the more pilings they found, tracing the outlines of more elaborate structures. Soon they were flying over the scattered foundations of a whole maze of buildings, long docks, and causeways. Moon cupped his wings and dropped down to land on a broken pillar more than three paces across. The stone was chipped and coated with moss. Tiny blue fish darted in the water just below. Chime managed to land on another piling nearby and flailed his wings for balance. "This was a huge city," Chime called.

Moon turned to look down the shore. He had been so focused on what was below them, he hadn't noticed what was ahead. "Looks like some of it's still there." Some distance down the shoreline, he could just make out structures, round beehive shapes, standing high above the water. They might be a part of the ruined city still standing, or other inhabitants had taken over the old pilings for their own use.

"What?" Chime turned, his spines lifted as he spotted the distant shapes. "Huh. I wonder if they know anything about the groundlings out in the sea."

"We can ask," Moon said.

☾

As they drew near the beehive city, they turned away from the shore, into the forest. Flying under the cover of the tree canopy, they landed on a branch at the edge of the open beach.

From here, Moon saw the buildings were made of braided wood, some hundreds of paces tall. They stood on a wooden grid built out over the water, using the old pilings as foundations. A fleet of light woven boats were tied up under the grid, but the inhabitants seemed to be farmers rather than fishers. Vines grew up out of the water, trained to wind up wooden racks along the sides of the walkways, until some of the hives looked as if they were growing out of a miniature forest. He could see the inhabitants, too, paddling their boats, crossing the catwalks between the upper levels of the hives, picking some sort of fruit or pods off the vines. They were Kek, just like the ones who lived under the mountain-tree roots.

"This is no help," Chime said, disappointed. "They couldn't be the groundlings who came to our tree. The forest Kek would have known what they were."

He was right. It was vaguely possible that the forest Kek had told them an elaborate lie to cover up the actions of their seashore-dwelling cousins, but this was still far from where the seed was supposed to be. And these Kek looked a little bigger, but were still no match for the bones of the dead thieves. "Maybe they saw something. It's worth asking."

It was worth asking, but Moon still felt strange flying into a groundling settlement, even a Kek settlement at the edge of the Raksuran Reaches. He circled over the area nearest the shore first, Chime following his lead, just to see what the reaction would be.

The Kek didn't seem frightened or angry at the sight of two Raksura in the air. They came out of the vine racks and the hives to look up, point and call to each other.

Bracing himself, Moon circled down toward an open section of platform and cupped his wings to land. The wood creaked as his weight settled on it; it was surprisingly spongy underfoot. Moon folded his wings to make room as Chime dropped down behind him. The Kek gathered around the edge of the platform and crowded the catwalks above. They kept their distance but still didn't seem afraid.

One Kek came toward them. Like the old leader in the forest, he had stringy white growths on his arms and a squarish head. In Raksuran, he said, hopefully, "Trade?"

Moon wished he had thought of that, but he had no idea what the Kek would want. He countered, "No. Talk?"

A little taken aback, the Kek looked from Moon to Chime. "Talk, yes?"

Chime tugged on one of Moon's spines and whispered, "Shift."

I hate this part. Moon was never going to get over feeling vulnerable in front of a large crowd of groundlings who knew what he was, not even the Golden Islanders or the Kek. Chime was still tugging. Moon shook off his grip and shifted to his groundling form. The cool wind off the water pulled at his shirt, and the bright sun, which he had barely felt on his scales, warmed the back of his neck.

Chime followed suit, and the watching Kek murmured to each other in what sounded like approval.

The leader gestured for them to follow and led them further into the city, between the high wooden hives. The heavy greenery grew everywhere, hanging from racks overhead, climbing the hive walls. The place smelled of sweet green plants and moss, combined with the clean acrid scent that came from the Kek themselves.

On the brief walk they mutually managed to establish that the leader was called Khitah, and they were called

Moon and Chime. Presumably the Raksura this city normally traded with could speak Kek, because Khitah had
as much trouble speaking Raksuran as the forest Kek, and
didn't know any other groundling languages. Listening to
him, Moon thought it was more the way the Kek's mouth
and throat were constructed; Khitah seemed to know far
more Raksuran words than he could manage to say.

Khitah led them under one of the walkways bridging two
of the hives and stopped to gesture up at it. Mounted along
the arch of the bridge were several wooden plaques. Carved
of warm-toned wood, they depicted views of the beehive
city, with Kek paddling boats and harvesting their plants. It
was clearly Arbora work.

Moon nodded, trying to look appreciative. Khitah
seemed pleased.

Keeping his voice low, Chime said, "We should have
brought them a gift."

Exasperated, Moon asked him, "Did you know we were
coming? Because I didn't."

"I'm just saying that next time we should—"

Moon turned to Khitah. "We want to ask about other
people who live out on the sea. Islands? That way?" He
pointed out toward the water, roughly in the direction the
mentors thought the seed lay.

"Islands. People," Khitah agreed, and made an expansive
gesture, indicating most of the sea.

"Good. But what about that way?" Moon pointed again.

Khitah considered it, as the breeze stirred the feathery growths on his arms and head. He waggled his stick-
like fingers in what seemed to be the Kek equivalent of
a shrug.

"Maybe they just don't know," Chime said, a little frustrated. "Those round boats couldn't make it very far out
into the water."

"But they trade." Moon had forced himself to shift in
front of a strange groundling settlement with only Chime
for company, and he was unwilling to give up so soon.
"They have to see who travels back and forth here."

Maybe some of those words struck a bell for Khitah, because he turned back to the passage and motioned them to follow again.

They wound their way further into the city, through the green shadows of the plant racks and into the bottom level of one of the hives. Overhead, Kek moved on the reed floors, called to each other in their soft voices, peered curiously down at the visitors.

They went down a ramp, then came out again to a dock area open to the sea. Partly sheltered from above by woven reed canopies, it had small wooden piers snaking out into the lapping water. Round Kek boats were tied up along most of the piers, except for one. Next to it was a large leafless tree, apparently growing up out of the water.

Not a tree, a boat, Moon realized, moving down the dock to get a closer look. It was round, the gray branches arching up from a thick mossy mat to form a bowl-shape. Something sat in the center, its form obscured by the branches.

Khitah pointed emphatically toward the strange boat. "Water traveler," he said. "Go long way. Know much." Moon started to step down onto the pier, but Khitah put a hand on his arm. His grip was light, like being caught by dry brush. He stared hard at Moon and said, "Careful."

Moon nodded. The warning just confirmed his suspicion. "I will."

"Why?" Chime squinted to get a better look at the shadowy shape inside the branches. "It's just a groundling in a boat . . . isn't it?"

"No. Stay here with Khitah." Moon stepped down onto the pier, the reeds creaking under his weight, and moved toward the water traveler.

Drawing closer, he could see root-like tendrils floating in the water, growing out from the underside of the mat. The gray branches looked less like wood and more like gnarled horn. They were connected to the being that sat in the center, growing out of its arms, legs, back, chest. It wasn't a groundling sitting in a boat; it was a waterling, and it was the boat.

A voice said, "Now what's this?" It spoke Altanic, low and sibilant. Something about it made the back of Moon's neck itch. The scent wafting toward him had a rank edge to it, odd for a water being of any kind. It was a predator's scent. "A curious groundling come to talk to old Nobent?"

"You could say that." Moon crouched on the pier, so his head was about even with Nobent's. It gave him a better view of the water traveler's face. It looked a little like a male groundling, his skin gnarled and gray like the horn structures growing out of his body. There were chips of the stuff above his eyes, down his cheeks, studding the curve of his skull. It wasn't that the growths or the gray coloring were particularly repellent. Stone was gray and a little gnarled too, though not to this extent. But this creature radiated menace. "I need to know if there are any groundlings living out on the sea, that might travel to this shore."

Nobent leaned forward. Out of the corner of his eye, Moon saw the outer branches of the boat stir slightly. Nobent smiled, deliberately revealing a toothless mouth. If he was meant to live like this, floating atop the sea, then there might be a second mouth in the bottom of the mossy-covered base that supported his upper limbs. *Top one for talking, lower one for eating,* Moon thought. It wasn't the oddest thing he had seen. The branches looked stiff, but he bet they could whip around, seize prey, and snatch it under water. Obviously the Kek didn't fear the creature, but there was hardly any meat on their light bones. It said, "Old Nobent doesn't hear well. Come closer."

Oh please, Moon thought. "Does that really work?"

Nobent hesitated, nonplussed, and something made Moon think that "Old Nobent" wasn't so old. Nobent's lips curled in derision. "You're not scared of old Nobent? Nobent isn't scary."

Nobent was, however, annoyingly single-minded. *This could go on forever.* Moon shifted, flared his spines, snapped his wings out so they were half-unfurled. "I am."

With a startled snarl, Nobent jerked back. His whole structure rocked and splashed water up onto the pier. Unimpressed, Moon flicked droplets off his claws. He said, mildly, "I'm not hungry yet."

Nobent crouched, tugged his branches in tightly and made a protective cage around himself. "What do you want?"

"You know what I want. Tell me about groundlings who live out on the sea. Are there islands out there? Cities, traders? Do they come to this shore?"

Nobent eased forward, the fear in his expression turning into crafty greed. "Are you Fell? I've heard of Fell. You want the sea-goers? I'll help."

Moon controlled the urge to leap forward and rip Nobent's head off. The fear of Fell had dogged him most of his life. All Fell were shapeshifters, all had black scales, and Fell rulers strongly resembled Raksuran consorts. It didn't help that once Moon had thought he might be a Fell, for a brief and self-destructive time that he was still paying for, all these turns later. His voice tight, he said, "If I were a Fell, I'd take your help and eat you anyway. Tell me about the sea-goers."

Nobent settled into his mossy bed and his branches relaxed a little. "The sea-goers don't come here. They're afraid of the forest." With an air of injured dignity, he volunteered, "The Kek trade their rushes and edilvine to me, and I trade it to the sea-goers."

That wasn't helpful, though it explained why the Kek didn't know much about what lay further out to sea. And if the sea-goers were afraid of the forest Reaches, it might be because they knew about the Raksuran colonies. "But other groundlings come to this shore, other traders?"

"Maybe." Nobent seemed uninterested, and it was the first time in the conversation that Moon felt the waterling was being honest. "Not in a long time. There's nothing here for them."

"What about the far side of the sea? Do groundlings live there?"

"Probably." Nobent leaned forward, eyes widening. "You want the sea-goers."

"Do they live in that direction?" Moon pointed with the tip of his right wing.

"Sometimes. They move around." Nobent was more interested in his own questions. "What do you want them for? Nobent can help you, whatever you want to do to them."

Moon couldn't imagine what form Nobent's "help" would take, and he didn't want to. He countered with, "What do you trade for from the sea-goers?"

For some reason, that one made Nobent more cagey than ever. Moon asked more questions about the sea-goers, about what they looked like, why they moved around. Nobent's answers were so cryptic it quickly became obvious that he had no intention of imparting the information. Moon decided to let it go, at least for now. He had found out what he really needed to know: there were groundlings living out on the sea at the point where the mentors' map said the seed lay. Nobent couldn't travel very fast, and now that Moon had his scent, he would be easy to track down again.

He stood, abruptly enough that Nobent sloshed backward again. With a somewhat nervous sneer, Nobent said, "You're leaving? Too bad."

"It's getting late, and I'm hungry." Moon cocked his head, letting the meaning sink in. He didn't usually threaten to eat people, but he was having difficulty classifying Nobent as "people." "I might be back."

He walked up the pier to rejoin Khitah and Chime. "Good?" Khitah asked.

"Good," Moon told him. "Thank you."

They started back into the green shadows and sweet scents of the Kek city, a relief after the miasma that hung over the water traveler. Chime looked back over his shoulder, frowning. "That was odd. What did it tell you?"

"Not much." Moon was certain Nobent had been lying, or obfuscating, for some reason. But it was some confirmation that they were in the right place, that the map hadn't led them astray. "We'll have to see what Stone finds."

☾

It was dusk by the time they returned to the camp on the tree branch and found that Jade and Balm were already back. They had found ruins along the shore too, but no Kek and no evidence of recent groundling habitation. Vine reported that his afternoon had been uneventful. "Flower slept the whole time," he said. "I think she needed the rest."

Flower, fidgeting around as if having trouble finding a comfortable spot on the branch, gave him an irritable glare. "No one cares what you think," she told him.

Vine said wryly, "I noticed that."

Chime handed her a pack to lean against. "Are you all right?" She hissed at him. "I'm fine."

No one was hungry enough to hunt again yet, so there was nothing to do but wait for Stone. The branch was more than wide enough for them all to sprawl on comfortably, and through the leaves they had a good view of the seashore. During the afternoon, Vine and Flower had built a little hearth: one layer of flat, water-smoothed rocks to insulate the wood, and a second smaller layer that Flower had spelled for heat, so she could warm water for tea.

The air was fragrant in the gathering twilight, scented with the flowers of the field and the leaves of their tree. The nightbirds and treelings and insects sang and hummed, and Moon tried to listen to the others talk and not be rabidly impatient for Stone to appear.

After darkness settled over the shore, Balm took the watch and they tried to sleep. Moon lay with his head pillowed on Jade's stomach, wide awake. He didn't realize he was tapping his fingers on his chest until her hand closed over his. She said softly, "It's not a long flight for Stone."

"I know." He made his hand relax. "Still."

Nearby, Chime said, "Pearl will know by now. I wonder . . . I mean, what will she do? Besides send someone after us."

Jade snorted, quietly. "I think we know what she'll do."

Just past Chime, Vine groaned.

Moon finally dozed off at some point, only to wake

abruptly some time later, when someone said, "He's back!"

Moon sat up and startled Jade awake. It was still dark but he could tell from the quality of the air that it wasn't long before dawn. Vine had taken Balm's place at watch and Moon scrambled forward to his side.

A darker shape hung against the starlit sky: Stone, flying back toward the shore.

By the time Stone reached them, everyone was awake. Flower was the only one who had slept heavily. Still bleary with it, she filled their kettle from the waterskin and put it on the hearth to heat.

Stone was just a big dark shadow as he landed on the end of the branch. The wood shivered with his weight, then went still as he shifted to his groundling form. He walked up the branch toward them, and Moon wished they had been able to camp on the ground, or anywhere else where they could have made a real fire. The heating rocks didn't give off light and he wanted to see Stone's expression.

Stone stopped a few paces away, and said, flatly, "I couldn't find it."

Jade stirred a little, and Moon knew she had just controlled the urge to hiss in disappointment. Chime shook his head, confused. "The seed? But—"

"The island," Stone corrected. He sat down, moving slowly, and Moon heard his bones creak. "There's nothing out there. I spent most of the night flying a spiral, looking for land." He rubbed his eyes. "What I'm afraid of is that these groundlings were on a boat that sank."

"Or the island moved," Moon said. Suddenly some of the things Nobent had told him made a lot more sense.

Even in the dark, Moon could tell that Stone was giving him a look that would have sent most of the warriors skittering for cover. But there was more life in his voice when he said, "What?"

Moon told him, "We found a Kek settlement, and talked to a waterling trader. It said there were groundlings called 'sea-goers' who lived on the water and moved around." He told the rest of it, with Chime inserting more details.

"That might explain it," Jade said. "If we knew how these sea-goers were moving, it would help."

Vine shrugged. "They could be on boats, or they could have a flying island."

"If they have a flying island, it must be moving fairly fast," Chime countered. "Too fast."

"That's right." Flower sounded thoughtful. "It moved out of Stone's range in only seven days. Flying islands drift slowly with the wind. Unless there was a big storm, and we've seen no sign of one, it would still be in the area. It's more likely to be a boat."

"Or a fleet of boats," Moon added.

"Maybe." Jade scratched her claws on the wood, thinking it over. "How does the water traveler find them?"

"That's . . . I don't know," Chime said slowly. "It has to be scent, doesn't it?"

"Something in the water." Moon shook his head. "The sea-goers leave a trail, somehow."

Stone sounded weary. "We'll figure that out when we get there. You all know how we're getting there, right?"

"An augury?" Vine asked, turning to Flower.

"No, we don't need an augury," Moon said before she could reply. He smiled. Old Nobent was going to help them after all. "We'll follow the water traveler."

CHAPTER EIGHT

Once everyone had agreed on a plan, Moon and Chime flew immediately toward the Kek city, following the dark line of the shore. The others were to follow later, after leaving a marker for whoever might be coming after them from Indigo Cloud. Stone, who would be doing the biggest share of the tracking once Nobent set out, needed to sleep before he started another long flight.

Before they left, Flower had asked, "If this creature does lead you to the sea-goers, do you have any idea what to look for?"

"Besides the seed?" Moon had to admit she had him there. "No."

Flower sighed and rubbed her forehead. "You'll need something to go on besides that. I'll augur again."

Chime frowned at her. "Are you sure that's a good idea?"

Flower stared hard at him. "Yes."

After they had taken flight away from the camp, Moon asked Chime, "Why didn't you think Flower should augur?"

"She hasn't been looking well," Chime replied, slipping sideways in an unexpected air current. "I just have a bad feeling about it."

Moon hoped he was wrong. Flower's augury was the only thing that had gotten them this far.

When they drew near the Kek city, Moon tipped a wing at Chime. Chime broke off and flew into the deeper shadows under the trees. Moon turned toward the city.

There were a few smudge pots and lights lit in the lower levels; by the smell they were using some kind of nut oil. Several lamps hung on the outer edge of the dock area Nobent occupied.

Moon had debated approaching underwater, and decided against it. He didn't know what kind of senses Nobent had for detecting prey in the water, and it was best not to find out the hard way. He was pretty certain he could take Nobent in a fight, but that wouldn't get him what he wanted.

He circled the city, playing the cool damp wind against his wings, dropping lower and slowing until he could catch the side of a hive-tower. He heard a slight stirring of movement through the woven reed wall, and a sleepy squeak, but no one gave the alarm. He climbed down the wall head first, found the heavier support for the half-roof that hung out over the dock, and eased out onto it.

This close to the piers and the surface of the water, he could scent Nobent's rank odor, but it wasn't nearly as strong as it had been before. Taking a chance, Moon crawled to the end of the roof and hung his head down over the edge.

The dock area was lit by three hanging lamps, the wan light showing him the empty pier where Nobent had rested. *Huh. Maybe he left as soon as we were out of sight.* That was a little odd. If Nobent only wanted to take his next cargo of edilvine and rushes to the sea-goers, he should have waited until morning. His eyes hadn't had the appearance of a nocturnal being's.

He could be rushing off to tell the sea-goers that Raksura were searching for them, but Moon didn't think Nobent could know about the theft. Nobent hadn't recognized Moon as a Raksura, hadn't seemed to know about the courts inhabiting the forest. But maybe the sea-goers were interested in anyone who asked about their whereabouts. *That's a good sign we're looking in the right place.*

Moon straightened up and pushed off the roof to catch the wind. He swept down low over the water, only ten or twelve paces above it. He cast back and forth over the sea in front of the city twice before he caught Nobent's scent again, traces of it carried by the constant breeze blowing in off the water. It gave him a direction and a faint trail to follow.

He swooped up again and curved over the city. Chime, watching from the forest, arched up out of the canopy to meet him. Moon twisted into a tight circle, matched Chime's slower speed, and said, "He's left already. I'm going to follow. Tell Stone to go northwest."

"Northwest," Chime repeated. "Be careful. Don't go too far!"

Like all good advice, Moon didn't think he was going to have much chance to follow it. He banked away and headed out to sea.

☾

Moon flew low over the water, following Nobent's scent on the wind. He lost it twice in crosswinds while it was still dark, and had to cast back and forth only a few paces above the water to pick it up again. After that he slowed his flight, going more carefully.

When the shore was far behind him, a dark band barely visible in the night, he realized this was the first time he had been really alone in . . . he had lost count of the days. Except for the day and night when he had tracked the kethel to the Dwei hive, he had been with other Raksura since Stone had found him in the Cordans' valley. He had been alone for turns before that, for most of his life, isolated even when he was living with groundlings. It was strange how quickly he had gotten used to constant companionship.

The sky began to streak with dawn, the light reflecting off long fingers of cloud, lightening the water to a crystalline blue. Moon was only about ten paces above the waves when he caught movement out of the corner of his eye, a shape under the surface. Concentrating on the scent, he reacted by instinct before the thought even formed. He twisted away just as something lashed up at him from below. It brushed his wing, hard enough to knock him sideways.

Badly startled, Moon flapped wildly through the spray,

shooting upward as fast as he could. He looked down in time to see a white shape, an arm with a clawed hand, sinking slowly down below the waves. The palm was at least two paces across. Moon swore, gained some more height and caught the wind again. He could see a dim outline just below the crystal surface, something pale sinking out of sight.

That was . . . exciting, Moon thought, his heart pounding as he corrected his wobbly flight. At least he was wide awake now.

After that he was a lot more careful about his distance above the water.

Clouds moved in to paint the sky with gray, but there was no smell of rain yet. He caught up with Nobent about mid-morning, and swept up high into the air so there was no chance of the water traveler spotting him. Nobent swam determinedly northwest, his branches open around him like a big ugly gray flower. Whatever he was paddling with was hidden by the tendrils of his mat.

Nobent moved at a good pace for a water creature or a rowboat, but not for a Raksura. Moon was able to glide after him, riding the wind. He couldn't see Nobent's destination yet, though far ahead there were drifts of mist near the surface that might obscure a small island or fleet of large watercraft. If the sea-goers lived too far away, the warriors wouldn't be able to make the flight.

Moon kept looking back, hoping to see Stone. When the sun was directly overhead, casting great cloud-shadows on the crystal-blue sparkle of the water, he was rewarded with a dark shape moving rapidly toward him. *Finally,* he thought. At least this part of their plan had worked.

Stone must have spotted Moon because he curved upward and vanished in the clouds. Moon shot up to meet him.

He passed up through the cold fog of a cloud and emerged in brilliant sunlight to find Stone circling overhead. "What took you so long?" Moon called to him.

Stone never spoke in his Raksuran form, so Moon was fairly sure he wouldn't dignify that with an answer. Stone just rumbled and tapped his chest with one claw.

"I'm coming." Moon hated being carried, but he wasn't staying back here, plodding along after Nobent. He flew up to Stone, matched his pace, then grabbed onto Stone's outstretched arm. Shouting to be heard over the wind, he said, "There's waterlings as big as major kethel hunting this sea. I don't know how Nobent survives." Possibly he smelled too bad for anything to want to eat him.

Stone grunted thoughtfully. Moon pulled his wings in and folded them tight against his back, then climbed up Stone's arm to hook his claws into the big scales across his chest. Stone reached up and closed a hand around him, holding Moon securely. Then they shot forward over the clouds.

☾

At Stone's speed, following the direction that Nobent had taken, it wasn't long before Moon saw the outline of an island. It was a series of seven rising hills in a half circle, and it was inhabited. He could see the glitter of reflected sunlight on the regular shapes of tall octagonal towers. Stone gained altitude, skirting the bottom of the clouds to lessen the chance of anyone looking up and spotting them.

This wasn't what I was expecting, Moon thought, as Stone tilted his wings to slow his flight. Maybe this was the sea-goers' home port, and they had fast-moving vessels to travel in. *They used something to move the seed away from the spot where the mentors saw it. They didn't* . . . Moon stiffened, eyes widening. *What in the Three Worlds* . . .

They were close enough now to look down on the island, to see that it wasn't an island.

The seven low hills formed a half circle, and were completely covered with the stone buildings of the groundling city. But the water was so clear Moon could see what was just under the surface. From one end of the island a long curving tail stretched out, tipped with giant fins. On each coast were three massive flippers, angled down to vanish in the blue depths. And at the other end, a huge triangular head, tilted down so only the brow ridge just below the waves was visible.

Above Moon's head, Stone hissed incredulously. Moon echoed the sentiment. He couldn't believe that groundlings had managed this. But there was the city, mostly composed of towers and bridges and raised plazas, as if built to stand as high above the surface of the creature as possible. He could see the sparkle of fountains, people moving on the bridges between towers. There was even a harbor, formed by the curve of one haunch, with sailing vessels docked in it. *They could have the seed.* A creature this size could have easily swum the distance between the point the mentors had augured and here in only a few days.

Moon looked up, though all he could see was the scaled underside of Stone's neck. "We need to talk to Nobent again."

Stone must have agreed. He banked away and headed back toward the shore.

☾

"While it sleeps, anyone can approach. When it wakes, it moves." Nobent sunk down further into his mat, his knobby brow furrowed in sullen dismay. "That's all Nobent knows."

"That's not what Nobent told us earlier," Moon pointed out. "Nobent's memory has improved."

Nobent sniffed self-righteously. "You didn't ask Nobent the right questions."

It was evening, the sun setting over the sea, and they stood on the forest beach, just out of sight of the Kek city. Stone had acquired Nobent by scooping him out of the sea with his free hand, and had flown back here at his best speed. They had told the others what they had found and, with difficulty, had gotten them past the initial "groundling city on a giant water monster" shock. Now they were trying to decide what to do and how to do it.

Flower was the only one not present. The warriors had built a small blind up on one of the mountain-tree branches, and she was inside it, sleeping. Chime had said she had been exhausted again after the augury and had spent most of the day asleep.

Jade cocked her head, watching Nobent, not hiding her skepticism. "And you say if we land on this thing, in the dark, it won't react to us."

Nobent eyed her nervously. "As long as it's sleeping."

"Do we seriously believe that?" Vine asked, waving a hand in frustration. "A giant water beast isn't going to notice if we land on it?"

Nobent grimaced. "It doesn't notice Nobent. Fools. Groundlings come all the time in ships. How could the groundlings live on it if it ate them?"

"How do they find it?" Chime asked pointedly. "If it moves?"

"They have a special magic. Or they ask a water traveler." Nobent sat up a little, sulky and contemptuous. "Ask, not snatch up off the sea."

"And how often do they get eaten?" Balm asked, her expression grim.

"It doesn't eat them!" Nobent snarled. "Nobent is not stupid!"

"If you're lying," Stone said, his voice even and thoughtful, "I'll find you. There's nowhere I can't find you."

If the threat had been directed at him, Moon would have found it very effective. Apparently Nobent did, too. The water traveler huddled, eyes widening with real terror. "Not lying," he said in a small voice.

Jade hissed and turned away to walk up the beach. Stone went after her. "Watch him," Moon told the three warriors, and followed.

They stopped out of earshot, in the shadow of a stray sapling mountain-tree that overhung the beach.

Keeping her voice low, Jade said, "When Flower augured this morning, she saw a metal ship. She said it would lead you to the seed. Did you see anything like that?"

"No. But we weren't looking closely at the harbor," Stone told her. "When we go back, we'll know where to start."

Jade looked up the beach, her brow furrowed. "Someone will have to stay behind with Flower. It would be good to have a mentor along, but she's just not up to it. I've never seen an ordinary augury affect her like that."

Moon glanced up at the shelter. He hoped Flower wasn't ill. Since leaving the old colony, they had all been on one long journey after another, and there had been no time for anyone to rest.

Stone followed his gaze. "She's pushed herself too hard." He turned to Jade again. "It's a long day's flight for a warrior, but if this thing moves further out to sea, they'd be stuck there. I couldn't carry all of them. The best option is to let me go alone."

"With me." Moon couldn't keep his mouth shut any longer. "I know more about groundlings than any of you. I know how to blend in."

"He's not wrong," Stone admitted.

"I know that." Jade shook out her spines, obviously unhappy with their lack of options. "But we're taking a chance that we won't need them to help fight when we find the damn thing."

Jade had clearly assumed she was going with them. Nobody appeared to have seen the problem with that. Moon said, "Jade, the thieves know what Raksura look like. They've seen the carvings in the colony tree. Even in your Arbora form, they'll recognize what you are."

She hissed, her expression turning sour. But she didn't try to argue the point. "So we're leaving me behind, then."

"Yes." At her glare, he added, "We can't help it."

Jade turned to Stone. "Before you leave, take Nobent off somewhere he can't cause trouble." Grimly determined, she added, "If you're not back in three days, we're coming after you."

"Fair enough," Stone said. Moon thought, *If we're not back in three days, we'll probably need the help.*

☾

Stone took Nobent some distance along the shore to the south and dropped him off. It would take him days and days to make his way back toward the sea-goers' island, the hope being that he would be too smart to try to go there immediately. After that, Moon and Stone rested and fed, then left in the early afternoon. They could go more quickly this time, at Moon's fastest pace, timing their flight to reach the city just after dark.

By the time the sun set, they could see the city's lights in the distance, dimmed by the heavy mist hanging over it. As they reached it, Stone broke off to circle and Moon dropped down for a closer view than he had gotten before.

The city was mostly composed of towers that rose up the flanks of the giant creature and thickly crowded along its hilly spine. There were big ones, octagonal with domed roofs, and smaller round ones. Light shone sporadically from windows and on the plazas and bridges. There were glass and metal lamps, on poles or hanging from chains, filled with a vapor that gave off a white illumination. There were no streets, just stairways and walkways, wreathed in mist. Some of the towers were topped with elaborate structures, domed roofs, smaller turrets, and colonnades with wide terraces overlooking the city. Some were brightly lit and occupied.

The illusion that this was just another groundling city was broken by the heavy, damp musk in the air—the scent of a huge, unimaginably huge, water creature.

Moon flew in close to a larger tower, catching hold of a lower ledge and climbing up. From the top he heard voices, and a thread of music from stringed instruments. He reached the stone railing and lifted himself up just enough to peek over the edge.

Past the terrace, through the heavy columns supporting the dome, Moon could see a large group of groundlings, talking, laughing, moving amid low fountains and tall potted trees. They were dressed in flowing robes in brilliant colors, the fabrics translucent or catching metallic glints in the light. Heavy lanterns hung from chains, wrought into elaborate shapes of fish and sea creatures. The groundlings held goblets of pure crystalline glass in rich colors. Moon wouldn't have thought living on a giant monster would be so lucrative.

He spotted four different races immediately; Nobent hadn't lied about that at least. One group was tall and willowy, with dark skin and darker hair. Another was a weathered gold color, with long golden hair. The largest group by far had light blue skin, with knobby, pearl-like lumps on top of their skulls. The ones who seemed to be servants, who moved among the others with gold metal trays of food and drinks, were all shorter, with gray-green scaly skin and boney crests that looked like fish fins.

Moon pushed away from the railing, dropped down, and spread his wings. He caught the wind and turned toward the harbor.

He landed on a conical roof to get a better view of the half-circle of the harbor. Ships lay several levels below, tied up to long floating pontoon piers. Past them a great barrier ridge loomed, tapering away to vanish under the waves. Knowing it was the leg of the giant creature beneath them made the skin under Moon's scales creep. Looking at the towers and other stone and metal structures made it easier not to think about what was below you. The leg was very . . . obvious.

The dock itself was narrow, built against the rising slope of the creature's side. Multiple stairways led down from the crowded huddle of buildings perched just below the city proper, lit by the vapor-lamps. They had to be warehouses, provisioners, places where the ships could be hired or cargos sold. Below them, big metal scaffolds clung to the slope, hanging out over the water. They supported what looked like metal cradles, which Moon found bizarre, until he spotted one that held a small fishing boat nestled in its grip. The smaller boats must be cranked up out of the water with the cradles, probably to protect them when the monster moved.

No one was around on this end of the docks. A few people climbed the stairs at the far end. The buildings along here all looked oddly off center, as if their foundations were unsteady and they were about to tumble off their perches. Considering what they were built on, their foundations probably did move periodically. Presumably the giant towers were built on more stable footing.

Moon leapt lightly down to the walkway and shifted to groundling. Immediately the mist was clammy on his skin, even through the tough material of his shirt. The metal surface of the walkway was cold under his feet. The trade-off was that the heavy odors of monster and fouled water and dead fish wasn't nearly as overwhelming. He took the first set of stairs, then worked his way down from walkway to walkway under the scaffolding, until he could step out onto the somewhat wider dock.

The green metal was rusty in places and puddles of water had collected in the worn spots. The vapor-lights were suspended on curving metal poles, the top of each one ornamented with a goggle-eyed fish head. The side of the monster was like a cliff stretching up from the water, the skin greenish and patterned with giant scales, crusted with little clumps of barnacle-like creatures. Moon stared at it in unwilling disgusted fascination. He couldn't see how these people could live like this.

He tore his gaze away from the monster's skin and walked down the dock, away from the fishers' scaffolds, toward the bigger trading ships. The area wasn't as uninhabited as it had appeared from a distance; the bundle of rags against a piling was a groundling, sleeping deeply. Another group of groundlings were in a shack built back against the cliff, having a desultory conversation. A few others moved around on the deck of a ship ahead, and some carried casks down into the hold. All the ships were wooden vessels, their sails furled or folded down. They were large and small, some plain and some painted, some with carved designs along the hulls. He could pick out the acrid scent of tar, and the wet weedy odor of the fibers used to make the ropes.

Then he moved past a large sailing vessel and saw a ship docked by itself, at a pontoon pier that stretched further out from the others. The vapor-lights caught the gleam of coppery metal on its tall hull.

There we go. Moon walked to the edge of the dock.

The metal ship was about two hundred paces long, but it was much wider than the sailing vessels. There were multiple decks above its bulbous hull, enough to make it look top heavy, and it had three wide chimneys across its width. It was also easily big enough to make a long sea crossing to the Reaches, and to carry a large party of groundlings and the supplies they would need to make the trek into the forest on foot. *This has to be it.*

It was dark, no lights showed in any windows or doors, and no one was out on the decks. The groundlings aboard must be sleeping soundly inside.

Moon turned away and walked down the dock toward the darker end, away from the vapor-lights. He sensed something big fly overhead, just out of range of the lights, and knew Stone had seen the ship as well. When Moon reached a shadowy spot, he ducked down, shifted, and slipped over the edge of the dock into the cool water.

Swimming in the dark, knowing what lived in these waters, was a nerve-racking experience. He stayed near the hulls of the other craft and worked his way back toward the metal ship. At least the water was fairly clean. The harbor area must get sluiced every time the creature moved, so it didn't have much time to collect layers of garbage and filth like other groundling ports.

He reached the metal ship's hull, and swam along until he found a boarding ladder on the side facing away from the dock. He climbed up onto the wide deck and paused to shake the water off his scales. Instead of wood, it was plated with narrow strips of copper metal. He listened for a long moment, and tasted the air, but there was no hint of movement, no scent of nearby groundlings.

There was a faint splash against the hull below, then Stone in groundling form climbed up the ladder, his clothes dripping on the copper deck.

Moon found a hatch, a heavy door with a thick crystal porthole. It opened into a wide interior corridor, dark except for what little light came through the doorway. It was lined with fine dark wood, with bright metal sconces holding white crystal globes for lamps. It was also utterly silent, and smelled faintly of must.

It felt empty, and Moon's heart sunk. He had hoped the groundlings would be aboard, that they could surprise them, get the seed, and be flying back to the others before dawn. Obviously coming to the same conclusion, Stone made a low-voiced frustrated snarl. He stepped past Moon and moved down the corridor.

They found a doorway that turned into the darker interior. Stone stopped to fish in his pack and pulled out a small cloth bundle. As he unwrapped it, light glowed. It was a little beach rock spelled to make light, one of two that he had gotten from Flower before they left. He handed Moon the other one and they followed the passage inward.

About midway through the ship, the corridor opened into a living area. It had deep cushioned couches and bookcases with clear glass doors, and a white porcelain stove painted with delicate flowers and vines. Moon saw a book left out on one of the couches, and picked it up. It had a leather binding, and delicate paper printed with even rows of characters. He couldn't read the language, and there weren't any pictures. He put it back on the seat and stepped over to touch the stove, just to make certain, but it was cold.

He looked at Stone. "No one's been here for a long time."

Stone grunted an acknowledgement. "Maybe they left the seed. Look everywhere."

They searched, opening every door, every cabinet, looking into every cubby. The cabins meant for sleeping had beds built into the wall, and cabinets for storage, so there were a lot of doors and cubbies to investigate. It didn't help that many of them were still filled with possessions. Clothing made of heavy fabrics, leather boots and shoes, more books in unfamiliar languages, some printed and some handwritten, strange tools that Moon couldn't guess the purpose of. Everything was as rich as the living area, with fine wood, polished metal, painted ceramic sconces over the lights. There were tiny rooms for bathing, the walls covered with painted ceramic, with basins for the water to be piped into.

Moon found a room that was meant for preparing food, with a long table and chairs, and a larger stove of metal. The cabinets there held white pottery dishes, and metal cooking pots and utensils, and containers of flour, salt, and other dry foodstuffs he couldn't identify. Some of it had been sitting long enough to get moldy. There was a bowl on the table, filled with fruit so old it had turned into desiccated husks. Moon poked it thoughtfully, trying to estimate the age. *Six changes of the month, maybe seven?* Stone walked in, saw it, growled, and walked out again.

Down below there were strange rooms filled with machinery, all of it cold and silent. One of the rooms held blocks of a mineral, with a scent and texture not unlike the one used as fuel for light and warmth in the Turning City, back in the eastern mountains. Moon assumed the blocks were used to make the ship move, somehow. But searching those areas told them nothing except that the seed wasn't hidden there. They found signs that the crew had left abruptly but meant to return: a jacket tossed over a chair, tools scattered on the floor in front of one of the machines, a writing book left out on a table with a wooden pen and an open ink bottle. The beds all had blankets and cushions, some tumbled as if the occupants had just gotten up.

They ended their search in the bridge at the very top of the ship. It was round, with big windows giving a nearly panoramic view of the harbor. They had to wrap their lights up again to keep the glow from being seen from the docks, so they had to search the large area by starlight.

Not that there was much here to search. There was a brass-bound wheel for steering and other devices Moon didn't recognize, and papers covered with unintelligible writing strewn carelessly around. Some of them had been stepped on and torn or stained with dirt.

In the center of the room was a narrow, waist-high pillar of polished wood, the top formed into a heavy glass hexagon. It reminded Moon of the mechanism that steered the Golden Islanders' flying ships, but there was nothing inside it and there was no handle to steer with.

Stone hissed in frustration. "The damn seed isn't here."

"It's the only thing that isn't here." Moon straightened up from peering into the bottom of the empty pillar. "They left food behind, and their books, their writings, clothing. If they left voluntarily, they meant to come back."

"Or somebody came aboard and killed them." Stone shook his head and paced to the window that looked out at the harbor and the misty city rising above it. "And took the seed away somewhere. Flower didn't say the seed was on the ship, just that the ship would lead us to it."

Moon scratched the back of his neck, thinking it over. "But somebody still pays to keep this ship here."

Stone turned back, frowning. "What do you mean?"

"Trading ports don't let ships dock for free." He had heard enough captains and sailors complain about this in the trading cities along the Crescent Coast to know it was a fairly universal practice. "Somebody has to own the pier, or be paying for the ship to stay here. And what about when the monster moves? The bigger ships can't just be dragged along, they'd get damaged. Somebody has to sail this one. Or tow it."

Stone turned to look out toward the city again. "So somebody must come down here to keep an eye on it."

☾

They wanted something fairly dramatic, something that would catch attention quickly. Setting the ship on fire was the first thing that occurred to them, but that might rouse the whole harbor. So Stone climbed down the hull again, slipped underwater and shifted, and used his claws to snap the heavy cable at the ship's bow.

Moon swam back to the docks, climbed a piling, and slunk through the dark to crouch among stacks of casks and boxes waiting to be loaded. Once his scales dried, he shifted to groundling and settled in to wait.

The ship was still attached to the pier by a few lighter lines and a cable in the stern, but without the bow cable it soon swung out from the pier and drifted sideways. It was a potential hazard to the big sailing vessel docked at the next pier, and it didn't go unnoticed.

After some time, the groundling who guarded the deck of the sailing ship passed by that side, stopped, and stared for a moment, then hurried away. Soon he was back with more groundlings. Two of them went down the gangplank to their pier and crossed over to the buildings just above the dock.

More groundlings came out to look, then went down the pier. They brought out a small boat and readied lighter cables to fasten the ship back to the pier again. Moon cursed wearily. It looked like the dockworkers were going to deal with the situation without summoning the ship's owner.

The lights and noise woke the crews sleeping on the ships nearby, and they started to come down onto the dock to watch. They were mostly of the dark and golden groundling races that Moon had seen in the top of the tower, though they were all dressed like sailors, in pants, shirts, and vests of rough cloth and leather. There were no blue-pearl people, and none of the sea-people with the grayish scales and head crests. Moon got up, wove his way through the forest of crates, and slipped into the crowd.

One thing Moon had wanted to find out, while it was still dark out and they were in a spot relatively easy to escape, was what the reaction would be to his and Stone's groundling forms. It looked like the people here were used to seeing a variety of groundling races, but you could never be too certain. He had been in situations where a settlement had seemed to welcome a large number of diverse races, only to find out that his groundling form looked just enough like their hereditary enemies.

But while some of these people glanced at him, no one seemed to find his appearance shocking. Several were having an annoyed conversation in Kedaic, mostly about the stupidity of whoever had tied up the ship.

Moon took a chance and said in the same language, "Who does it belong to?"

Without looking around, an older woman with weathered golden skin said, "It's been there a long time." She tapped her chin thoughtfully. "Most of the turn, I think."

One of the dark-skinned men said, "At least. It belongs to Magnate Ardan."

Someone off to the side said in a thicker accent, "Does it? I thought it was farcoast traders brought it here."

Another woman shrugged. "Maybe they sold it to him. His emblem is on the pier."

"Ah, you're probably right, then."

There was a pause, as everyone was distracted by two of the small boats almost blundering into each other.

"Magnate Ardan?" Moon repeated, hoping that was enough to get them started again. He didn't want to say too much or show particular interest. They didn't need any rumors spreading about the funny-looking stranger asking questions about Magnate Ardan's ship.

"I didn't know he was a trader," someone said.

"I don't know that he is." The gold woman turned to point. "He has that tower, right up there. The one with the gold turret."

CHAPTER NINE

O nce the metal ship had been secured again, the excitement died down and everyone wandered back to their ships or the dock buildings. Moon lingered, just in case the ship's owner belatedly appeared, but finally gave in.

He took the first stair upward, where it wound up among platforms braced atop the knobs and swellings in the monster's side. As the stairs curved inward, he saw someone standing on the platform above, under the vapor-light, waiting for him. It was Stone, radiating impatience.

"Well?" Stone asked, as Moon reached the platform.

"It didn't work like we thought."

"I noticed."

Moon ignored that in the interest of not spending the rest of the night fighting. "I heard the other crews talking. They think the ship belongs to somebody called Magnate Ardan. He lives up there." He jerked his head up toward the tower, the gold top barely visible from this angle.

Stone turned to look. Then he hissed out a breath and started up the stairs. "That's going to be a problem."

Following him, Moon agreed. They had a whole tower to search now, and it would probably be occupied by a large number of groundlings. And they didn't know for certain that the seed was there, just that this Ardan now owned the ship, so he must know what had happened to the crew.

The steps twisted up through a heavily shadowed, unlit walkway. Stone kept walking, but Moon shifted and scaled the nearest wall, then climbed up to the rust-streaked metal roof of the house that overhung the walkway.

He had a better view from here. Above the crowded buildings overlooking the dock, the walkways turned to narrow caverns, winding their way past the feet of other towers, far smaller than those toward the center of the city. It was well past the middle of the night, and many of the lights had gone out. He didn't see much movement on the walkways and bridges in this area, either.

He could understand why groundlings might be reluctant to venture out into the night. The mist had sunk into the low spots of the city, the walkways and lower platforms, so heavy it obscured everything but the brightest lights. Unless these people had a Raksuran-like sense of direction, they could easily become lost in their own city. He sprang up from the roof, spreading his wings to catch the strong wind, and turned toward the city's central ridge and Ardan's tower.

It loomed out of the misty dark, a tall octagonal structure with a domed roof of green-tinged copper topped by a slender gold spire. But there were no open terraces and balconies like the other big towers. He flew closer, slipping sideways in to make a wide circle around it. There were windows, narrow arches set deeply back into the heavily carved façade, but they all seemed to be covered by metal shutters. *That's not helpful.* He had hoped to at least get a glimpse of the inhabitants—

He slammed into something and the stunning blow sent him spinning away. Dazed, he plunged down, falling toward the rooftops. He struggled to extend his wings, then managed to roll out of the dizzying tumble and caught the air just in time to break his fall.

Moon glided down, then dropped onto a slanted rooftop. He hooked his claws in the slate shingles as he folded his wings and pulled them in protectively. The skin under his scales tingled, as if he had fallen into something acidic. He shook his spines out with an angry rattle, but he wasn't sure who he was more mad at, himself or the damn groundlings.

Still shaken, he crept to the edge of the roof, climbed down to a lower rooftop, and finally down a wall to a walkway cloaked in mist. There, he shifted to groundling. The sudden change in sensation made him stumble; the tingling was worse, like being bitten all over by firebugs. And he had a headache.

Snarling under his breath, he found his way through the narrow caverns of the walkways. The damp air seemed to congeal on his skin, weighing his clothes down. He crossed a bridge over a mist-wreathed chasm and came out onto the open plaza at the base of the tower.

Two bridges led off from the plaza and several stairways wound up and away from it amid the smaller buildings clustered around. Vapor-lights hung from arches and eaves over some of the ground-floor doorways. The doors were all sealed, except for one. It was off the second landing of a stairway, and was lit and open; piping music came from it, and an occasional muffled voice.

From this angle, the tower itself looked even more like a blocky, windowless fortress. The entrance was large but sealed with heavy ironbound doors and there was a big vapor-light mounted on each side.

The plaza wasn't uninhabited. Moon immediately sensed movement down several of the byways. And Stone, still in groundling form, was just across the way, sitting back against the wall, near a bundle of rags. Swearing silently, Moon crossed over to him.

"So they don't want visitors," Stone said, apparently having decided to be unperturbed by this development.

"I'm fine, thanks for asking." Moon leaned on the wall and eased down to sit. The paving was gritty and smelled of mold. The shock of running into the tower's barrier had left him feeling every moment of all the days of long flights, tension, and little rest. "Who's that?"

The bundle of rags was peering around Stone, staring at Moon. Its eyes were big, dark, and slightly mad. It smelled like a groundling; based on the size, Moon was guessing one of the gray ones with the waterling scales and crest.

"This is Dari." Stone jerked his head to indicate his new groundling friend. "They threw him out of that wine bar up there."

"Halloo," Dari said, or something similar. Moon realized that Dari wasn't mad, but just very, very intoxicated.

A group of blue groundlings tumbled out of the wine bar's doorway, the vapor-light gleaming off their pearly skull-caps. They careened down the steps, talking loudly. Moon leaned his aching head back against the wall. "The crewmen were speaking Kedaic. They used a word I thought meant 'magnate,' but maybe it means 'magister.'" That would explain how the thieves had found the colony tree, why they had been so bent on getting the seed. If Ardan was a powerful groundling shaman, he could have wanted the seed for magic, used his powers to locate it, and sent the thieves after it. Moon just hoped Ardan hadn't noticed that something had flown into his damn magical barrier.

Stone said, dryly, "That would agree with Dari, who says a powerful magic-worker lives in that tower, and that everyone's afraid of him." Dari nodded emphatically.

Stone added, "I checked. That barrier goes all the way down to the pavement in front of the doors."

The drunken groundlings staggered across the plaza. Two spotted Moon and Stone, and broke off to rush aggressively toward them. Dari yelped and cowered.

When they were less than ten paces away, Stone growled, a low reverberation that Moon felt through the paving. The two groundlings stumbled to an abrupt halt and peered uncertainly. Groundling eyes often weren't as good in the dark as Raksuran, and they probably couldn't see much except three shapes sitting against the wall. They hesitated, wavering, then retreated, throwing uneasy looks back. They rejoined the rest of the group, which was making its way loudly and erratically across the plaza.

Dari made a noise of relief, pulled a pottery jug out of his rags, and drank deeply.

Stone waited until the groundlings had wandered out of sight, before he said, "He's had our seed most of a turn, depending on how long it took his thieves to get back through the forest. We need to get in there."

"But not tonight." Moon had had enough for now. They needed to rest, get more information about Ardan, then think of a way to get past the protective barrier. "Dari, show us where the nearest abandoned house is."

☾

There were several not far away, a crowded huddle of houses around a dark octagonal tower. Dari pointed it out for them, then wandered off back toward the wine bar.

They made their way down a little alley that wove between the other buildings. It opened occasionally into small courtyards, barely thirty paces across. Moon could hear people sleeping in some of the houses, but others sounded empty. The odor of mold was worse here, almost as bad as the musky stench of the monster. The rock everything was built from seemed too strong to crumble, but the perpetual damp caused mold and mushroom-like plants to grow on it.

They came to the tower's base, and there was no mistaking the fact that it was abandoned; the entrance archway was bricked up.

Moon glanced around, making sure the houses overlooking this plaza had either blocked windows or blank walls. Then he shifted and jumped up onto the side of the tower.

The openings below the third floor had all been blocked up, the seams filled with layers of dirt and mold. He climbed up to the first open window. Stone flowed past him and disappeared into an opening on an upper floor. Moon slipped inside, scenting nothing but rot.

The room was large and high-ceilinged, the floor strewn with broken furniture mixed with shrouds of disintegrating fabric and rotted trash. It was too dark to make out the carving on the pillars and the walls. Moon explored, finding that the layout was fairly simple, with big rooms on each floor around a central staircase. Prowling around each level to make certain nothing else was living here, he kept stepping on odd indentations in the floor. They were small and round, and there were a lot of them. He wasn't sure what they were for, except to trip the unwary, until he found the rusted broken remnants of a metal clip in one. *Huh,* he thought, flicking the metal with a claw. They must be for anchoring down furniture, and anything else that might fall over when the leviathan moved.

There was also a big ceramic cistern on the fifth floor, filled by a pipe that ran out through the wall, and probably up to funnels on the roof. He opened the lid and sniffed cautiously. The water smelt stale, but not like anything had died in it.

Climbing up the stairwell, Moon wondered if the city wasn't as populated as it had looked at first. If the empty walkways and sporadic lights weren't a sign that the inhabitants were asleep, but a sign that many of them had long since left. The harbor had seemed well occupied by ships, if not crowded, but then with no room for crops or herds, the city must get all its food by trade and fishing.

He found Stone on the top floor, in a big room with two walls open to the wind and the night. Columns in the shape of groundling women supported the roof on that side, and a terrace with a high balustrade extended all the way around the tower. The weather had washed any debris down the stairs or back into the corners, so the cracked tile floor was almost clean.

Stone was in groundling form, sitting on the floor, digging through his old battered pack. Moon shifted to groundling too, and sat next to him, smothering a yawn. Stone pulled out a redfruit and offered it to him. Moon shook his head. He was a little queasy from his encounter with the barrier and he didn't think a sweet redfruit would help.

Tomorrow they would have to find food, as well as a way into the Magister's tower. They had some loose gems, sunstones from an old consort's bracelet of Stone's, brought along for him to wear at Emerald Twilight. Stone had refused to wear it, and apparently wasn't at all reluctant to use it for trade.

Moon looked out into the dark sky, streaked with drifts of mist. *How do we get into that tower?* he wanted to ask. Instead he said, "If we can't get the seed back, where do we go?"

Stone contemplated the redfruit, then put it back in his pack. "We look for another colony."

"I know that." Moon scrubbed a hand through his hair, and told himself not to try to pick a fight with Stone. Exhaustion and impatience and growing despair weren't a good combination for this conversation. "Blossom said if we took another deserted colony, we could be attacked by other courts."

"Blossom's right." Stone pulled out his blanket. "They can accuse us of stealing territory and attack us for it, drive us out of the Reaches."

It sounded so wearily familiar to Moon. "Would they do that?"

"Yes. Emerald Twilight knows our situation. And if they know it, all the courts in the Reaches will know before the next turn. Some of them would be sure to decide that they don't want a vagabond Fell-cursed half-dead court wandering around taking territory that doesn't belong to it."

"So they'd treat us all like solitaries."

"Yes." Stone straightened the blanket, and moved around to lie down on it, grimacing as he settled himself on the hard tile. "The colony tree isn't just a place to live, it's our heritage, our bloodline, our right to take our place among the other courts." He patted the blanket. "Go to sleep."

Moon lay down next to Stone, twinges of pain in his back and shoulders making the process more difficult than usual. Even when he was settled comfortably, his thoughts chased in circles and it seemed a long time before he could sleep.

He woke just before dawn. He was lying on his stomach, and Stone was using his back and shoulder as a pillow. Stone was heavy but also very warm, a contrast to the damp cool of the morning. Moon just lay there for a moment; sleep had helped cure the exhaustion but not the impatience or the despair.

Reluctantly, Moon nudged Stone over and climbed to his feet to stretch. In the daylight he could see the walls were covered with splotches of peeling paint worn away by the weather, old murals too faded to make out. He went to the big window and leaned against the side, yawning, looking out into clouds of white mist, much heavier now than it had been last night.

They would have to go through the city today, which meant talking to strange groundlings. He remembered he was still wearing his consort's gifts, the belt and knife, and the gold wristband. They weren't obvious, and the wristband was normally hidden by his shirtsleeve, but it didn't pay to take the chance. Groundlings who had been to the colony tree to steal might recognize the Arbora's designs. He took both off and tucked them into a handy chink in the wall.

He went out onto the terrace and stepped up onto the low balustrade. His toes hanging out over the precipitous drop, he looked out over the city again. The mist hung like a heavy blanket over the smaller houses around the tower, obscuring any view of the alleys, the walkways. Sound was muffled, but there wasn't much to hear: some distant clanking and banging from the direction of the port, the call of a food peddler. Any signs of movement or life were buried under the fog.

Moon decided to take a chance. He shifted and jumped off the balustrade, hard flaps taking him up until he could catch the wind.

He flew out past the edge of the mist, which clung to the edges of the giant island-monster but faded away over the open sea. He took a long circuit around the shoreline, just to see if anything had changed. No ships had put out yet, but he did see three shapes swimming toward the harbor: water travelers, plodding steadily over the waves. He didn't want to go any closer, but he was pretty certain Nobent wasn't one of them. If Nobent was foolish enough to head back here, it was going to take him a lot longer than a day to make the journey.

Moon turned away and headed for the opposite coast from the harbor. Once there, he went towards the long reef formed by the tail and dipped down to fly low over the water. He eyed the waves cautiously; he hadn't forgotten the large size of the predators, though he hoped the close proximity of the monster would keep them away. Perhaps it would attract some variety of suckerfish, the larger the better.

He found several, big gray ones about four paces long. They swam close to the surface near the tail, clustering in an area where, judging by the flotsam caught in the waves, the islanders must dump their garbage. He caught one, snatching it out of the water, and flew back to the tower with it.

When he dumped it onto the terrace, Stone sat up with a grunt of surprise. Moon told him, "That's yours," and flew back to get one for himself. The sky was lightening as the sun rose and, fog or not, flying over the city would soon be too chancy.

By the time he got back with the second fish, Stone was gone. So was the first fish. Stone must have shifted to eat it because there was literally nothing left but a wet spot on the floor and a few stray scales. Moon ate his fish, leaving the bones, the scales, and sharp tail fins behind. He didn't have Stone's digestion.

He went down to the fifth floor and used water from the cistern to wash the guts off his claws, then stopped to listen. He could hear distant voices, including Stone's. *He would,* Moon thought, half wry and half bitter. Moon had always approached new groundlings cautiously, spending a few days observing them if possible before venturing to draw near. Stone apparently just sauntered into their camps and sat down. Shaking his head, Moon climbed out the window.

At the base of the tower, he shifted to groundling and followed the voices through the maze of alleys. Stone was in a little court, sitting on the paving with three groundlings. One had brought a metal brazier and from the smell, it was burning a fuel made from fish oil, unless that odor was

coming from the clay pot set atop it. Two of the groundlings were the short fishy-gray variety, the third was larger
with orange-tinted gold coloring, though his hair and beard
had streaks of gray. All three wore gray and brown clothing,
ragged and worn.

As Moon stepped into the court, the groundlings looked
up, startled. Stone obviously hadn't told them he had
brought a friend.

Ignoring the stares, Moon went to sit next to Stone. Stone
nodded to the gold man, then to the gray groundlings, who
were both female. "That's Enad, and Theri, and Rith. This
is Moon."

Enad lifted his brows at Stone, saying, "Where did you say
you were from?" He spoke Kedaic also, with a thick accent.

Stone, scraping tea into the steaming clay pot, didn't look
up at him. "I didn't."

"We came on that trader ship," Moon said. Every ship of
any size in the harbor had been a trader ship, and he didn't
intend to be more specific. His travels had given him a lot
of experience with how to appear to be willing to answer
questions without actually answering them.

Enad nodded, his gaze flicking curiously from Moon to
Stone and back. "The one from Bekenadu?" He didn't wait
for an answer, turning to the two women. "Times are hard
for traders, too."

Rith, the second gray groundling, regarded Moon skeptically. She looked older, and the blue-tinged gray of her
skin was marked with creases, the scales at the base of her
forehead crest turning white. "You're traders?"

"No. When they stopped here, the traders upped the passage price." Moon shrugged, leaving them to fill in the rest.
Obviously traders would sleep on their ships, or pay for
shelter near the harbor, and wouldn't need to live in abandoned houses.

The skepticism faded and Rith nodded understanding.
"There's not much work here, except at the harbor."

"Or the towers," the younger one, Theri, said. Her mouth
twisted. "But they're particular about their servants."

Stone caught her eye, and said, deadpan, "We're not pretty enough?" His lips twitched in a smile.

She smiled back, laughing. "Too big, too . . ." She made a vague gesture.

"They like their servants to look helpless," Rith added, rueful and bitter. "You look . . . not helpless."

Enad nodded confirmation. He thumped himself in the chest. "Me, too."

"All of them?" Moon asked. He hadn't seriously considered taking work as a servant to get into Ardan's tower, but it was a thought.

"All I've ever heard of," Rith said. "Better to get work in the harbor."

Enad began to elaborate on this, listing the various cargo factors he had worked for and how much coin they paid and what bastards they were. Moon considered how to turn the conversation back to the towers, then decided there was one question newcomers couldn't fail to ask. When Enad stopped talking, Moon put in, "Who builds a city on a monster?"

All three sighed, and the two women exchanged weary looks. "Everyone asks that," Theri explained.

Rith took up the story, cutting off Enad's attempt to tell it. "Long ago, before we were all born, the leviathan slept in a cove, not far off the shore of Emriat-terrene. Great magisters held it with their magic and built this city on its back—no one knows why," she put in to forestall the obvious question. "To show their power, maybe. They carried all the building stone and metal over on barges from the mines in Emriat-terrene. They say the mountains were stripped to the bone before they were done. But the turns went by and the rulers of Emriat-terrene were overthrown, rose again, were overthrown, and the magisters lost their skill, or much of it. The leviathan woke and swam away, taking the city with it."

Moon exchanged a look with Stone, who lifted a brow and shrugged. He was right; it wasn't the oddest thing either of them had heard.

Rith continued, "The magisters found ways to keep the city together. They gave the traders spelled direction-finders, so they could still find the city when the leviathan moves. They made a warning bell that tolls when the leviathan grows restless so the fishers know to come back to port and to lift their boats from the water, and the traders know to cast off."

Moon read the resignation in her expression. "It doesn't sound like a good life." It sounded as if the magisters controlled everything, and unlike most other cities, you couldn't simply walk away.

Enad looked bleak. "It's all right."

Rith said, "Many of those who have the coin to buy passage leave." She grimaced, dispirited. "The traders know how much they can charge now, and few can afford it."

Theri leaned her head on Rith's shoulder. "It would be easier if the leviathan went back to sleep for good, or went closer to the western shore."

"The western shore?" Moon asked.

"That's where most of the traders come from." Enad admitted, "If all of them could find us, and not just the ones the magisters give the trade-right to, it would be easier to leave. Or stay, if more people came back to live here."

Stone dipped a cup out of the pot and handed it to Rith. "What about the eastern shore, where the forests are?"

Theri laughed. "Everyone knows monsters live there."

☾

After the tea was finished, the groundlings went on their way, and Moon and Stone walked toward Ardan's tower. Moon hoped it was open during the day, and that they could at least get a look at who went in and out of it.

If the doors never opened at all, he wasn't sure what they were going to do.

The walkway they were on, a narrow passage winding between the tall gray walls, was empty at the moment. They had passed a few groundlings earlier, all hauling two-wheeled carts, heading toward the harbor, and Moon had heard a few others on the bridges and balconies they had passed under.

"You didn't ask them about Ardan," Stone said.

He didn't sound as if he was arguing the point, just curious. He had been letting Moon take the lead in finding things out, something which Moon had noticed and appreciated. Of course, if they failed, it would be mostly Moon's fault. "I didn't want them to get suspicious. If we just got here, we shouldn't know who Ardan is yet." Also, Enad was a talker, and Moon could too readily imagine him repeating the conversation to anyone who would listen. If Ardan was aware that something had tested his barriers last night, he might well be listening, and willing to pay for information. "I might ask them about the metal ship, later. It's different enough from the others in port that people must notice it."

Stone snorted in amusement, and Moon said, defensively, "What?"

"You talking to groundlings. That's a change."

Moon set his jaw, annoyed. "We are not flying up to them in the middle of nowhere. These people have no reason not to think we're groundlings. There's a difference."

They reached the plaza at the base of Ardan's tower. It wasn't much more occupied than it had been last night. A few people were crossing the paving, but all seemed to be heading for the walkways or stairs, just passing through. The tower itself was still tightly shut.

The second story wine bar on the east side of the plaza was still open, or at least the door stood open and the music still played. Groundling places that sold liquors or drugs usually only opened in the evening, but maybe living on a restless leviathan required constant access to intoxicants. Moon started toward it. "Maybe we can talk to somebody in there."

"If they're all like Dari, that might not be so helpful," Stone said, but followed him anyway.

The stairway climbed over another house's roof, and the gray tile steps had a few recent stains that stunk of vomit and some kind of sweet liquor. Words were painted on the wall in several different languages, one of them Kedaic, advertising wine and smoke.

Moon stepped into the doorway. The place was bigger than it looked on the outside, winding back away in a series of oddly shaped rooms. Cushioned benches were built into the walls, groundlings sprawled on them, most asleep or barely stirring. The whole interior was filled with drifts of variously colored fog. The cloyingly sweet odor made Moon sneeze. Groundling drugs and alcohol had never worked on him, and he didn't expect this would, either. He moved further in and Stone trailed after him.

As the main room curved away from the doorway, it widened out to a space where there was a small platform. Around it sat three fishy-gray groundlings, two playing stringed instruments and one a set of wooden pipes. On the platform, a golden-skinned groundling woman, dressed only in wispy scarves, moved to the music, though she looked half asleep. Dancing was another groundling thing that left Moon cold. The quick movements were often distracting and made him twitchy with the urge to hunt, and the slow movements were just boring. It was more fun to watch grasseaters graze.

Nearby stood an elaborate metal stand with a glass globe of blue water. The stands were scattered all over the room, fastened to bases built into the floor, and seemed to be the sources of the mist. Moon stepped closer and saw a little creature inside, a tiny amphibian with big eyes and feathery fins, gazing brightly back at him. *That's new,* he thought, and looked around again at the semi-conscious groundlings. Whatever the fog was, all the patrons looked too far gone to be of any use. *Dari was coherent compared to these people.* That was a scary thought.

A woman stepped out of the fog and moved toward him, watching him inquiringly. "You want to buy some smoke?" she asked. She was tall and slender, her skin a smooth matte black, and she had a shock of short white hair. White brows outlined her dark eyes, and she had gold paint dotted on her forehead, nose, and chin. She was wrapped in a silky blue robe that covered her completely, but she was much more attractive to look at than the sleepy dancer. It took Moon a moment to remember to answer her question. "Uh, no, not smoke." She seemed more amused than anything else, so Moon added, "We were looking for a place that sold food." Not true, but it was a good excuse for wandering in here.

"Not here." She nodded toward the door. "You'll need to go back toward the harbor. There's a market on the main walkway."

"Sorry." Moon turned to go.

She walked with him. "It's all right. I don't often get to speak to people who aren't sodden with drink or smoke." Stone, who had been wandering the shadowy areas, came back to Moon's side. She looked him up and down and lifted a brow. "That's your father?"

"Grandfather," Stone corrected, and looked her up and down in return. It was as close to true as it was safe to get; most groundlings didn't live to be Stone's age.

Her mouth quirked in a smile. "Interesting family."

She seemed to be finding them odd but not dangerous, which was the best they could probably hope for. It also meant they could ask questions without looking any stranger than they already did. As she led them out, Moon asked, "We're looking for work. Does that tower hire laborers?"

"You don't want to work there. It's a strange place. It belongs to a magister. You stay away from them." She stopped just outside, but leaned in the doorway and didn't seem in a hurry for them to go. "They like their own way. Anybody like that is dangerous."

She was right enough about that. "What does he do in his tower that's so strange?"

"He collects things." Her brow furrowed, and she tried to explain, "Trinkets and art. Things from far places. Some of it makes your flesh crawl. You can see for yourself. The tower will open at midday."

"Open?" Stone asked.

"For anyone to go into the lower floors, to show off his collection and offer him new things. He does it every day.

Likes to frighten people, probably." She pushed away from the door, turning to go back inside. "You go see for yourself—just don't ask for work there."

"We will," Moon said to her retreating back. "Thank you."

☾

It was still early, so they went to the market the woman had spoken of. Moon couldn't count on being able to fly out to fish for remoras every day, and they needed to stay as well fed as possible. Moon traded one of their small sunstones for a couple of pots of cooked fish and clams, and a small pile of the marked metal bits that served as the local coinage. They sat down on the steps at the edge of a little plaza to split the food, watching the people in the market pass by.

It was busy, with stalls set up under the eaves of the buildings on each side of the walkway. Besides food, the stalls sold metalwork, pottery, a local cloth made of dyed fishskin as soft as the finest leather, and trade goods like silks and scented oils. Moon had looked at the roots and fruit, but they were all small, old, and far more expensive than the fish. But then they all had to come in on the traders' ships.

The groundlings browsing the stalls were all better dressed than Rith, Enad, and Theri, but not in a much better frame of mind. Talk was muted, and people picked over the goods in a desultory way.

"Not very lively," Stone commented. He hadn't balked at the idea of eating cooked fish, but then Stone was odd for a Raksura. Though Moon did have to remind him not to gnaw on the clam shells in public.

"They can't afford the roots." Moon scraped up the last of the sauce. The stall holder had promised them four more bits for bringing the pots back. "Like Rith said, most of them probably want to leave." They were speaking Raksuran, and Moon kept an eye out for anyone showing undue interest, but everyone seemed wrapped up in his or her own concerns.

"There's something funny about all this." Moon lifted a brow, and Stone added, "Besides the fact that they built their city on a leviathan, even if it was sleeping at the time."

"What do you mean?"

"I don't know." Stone spit out a piece of clamshell. "Maybe I'll know when I see Ardan."

"Planning on having a long conversation with him?" Moon asked. They couldn't afford revenge; the only thing Moon was planning on was getting the seed and getting out.

"A pointed conversation," Stone said, and smiled.

CHAPTER TEN

When the sun was directly overhead, something Moon could sense rather than see through the heavy mist and clouds, they went back to the plaza.

A small crowd had gathered near the tower. Some were wealthy local groundlings, all dressed in rich fabrics and smelling strongly of flower perfumes. Many had small ivory fans, though the day wasn't warm. The fans, and the perfumes, might be a defense against the humid fog, which compounded the leviathan's stench and absorbed every odor of the city. The others waiting to enter the tower wore subdued, work-roughened cloth and leather, and must be traders up from the harbor.

Moon and Stone joined the back of the crowd. A few of the traders glanced at them, their expressions ranging from thoughtful curiosity to annoyance, as if they feared competition. The locals ignored them, which was just as well.

Before they had left the market, Moon had taken another precaution. From a used clothing dealer he had bought battered pairs of boots for himself and Stone. They were just soft squares of fishskin that wrapped and tied around your foot and ankle. Stone had put them on without vocal protest, affecting an expression of long-suffering.

Raksura normally didn't wear shoes. Even in groundling form, the soles of their feet were as hard as horn, and Moon had always found shoes impossible to shift with. Most groundlings didn't notice, considering it just a physical quirk of another race. But if Ardan and his thieves had ever managed to see any live Raksura, they might be looking for such telltale signs.

As the doors opened, Moon sniffed, then unobtrusively tasted the air. There was a hint of decay, of death, under the rush of stale scents. It disappeared into the miasma of leviathan, perfume, smoke, fog, and anxious groundling before he could be sure it was more than his imagination. Moon flicked a look at Stone, but his eyes were on the doorway. There was no hint of the magical barrier. Either it had been taken away so the doors could be opened, or it was only in place during the night.

They followed the traders through an arched entrance hall, the white walls carved to look like long drapes of fabric. Guards wearing coats of reptile hide and armed with short metal-tipped spears stood at frequent intervals. They wore weapons at their belts that looked like small crossbows, just from the brief glimpses Moon was able to get. *Good,* he thought sourly. *First we have a groundling shaman, and now we have projectile weapons.*

He had been expecting the inside of this place to be something like their abandoned tower, if on a larger and less decayed scale. But the size of it caught him by surprise.

The entryway opened out into a large circular hall, with a wide stairway curving up to the level above. The walls were set with alabaster panels framed by heavy carved drapery. Vapor-lights hung from sconces made to look like water serpents.

The knot of groundlings in front spread out a little, staring upward in astonishment. Moon looked up and froze, a quiver traveling down his spine.

Suspended high overhead was a giant blue-scaled waterling, its body a good sixty paces long. It was half-fish, half-groundling, with groundling-like arms and a scaled torso ending in a long tail, its fins as large as the sails of a small fishing boat. Its huge clawed hands dangled and its head pointed right down toward them, glassy eyes staring angrily, open jaw big enough to walk upright through, teeth stained yellow and black. It was dead—it had to be dead—stuffed and preserved and slowly decaying.

Stone bumped his arm, impatience mingled with reassurance, and Moon made himself move forward into the hall. That, or something very like it, was what had nearly grabbed Moon when he was flying low over the sea. The traders just ahead of them murmured in uneasy awe and discomfort. Moon was glad he wasn't the only one.

The local groundlings, apparently used to the sight, had already started up the stairs. Stone followed and Moon trailed after him. He had a bad feeling the giant waterling was only the beginning. At least he knew now what the woman in the wine bar had meant when she said the display in the tower was disturbing.

Preserved carvings hung along the inside stairwell, large sections chipped out of the walls of some other building. The faded paint showed groundlings with elaborate jeweled headdresses riding in procession on giant grasseaters, taller than the trees along the side of the avenue. In any other circumstances, Moon would have stopped for a closer look, but this place was making his skin twitch. Most of the groundlings passed the carvings with only brief glances as well, their attention on the gallery above the stairs.

The next level held far more exhibits. Carvings of stone and wood, all obviously cut or chipped out of their original locations, some painted or set with jewels. Some statues were rough and crude, others were beautifully carved, of strange types of groundlings, of other creatures Moon had never seen before. There were metalwork panels, shields, weapons, a whole row of full sets of armor, inlaid with gold, silver, and gems, the helmets formed into snarling animal masks. But next to all the wonderful things there were cubbies in the walls, and in each one was a dead creature, stuffed and posed in a horribly lifelike position. Standing on a low plinth in the center of the hall was the skeleton of something like a branch spider, standing more than fifteen paces high. The bones had been rearticulated somehow, maybe with wire, and the effect was eerily lifelike.

Moon and Stone moved out into the room, as the ground-lings wandered and pointed and exclaimed. It looked like this was as far up into the tower as they were allowed to go. A shorter open stairway led to a set of doors, but they were tightly shut and watched by two guards.

Stone stopped suddenly. He was staring at a stand with a large jar set atop it.

Moon's breath caught. *We're in the right place.* The jar was carved of rich dark wood, and it had obviously been made by Arbora. The sinuous shapes of winged Raksura wrapped it, their claws hooked over the rim. The wide opening was sealed with a single piece of polished onyx. Stone turned away from it, and said, low-voiced, "It's a queen's funerary urn."

Moon looked down, biting his lip, trying to conceal his start of shock. "From Indigo Cloud?" he muttered, speaking Raksuran.

Stone shook his head. "Ours were put into hollows in the wood of the tree, and the mentors made it grow around them. No one could get to them." He looked at it again, eyes narrow. "This came from another colony."

Moon swallowed, relieved. At least it wasn't one of Jade or Stone's ancestors. "Ardan's been to the forests. The seed has to be here somewhere."

Stone strolled away toward one side of the room. Moon took the other.

Delin, Niran's scholarly grandfather, had a collection from his travels too, but it had been limited to pretty sam-ples of pottery and other trinkets, and his books of notes and drawings. Ardan had sea creatures with maws of teeth and staring eyes, a flightless giant bird like the vargits that stalked the jungles far to the east, and something that was just a bundle of tentacles with mouths on the ends. There was a Tath, standing upright and pinned to a wooden post, the boney mask that protected its face making it look sight-less. Its jaw hung open and its long clawed hands dangled uselessly, and Moon still had the urge to rip it apart. He was half-afraid to look into an alcove and discover that Ardan had collected a Fell. Though he supposed the Fell would have long since found a way to reach the island if Ardan had been fool enough to stuff a ruler or a major kethel.

Then he walked past an alcove with an occupant that stopped him in his tracks.

A waterling lay stretched out on a plinth, but it was nothing like Nobent or the monstrous creature downstairs. This was a sea realm dweller. Her skin was pale green, with a pattern of opalescent scales. The heavy ribbons of her hair were dark green, like sea wrack, and there were sharp fins along her calves and thighs. Her fingers and toes were webbed, and tipped with deceptively delicate claws.

Moon stepped closer, unwillingly fascinated. She still wore her jewelry: a belt of pearls, white metal armbands shaped like water snakes. He couldn't see the death wound; possibly it was in her back. Whatever preserved her maintained the appearance of life, betrayed only by the faint scent of corruption and the sunken, bruised skin around her closed eyes. Moon had never seen a sea dweller this close before. He would have much preferred to see this one alive and swimming.

He turned away to see Stone regarding it with a grimace of disgust. "I'm surprised he doesn't have any stuffed groundlings," Moon said. There was no way Ardan could even pretend to classify a sealing with the Tath, the branch spider, and the other predators.

Stone gave the dead woman one last dark glance. "He doesn't have them down here, where the others can see."

He had a point. "Have you found anything?"

"It's not here." Stone's jaw set, as if it took all he had to suppress a growl.

"It's not on display," Moon corrected. The next step seemed obvious. Tricky and potentially dangerous, but obvious. "I'll say I want to see Ardan, tell him I know where he can find more Raksuran treasures."

Stone shook his head. "Moon—"

Moon explained impatiently, "If he believes me, maybe I can look around inside the—"

"Moon, if he finds out what you are, he'll collect *you*."

"I know that." With effort, Moon kept his voice low. "He won't find out. I'm good at not being caught."

Stone was more skeptical. "I saw how good you were at it when your groundling friends staked you out to be bird bait."

It was unfair to bring that up. "That was different." It was different in a hundred ways. Ilane had wanted to get rid of Moon somehow; if he hadn't turned out to be a shapeshifter she could accuse of being a Fell, she would have thought of something else. Presumably Ardan wouldn't have that kind of personal malice towards him. Not on such short acquaintance, anyway. "And he's not going to have Fell poison."

"You don't know that."

"Fine, so what do you want to do?"

Stone didn't have to think about it. "I'll tell him I know where to find the treasures."

"You can't. The rooms upstairs could be too small for you to shift in. You'd be stuck." Obviously Stone didn't object to the plan, just the fact that Moon was the one implementing it. He stifled the impulse to feel hurt; Stone couldn't think he would betray the court to some random groundling sorcerer. Still . . ." What, you don't trust me?" All right, maybe he hadn't quite stifled the impulse.

Stone gave him a withering look. "Jade made me swear to take care of you and not let you do anything crazy."

Moon stared at him, torn between extreme pique and gratification at the show of concern. And there was always the chance that Stone was just making it up, to justify him taking the risk instead of Moon. "I don't do crazy things. I don't need to be taken care of. And since when do you listen to Jade? Or anybody?"

"I'm a consort, I listen to queens. Something you might consider at some point."

How Stone managed to say that with a straight face, Moon had no idea, and he wasn't going to dignify it with an argument. Instead, he pointed out, "None of the others can do this." In either of her forms, Jade would be recognized as a Raksura by any of the thieves who had been to the colony tree and seen the carvings. None of the warriors had ever had to hide what they were. The only groundling they had spent any time with was Niran, and he didn't count. "It has to be you or me, and it can't be you."

Stone folded his arms and stared at the wall. He said, "You don't know I'd get stuck," but Moon knew resignation when he heard it, even from Stone.

☾

First, they made a quick trip back to their tower so Moon could retrieve his consort's gifts from their hiding place. If he was going to convince Ardan he knew where Raksuran treasure lay, it would be handy to have proof. He convinced Stone not to return to Ardan's tower with him; if something went wrong, then at least only one of them would be caught, and Stone would be free to find a way to rescue Moon—before Moon's dead body turned up in Ardan's collection.

Stone agreed reluctantly, and didn't tell Moon to be careful. They both knew that being careful wouldn't get them the seed.

By the time he returned to Ardan's tower, most of the locals had gone, but the traders seemed to be waiting for something. Moon hoped it was for Ardan to make an appearance.

Finally, the doors at the top of the stairs opened and a group of groundlings came out. Some were guards, some obviously servants, and one, a short blue-pearl man dressed in rich gold and green robes, was obviously the leader. *That has to be Ardan.* Moon followed the other traders over, trying not to show the tension that was making his teeth ache. This was the one thing he was most worried about; if Ardan was very powerful, he might be able to tell Moon was a shifter just by looking at him.

As an ivory-inlaid folding table and a chair were whisked into place for the leader, one of the servant groundlings announced, "This is the Superior Bialin. He speaks for Magister Ardan."

Of course he is, Moon thought sourly, disappointed. Ardan couldn't come down here, where the big doors downstairs were still open and Moon could leap the gallery and have a straight path outside if anything went wrong.

There were several traders here to offer objects and information, and Moon let them go first so he could watch what happened. It was a simple procedure: the traders each presented their objects to Bialin, who examined them, and then told the trader it was garbage and to go away. Moon wasn't close enough to get a good look at the objects, but from what he overheard, most were either jewelry pieces or small carvings from distant groundling cities—the kind of things that would have pleased Delin, but that were far too prosaic for Ardan's taste.

Two traders had a small chest, which they opened to reveal the preserved body of a little creature. Moon stood on tiptoes to catch a glimpse and thought it looked like a treeling sewn onto a lizard.

Bialin gazed at them tiredly. "This is a treeling sewn onto a lizard. Get out."

Finally it was Moon's turn. He stepped up to the table and Bialin said skeptically, "And what have you got to offer?"

Watching the others fail had made Moon more confident. "I can tell the Magister where he can find more Raksuran treasure."

"Raksuran? What is—" Bialin's gaze sharpened and suddenly Moon had all his attention. He leaned back in his chair, trying to look uninterested. "What is that?"

Bialin had already lost the chance to play coy. His first reaction had been telling. Moon said, "They live in the forest Reaches on the eastern coast. He already has that wooden pot with the onyx lid. It's a Raksuran queen's funerary urn."

Bialin leaned forward, giving up his skeptical pose. "How do you know this?"

"I've been to the forest."

"Can you prove it?"

Moon unbuckled his belt, and laid it and the sheathed knife on the table.

Bialin leaned over it, frowning. Then he snapped his fingers at his subordinate. The man handed him a heavy glass lens, and Bialin held it to his eye to study the leather more closely. He traced the pattern of lines, then drew the knife partway and fingered the carving on the hilt. Moon pulled his sleeve up and held his arm out, holding the red-gold consort's wristband almost under Bialin's nose. Bialin just blinked and switched his scrutiny to it.

Finally he sat up, lowering the lens. "Yes." He nodded to himself and smiled faintly. "I think the Magister will be very interested."

☾

Moon followed Bialin and his attendants and guards up the short flight of stairs and through the double doors, into the private recesses of the tower. When the heavy doors closed behind him and the guards turned the lock, Moon took a deep breath. He was committed now.

They didn't go far, down a high-ceilinged corridor and then into a large room. The decoration was all heavy, the alabaster carving full of staring faces, reflecting cold light from the vapor-lamps. The ceiling was just as heavily carved as the walls, with inset squares and circles, the edges made to look like bunched fabric. Moon scanned just enough to note there was nothing lurking in the corners, and focused on the man seated at the table in the center.

Like Bialin, Ardan was one of the blue-skinned groundlings, but he was younger than Moon had expected. His features were even and handsome, and there were faint lines of concentration at the corners of his eyes. He wore a silky gray robe shot with silver, simple compared to how some of the other wealthy locals dressed. He was reading a roll of white paper spread out on the ivory-inset surface of the table, and didn't glance up at them.

Bialin stepped around the table, leaned over and whispered to him. Finally Ardan looked up. His gaze was sharp but faintly skeptical, as if Bialin had erred in the past and his expectations were not high. In a voice so dry it was dusty, he said, "Let me see these objects."

Bialin gestured impatiently. He looked nervous, and it was probably his head on the block if Ardan wasn't pleased. Moon could sympathize; his nerves were jumping, but Ardan didn't seem to know he was in the room with a shifter. He put the knife and belt down on the table, hesitated for a moment, then slipped off the wristband and set it next to them.

Ardan leaned forward, took the glass lens Bialin held ready for him, and began to examine the objects. The rough skin just below the edge of his pearly skull started to furrow with interest.

The vapor-lights hanging overhead misted in the cool damp air, and Moon waited, tracking the bead of sweat working its way down his back. With the sea kingdom woman lying stuffed in his grand hall like an animal, Moon had half-expected Ardan to look like a monster. He didn't. He just looked like a clever man.

He's not a monster because he doesn't see that woman as a person, Moon thought. If he had known Moon was a Raksura, he wouldn't see him as a person, either, just another potential collector's item. Moon was suddenly glad he had bothered with the boots.

Ardan examined the knife, belt, and wristband for a long silent moment. Then he looked up and studied Moon, his hooded eyes thoughtful. "What are you called?"

"Niran." Giving a fake name might be overcautious. In both Kedaic and Altanic, Moon's name was just a random sound, meaningless. But Moon looked into Ardan's eyes again and decided he couldn't be too careful.

He gestured to the collection on the table. "You're selling these things?"

"No, I'm selling the information." He would hand over the knife and the wristband if he had to, but he didn't think a real trader would be eager to part with them either. "You're not interested in trinkets."

Ardan conceded that with a faint smile. "No, I'm not." He was now clearly intrigued. "How did you know that container was a . . . queen's funerary urn?"

Moon had absolutely no idea how Stone had identified it as a queen's urn, but then it didn't matter if Ardan thought he was lying for effect. "It was like the others we found. The scholar I was with said that's what they were. His name was Delin-Evran-lindel, from the Golden Isles in the Yellow Sea."

"You found other urns?"

"In an abandoned Raksuran—" Moon reminded himself not to be too exact with the terminology. "Hive."

Ardan nodded. "And where was this abandoned hive?"

"Near the edge of the Reaches." And Moon began to describe a journey on a flying boat to the old Indigo Cloud colony, the one that had been built into the groundling ruin straddling the river valley, but with the location transposed to the lakes they had passed before entering the forest.

As Ardan's expression grew even more intent, Moon populated this version of the colony with scattered bones and other grisly remains, to explain why these Raksura had left all their belongings behind. Finally Ardan lifted a hand. "Stop. I wish someone else to hear this." He called one of the guards over and spoke to him briefly. Moon caught the words, "Bring Negal."

Bringing someone else in to listen was possibly a trick to catch Moon in a lie, to see if he changed his story with repetition, or if the details sounded memorized. He wasn't worried; the details were all true, just arranged in different ways from how they had actually happened.

As they waited, Ardan set the knife aside, saying, "You'll get this back when you leave here." He handed the belt and wristband to Bialin, who handed them to his subordinate, who handed them back to Moon. Moon buckled on the belt, then slipped the band back onto his wrist, pulling his sleeve down over it. He hoped this was a good sign.

After a short time, another groundling was led into the room. He was from a different race than those common to the leviathan, with light brown skin, curly gray hair, and a trim gray beard. He wore dark pants and a shirt of a knit material in a coarse weave, a short jacket, and heavy low boots. Clothes meant for colder weather, and bearing a close resemblance to the kind of clothing left behind on the metal ship.

We were right, Moon thought. His skin prickled, something that happened when prey was in sight. He folded his arms, hoping he looked bored and impatient.

The man's eyes were dark and wary. From the tension in his body he didn't appear eager to be here. Ardan said briskly, "Negal, sit down. This man is called Niran. He's an explorer who has been to the fringe of the eastern forest."

Negal's expression relaxed slightly. Whatever he had been afraid to hear, that wasn't it. He took a seat on a stool, saying with some irony, "Ah, how interesting." He spoke Kedaic too, but with a different accent than the others.

At a nod from Ardan, Moon described the old colony again, throwing in a few additional details.

Negal sat forward, listening with growing interest. When Moon paused for breath, he said, "Were there carvings of both types of Raksura, those with wings and those without? Was there anything to indicate what the relationship between them was?"

"I saw some carvings of wingless Raksura." Moon didn't think a trader would be much interested in what Raksuran daily life was like. "I didn't pay attention. I was more interested in the jewels and metal."

Negal leaned back, clearly displeased by that answer. Ardan eyed Negal with an air of satisfaction. He seemed about to end the interview, and Moon took his chance. Trying to keep his tone even, he said, "There were these things, like big seeds." He held up his hands, shaping something the right size. "Three of them. They were wood, or shell, with a rough surface. The scholar I was with said they could be valuable, but not to him."

Negal glanced at Ardan, as if expecting a reaction. Ardan only looked thoughtful, and said, "Did you take them?"

"No." Moon hoped that Ardan had no extra-keen senses and couldn't hear his pulse pounding. "The others wanted to leave them there. I couldn't see a use for them, so I didn't argue."

Ardan nodded, still thoughtful. "Thank you for bringing me this information. You'll be paid well, but we'll have to speak of all this further. You will stay the night here."

Moon didn't want to appear relieved. He said, "I have friends waiting for me outside."

"Surely they knew it would take you some time to convince me to pay for your tale." Ardan smiled, and it even reached his eyes. "Let them wait."

☾

Bialin and two guards took Moon up a large winding stair. The walls were covered with carved figures, mostly male groundlings dressed in elaborate robes, staring down with grim expressions.

They passed landings with big double doors, all tightly closed. Finally they stopped and Bialin took out a ring of large keys, unlocked the doors, and stepped back for the guard to push them open.

They walked into an anteroom with yet more closed doors, with an arch opening into a hallway.

"You'll sleep here." Bialin gestured briskly and the guard opened a door. "You will not be allowed to leave this level. The Magister will send for you when he wishes to speak to you again."

Moon stepped into the room. The guard shut the door behind him and he listened for a bolt to click. It didn't. So Ardan allowed his guests at least limited freedom of movement. That was a relief.

The room didn't look like a cell, either, except for the general oppressive air of the heavy carving. There was a bed with dark blankets against the far wall, and a woven rug to warm the gray slate floor. In a curtained alcove there was even a metal water basin with a tap, and a wooden cabinet that probably held a chamber pot. There were also clips that held the furniture fixed to the stone floor, like the broken ones in the abandoned tower. A vapor-light in a chased metal holder hung from the high ceiling. There was no window, no bolt on the inside of the door, but there was a narrow opening at the top. It might be meant for ventilation, but anyone standing in the hall would be able to hear what the occupants were doing.

Moon stood still, listening to Bialin and the guards move away, then he tasted the air. It wasn't stale, though not terribly fresh, and clouded with the scent of the local perfumes and of unfamiliar groundlings.

When the anteroom sounded empty, he opened the door and stepped out. The heavy double doors to the stairwell were closed. Moon moved close enough to hear the breathing and faint restless movement of at least two guards stationed on the other side. He turned down the hallway, toward the sound of voices.

The doorways he passed all had the gap at the top, and he didn't hear any movement within, but there were low voices somewhere ahead. Then the hall curved and an archway opened into a larger room.

Like the rest of the tower, it was grim, high-ceilinged, and cold, but it looked a little more like a place people actually lived in. The vapor-lights were suspended over cushioned couches. There was a circular hearth in the center, with a slate-sheathed chimney that stretched up into the high ceiling. Negal, two other men, and a woman sat on a couch and a couple of stools, having an anxious, whispered conversation. They all looked to be from the same race of groundlings as Negal, and all dressed in the same type of clothes, pants, shirts, and jackets, thick soft material or knits.

It took them a moment to notice Moon, standing silently in the doorway. When they did, one man started in alarm and fell off his stool. The others stared at Moon. Moon stared back.

Negal recovered first, saying in Kedaic, "This is Niran, the explorer I was telling you about."

The man still on the couch dug a small object of glass and wire out of his jacket pocket. They were spectacles, lenses meant to go over the eyes; Moon had seen them used in Kish. The man put them on and stared at Moon some more. He had stringy dark hair and a belligerent expression.

Negal cleared his throat. "This is Esom, our deviser, and Orlis, his assistant." Orlis was the one who had fallen off the stool. He was younger, with thinner features, a more diffident expression. "And Karsis Vale, our physician." She had long curly hair tied back under a dark cap. Her features were sharp, and her sober clothes didn't quite fit, making her look gawky and awkward. She also wore spectacles like Esom, which made Moon think there was a resemblance. The Kedaic word for *physician* meant the same thing as the Altanic *healer*, but Moon had no idea what a *deviser* was.

"He won't let you leave, you know," Karsis said, tense and a little angry, either at Ardan or Moon or both.

"He will if he wants to find the ruin," Moon said, moving to the center hearth and sitting down on the stone rim. He didn't have to fake an air of unconcern. Escaping was something he would worry about after he found the seed. He would probably worry really hard about it at that point, but not just at the moment.

"That's what we thought," Esom said with bitter emphasis.

There was another archway in the far wall, open to a corridor, but it looked like it just circled around toward the main foyer. The hearth was more promising. The stone-lined bowl in the center was set up to burn some sort of oil, though it was unlit now. He leaned back and looked up the chimney. *That's a possibility.* "Is that your metal ship, down in the harbor?" If these weren't the thieves, he would let River call himself First Consort.

"Yes," Negal answered, his voice sharp with interest. "It's still there?"

Moon said, "It was yesterday," and they all turned to each other, talking in their own language again, agitated but keeping their voices low. Moon sat back and looked them over. They weren't quite what he had been expecting, and he couldn't decide why. "Did Ardan hire you to go to the eastern coast and loot the Reaches?"

They all stared again, and Esom actually seemed offended. "We didn't *loot* anything," he said tightly, "And we weren't hired by Ardan, we're his prisoners. He's killed five members of our crew."

That was no more and probably much less than they deserved. Moon glanced at Negal, and said carefully, "Ardan seemed interested in those wooden seed things. You found some?"

Negal hesitated, his lips pursed, as if trying to decide whether to answer. But Orlis nodded glumly and said, "We found one. Ardan wanted it—"

Esom hit him in the shoulder. "Why are you talking to him?"

Orlis winced away and gave him an irritated glare. "Why not?" he said, with more life in his voice. "What does it matter to us? We're still stuck here."

Karsis stirred, saying thoughtfully, "Maybe if Ardan knows where to find more of the things, he'll send us after them."

Moon looked down, scuffed at the gray tile with his worn fish-skin boot. *So close.* It wouldn't be in these rooms, where Ardan kept his guests/prisoners. He could ask where it was, but that would just make him look like exactly what he was, a thief who had tricked his way in here to steal from Ardan's collection. He thought he had already shown too much interest in it. He didn't want these people trading him to Ardan for their freedom. Better to keep them talking about themselves. "Why is he holding you prisoner? What did you do to him?"

Orlis started. Karsis stared at Moon, lips thin with annoyance. Esom took a breath for an angry answer, but Negal stopped him with a hand on his shoulder. Negal said wearily, "We did nothing to him. Apparently he finds us . . . interesting company."

So Ardan had collected them, as well. Moon didn't feel terribly sympathetic. They weren't dead and stuffed, and if not for them he would be back at Indigo Cloud Court in a bower with Jade, making clutches. Trying to keep the irony out of his voice, he said, "What makes you so interesting?"

Negal watched him for a moment, as if trying to decide if Moon wanted a serious answer or not. Finally he said, "We come from a land far to the west. It lies atop a tall plateau, isolated by boiling seas, impassable cliffs, rocky expanses with steam vents and chasms. We had legends of other lands, other peoples, but they were only legends. No one believed it was possible to leave our plateau. Or that if we did leave, we would find nothing but an endless lifeless sea." He smiled ruefully. "We thought the boundaries of our little existence formed the entire world."

Esom slumped, anger giving way to resignation. He muttered, "The plateau is not that small. It's four thousand pathres across, easily."

Negal continued, "Our Philosophical Society had long been exploring different methods of leaving the plateau as an intellectual exercise. Until we discovered one that actually seemed to have a chance of success. We built prototypes, experimented, and finally developed the *Klodifore*, the metal ship you saw in the harbor. Our crew of volunteers sailed away on what we thought would be a voyage of great discovery."

Karsis touched his hand. "It has been that." Defensively, she added to Moon, "We traveled for six months with no real trouble, visiting the different civilizations along the coast, learning this language so we could communicate. Then we ran into this island."

Esom said, "Literally. We were plotting a course back across the sea toward home, and the leviathan swam into sight. So we decided to stop and see what kind of people lived on it." He sounded so bitterly ashamed of the decision, it was likely he was the one who had pressed for it.

All right, so their story was more interesting than Moon had thought. "Then why did you go to the Reaches with Ardan?"

Orlis said bleakly, "He tricked us. He courted us, showed us things in his collections, talked about the trip he was planning to study the strange creatures who lived in the forest Reaches." He shrugged. "He said it was a long way, and that as a magister he could only spend so much time away from the leviathan or the city would be in danger. Our ship was the only one that could make the journey in a short time."

"It's not that far to the forest coast," Moon said, and then remembered that the leviathan might have been much further out to sea. And that maybe he shouldn't seem to know exactly how far it was to the forest coast.

But Orlis said, "Not the journey to the coast, the journey inland."

Esom said, with a faint sneer, "You probably won't understand this, but our ship is capable of flight."

"It's a flying boat, a wind-ship?" Moon said, startled. "It has a sustainer?" That . . . explained a lot. Why Ardan had needed these people, why he couldn't simply have gone with his own men. How they made it over the forest floor without being killed, how they had gotten up to the knothole entrance. The Kek hadn't seen the ship, but then most of them had been on the other side of the tree in hiding. *They didn't see our flying boats either.* It didn't explain why they had bothered to open the tree's root entrance, but maybe they hadn't been able to keep the heavier metal ship that high in the air long enough for everyone to disembark.

Esom was blank with astonishment. "Uh . . . it's not called a sustainer, but—"

"Apparently a civilization called the Golden Isles also has flying craft," Negal told Esom kindly. He turned to Moon. "I wanted to ask you—"

Moon heard a door open and three people approach briskly down the hall. The others immediately fell silent and waited tensely. One of Bialin's servants appeared in the doorway with two guards. He was an older blue-pearl man with a harried expression, and under his perfume he smelled of fear-sweat. To Negal's group, he said, "The

Magister wants you for the evening meal in three callings of the hour."

Nobody seemed horrified, so Moon assumed the man didn't mean that the way it sounded. Then the servant looked at Moon and, in a tone that conveyed how doubtful he found this, added, "The summons includes you."

Apparently Ardan's invitations didn't normally include scruffy foreign traders who came to sell information. Moon was certain this one included him because of one thing: Ardan wanted more seeds. *If I can just get him to show me the one he already has.*

CHAPTER ELEVEN

The dinner was odd, though not as fraught for Moon as the one at Emerald Twilight.

It was held in a large room a few levels above the guest quarters. Giant carved images of dour blue-pearl groundlings stared down from the walls, all more than thirty paces high, some forming columns supporting the arched ceiling. Their expressions gave Moon the impression that was he was being watched with disapproval, but he felt like that a lot, so it was probably just him. There was a small pool with a fountain at one end of the room for show, not for drinking or swimming. The large hearth at the other end was big enough to roast a bando-hopper. Like the one down near the guest rooms, it was unlit.

For the dinner, polished stone benches were arranged around a low marble-topped table at the hearth end of the room. They were draped with fine linen and softened with brocaded cushions. The heavy furniture wasn't fastened to the floor, but Moon noticed the table had ridges carved in it to help keep the plates and cups from sliding. Efficient servants placed the food on the table. Unlike the party in the other tower Moon had spied on, Ardan apparently only hired young male blue-pearl groundlings.

Negal and his people were the only other guests, sitting uncomfortably around on the benches. From remarks Moon overheard from the servants, Ardan had a family stashed away somewhere in the tower. He just didn't let them mix with his "guests."

As the food was served, Ardan spoke with Negal, mostly about the cities along the coast that Negal's ship had visited. The other three just sat there and ate mostly in silence, looking and acting like captives, grim and suspicious. Negal spoke easily enough, but his eyes were weary, as if the conversation was just another facet of his captivity. Moon told himself it was foolish to feel sorry for them. *So they say they were tricked into going to the Reaches.* They had still helped loot the colony tree.

The food was far better than what had been on offer at the market. There were several unfamiliar varieties of preserved fruit, different types of fish and shellfish cooked in various sauces, and sweet breads that had to be almost as expensive as the fruit, since the grain would all have to be shipped in. Moon didn't have to force himself to eat. It was all so good he could have finished everything on the table, but he managed to confine himself to only two servings. The wine they had been provided with had no effect on him, but he drank it anyway.

As the meal came to an end, Ardan toyed with his goblet and said, "I've invited other guests, who should be arriving soon." The others were sitting upright on the benches; Moon took a cue from Ardan and lounged back on the cushions with his wine goblet. It was easier to pretend to be relaxed that way. His apparent ease made Esom stare at him in annoyance.

"Showing us off again?" Karsis said to Ardan, affecting boredom in a deliberate way. She jerked her head toward Moon. "Or your new acquisition?"

"My guests are all seekers of knowledge," Ardan answered mildly. "But I'm afraid they're more interested in my collections than in intellectual discourse." Esom snorted in derision, and was ignored. Then Ardan turned to Moon, and asked, "How did you come to be on your expedition to the forest?"

Good question, Moon thought. "The Islanders were hiring hands. I needed the work."

"The Golden Islands are not your home, then?"

The Islanders were all like Niran, smaller people, with golden skin and white hair like silken floss. Niran had said the maps aboard the *Valendera* didn't range this far, but Ardan might know more about the eastern region than he pretended. "No. I was working on a Yellow Sea trading barge that came to port there. The expedition offered better pay."

"But more danger."

Moon shrugged. "They didn't explain that part."

Ardan chuckled indulgently. "Sometimes a little deception furthers the course of scholarly pursuits."

Karsis stared, Esom and Orlis exchanged an incredulous look, and even Negal's stoic expression turned sardonic. Apparently oblivious, Ardan asked Moon, "Where do you come from?"

"The east, near the gulf of Abascene." This was, technically, true, and Abascene had the extra benefit of being even further from here than the Yellow Sea. "The place we were living was destroyed by Fell, turns ago. I left with the other refugees and I've been traveling ever since." This wasn't quite as true but Moon had lived in enough places that had been destroyed by the Fell to supply convincing details, if he needed to.

Ardan frowned in thought, as if honestly interested. That wasn't something Moon had expected. Ardan said, "I've heard of the Fell, but never seen one."

"You're lucky." Moon decided it was time he asked a question in return. "Why did you go to the Reaches?"

Ardan lifted his brows as if amused by Moon's presumption. Moon suspected the conversations with Negal and the others tended to be one-sided. Ardan answered, "I was curious. I had heard intriguing things about the area."

Esom said abruptly, "What are the Fell?"

Moon felt his jaw tighten; a dramatic change of subject was exactly what he didn't need. Ardan gestured for him to answer, and he said, reluctantly, "They're shapeshifters that travel in large flights. They eat people and burn cities because they enjoy it." He had everyone's attention; even Karsis had lost her cynical expression. "Some are as big as the sea monster hanging down in the first floor hall. Others are smaller than you. When they shift, they look like ordinary groundlings. One could walk through the streets of this city and no one would know."

"Like the Raksura," Karsis said.

Moon leaned back against the cushion and took a drink of wine, just in case he didn't have his expression as under control as he thought. If the Raksura had had anything but a distant kinship with the Fell, the leviathan's inhabitants would have long since found out about it.

"Not at all." Ardan turned to her, his expression serious. "The Fell are thieves, predators, parasites. They build nothing, make nothing, grow nothing, have no art, no written language. They loot their victims' habitations for everything they need. You saw the artwork in the Raksuran hive. Creatures who could create such as that have no need to steal."

Karsis sat back, thwarted from starting an argument. Negal said, wryly, "Then it's a pity your men destroyed some of the images, removing the inlay."

"Not many." Ardan eyed him. "And they were punished."

Karsis took a sharp breath, Esom and Negal looked grim. Orlis set the pastry he had been nibbling down on his plate, as if the memory had taken away his appetite.

Moon took it that the punishment had been extreme and effective. He was surprised the hunters hadn't found more bodies. But at least they were back on the right subject. "I take it you weren't interested in the gems and metal." He glanced around, pointedly indicating the room and the wealth it represented.

"No, you're quite correct, I already have more of that than I need." Ardan lifted his goblet and studied the purple-tinted glass pensively. "I am the youngest magister in the city. I took my father's place when he died, several turns ago. The competition between myself and the others, as well as our duty to see to the city's survival, drove me to seek knowledge and avenues to greater power."

Yes. Moon held his breath. If Ardan would elaborate, mention the seed, if Moon could ask to see it . . .

Then Ardan set his goblet aside and glanced up as Bialin approached the table. "Ah, I believe my other guests have arrived."

☾

The other guests turned out to be a large group of wealthy local groundlings and their servants and hangers-on. The big chamber rapidly became well-occupied.

They seemed to be in a contest to outdo each other with the richness of their clothes. There were silks in every color, sheer gauzes, black and gold brocades. There were also some traders, all looking much more prosperous than the ones who had come to sell trinkets today. There was apparently nothing else to do in this city in the evening except go to parties in the big towers or drug yourself unconscious in the wine and smoke bars.

Servants put out more food and drink, but people didn't sit to eat. Instead, they walked around to mingle and talk. Moon was able to fade into the background as the crowd grew, watching and being watched in turn.

There didn't seem to be much to discover. The conversations Ardan had were all brief, all apparently casual. The point of all this seemed to be showing his wealth off to the other groundlings. At the moment Ardan stood with a richly dressed old man, surrounded by a small audience of lower-ranking groundlings. Ardan was at ease, as usual, but the old man simmered with anger.

"Trader Niran."

Moon glanced around even before he remembered that was supposed to be him, which was why he had taken the name of someone he knew. It was Bialin, who motioned urgently for him to follow. "The Magister would like to speak with you."

"Who's that with him?" Moon asked.

Bialin pressed his lips together in dissatisfaction at Moon's lack of instant obedience, but answered, "Lethen, another magister."

Moon followed Bialin over to the group. Unlike Ardan, Lethen was ruinously old. The pearly surface of his skull was dulled and worn, disturbingly like raw bone. Deep lines were etched around his mouth and eyes, and his blue skin had an unhealthy, pale tinge. He was dressed in blue and gold brocade, and leaned on an ornate ivory cane. He had blue gems somehow mounted in the age-yellowed base of his skull cap. Judging by his pinched expression, the process had been painful.

As Moon and Bialin arrived, Ardan said to Lethen, "Trader Niran has brought me word of another site of interest." He nodded to Moon. "Show him the bracelet, if you would."

Moon pulled the cuff of his shirt up and held out his arm. The red gold gleamed on the entwined serpentine forms.

Lethen leaned in to look and his hands tightened on his cane. His nails were like gray horn against his lined blue skin. He said, tightly, "I see."

There was an undercurrent here, a strong one. *Lethen wants Raksuran treasure? Or he knows about the seeds and wants one?* Moon wondered, and watched Lethen regard Ardan with a bitterness bordering on hate. Ardan definitely had some hold over him. Just to stir the pot a little, Moon said, "Do you want me to tell him what I found in the ruin?"

Ardan flicked him a look, part surprise and part amusement. "Not necessary." He gave Moon an ironic nod. "You may go."

Tugging his sleeve down, Moon wandered away, circled the nearest statue-pillar, and stopped just within earshot. He was mildly surprised to find Karsis already there, eavesdropping. She glared at him, not very pleased to be caught.

Sounding as if it was a wonderful joke, Ardan was saying to Lethen, "So, will you mount your own expedition to the coast?"

Lethen snapped, "I want you to allow another trading clan access to our harbor."

"Your wants are immaterial." Ardan was clearly bored with the change of subject. "There's no need."

"There is need. My artisans can't produce anything when they can't get raw materials."

The boredom was turning into annoyance. "I'll consider it."

"There's no need to keep this stranglehold—" Ardan was already walking away, stubbornly pursued by Lethen.

Karsis let out a frustrated breath. "Well, that was pointless." She flicked a grim glance at Moon. "Eavesdropping makes me feel like I'm at least trying to do something."

"Ardan controls the traders?" Enad had said something about trade rights, that things would be better if the magisters gave them to more traders.

"Most of them. He controls their ability to find the island," Karsis corrected, and stepped out to watch Ardan move away. Moon thought she was being far too obvious about it. She must not do much hunting on her people's isolated plateau. "The leviathan moves at random. The traders all have magical tokens that allow them to find it again. They have a monopoly, and can charge whatever they like for their goods and foodstuffs."

"What about the other magisters?" Moon followed her. Ardan headed toward the far end of the room, past the pool and the fountain, where a set of stairs went up to a gallery along the back wall. There was an archway up there, surrounded by elaborate scrollwork carving, an entrance to another grand hall. Guards were posted, but Moon had assumed they were there to keep Ardan's involuntary guests from slipping away.

"Several of them have died off from old age, from what we've heard. Ardan is the most powerful." Karsis sounded bitter about it. "He seems to be instrumental in keeping the beast from sinking, or shaking the city off."

"But he can't put it to sleep again, or send it back to the coast of Emriat-terrene."

Karsis made a faint derisive noise. "Why would he bother? He has everything here just as he likes."

Ardan climbed the stairs to the gallery and vanished through the archway. "What's up there?"

She sighed. "Another exhibit hall full of his acquisitions. Those are apparently more precious to him than the ones downstairs." Her tone turned contemptuous. "I suppose you'll be helping him to add to it with this ruin of yours." She hesitated. "He will kill you, you know."

Moon's attention was on that tempting archway, so carefully guarded. He turned to her abruptly. "Is that where he keeps the seed? The wooden thing you found?" His expression must have been too intense because she fell back a step.

Sounding uncertain for once, she said, "I don't know where he keeps it." She recovered quickly and lifted her chin. "Why do you want to know?"

Yes, why do you want to know? Idiot. He said, "I wanted to see it, make sure it's the same as what we found in the ruin."

"I see." She studied him a moment. "What do you know about these seeds?"

At that point, Esom arrived, saving Moon from an answer that probably would have been suspiciously inadequate. Esom took Karsis' arm firmly and said, "Karsis, Negal needs to speak to you."

"What? Oh—" Esom tugged and Karsis went reluctantly. Moon took the opportunity to vanish into the crowd. He had some planning to do.

☾

Ardan's withdrawal must have been a signal, because it wasn't much later in the evening when the invited guests began to leave, and Bialin and his guards herded Moon and Negal's group back down to their quarters. As the stairwell doors were securely locked behind them, Negal turned to Moon and said, low-voiced, "Guards walk the halls at odd intervals. We are not locked in our rooms, but movement is discouraged."

That was good to know, and unexpectedly generous of Negal. Moon didn't want to feel like he owed these people anything, but he managed to thank Negal without irony.

Orlis and Karsis were already moving away down the hall, both seeming tired and dispirited. But as Negal went to join them, Esom stopped Moon and said, with stiff aggression, "And in case you found yourself curious, Karsis sleeps in my room."

Moon had no idea why he was being given this information. Hoping to discourage further disclosures, he said, deadpan, "That's nice for you."

Esom stiffened even further. Through gritted teeth, he said, "She's my sister."

It occurred to Moon, belatedly, that Esom was trying to warn him off approaching Karsis for sex. *Groundlings,* Moon thought in sour disgust. It must have shown on his face, because Esom's expression turned defensive and confused. Moon just walked away toward his room.

He closed the door and sat down on the bed, wincing at the faint odor of scent-concealing oils that came up from the blankets. After all the smothering perfumes upstairs, his sense of smell was next to useless. He pulled his boots off, lay down, and waited.

Listening to the groundlings' conversations upstairs had netted a little more information. Ardan was more powerful than Moon had thought, and everyone there had been afraid of him, hating him, or courting him, or a combination of all three. Moon would have thought a magister's business was to make magic, but Ardan seemed intimately concerned with the working of the city and its trade concerns.

After a time, he heard the others stop moving around. Various doors shut. He hadn't noticed earlier how dead the tower was to sound; he could be the only one alive in it. He thought of the colony tree, how despite its size you could feel it move and breathe and rustle, sense the faint presence of all the smaller lives inside it. *Stop it,* he told himself, annoyed. He refused to be sick with longing for a place he had barely spent two nights in.

Sometime later, out in the foyer, the heavy door to the stairwell opened, someone walked through, and the door was closed and locked again. Quiet footsteps moved away down the hall. That was the guard who patrolled the public rooms on this level. There had been no click of a key, so another guard in the stairwell had unlocked and locked the door for him. But Moon wasn't planning to use the stairs.

Moon listened to the guard make several slow circuits of the level. Finally the man's steps returned to the stairwell door, there was a quiet knock, and the door opened and closed again. Presumably the guard wouldn't return for a while. Moon shoved off the bed and reached the door. He eased it open silently, stepped into the corridor, and pulled it shut behind him. The corridor lights had been turned down until they gave off only a dim light and a faint trace of mist. Shifting in a blur of motion, he bounded down the corridor. He kept his claws carefully sheathed so they wouldn't click against the tile and betray him.

The first thing he did was rapidly search the rest of this level. He found two other corridors, both with closed doors. By the sound of breathing, only three rooms were occupied. He couldn't tell which two held Negal and Orlis, but a low whispered conversation marked the one with Esom and Karsis. There were two other open sitting areas, and a larger room with a cold bathing pool, but no other doorways to the stairwell, and no windows.

He whipped back through the door into the big common room. The vapor-lights here were still bright, lighting the empty room and making him feel exposed to the entire tower. Ignoring the sensation, he went to the hearth, stepped over the rim, hooked his claws into the mortar between the sooty stones, and wriggled up into the chimney.

Climbing the dark shaft, he peered upward. His eyes adjusted quickly, but there wasn't much to see. The chimney wasn't straight and shunted sideways at intervals to work its way up through the tower. He passed openings for several other connected shafts, too narrow for even a slender Raksura to climb down. At least it was a sign that all the hearths in this side of the tower connected to this central shaft.

When he was high enough to be above the big meeting room, he hit a junction with another large shaft. *Hah,* he thought, quietly satisfied at guessing right, and climbed headfirst down it.

He reached the bottom, where it opened into the hearth near the far end of the large chamber. He hung his head down and peered cautiously out, every nerve alert.

The vapor-lights had been turned so low they were nearly out, and the place seemed even more cavernous, the statue-pillars looming life-like in the shadows. He tasted the air and caught lingering scents of perfume, stale food, and wine. Nothing moved, and it was almost unnervingly silent.

He slid out of the chimney and stepped down off the big empty hearth, lifting his spines a little to dislodge some of the soot. Ghosting across the marble floor, he bypassed the stairs to jump up to the railing of the gallery.

The hall beyond the archway was smaller than the one down on the second level of the tower, with no alcoves. Ardan's acquisitions hung on the walls or stood on plinths. It was all artwork, wall carvings, pieces of sculpture, the gems and metal glinting faintly in the dim light. Moon walked through rapidly, reached the end, then turned back. He forced himself to move slowly, to look at each display more closely. *It has to be here.* It wasn't sitting by itself on a plinth, but it might be stuck in with one of the other objects.

He stopped abruptly as the skin under his spines prickled with unease; he wasn't alone in here anymore. He turned, slowly.

Barely ten paces away a mist hung in the air, and something formed rapidly inside it.

Moon snarled under his breath. He had forgotten Ardan's magic. Groundling guards were probably posted in any area where the inhabitants of the tower might move around during the night. In the chambers that were supposed to be empty, the guards could be more deadly.

The mottled green shape that emerged from the mist stood almost as tall as Moon. He could see the outline of long arms and clawed hands, but no head. *That could be a problem,* he thought, and crouched to spring.

It snapped into solid form, a bulbous muscular body with barely a lump for the head. Its eyes were small, yellow, and mean. Then a huge mouth opened, more than half the width of the body, and displayed an impressive array of yellow fangs. It surged forward and Moon sprang to meet it.

As it reached for him he grabbed its arm, swung up and slashed its face with his feet and free hand, then leapt away. Quicker than thought, it slapped him out of the air.

Moon bounced off the stone floor, then caught a blow to the head that knocked him back into a plinth. The creature charged toward him again, its goal apparently to grab him and stuff him into its huge mouth. Scrambling back, he thought, *I don't have time for this,* and bolted out through the archway to the gallery. Instead of going over the balustrade, he jumped straight up in the air. As the creature barreled out after him, he dropped and landed on its back. It roared, loud enough to deafen him, and reached back to claw at his head. Moon sunk all four sets of his own claws into the creature's rubbery flesh and bit down on the back of its lumpy head.

Still roaring, it staggered forward and tumbled over the rail. It hit the floor first and rolled, but Moon held on with grim determination. Even as it crushed him between its back and the floor, he kept his jaws clamped down. Its tough hide gave way abruptly and he got a mouth full of foul blood. The thing tasted terrible, like rot and mold.

It bucked, thrashed, and finally went limp. Moon shoved it off him and staggered upright. He spat out blood, stumbled to the fountain, and scooped up a double handful of water to scrub the acrid stuff off his face. Then he looked up at the gallery.

Three—no, four more misty shapes formed in the air. The creature's death must have triggered the appearance of reinforcements. *Damn things, how many does Ardan have?* He could stay here and take them all on, until the groundling guards and Ardan showed up. It wouldn't buy him any time to look for the seed. He turned back for the hearth and crossed the floor in long bounds.

A groundling couldn't have killed that creature. If Moon got down to the guest quarters again and shifted, he might be able to bluff this out. They wouldn't know they were looking for a Raksura. He hoped.

He reached the hearth, scrambled up into the chimney, and climbed rapidly back to the central shaft. At the junction he hesitated. He could keep going up until he found the outlet to the outside, if it was large enough to get through, if it wasn't sealed by the barrier that protected the outside of the tower. No, he had to take the chance to stay and keep looking for the seed.

He climbed down quickly and quietly until he heard a scrabbling noise, claws scratching against stone, somewhere above him. Moon continued to climb, and tasted the air as he went, but the stink from the creature's hide still clung to his scales and he couldn't scent anything. He glanced down and saw he didn't have far to go. Faint light marked the opening into the guest-level hearth perhaps twenty paces below him.

Then he heard a bang and a loud crack, and looked up to see a dark shape descending rapidly toward him. One of the creatures was in the shaft. Moon gasped a curse and dropped. He plunged down and caught himself just at the bottom of the chimney.

As he stood in the hearth, he saw the creature stop abruptly, still some distance above him. *The stupid thing is stuck,* he thought incredulously. And it was cutting off any chance of retreat up through the shaft. Hissing in frustration, he ducked to climb down out of the hearth basin.

At just that moment he heard voices and footsteps, about to turn through the door into the common room. By instinct Moon shifted. But when his claws vanished, he lost his footing on the edge of the hearth and tumbled to the floor.

Esom and Karsis stepped into the doorway just in time to see Moon roll across the tile. They stopped, staring. Esom demanded, "What are you doing?"

"Nothing." Moon sat up on one elbow and glanced warily back at the hearth. A little soot trickled down, but no creature appeared. It must be jammed tightly in the shaft.

"Were you—" Karsis looked at the hearth, then at Moon, obviously taking in the soot stains on his clothes and hands. At least his face wasn't covered with monster blood, though there had to be flecks of it all over him. He had been counting on a chance to thoroughly clean off his scales in his room before he shifted. She shook her head in disbelief at her own theory. "You couldn't have been—"

"What do you mean, nothing?" Esom persisted. "Why were you standing on the—"

Moon pushed to his feet, half-ready to answer Esom's question by hitting him in the head. Then far down the hall the stairwell door crashed open. He heard shouts and footsteps as the guards swarmed in. *That's that,* Moon thought. He couldn't retreat up the chimney, and there was no other way out of this level. He should have tried to go up and out when he had the chance. He said, quietly, "Get away from me."

"What?" Esom blinked in confusion but Karsis took his arm and tugged him back.

Several guards burst into the room, their javelins and small crossbow weapons held ready. They all looked angry, and the anger had an even more dangerous tinge of fear. "Was it here? Did you see it?" one shouted. Others raced by in the hall toward the other guest quarters.

"See what?" Esom said, sounding affronted. "We've been locked up here. Of course we didn't see anything!"

Then the guards hastily made way and Ardan walked into the room. Moon had expected him to be angry, but Ardan's expression was grimly pleased. The realization was like a dash of icy water. *He suspected all along,* Moon thought, eyes narrowed. *And now he knows.*

Watching Moon carefully, Ardan said, "So you've been exploring. I wonder why."

Karsis said quickly, "No, he was in his room, we went there to speak to him. We came out here to talk—"

"Quiet." Ardan didn't spare her a glance.

Moon bared his teeth in something that might possibly be interpreted as a smile. "You don't look surprised."

"Let's say I was hopeful." Ardan's smile was dry. "I have someone I'd like you to meet."

Another groundling came down the hall, light footsteps at a deliberate pace. The guards stirred uneasily.

"It's him," Esom muttered and glanced toward the door in fearful anticipation. "That's all we need."

Karsis said, low-voiced, to Moon, "Watch out, he's dangerous. He's not what he seems—"

Moon stopped listening when the newcomer stepped into the doorway. He was younger than Moon, with a slim build, light bronze skin, and dark hair, sharp features. He wore a loose light shirt and dark brown pants of the local fishskin cloth, but his feet were bare.

Despite it all, Moon had a moment of doubt. Then their eyes met and he knew for certain. *Well, that does explain a lot,* he thought, suddenly cold with fury. How Ardan had found the tree, how he had known about the seed. He hadn't even needed a flying ship to get inside the colony tree's high knothole entrance.

The man turned to Ardan, fury twisting his handsome features. "Why didn't you tell me about this? Were you planning to play us off each other? Get rid of me?"

Ardan turned to him in fond exasperation. "Of course not. I wasn't certain what he was. I wanted to be sure before I told you." Of course Ardan had suspected Moon all along; with a live Raksura in groundling form at hand to compare him to, he could hardly help but be suspicious. Add to that Moon's knowledge of the mysterious ruin, his questions about the seed. Ardan looked at Moon. "This is Rift, my friend and guide." He managed the Raksuran pronunciation without difficulty. "I assume your name is not Niran."

"It's Moon, of the Indigo Cloud Court." Karsis and Esom stared at him, Karsis in astonished realization and Esom in growing horror. "That's the colony tree you stole the seed from."

Rift twitched, and hissed. "You're lying. It was empty. It was a dead court."

"It's not empty now," Moon said. "You led him to the seed, you know what that means."

Ardan watched them with a narrow, speculative gaze. He said, "Rift, calm yourself. I thought you would be pleased, to have another member of your race here."

Moon snorted. Ardan obviously didn't know as much about Raksura as he thought.

Rift grimaced in disgust at Ardan. He shifted, his groundling body vanishing in a dark mist, resolving into a warrior with dark green scales. He flared out his spines, and snarled in Raksuran, "You're lying. That colony tree was abandoned. I don't know what you want here, but if you want to live, go away. Now."

Moon barred his teeth. *He thinks he's looking at another warrior.* In groundling form, it was hard to tell young consorts from male warriors. Until it was too late. Moon said, "Come and get me."

Rift sprang toward him. Moon shifted, flared his spines out, and lunged forward. They grappled, tumbled across the room, slammed down onto a bench, bounced off a pillar supporting the chimney. Moon was bigger, stronger, and much more angry. He barely felt the smaller warrior's claws.

Around them, groundlings shouted and fled. Rift's growls went up in pitch as he realized he was overmatched. Wrenching free, Rift tried to bolt. Moon caught him again and flung him toward the knot of guards in the opposite doorway. They scattered as the warrior slammed through them. Claws scraping the floor, Rift scrambled away down the corridor. Moon jumped over two fallen guards, bounced off the ceiling, and pelted after him. Moon was peripherally aware of running, shouting, confusion, but the only thing he could see was Rift.

Rift slammed through an archway into another small sitting room just as Moon caught him. He grabbed Rift's spines and yanked him around. Rift clawed for Moon's eyes but Moon slammed him down to the floor. Kneeling on the warrior's chest, he seized him by the throat. Then Rift croaked, "Don't. Please."

Moon, just about to tighten his grip and rip Rift's throat out, growled in pure frustration. He was breathing hard, his skin stinging from scratches on his hands, arms, and chest that had penetrated his scales. Rift's eyes pleaded, and Moon couldn't kill him. "Where's the seed?"

He gasped, "I don't know. He took it away, out of the tow-er— Watch out!"

Moon twisted in time to see a guard in the doorway, lifting his little crossbow. Moon snapped out his right wing in a sharp punch. He struck the man in the chest with the tip and flung him backward.

Taking advantage of the moment of distraction, Rift said quickly, "I'll show you the way out, through the bottom of the tower. The barrier stops at the ground."

Shouts and crashing echoed from up the corridor. Ardan shouted, "Where are they?"

"You swear it's not here," Moon hissed.

"I swear." Rift's eyes burned with sincerity. "He took it away somewhere."

There wasn't much of a choice. Moon let Rift go and rolled to his feet. More guards rushed the door, and Moon slammed through them, knocking them sprawling. Rift jumped over his head, clung to the ceiling, then leapt down the hall. Moon tore after him and rounded the corner just as a chorus of crossbow bolts clattered against the stone wall.

He caught up with Rift in the foyer as three of the bulbous guard-creatures barreled in through the stairwell doorway. Rift threw himself at the first, hands and feet ripping at its face. The other two tried to crowd past. Moon jumped and landed on top of the first one's head. He slashed at the clawed hands that reached for him and dove forward, over their heads and out the doorway. Out in the stairwell, he whipped around and ripped open the back of the one still trapped in the door. All three creatures roared. Ardan's groundling guards, stuck in the foyer with their path blocked, shouted. Then Rift tore his way out over the creatures' heads.

Rift bounded down the stairs, Moon right behind him. But Rift turned off at the next landing and slammed through a door. Moon hesitated. It led into a foyer and hall not much different from the one they had just escaped. Rift stopped to whisper, "This way—we can't go down the main stairs. He'll order his men to shoot us."

Moon's nerves were as tight as wire at the idea of trusting Rift, but he heard the guard-creatures clumping down the stairs, and there was no time to argue. He ducked through the door, dragged it closed behind him, and ran after Rift.

They passed more doors, a confusing maze of empty rooms, then Rift took a smaller door into a plain room that held only a big iron stove. It was almost as tall as Moon, but cold and dusty with disuse.

Rift climbed up to stand atop it, and explained, "This makes heat for the bathing rooms above. They only use it when it gets cold."

A copper-sheathed chimney led up from it, and for a moment Moon thought Rift meant them to escape through that. It looked far too small and it was going the wrong direction. But there was a grate in the wall behind it, and Rift pried it open with his claws. It opened into a much larger shaft that led down through the wall of the tower. A cool breeze flowed from it, carrying the faint odors of outside air. "This is for ventilation," Rift said as he climbed inside. "Ardan doesn't know I've been down here."

"Then why didn't you escape before?" Moon followed him reluctantly. There were so many things he didn't like about this that he couldn't settle on which was the worst.

Rift hung from chinks in the wall, let Moon get through and then, one-handed, he tugged the grate back into place. "I didn't have anywhere to go."

Moon helped him pull the grate closed, which left the shaft with only the small amount of dappled vapor-light that shone through the bars. "What court are you from?"

Rift eyed him uncertainly as he clung to the grate. "I don't have a court. I was traveling alone."

Moon's spines snapped up, his first impulse a renewed fury. *He's lying, he's lying to make me think—* Except Rift couldn't know anything about Moon's past.

Rift shrunk back against the wall at Moon's reaction. Moon made himself lean back, settle his spines. He started to climb down and after a moment, Rift hurried to catch up. Moon asked, "How did you get here?"

Rift hesitated, as if afraid to provoke another angry re-action. It was already too dark to read his expression. He answered, "I came here a couple of turns ago, not by choice. I was traveling along the eastern shore and got caught in a storm. I got blown out to sea and couldn't fly against the wind. I was exhausted, about to fall out of the sky, and I saw a trading ship. I landed on it. They locked me in the hold, chained me up, and brought me here to sell me to Ardan." He took a sharp breath. "I know I should have let myself drown, but I wanted to live."

Moon had wanted to give up more times than he could remember, and he was ten turns older than Rift, at least. He muttered, "You shouldn't have let yourself drown." He heard Rift miss a handhold and scrabble to recover. Moon added, "You're lucky Ardan didn't stuff you and stick you in his exhibit."

"He had other plans," Rift said, still sounding wary.

Moon clamped his claws into the stone and waited until Rift drew even with him. Going by sound and instinct, he grabbed Rift's shoulder and felt the young warrior's spines flatten into instant submission. He said, "You went to the Reaches with him. You led him to the Indigo Cloud tree. You could have escaped any time while the groundlings were traveling through the forest."

Rift wriggled to get away, then made himself stop. He said tightly, "I didn't want to leave him then. He was kind to me. He helped me."

"You're eager to leave him now."

Rift sounded genuinely anguished. "I'd been to that colony tree ten times over the turns, I used to shelter there. That court must have been gone for generations—"

Moon let go of him and started down again. Rift's story cut far too close to the bone. "It was. But they were attacked by Fell. They— We had to move back to the colony tree."

Rift caught up with him, his claws scraping the wall. "You're a consort. What are you doing here alone?"

Moon didn't answer, and Rift froze for a moment in startled realization. "You're not alone. There are others."

Chapter Twelve

Not much further down the air shaft, they reached a grate that opened into a small dim room, most of it blocked by the bulk of another stove. Unlike the one on the upper floor, it was giving off warmth, and it smelled faintly of fish oil. "This way," Rift said, tugging at the grate.

Moon set his claws in a crack in the wall and looked down. The scents of outdoor air still came from below them. "There's a way out further down."

"It's too small. And the warding barrier blocks it, like the big doors on the ground floor." Rift eased the grate open and climbed out to clamber over the stove. "We have to get to a passage under the tower."

Moon growled in the back of his throat, mostly in frustration. He believed in the barrier outside the tower. After running into it yesterday, he knew how effective it was. But he wanted to get out of here and figure out where the seed was before Ardan moved it again.

He climbed out after Rift, over the top of the big metal stove. It was hot, but not enough to burn Raksuran scales. The pipes from it led into the dirty patched walls, not up through the ceiling. It might be keeping the air in the exhibit hall dry to help preserve Ardan's collection.

Rift jumped from the top of the stove to land near the heavy door. He opened it just enough to peer out. Easing up behind him, Moon stretched to see over his head. The door opened into a gray stone corridor, high-ceilinged and a little better lit. They were somewhere under the main stair-well, on the second level. Moon caught the distinctive odor of decay from the stuffed specimens in the exhibit hall.

Rift slipped out and led the way through a maze of hallways, passing closed doors. They came out on a little balcony and crouched to see over the heavy balustrade. It overlooked the shadowy first floor hall, lit by only a few va-por-lamps. They were distressingly close to the angry face of the giant waterling. Its dead, frozen eyes gleamed in the dim light, its fanged mouth a dark cavern.

Moon sensed movement immediately, and spotted one of the bulbous guard-creatures on the floor below. The thing paced back and forth not far from the bottom of the long sweep of stairs, half-hidden by the bulk of the waterling's tail. Making an impatient snuffling noise, it looked and sounded exactly as if it was casting for a scent, but no one else moved in the shadows.

Rift leaned close and said in a breathless whisper, "Some-one's down there. The wardens don't appear unless some-one comes into the area they're guarding."

Rift was right. If the thing had appeared in response to their arrival, it would know where they were. And it seemed certain there was someone near the stairs. Moon whispered back, "We have to get through that room?"

Rift jerked his chin toward the far end of the hall. "The door is behind those stairs."

Moon motioned Rift to stay back and eased up to perch on the railing, watching the warden pace. This would be tricky. As soon as they killed the thing, it would trigger the appearance of others and likely send some sort of warning to Ardan.

Moon waited until the creature moved out of sight, his view of it blocked by the waterling's right tailfin. Then he jumped, landed on the waterling's back, and ran lightly down its body. The decaying scales squished unpleasant-ly underfoot. Peering over the side of the tail, he saw the guard-creature standing at the base of the stairs. Its arms were out and it was moving slowly forward, as if trying to corner something. *Except nothing's there,* Moon thought. At least nothing he could see at the moment.

He made a sharp gesture at Rift. Rift vaulted the balcony railing, landed on the floor, and snapped his wings out for maximum noise. The guard-creature whipped around toward him and Moon leapt to land right on its oversized head.

The creature staggered and roared, clawed for him, and he ripped, tore, and wrenched. Rift hit it an instant later and tore its legs out from under it. The thing collapsed.

Moon shoved away from it, letting Rift finish it off. He turned toward the stairs and the supposedly empty shadow. Cautiously he tasted the air, but between the decaying waterling and the dying creature, scent was useless. But instinct told him something was there, something was occupying space that should be taken up by air.

He lunged forward, slapped at the shadow, and hit solid flesh. A groundling yelped, and suddenly Esom and Karsis sprawled on the steps.

Moon snarled. "So you're a shaman, too." The two had been using some sort of spell to conceal themselves. They must have used it to slip away from the guest level in the confusion and flee, while Ardan searched for Moon and Rift. He tilted his head toward Esom. "Is that what 'deviser' means?"

Karsis struggled to sit up, shoving her brother off her. Esom stumbled to his feet, "You can't stop us, we—"

"No time," Rift told Moon as he shook the creature's blood off his scales. A clatter sounded from overhead as groundling guards ran across the second level hall to this stairwell. At least two misty shapes forming in the air nearby meant more wardens were about to appear. Rift started toward the curving passage that led under the stairwell.

"Come on," Moon snapped at Esom and Karsis, knowing if he left them behind, they would point the way for the guards.

Fortunately they didn't argue. Esom pulled Karsis up and they both ran after Moon.

The passage wound under the bulk of the stairwell, apparently a back way to the service areas behind the hall. Rift stopped at a spot where there wasn't a door, just a carved panel that looked like part of the wall decoration. But there was a faint line of mold along one edge, showing that there must be something behind it. Rift grabbed the edge, worked his claws under it, and popped it open.

It led into a dark space lit by greenish light that released a breath of dank air carrying a truly foul odor. Rift stepped inside, Moon pushed Karsis and Esom in after him, then stepped through himself.

Moon helped Rift maneuver the panel back into place. There was no lock. He looked hurriedly around the small space. The dim greenish light came from odd little pockets in the stone walls; it was hard to tell if it had been intentionally placed there or was just a lichen or moss that grew naturally. There was nothing to wedge against the panel, nothing to keep the guards from prying it open once they realized it was an escape route.

"We can't seal it," Rift told him, low-voiced. "We need to move away, or the wardens will hear us."

"Can Ardan send those things after us?" Moon asked in Raksuran. They started down the passage, which sloped downward in a long spiral. Karsis slipped a little on the slimy paving but caught Esom's shoulder to steady herself. Both of them watched Rift warily.

Rift replied in the same language, "He can send them, but he has to figure out where we went, first. They can't appear out of nowhere. He has to put the guard-spells for them in place. I don't think he knows about these passages."

"You don't think." That wasn't reassuring, but then nothing about Rift was. "How did you find the way down here without killing the guard-things in the main hall?" That would have had to alert Ardan that Rift had been poking around down here.

"I found it during the day," Rift said. He jerked his head toward Esom and Karsis. "What are we going to do with them?"

That "we" was awfully confident. Switching back to Keda-ic, Moon asked Esom, "If you're a shaman, why didn't you escape before?"

Stiffly, Esom said, "I've tried, but I knew the wardens would stop us. As you saw, the sight-spell doesn't work very well on them."

"We weren't very organized," Karsis admitted. "We tried to get Negal and Orlis, but the guards had already locked them in. And we aren't even certain where Ardan is keeping our other crew members."

"How were you planning to get through the barrier?"

Esom started to speak, then hesitated, and Moon saw Karsis dart a look at him. Esom said, "With all the confusion, I thought we might be able to conceal ourselves down here until morning, when the barrier goes down and the outside doors are opened."

They were terrible liars. "Hide from that creature till morning? I don't think so. I think you knew you could get through the barrier."

The two groundlings exchanged a grim look, and Esom said, "All right, yes. I think I can get through the barrier, but I'm not certain. I've never had a chance to escape from the upper level and test it."

Rift told Moon, "I knew he was a wizard all along, but he can't do much. He's not nearly as powerful as Ardan."

Esom stopped abruptly and stared at Rift. He said, "You knew?"

Karsis demanded, more to the point, "Why didn't you tell Ardan?"

Rift bared a fang in an ironic smile. "I'm not Ardan's servant."

Esom sneered back. "So you're his pet?"

Growling, Rift reached toward him and Esom jerked back. Moon hissed and flicked his spines. Rift glared resentfully, but eased away from Esom.

Esom looked from Rift to Moon, then wet his lips and said, "If you don't help us escape, we'll tell Ardan's men which way you went."

Karsis cleared her throat, a little embarrassed. Apparently she had seen the flaw in her brother's plan. Moon said, "Or we could just kill you."

Esom blinked, then grimaced. Karsis elbowed him and he glared at her. "All right, fine." He took a deep breath. "I think I know where the seed is, the one you've been asking about, that Ardan took from the giant tree. I'm not certain, but I have a good idea."

That was different. Moon took a step nearer, looming over him. "Where?"

Esom lifted his chin and squared his shoulders, the groundling equivalent of lifting his spines. "I want your promise to help us escape, and to help us get our friends away from Ardan."

Moon thought it over fast, flicking his spines. "I can take you out of here with us now, but I can't go back for your friends. Ardan will search the city for us and there's no way we can get back inside this tower." That might or might not be true, but he wasn't going to make promises he couldn't keep.

Esom looked at Karsis, who gave him a helpless shrug and said, "At least we'd be free to try to help the others."

Esom, jaw set and ready to argue, visibly deflated. "All right, I'll—"

A thump somewhere above interrupted him. Rift twitched in alarm. "They're coming."

"Come on, move." Moon gave Rift a push and started away down the passage. Motioning Karsis and Esom to follow, he whispered, "You keep talking."

Keeping his voice low, Esom said rapidly, "When we first arrived in the city, Ardan let us explore at will. Towards the front of the creature, near a flooded valley where its left front leg dips down, there's a domed building that looked as if it had some important purpose. Negal and I went there. Part of it is apparently used as some sort of mortuary temple, but the public area was covered with carvings showing what seemed to be early magisters taking control of the leviathan by placing an object in contact with its body. These carvings led toward a doorway, with a stairwell down. Guards prevented us from going any further, but . . ." He hesitated, and Karsis nudged him impatiently. "Part of my ability . . . I can see and feel emanations from magical artifacts. That's how I found the metora stone to power our vessel, the *Klodifore*. And I'm sure there's something down there, some source of magic," Esom finished.

Moon managed not to hiss impatiently. He was glad he hadn't made them any extravagant promises in a moment of weakness. "Ardan didn't have the seed then. Why do you think it's there now?"

Esom said, "On the journey through the forest, he kept talking about how urgent this was, that the survival of the city depended on it, that they were in danger of losing control of the leviathan."

Karsis added, "When we reached the tree, we only spent one day there. Once he found the seed, he wanted to leave immediately."

Esom continued, "We haven't seen the seed since we got back to the city. It stands to reason, if he wanted it to help him and the other magisters with the leviathan, it must be in that building, in the place where they control the creature."

If it was a lie, it was an odd one. Esom could have said the seed was still in the tower, to trick Moon into going back for his friends.

Then Rift said, "He's right. Ardan took it there the day we got back from the Reaches."

Moon stared at him. He said through gritted teeth, "You said you didn't know where it was."

Rift turned back to give Moon a look of impatient innocence. "I knew it wasn't in the tower. I didn't want to waste time trying to convince you to leave."

Moon switched to Raksuran to say, pointedly, "If you knew this, why did you let me make a bargain with him?" He would have taken Esom and Karsis out with them anyway, as long as they were here, but he wanted to know what Rift was playing at.

Rift paused at an intersection in the passage, where another ramp spiraled more steeply down. The flow of damp, foul-smelling air hadn't increased, but Moon could hear the growing sound of rushing wind, rising and falling in oddly regular gusts. In the same language, Rift said, as if it was obvious, "We don't need them. You don't have to keep the bargain."

This was an interesting insight into Rift's thought processes. Moon said, "If you expect me to trust you, you might want to stop lying and betraying people in front of me."

Rift twitched, watched him uncertainly, then turned to lead the way down the ramp.

Moon couldn't trust what Rift told him and he couldn't trust Esom and Karsis, but with all three together, he might be able to get something close to the truth out of them. Though if Esom had really concealed his power from Ardan all this time, he was a better liar than Moon would have thought.

Running footsteps from somewhere far up the passage suggested that Ardan's men had found the panel and opened it. They didn't have much time.

Two more spirals down, and the ramp ended in a low-ceilinged chamber, sparsely lit with the green mold, with a large round hole in the center of the floor. Moon stepped to the edge. The shaft plunged more than a hundred paces down, the bottom lost in the dim greenish light. The wind sound came from somewhere below, and the smell was horrific.

"Down there," Rift said. He glanced worriedly back up the ramp. "We need to hurry."

Esom and Karsis exchanged an appalled look. *Wonderful,* Moon thought, privately agreeing with them. To Rift he said, "You take her, I'll take—"

"No," Esom interrupted. He told Moon, "You take Karsis."

It was an interesting point, that Esom felt his sister was safer with Moon, another Raksura and a stranger, than Rift. In Raksuran, Moon said to Rift, "I want them both alive. Drop him, and I'll gut you."

Rift hissed in exasperation. "I won't. I told you, I want to help you."

Moon caught Karsis around the waist and jumped down into the shaft to catch the edge one-handed. She made a noise like a short shriek and grabbed his shoulders. His claws hooked on a gap in the mortar, Moon said, "Put your arms around my neck and hold on. Watch the spines, they're sharp."

"Yes, I see." Karsis wound her arms around his neck, holding on tightly. Moon planted his feet on the wall and pushed off, falling to catch hold of another gap further down. Karsis' shriek was closer to a strangled yelp that time. "Sorry," she gasped.

Moon glanced up, saw that Rift had Esom and hung from the upper ledge. Moon cautiously let go of Karsis, made certain she had a firm hold on him, and began to climb down the wall.

Keeping his voice low, Moon said, "Tell me about Rift."

She whispered, "We didn't know what he was, at first. He came on the voyage to the forest coast with Ardan and his other men. Ardan said Rift would be our guide. He didn't reveal himself until Ardan needed his help to force us to keep going inland." She hesitated, then added, "We thought he was one of a kind, a . . ."

"Monster," Moon finished for her.

"Yes, until we reached the tree and saw the artwork. It looked as if it had been abandoned for ages. We didn't— And even Ardan and Rift didn't think anyone lived there anymore."

"It wasn't abandoned, just . . . waiting." The last thing he wanted at the moment was an apology. "Where is Rift from?"

"He's never said." She gasped as he had to drop for the next handhold, but recovered quickly. "Is it important?"

Moon couldn't answer that right now either. He wanted Rift to be from a rival court, a place hostile to Indigo Cloud. He wanted him to be in the power of the Fell. "Why didn't you mention that Ardan had a pet Raksura?"

"Ardan has six members of our crew locked up some-where in the tower. He said if we spoke about Rift to anyone he'd order them killed. We know he's serious. Five of our crew tried to escape in the forest, and he had them executed. He let Rift kill three of his own men when we were at the tree."

That explained the bones left behind in the root passage. "What for?"

"Rift caught the men destroying some of the wall carvings, trying to take the inset gems."

Moon snarled under his breath, incredulous. "What?" Karsis asked nervously.

"He showed Ardan how to take the seed; that's killing the tree. Those carvings were all going to rot away with the rest of the tree without it." If Rift knew where to find the seed in its hidden cradle in the colony tree, then he had to know what it was, what it meant to cut it out.

"I see," Karsis muttered. "Or, I don't see. I don't understand his thinking."

That makes two of us. The stench was getting worse; Moon couldn't have scented a major kethel if it was breathing down his neck. The regular rush of wind grew louder as well. Moon reached the bottom of the shaft and hung there, trying to see what lay below.

The drop was about two hundred paces to an uneven surface that looked like pitted and scarred paving. Heavy round pillars and blocky columns supported the foundations of the tower. In the dim green light he could see they were heavily covered with patchy molds and odd dark growths. Rift and Esom arrived just above them, and Esom said, "Karsis, are you all right?"

"Quiet!" Karsis snapped, before Moon could. He listened intently to the wind. It had been repeating the same pattern the entire time they had climbed down the shaft: the sound would stop, there would be a long low rush, like something drawing breath, then it resumed. *Like something drawing breath,* Moon thought. *Right.*

Karsis whispered, "That's not what I think it is, is it?"

"The leviathan. We're right above its back." Now that Moon knew what he was looking at, he could see that the pitted, scarred paving was actually the giant scaled hide of the leviathan.

Karsis made a noise eloquent of disgust.

From above them, Rift whispered, "It's all right to walk on it. Its hide is too thick, it won't feel us."

"How do you know that?" Esom asked.

Rift didn't reply, and Moon said, tightly, "Answer him."

Rift said in annoyance, "I've been down here before. How do you think I knew the way?"

"That's reassuring," Moon said under his breath. He would just have to trust Rift now and beat the truth out of him later.

Holding on with one hand, Moon wrapped his arm around Karsis' waist again. Then he let go of the wall. As they dropped he snapped out his wings to soften the fall. They landed on one of the big scales. He was braced to leap back up to the shaft, but nothing happened. The whistling rush of the creature's breathing continued undisturbed.

He set Karsis on her feet. It took her a moment to unclench her hands from his collar flanges, and she wobbled on the uneven surface. He turned and scanned the dark space. It went on for a long distance. Apparently this area was the underpinnings of the city. It wouldn't be the leviathan they had to worry about, but the parasites that might live down here, feeding off the garbage dropped from the buildings above and the growths on the leviathan's hide. The creature's stench made Moon effectively scent-blind, and the rush of its breathing masked slight sounds of movement.

Rift dropped to the ground a few paces away, and dumped Esom on his feet. Esom staggered into Moon, jerked away, then self-consciously straightened his jacket. Rift pointed roughly east, back toward the tail of the creature. "That way. There's a passage to the outside up there."

"Lead the way," Moon said, pointedly.

Rift flattened his spines in a way that suggested he was hurt at Moon's distrust, and started away through the shadows. Moon controlled the urge to slap him in the head and followed.

It was a long walk, nearly half the length of the city. They had to go at the pace of the two groundlings, who were moving as fast as they could, but the rough scales made for uneven and difficult footing. The vast support pillars loomed overhead, blossoming with ugly, bulbous growths, and several times they crossed broad, slimy trails, though they never saw the creatures that were leaving them. There were also gray shapes clinging to the ceiling that looked like giant tree frogs, like the ones in the suspended forest. They might be just as harmless, but Moon doubted it on principle. Nothing attacked them, but Raksura were different and unexpected enough that the predators here might be cautious. For now, at least.

Ardan's men would have had to fetch ropes to get down the shaft, so they had a good lead by the time Moon caught the sound of voices. And unless Ardan had a way to magically detect them, there was nothing to show which way they had gone.

Finally the space around them became more closed-in, the foundation pillars and supports much closer together.

"There it is," Rift said, "Do you smell it?"

"Smell what?" Esom asked, stumbling.

"Fresh air," Moon told him. It was a draft scented of outside air, damp and fresh, an intense relief after the leviathan's stench. "There's an opening somewhere ahead."

"Finally." Esom wiped sweat off his forehead. "I thought we were going to be stuck down here forever."

"I'd prefer it to going back to Ardan," Karsis added.

"Now do you trust me?" Rift said.

"We'll see." Moon had no intention of committing himself on that point.

Finally they were close enough for Moon to actually see the opening. The chamber narrowed to end at a bulwark of heavy stones, and there was an irregular patch of lighter darkness about midway up, just above a mound of rubble.

But as they drew closer, Moon realized he could hear something else besides the rushing wind of the leviathan's breath. It was a deep, hollow sound, regular and even. "Do you hear that?" he asked the others. His first thought was that it was something the leviathan was doing, though he didn't even want to guess what bodily function could produce that sound.

Rift stopped to listen, then said, startled, "It's the bell. The warning bell. The leviathan's going to move."

Esom swore in a strange language, then added in Kedaic, "There's no telling how long it's been ringing."

The magisters' enspelled bell, that rang to warn the city that the leviathan was about to move. It would call the fishers to lift their boats out of the water and the traders to cast off. Moon said, "How long does it—"

The ground lurched under him; he and Rift swayed, using their foot claws to stay upright. Esom and Karsis both stumbled and fell.

The whole underground shook, moss and debris rained down from the ceiling. Beneath them the leviathan's hide pulsed and shuddered. Moon leaned down, caught Karsis around the waist, and started up the pile of rubble. Rift followed, hauling Esom with him.

At the top, they climbed out through the jagged gap into a windy night, alive with the crash of the surf. There were hanging vapor-lights below them, rocking wildly with the leviathan's motion. Moon squinted to see, realizing they were at the far edge of the city. A giant stone bulwark rose up behind them, and the leviathan's immense tail stretched out below, like the surface of a reef. It moved now, migrating back and forth across the waves and tossing up fountains of spray as the creature swam.

"What do we do now?" Karsis shouted in his ear.

The leviathan moved at a good speed, but not faster than a Raksura could fly. The sky was starting to gray towards the east and they didn't have much darkness left. They would be fighting the wind the whole way, but they had to go now. Moon turned to Rift, and shouted, "You take him, and follow me."

Esom's "Where are we going—" was cut off with a yelp as Rift grabbed him. Moon tightened his hold on Karsis, snapped his wings out, and jumped into the wind.

Both he and Rift were blown backwards, out over the moving tail. Hard flaps took them back over the creature's hindquarters, Moon leading Rift upward to gain altitude.

Moon played his wings against the wind, riding it to keep moving forward. Karsis clung to him, her hands gripping his collar flanges tightly, and buried her face against his scales. A few vapor-lights were lit in the streets and in the windows of the towers, but the city looked empty; everyone must be huddling inside.

Moon banked away to avoid the area near Ardan's tower. The wind drove him further than he intended, and he skirted the harbor. It was empty of the big trading ships, the pontoon docks churning up waves as they were dragged through the water. Little fishing boats swung from the cages that had lifted them to safety. The metal ship, the *Klodifore*, had been moved close to the dock, but was still floating . . . *No, it's hovering*, Moon thought, realizing it had no wake. When the bell had started to sound, Ardan must have sent someone to the harbor to raise the ship.

He fought the wind to curve toward the abandoned tower where he and Stone had camped.

The wind sheared around the roof of the tower and Moon made a dive for the open terrace on the top floor. He made it and bounced lightly off the tower wall. Rift managed it too, though he bounced a little harder and staggered across the terrace.

Moon stepped between the columns into the shelter of the big room, expecting to find an impatient Stone. It was too dark to see much, but the Raksuran figure waiting there was much smaller. It said, "Moon?"

"Song?" It couldn't be Song, except it was. Startled and a little appalled, he set Karsis on her feet. "What are you doing here?"

Song explained, "Pearl sent us. We caught up with Jade and the others late yesterday, and just reached this place a little while ago. Stone saw us and guided us here. They're all downstairs. Why do you have a groundling—" Rift stepped in and Esom staggered after him. Startled, Song stared at him. "Who's that?"

Rift hesitated, then stepped back toward the balcony. "No," Moon said sharply.

Rift quivered, on the verge of bolting. If he fled, Moon would have to catch him again, if the wind whipping around the tower didn't kill them both. On impulse, he shifted to groundling. It was Raksuran etiquette that when the highest-ranking person shifted to groundling, everyone around them did as well. Song followed suit immediately, and Rift, by habit too ingrained to break, shifted too.

Moon reached, caught Rift's wrist, and towed him toward the door. He could deal with Esom and Karsis later.

They passed Root in the dim stairwell; he was hanging from the ceiling. He saw them and shouted, "Moon! Moon's back!"

Light shone up from the room on the level just below, and Moon heard familiar voices raised in argument. It was an interior room, no windows, so no one venturing out into the streets would see suspicious light from an abandoned and inaccessible tower.

Moon stepped into the doorway. Some broken tiles had been spelled for light and tucked into various wall niches, so he could clearly see Stone, Jade, Chime, Vine, Balm, and Flower. But the other three warriors were Floret, Drift, and River, which was a surprise of a whole different kind. *I can't believe Pearl sent River,* he thought incredulously. *That's all we need.*

He couldn't believe they were here at all. It was a bad idea, it was going to cause trouble, and Jade should have waited before leading the warriors to the leviathan. But Moon couldn't help a warm swell of relief at seeing them all. He said, "I thought you gave us three days."

Everyone's attention snapped to the doorway. Jade stared. "Moon—"

Moon said, "This is Rift. He helped Ardan get the seed, and he's going to help us get it back."

☾

Esom and Karsis sat on a marble bench built out from the wall, watching nervously, but then the conversation was in Raksuran. Rift's presence had caused some awkwardness. Most of the others had stared at him, then looked away. Stone hadn't betrayed any reaction, and Balm was expressionless, but Chime kept looking anxiously at Moon.

Moon had explained something of what he had found out about Ardan and the tower, and where Rift and the two groundlings had come from. They had also established that by everyone's sense of direction the leviathan was moving further west, away from the coast, and the distance was probably already too great for the warriors to make in one flight. *They were lucky,* Moon thought grimly. If the creature had chosen to move while they were still flying towards it, they could have all drowned.

How they would get back to the coast was another question.

River swung around and snarled at Moon, "This is your fault."

Moon regarded him. All things considered, he had had a hard day. "If you're not careful, Floret is going to be taking you back to Pearl in a basket."

Floret lifted her hands, protesting, "I didn't say anything!"

Jade said, deliberately, "If I have to tell you all to stop fighting one more time, I'm going to beat every single one of you senseless."

There was a short silence. Then Karsis whispered to Flower in Kedaic, "What are they saying?"

"It's not important," Flower said, wryly. She sat next to them on the bench, her legs drawn up under her smock. Her face was drawn and weary, but that must have been from being carried on the long flight out here.

"Esom knows where the seed is," Moon said, speaking Kedaic so the groundlings would understand him.

Everyone turned to Esom and he recoiled a little under the concentrated predatory gazes of a roomful of Raksura. Even though most of them were in groundling form, it was a little intimidating. Even Karsis flinched. Jade said, "Where?"

Esom coughed, and uneasily repeated the story he had told Moon. He finished, "So, I think you should search that building."

Jade took a step forward to stand over him. "Why are you certain it's there?"

Esom blinked up at her and appeared to have difficulty answering. Considering how many clothes his people wore, Moon thought it was probably due to the fact that she was dressed only in jewelry. Even with the scales, it had to be distracting. Esom managed, "Ah—"

Karsis put in, "Rift said that's where Ardan took it."

Everyone looked at Rift. He twitched uneasily and stared determinedly down at the dirty floor.

Jade watched him for a long moment, her spines flicking. Rift wouldn't meet her eyes. Finally she turned to the others. "We need to look for this place, see how well-guarded it is."

River folded his arms. "And make sure it exists at all."

Moon ignored that. "We'll need to go on foot. Dawn's breaking, and the wind is keeping the mist from forming."

"Not you. This Ardan will be looking for you now." Jade glanced around at the others. "Vine and Floret? Can you walk through a groundling city without letting anyone know you're Raksura?"

The two exchanged a worried glance. Vine said, "I think so, yes. Probably."

Moon looked them over critically. They were dressed like the others, pants and a shirt, a sash and belt at the waist. The fine fabric was sun-faded and a little dirty from their long journey, so they didn't look overly prosperous. He said, "Take off anything that looks like Arbora-work, especially your jewelry. And put something on your feet, a cloth or leather wrap, to make it look like you're wearing shoes."

Both looked down at their feet, a little dubious, but neither argued with him.

"Go now," Jade said. "Don't try to fly. Climb down the outside until you're out of the wind. Find the building, but don't try to go inside without us."

Floret nodded soberly, but Vine said, "If we find the seed lying around unguarded, can we—"

"Yes." Jade added, "If you do, I'll be very surprised, since nothing so far has been easy."

"Good point," Floret muttered, and gave Vine a nudge.

As they headed for the stairs, Moon let his breath out in relief. At least they were moving forward again, even if they didn't know exactly where they were going.

Stone had been leaning against the wall, taking it all in with an expression that could best be described as satirical. Now he pushed himself up with one shoulder and said, "Who let you into the tree?"

Both groundlings stared up at him, and Esom's throat worked as he swallowed. There was no space in here for Stone to shift, and he still looked like an older groundling man, battered and gray, wearing battered gray clothes. But he seemed to be taking up far more space in the room, and the air was suddenly heavy. Esom said, "It was him." He pointed toward Rift.

Watching Stone uneasily, Karsis said, "Rift flew to a large doorway high up in the trunk. We couldn't have reached it. Our ship can only lift about forty paces off the ground."

Stone turned to regard Rift, who shrank back against the wall. Stone started across the room toward him, slow deliberate steps.

Moon said, "Leave him alone." The words were out before he thought.

Stone stopped, cocked his head. His expression was opaque. He said, "I need to take care of this now."

Moon looked at Jade, but she watched Rift. None of the others were looking at the warrior; they were waiting, stiff and tense, anticipating violence. Moon flushed cold in realization. *Take care of this* meant *kill the solitary*. Moon growled low in his throat. "No."

Stone was fast in his groundling form, but it took Moon's breath when he was suddenly across the room, face to face with Moon, between one heartbeat and the next.

Moon fought down several impulses, to shift, to fall back,

to squint to protect his eyes; he held his ground. Jade gave a startled snarl, a thick, rough sound like rock scraping. The others were dead silent, frozen in place. Rift had flattened himself back against the wall.

Ignoring all of them, Stone said, "This needs to be done. He betrayed us to groundlings."

Moon said, "He didn't know we were coming back to the tree. He didn't know we existed."

"And we don't know what he did to get thrown out of a court. He's a solitary and he can't be trusted."

Moon held his gaze. "Like you couldn't trust me." His voice shook, but it wasn't from fear.

"What?" Stone's eyes went hooded, but not quite in time to conceal his start of shock. He knew Moon meant the day Stone had found him with the Cordans and had taken him up to a ruin in the mountain valley. "No."

Yes. Moon had always known that the only reason Stone had bothered to save him was because he was a consort. But he had been naive enough to think that if Stone had decided that Moon was a real solitary, thrown out of a court for some terrible reason, Stone would have just left him behind somewhere. If he was willing to kill Rift just for showing Ardan the location of an empty colony tree . . . "You said you wanted to help me. If you hadn't believed what I told you— You took me up there to kill me."

Stone recoiled, snarled, and flung himself out of the room.

Everyone stared. Balm, Chime, and even Drift were appalled, Esom and Karsis confused and frightened. Flower just sighed, tired and disgusted. River looked as if, much against his better judgment, he was reluctantly impressed.

In the silence, Jade stepped forward. She jerked her head toward Rift, and told the warriors, "Watch him." Then she caught Moon's arm and pulled him out of the room.

CHAPTER THIRTEEN

J ade hauled Moon across the stairwell to a room on the
far side. Root, who still hung from the ceiling, stared
curiously as they went past but didn't speak.

The room had a wall of tall windows, sheltered by the
terrace on the floor above. Dawn was breaking, the first
light spreading gray-blue across the dark sky. There was
just enough light to see the carved figures in the walls glaring down with sightless eyes. Wind whipped through the
room, scouring away the scent of mold.

Jade dropped Moon's arm and went to the window. She
faced away from him, her spines still quivering in agitation.

Moon watched her warily. He couldn't tell who she was
most angry at, him, Stone, Rift, or all three of them. He said,
"I'm not going to let Stone kill him."

Jade flicked a look at him. "He's a solitary."

Coming from her, that hurt. "So was I." Rift had inadver-
tently betrayed Indigo Cloud to Ardan, not knowing the
colony tree was soon to be occupied. Moon had inadver-
tently betrayed Indigo Cloud to the Fell, not knowing they
had been waiting for turns for vengeance. Moon didn't see
much of a difference, except that he was a consort, and the
court had needed him.

Jade turned to face him. He couldn't see her expression
with her back to the light, but her voice was still taut. "You
weren't thrown out of a court, Moon. It's not the same
thing."

It felt like the same thing. "If I'd been born a warrior—"

"Moon." Jade moved to him and grabbed his shoulders. Moon was braced for just about anything, except what she said. "Stone likes you. He likes you better than most of his natural descendants."

He tried to pull away but she didn't let go. She said, "You didn't give me a chance to tell you I'm glad you're alive. I get here and find out you've talked your way into a groundling wizard's tower, a groundling wizard who collects the decaying bodies of rare creatures—"

"You were supposed to give us three days."

"I couldn't wait." She let him go and turned away with a distracted hiss. "Now the warriors are probably trapped out here and this damn thing is still moving. If we go further out than even Stone can fly, we can't even—" She bit the words off.

Moon rubbed his arms where her hands had pressed into his groundling skin, jolted into remembering that Rift wasn't the only issue. If they all died here, unable to escape, or drowned trying to reach the forest coast, it would be Jade's fault for not waiting. That would please River, though probably not much, what with being dead himself. And why had Pearl sent River after them and not one of her other warriors? As far as Moon had been able to tell, she had always kept her favorite warrior-lover close at hand. Maybe River had wanted to prove himself. Things had changed in Indigo Cloud, and maybe River couldn't hold on to his status without showing he was willing to risk his life for the court like Vine and Floret and the other warriors.

He could worry about River's motives later. Jade was too much of a Raksura to remember there were other ways off this leviathan than flying. Moon said, "The groundlings— Esom and Karsis—have a boat."

Jade's spines twitched. "Of course," she muttered. She turned to him, her brow furrowed. "They've said they won't leave without their friends. We'd have to take it from them."

Moon shrugged uncomfortably. "I know." Negal and his crew had helped steal the seed. But telling Esom and Karsis they were on their own was one thing; forcing them to abandon their people to die was another. *Maybe we could work something out.* They didn't need a boat for the whole trip, just to carry them far enough that the coast was within a safe flying distance for the warriors. "Maybe . . ." He let the word trail off as he realized the subtle sway of the tower, the sense of motion, was dying away with the howl of the wind.

Jade went to the window. Moon reached her side and looked over the rooftops out to the sea. The rising sun broke through the streaked clouds and glanced off the water, glittering on the roiling whitecaps stirred by the leviathan's fins. But the waves died down and settled to swells. The leviathan was gliding to a halt.

Jade hissed in bitter amusement. "You and Rift escape Ardan, and suddenly this creature moves further out to sea? It can't be a coincidence."

Moon leaned on the windowsill. "It has to be. The whole reason the city needs the magisters at all is because the leviathan moves . . . at random." *Huh.* That was what all the groundlings thought, anyway. *Because that's what the magisters tell them.*

Jade's expression was thoughtfully skeptical. "How convenient for the magisters."

Moon looked out to sea again. "Some groundlings who live here told us that turns ago the magisters started to lose their power, and the leviathan woke and swam away. They can still keep the city together, but they can't make the leviathan go back to the shore."

"Or they let the leviathan swim away, so they could keep control of the city," Jade said.

"Maybe. Maybe they have just enough power to make it move when they want." Ardan clearly had some hold over Magister Lethen, a hold that Lethen bitterly resented. "Or when Ardan wants. Maybe he's the only one with the power to make the leviathan move anymore. He's the youngest magister." He turned away from the window, thinking over what Ardan had said, and not said.

"We know he thought our seed would help him some-

how, give him power. We don't know if he was right or not."
Jade shook her spines, irritated. "We won't know until we
find this mortuary temple."

Moon hesitated, but he wanted this point settled. "Are
you going to let Stone kill Rift?"

Jade twitched at the question. But she said, "Not today."
Her voice hardened. "That's as far as I'll go."

Moon set his jaw, forced himself not to argue, and walked
out.

☾

Moon went back into the main room. Rift sat on the floor
in the far corner. Esom and Karsis were still seated on the
bench, and Chime, Balm, and Drift stood around looking
uncomfortable.

Moon asked, "Where's Flower?" River was missing too,
but he didn't care if River had gone up to take a turn on
watch or had flown away to die somewhere.

He had spoken in Kedaic, and Karsis answered, "She said
she was going to talk to the older man who stormed off earlier."

"Is Jade all right?" Balm asked, a little hesitantly.

"Yes." Moon was hesitant too. "She's . . . resting."

Drift sneered. "She should give you a beating."

Moon took a step toward him. His expression must have
made his first impulse clear. Drift flinched back and hissed.

Balm hissed at Drift, and Chime threw him a glare, saying,
"Why don't you go say that to Jade and see what happens?"

Apparently declining to follow that advice, Drift subsided. He retreated to lean against the wall with his arms folded, and eyed Moon resentfully.

Esom and Karsis sat stiffly, trying to look as if they weren't
tense to the point of rigidity. It seemed cruel to expose
them to any more of Drift than absolutely necessary, but
they had to be watched. Moon nodded toward an alcove
on the other side of the room. It had another stone bench
and room to stretch out on the floor. The two groundlings
had been awake all night, too, and had to be weary. He said,
"You can go over there to rest, if you want. Chime, do you

have spare blankets?"

Chime turned to one of the packs lying against the wall. "Yes, I'll find some. And some water, and I think we have some dried fruit and roots they could eat."

Relaxing a little, Karsis said, "Thank you," and Esom nodded, still stiffly.

Moon went over to where Rift was crouched in the corner and sat near him. Rift watched him warily, his body tight with tension. This close, Moon could scent the fear in his sweat. He said, "They won't kill you."

Rift's shoulders slumped and he closed his eyes for a moment. He made a noise that was between a sob and a harsh laugh, and looked up at Moon again. "Your queen does whatever you want?"

Moon stared him down, until Rift dropped his gaze. "Sorry," Rift muttered. "I didn't mean . . . The consorts at my court weren't like you."

That was probably true. "Did Ardan think I was here alone?" Yesterday Moon had told the magister that he had friends waiting for him, but he was hoping Ardan had taken that as a lie, part of Moon's persona as a trader.

Rift shook his head. "I don't know. He didn't even tell me that he had another guest."

Moon let out his breath. He didn't think that was a lie. Rift's shock at seeing another Raksura had been genuine. "How much does Ardan know about Raksura? When he saw me shift, would he have known I was a consort? That a consort wouldn't be here alone?"

Rift's brow furrowed as he considered it. "He knows what a consort is, but . . . I'm not sure he really understands, not well enough to realize you wouldn't be traveling alone." Rift hesitated and watched him uneasily. "Why did they send you to the tower? Why not one of the warriors?"

Moon drew back. "I've been around groundlings. The others haven't." He wasn't ready to say more than that. Rift already had a hold on him, he didn't need to know details. He countered, "What did you do to get thrown out of your court?"

It was Rift's turn to recoil. After a moment, he said, "The

queens didn't like me."

The flicker of hesitation in Rift's eyes told Moon it was a lie. And if that was a reason to be exiled, half of Indigo Cloud would be wandering the Three Worlds. "Were you from a royal clutch?"

Startled resentment crossed Rift's expression. "Yes," Rift admitted, biting the word off as if it hurt to tell the truth. "How did you know?"

There was something about Rift's attitude that suggested it. The warriors born out of royal clutches always seemed to be the troublesome ones. "Just a wild guess," Moon said. Across the room he saw Drift, who had been pretending not to listen, roll his eyes in derision.

Rift's sideways look was dubious. Moon said, "Why didn't the queens like you?"

"I had a fight with one of the reigning queen's favorites." That wasn't a good reason to be exiled, either. Moon hadn't even been in the court that long, and he knew young warriors frequently attacked each other. River and Moon had tried to kill each other right in front of Pearl and Jade, and nobody had suggested exiling anybody.

Moon asked, "Did you kill her?"

Rift flicked his spines. "Of course not."

Moon sensed the story had just veered off the truth again. Rift's answer had been too easy. Moon thought an adult female warrior, especially a favorite probably from a royal clutch herself, could have beaten Rift into the ground. And if the fight was so violent that Rift had killed his opponent in self-defense, that wouldn't be such a terrible thing to admit. Moon said, "So they threw you out of the court for losing a fight with a queen's favorite?"

Rift's jaw set as if he suppressed some strong emotion. Moon knew in his bones that this was play-acting. Rift said bitterly, "If that's how you want to describe it. It wasn't fair, but it's what happened."

Moon watched him for a long moment, but Rift's gaze didn't waver. He knew he hadn't gotten the truth yet, but Rift seemed committed to this story, at least for now.

He got to his feet and walked out, randomly picking another doorway off the stairwell. The room within was thankfully empty, a little smaller than the others on this floor, with long narrow windows letting in light and the damp air.

There was a quiet step behind him and he glanced back to see Balm.

She stopped and said, "He's not like you, Moon. He's a real solitary, exiled from his court for a good reason."

Moon rubbed his eyes, trying to be patient. He suspected he was going to be having this conversation a lot. "You don't know he's not like me," he said, aware he was just being difficult. "I could be lying."

Balm shook her head in exasperation. "You don't know anything about living in a court. You have to have everything explained to you, and when we do explain it, you look like you think we're crazy. Everyone who speaks to you notices that. No one is that good a liar."

Moon turned away abruptly and sat down against the wall, folding his arms. He had expected to have the conversation, but not that it was going to be about him. Balm followed and sat on her heels in front of him. He said, reluctantly, "It could have been me. Everything Rift did. When I was alone, I was just looking for a place to live. If I'd been hurt, trapped, and been found by someone like Ardan, who was kind to me . . . Even if he wanted to use me, I might have gone along with it, just to belong somewhere." He waved a hand in frustration. "That's exactly what happened with Stone. I crossed the Three Worlds for the first person who asked me."

"The first Raksura who asked you," Balm corrected, unconvinced. "Back at the colony tree, you told me what I should do. Now I'm telling you. This solitary is not like you. Thinking of him that way is a mistake." She sat back. "He's even changed his name. No one calls a child 'Rift.'"

Stone had said much the same thing about Sorrow, the warrior whom Moon had thought of as his mother. But a warrior who changed her name to Sorrow because her court had been destroyed and she was left alone with four small Arbora and a fledgling consort to care for was understandable. A warrior who left his court and called himself "Rift" . . . "I know. I know I can't trust him."

Balm watched him. "Do you trust us?"

Moon couldn't answer. Maybe he didn't trust them. Maybe he was pretending they were his family, going through the motions, but deep in his heart he didn't really believe it. *It would explain a lot,* he told himself. *Like why you keep acting like an idiot.*

Balm shook her head regretfully. "Sometimes it doesn't seem like it. Did you think we would have let that noisy little Emerald Twilight queen touch you?"

It had never even crossed his mind that they might defend him. From a Fell or a predator or some other common enemy, but not from a Raksuran queen, even one from a strange court. It was an uncomfortable insight.

His inability to answer told Balm all she needed to know. She sighed and squeezed his knee sympathetically, then pushed to her feet and walked away.

Chime passed her in the doorway, and Moon hunched his shoulders, feeling beleaguered. "Don't say she's right. I know she's right."

"That wasn't what I was going to say." Chime sat down, settling uneasily on the cracked tiles. "She is right, though."

Moon rubbed his forehead; the tension and the long night underground had given him a headache. "What were you going to say?"

"Nothing. I just . . . I don't want to worry Flower. Especially now, when she's trying to talk to Stone."

Moon squelched a surge of guilt at the mention of Stone. "Worry her about what?"

Chime sighed. "I keep having these . . . odd feelings."

"Odd how?"

Chime made a vague gesture. "Like I can feel water moving, and . . . cold and weight and rock. I'm twitchy, like I can just catch glimpses of things that flick away before I can focus on them. The feelings come and go, in bursts—which is good, because otherwise I'd go out of my head."

That definitely sounded odd. "When did it start?"

"Since just before dawn, when we landed on this creature." Chime shrugged, obviously uncomfortable with the whole idea that he might have some sort of heightened awareness of the leviathan. "I know. If it's a coincidence, it's a strange one."

"Is it a mentor thing? I mean, are you . . ." Knowing how badly Chime felt about his involuntary change to warrior, Moon hesitated to suggest that Chime might be getting his abilities back. If he wasn't, if it was just his imagination . . . Hope was painful.

But Chime shook his head. "No, it can't be. Augury isn't like this. This is different."

"Then you should talk to Flower."

"I know." Chime slumped. "I'm tired of strange things happening to me. I just got used to being able to fly, and to hunting, and all the other things I'm supposed to do now. I know this is the only way you've ever seen me, but to me it still feels like it just happened."

"No, I know what you mean." Moon felt like he was reliving his past at regular intervals, whether he liked it or not.

Flower stepped into the doorway, gave the room a sour look, then came to sit down next to Moon with a grunt of effort. "Consorts," she said, in a tone that made it sound like an insulting epithet. "Old, stubborn, obstinate consorts." She eyed Moon without favor. "And you. You have to be coaxed to do everything except risk your life."

Moon fumbled for a rebuttal as Chime said, "Are you all right? You look terrible."

Flower transferred her glare to him. "If you ask me that one more time, I will curdle your liver."

"Hah, good luck trying to slip me the simple to do it with." Chime leaned close to her, despite her attempt to bat him away. "You've got blood trails in your eyes."

Moon took her hand. Her skin was the matte white of extreme age, no trace left of its original color, though there were traces of gray in the creases around her wrist and on her palm. He wondered how many Raksura were left in the court who remembered what Flower had looked like in her youth, if her skin had been bronze or copper or some shade in between, if her hair had been black or red-brown. Stone was more than old enough, and maybe Bone. Pearl might be, but he wasn't sure. He hadn't learned to judge the age of queens yet. He said, "You should rest."

She freed her hand. "I'll rest when we get the seed."

"Yes, that's why I'm risking my life," Moon said pointedly. "We knew what we were doing. You shouldn't have let Jade bring the warriors."

"I know." Flower rubbed her eyes. "I advised her not to go."

That didn't make Moon feel any better. Worried, Chime said, "I didn't know. Did you have a vision that we shouldn't go? And Jade didn't listen?"

"No, it wasn't a vision," she said, annoyed. "I just thought we should wait. Sometimes I don't have visions; sometimes I have common sense. Not that any of you listen to me."

"You could have lied and said it was a vision," Moon said. They both looked at him, nearly identical exasperated expressions. "What?"

"Mentors don't lie about visions." Flower sighed. "I'm going to rest now, hold still."

"What? No, I can't—" Flower climbed into Moon's lap, ignoring his protests. "I need to keep an eye on Rift."

"Balm and the others are watching him and the groundlings. Root is going to come get me when it's my turn," Chime said and settled against Moon's shoulder.

Flower had buried her face against his chest and he automatically put his arms around her. She felt like she was all sharp bones under the light material of her dress; it was like holding a Kek. He didn't remember her feeling this insubstantial. In fact he was fairly certain she had had more solid muscle, like the other Arbora, not that long ago. But before he could think of a way to frame a question, she said, "Stone won't kill him. Not now. You two can fight that out later."

Moon leaned back against the wall. He was painfully sensitive to any mention of Stone at the moment, angry, guilty,
and angry at himself for feeling guilty.

He didn't mean to rest, but he hadn't slept since last night,
so he ended up dozing for a while. He woke when Root
came to get Chime for his turn at watch. Too anxious to stay
still, Moon handed the still-sleeping Flower over to Root.

Everything was quiet. Chime and Song settled down
to watch Rift, who had fallen asleep. Jade was in the other room, sleeping with Balm, and River was up in the top
room on watch. Esom and Karsis had even dozed off, lying
in a corner of the main room on borrowed blankets.

Moon paced an empty room on the far side of the stairwell, thinking of everything they needed to do. Jade and
the warriors had eaten heavily before they left the main-
land, and had brought meat in their packs, wrapped in the
big leaves of the mountain-saplings. It was enough for the
moment, but they were going to have to feed everyone in
the next couple of days. They still had enough metal bits
to buy food, but the market he and Stone had used was too
close to Ardan's tower. Looking for another one would be
a good use of Moon's time, except he couldn't go outside in
the daylight for fear that Ardan's men might be searching
for him.

He had reached a peak of frustration when Song ducked
into the doorway. She said, "Floret's back. She says they
found the place."

☽

"It was just like the groundling said," Floret reported,
when they gathered in the main room again.

Stone had returned from the depths of the tower and
leaned against the wall, as calm as if nothing had happened.
That made Moon's jaw so tight his back teeth ached. Rift
hunched in a corner, with Chime and Balm nearby. River stood near Jade, with a grimly skeptical expression that
seemed to be trying to indicate that he was a leader but not

responsible for anything that went wrong. Esom and Karsis had taken seats on the bench again, and watched anxiously. Flower sat nearby, still trying to wake up. Drift was on guard now, up on the open top floor, and Root and Song stayed near the doorway, as if ready to make a quick escape if there was another fight.

Having left before the argument broke out, Floret didn't notice the undercurrents, or if she did, she was too excited by her news to worry about it. "A big round building, near a flooded part of the city, towards the front of the leviathan. There weren't many groundlings living nearby, and they all seemed to be sick or sleeping, and they smelled funny." *Or drunk,* Moon thought. Floret had probably never seen anyone intoxicated before. She continued, "The only ones who looked normal were guarding the round building's doors. Vine stayed behind to keep watch on it, in case anyone comes to take the seed away."

Jade asked, "There was only one way in?"

"That we could see." Floret glanced at Moon. "Vine and I thought that since you and the two groundlings found an underground passage out of that tower—"

"There could be one into this mortuary." Moon looked at Rift. "Is there?"

Rift shrugged helplessly. "There could be, but I never went there with Ardan. I don't know where the entrance would be."

"If it's guarded on the surface, wouldn't it be guarded underground, too?" Chime ventured, with a cautious glance at Stone.

"The passage down from Ardan's tower wasn't, but then groundlings would have needed ropes or ladders to use it," Moon said. It had looked more like a handy disposal area for garbage or waste. Whatever its original purpose, it had fallen into such disuse it had been nearly forgotten. He didn't remember seeing any other shafts upward to other structures, not that he had been looking closely. "We could try going back and working our way toward the mortuary, but Ardan might still be searching down there for us."

Stone said, in Kedaic, "Why did you think it was a mortuary?"

Moon looked up, startled. Stone watched Esom and Karsis. Confused, since no one had translated the other part of the conversation for them, Esom said, "The building I described, where we think your seed is? Oh, well, Negal and I saw what seemed to be a funeral procession going inside. We asked one of the local men, and he told us the dead were carried there." He looked around, and explained, "We had been trying to find out about the burial customs of the city."

"Why?" Balm asked, her expression critical. She seemed to find this a dubious pursuit at best.

Karsis explained, "Negal believes that it tells a great deal about a people, how they dispose of their dead."

"So they've been storing all the remains of everyone who died on this leviathan for however many turns?" River said, skeptical. Then he added, "Maybe that's what the underground area is for and there is a passage up into the place from there."

Moon was too struck by River actually saying something helpful to reply immediately. Jade turned to Rift. "Is that what they do with their dead?"

"I don't know." Rift twitched uncomfortably. But after a moment of reluctant thought, he added, "I never saw anything down there that looked like a place for burials, but I didn't explore very far. Once I found a way to the surface, I didn't want to risk Ardan finding out where I'd gone."

Jade nodded, her decision made. "We won't go back through the underground, not unless there's no other choice. Moon's right. Ardan might still be looking for you down there. We'll search around this temple." She glanced toward the stairwell, the fall of gray light still illuminating it, and amended, "Some of us will search around it. Unobtrusively, as groundlings. I'll join you when it gets dark."

"I'll go," River said.

Of course you will, Moon thought. He was trapped here

until dark.

Stone pushed away from the wall. Moon tensed all over, but Stone only said, "I'm going out to talk to some groundlings, see what they know about this mortuary place."

It wasn't a bad idea. In fact, it was such a good idea, Moon wished he had thought of it. There was Theri, Rith, and Enad to ask, if they were back from their daily work, or the woman who ran the wine bar. But it was a much touchier subject than how strangers found work in the city. Moon asked, "How are you going to work 'What do you do with your dead?' casually into a conversation?" Tension made the words come out sharper than he meant.

Everyone seemed to tense in apprehension. But Stone just said, "I thought I'd ask somebody who won't notice. Like Dari."

☾

As soon as the sun sank out of the cloudy sky, Moon and Jade left the tower, flying toward the coastline near the leviathan's head.

All through the afternoon, the warriors had taken turns surreptitiously searching the empty buildings in this area, looking for passages down to the underground space. Root, Song, and Floret had been left back at their tower to keep watch over Rift and the two groundlings.

The mortuary temple lay in a shallow valley between the leviathan's shoulders, surrounded by crowded, crumbling stone structures only a few stories high. There weren't many vapor-lights and the empty streets were deeply shadowed, except for the gleam of water. The sea must wash up over the leviathan's head whenever it moved, flooding the streets and leaving puddles behind. Moon could pick out only a few lit windows here and there. This was obviously not a highly prized neighborhood, if it had ever been one.

To the northwest, he could see where the creature's body dipped down, just below the ridge formed by its right arm. The roofs and top stories of flooded buildings were just visible above the dark water.

They banked in to land on the peak of a roof, and Jade climbed down to the alley. Moon paused to watch a groundling lamp-tender make his way across the open plaza in front of the temple's entrance. It was a big, round structure, at least four stories tall, topped by an octagonal dome. A wall formed a roofless court before the entrance, and inside it several blue-pearl guards, probably Ardan's men, stood in front of the metal-bound double doors. The night was cool, and they had gathered around a waist-high brazier. From their postures, they were very bored.

The lamp-tender reached the stand at the far end of the plaza. He filled the well in its base from the heavy canister he carried, closed it, and went on his way. The sputtering vapor-light in its glass cage at the top of the stand brightened noticeably.

"Moon," Jade whispered from below.

Moon climbed down the pitched roof to a ledge where Chime and Balm waited. Chime reported quietly, "Stone just got here. He said he thinks there's something over in that part that's underwater."

"We hadn't looked there yet," Balm said, frustrated. "We thought if there was an open passage, the water would have drained away."

They took flight again, Chime following them toward the flooded section. Balm went to gather the others back from their fruitless search.

They circled down to the flooded street, and Moon landed on a roof and crept to the edge. The street formed a dark passage below, lined with empty stone houses, their doors long ago washed away. Stone was in groundling form, standing balanced on top of a low wall just below this house. The water was as dark as obsidian and gleamed in the moonlight. The place smelled of dead fish and silt and . . . "Do you smell that?" Moon whispered.

Jade answered, "Yes, it's water traveler. There must have been one through here at some point."

Moon hooked his claws into chinks in the mortar and

climbed down the wall. "I saw some yesterday, heading toward the city. But why is the scent here, and not at the harbor?"

Following Moon and Jade, Chime said, "This must be where they do their trading, to keep them away from the groundlings in the harbor. After all, Nobent wanted to eat you when he thought you were a groundling."

Then from below Stone said, "The rumor I heard from Dari is that the city trades the dead bodies of the poor to the water travelers in exchange for edilvine."

"They trade their dead?" Moon stepped cautiously into the water and his claws slipped on the slimy pavement.

"For vines?" Jade added skeptically, hanging from the wall as she waited for Chime to climb down.

"That's the part I haven't figured out yet," Stone admitted, and turned to lead the way along the flooded street.

Behind them, Chime muttered, "The more I hear about this place, the less I like it."

If this was true, the vines had to be something the city wanted or needed, badly. "Maybe they make a drug out of it. Like that smoke, and whatever it is that Dari drinks."

Stone made a noncommittal noise and turned a corner to follow the street as it passed under a high, curved archway. It led into what had been an open court with a covered terrace at the back, supported by pillars carved in the shape of giant lily stalks. Like the street, it was flooded, the water washing the broad steps up to the deeply shadowed terrace. "How did you find this place?" Chime asked.

Stone said, "Once Dari mentioned water travelers, I just followed the scent."

Moon tasted the air as he and Jade followed Stone up the steps and past the columns. The scent of water traveler was much heavier here, clinging to the damp mortar and the furry plants growing across the vaulted ceiling. Stone dug in the pouch at his belt and pulled out a faintly glowing object—one of Flower's spelled rocks.

It cast a dim light over the cracked, stained paving and up to the far wall, revealing a carved scene with life-size groundlings in a procession, carrying a body on a bier. The carving framed a doorway, rusted metal figured with elaborate curving designs. "It's locked, maybe barred on the inside." Stone tugged on the handle, demonstrating.

"Let me see. If you shift under here, you'll break the roof." Jade stepped forward and took the handle.

"Don't break it off," Moon said.

"Moon—" Jade jerked at the door and it yielded with a loud crack. Pieces of a broken lock fell to the ground as the door swung open. Stone lifted his light and it shone down a long ramp that led into darkness.

Stone started to step forward and Chime snapped, "Stop!"

They all froze. Moon flicked a quick glance around the doorway, but he didn't see anything but dark patches of mold. He whispered, "What?"

"I— It's— I've got a funny feeling," Chime said, sounding mortally embarrassed. "Like there's something there."

"A mentor feeling?" Jade asked, and crouched down for a closer look at the pavement just inside the door. Careful not to let any of his frills fall past the threshold, Moon joined her.

"Maybe," Chime admitted.

"I thought all that didn't come back after you changed," Stone said, his tone carefully neutral.

"Well, it hadn't." Chime twitched uneasily. "Until . . . Look, I'm probably wrong."

Jade nudged Moon and nodded toward something on the pavement inside the doorway. "No, you're right," Moon told Chime. About a pace past the threshold was a line of dirt and flotsam that had washed up under the door. It had formed a straight line across the ramp, as if it had encountered some solid object, except there was nothing there. "It's one of Ardan's barriers, like the one around the tower."

Jade sat up, her spines flicking impatiently. "This could be a trap. If they trade with the water travelers, groundlings must come and go through here, and the lock would be enough to keep thieves out. The only reason to put a magical barrier here is to catch us."

"Trap or not, we still have to get in there," Stone said.

"Esom said he could get past the tower barrier without Ardan knowing," Moon said. "If he wasn't lying."

"We'll find out." Jade turned to Chime. "Bring him here."

☾

"It's an untested theory," Esom said, though at least he kept his voice low as he sloshed through the water up the terrace steps.

"Then we'll test it," Chime told him as he climbed down a column from the roof.

Balm and River waited here now too. Drift was on watch, posted on a rooftop above the flooded street, and Vine on the roof of the terrace.

"Finally," Jade muttered, and pushed to her feet. It hadn't really been that long. Moon and Stone had spent the time exploring the terrace, carefully not speaking to each other. Moon had found wilting scraps of a plant that smelled like the vegetation that had grown all over the Kek town on the coast, more evidence for the idea that the water travelers traded here.

River hadn't been in favor of the plan. "You're trusting a groundling thief," he had said. "That's almost as bad as trusting the solitary."

Jade just ignored his objections, and Moon didn't have an argument either. The only basis they had for trusting Esom was that he would be a fool to betray them to Ardan.

Then Floret climbed down the wall, followed by Flower. Jade hissed, startled and angry. "What are you doing here? Who's watching the solitary?"

"Root and Song and the groundling woman," Floret said, her flattened spines conveying guilt and chagrin.

"The groundling woman?" Jade repeated incredulously. "Are you—"

"I made her bring me," Flower interrupted, sounding brisk. She shifted to groundling and shook out her dress. "It smells foul here. Where's this barrier you're all babbling about?"

Silence fell. Moon scratched under the frills behind his ear and kept his mouth shut. After a moment, Jade said through gritted teeth, "Floret, get back to the tower."

Floret fled.

Jade made an effort to drop her ruffled spines. She said, "You should be resting. You've been ill since we reached the coast, whether you'll admit it or not."

"I can rest later." Flower crossed the terrace to the threshold of the doorway, and Stone shone the light on it for her. She nodded and glanced at Chime thoughtfully. "Something's there, all right. It smells of groundling magic."

Chime shrugged uneasily. "I don't know. Maybe it was just a good guess."

Stone snorted, but didn't otherwise comment.

Esom edged forward and frowned at the barrier. Moon switched to Kedaic, asking him, "Can you see it?"

"No, but I can feel it." He held out a hand, carefully not reaching past the doorway. "It's similar to the barrier around Ardan's tower."

"Can you get us past it?" Jade said, her voice tight with impatience.

"I can try." Esom looked around at them all, his expression grim. "I was never able to get outside Ardan's tower to try with that barrier. Tampering with this one could alert Ardan."

River hissed angrily, as if they hadn't all thought of that earlier. "If it does—"

"If it does," Moon cut him off, and finished to Esom, "Then you'll know, for when you go back to his tower to get your friends."

Esom glanced nervously at River, but said, "That's a good point." He stepped forward, hands out, and eased across the threshold, right up to the line of debris that marked the barrier. He crouched down and slid his hands along the pavement.

Moon stepped to the side to see his face. Esom's eyes were shut in concentration, and sweat beaded on his forehead despite the cool air. Flower cocked her head, as if listening to something the rest of them couldn't hear. Chime watched intently, obviously straining his senses to feel what Esom and Flower felt.

Esom turned his head, and said in a hoarse whisper, "Be ready. I won't be able to keep it open very long."

Jade turned to the others. "Vine and Drift will stay here on watch. The rest of you will come with us."

Vine, hanging upside down from the edge of the terrace roof, said worriedly, "Be careful."

Moon happened to look at Balm in time to see an expression of relief cross her face. She had been afraid Jade would leave her behind.

Then Esom slowly eased to his feet and held his arms out as if lifting an invisible curtain. As Esom stood, Moon felt a breath of cooler air, tinged with decay and incense and mold. It was a draft that had been held back by the barrier, now flowing from the doorway. It was more confirmation that Esom was performing as promised.

Esom stepped in, pushed the barrier above his head. He gasped, "Now!"

Moon lunged forward, halted at the threshold as Jade beat him there and slipped past Esom. He followed her, Chime and Flower behind him. River and Balm ducked past Esom, then Stone. Esom stumbled suddenly, staggered forward as if something heavy had fallen on him. Breathing hard, he moved further down the ramp, away from the barrier. "I think . . . I think it's all right. Hopefully Ardan didn't sense that."

Jade said, "You didn't have to come in here. You could have waited outside with Vine."

Esom leaned against the wall, still catching his breath. He made a helpless gesture. "I meant to, but it got a little much for me. It was easier to go forward than back."

"You can say that about a lot of things," Flower said in an aside to Chime.

"Then you'd better come with us," Jade told Esom. She took the light-rock away from Stone and started down the ramp.

Moon had somehow assumed Stone was staying behind. Unable to stop himself from sounding accusing, he said, "Why did you come? This place is too small for you to shift."

Even in the dark, he could tell Stone was giving him that look. "That's none of your business."

"It's my business if you collapse the ceiling on us."

"Both of you, quiet," Jade snapped.

CHAPTER FOURTEEN

The ramp curved down into darkness, the stale air heavy with the scent of old and new decay. The light caught carvings rimed with mold: processions carrying biers, faces twisted in pain and grief. In the dark it was it hard to tell, but they all looked like the blue-pearl groundlings. *Maybe they lived here first*, Moon thought, *and the others all came later.* Maybe it was their crazy idea to tame a leviathan. He suspected many of their descendants had cause to regret it.

They were some distance below street level when their light fell on an opening in the wall that looked as if it had been roughly chiseled out. It stank of edilvine that was gradually fermenting into something else, and as Jade stepped inside they saw bundles of the vine, stuffed into vats filled with dark liquid. Esom made a gagging noise, clapped a hand over his mouth and nose, and retreated back to the corridor.

"That's the drug," Stone said, and stepped past him. "It smells like that wine bar."

The stink of it was intense, but it wasn't having any ill effect on Moon or the other Raksura.

"That's not what we want." Jade turned away, hissing in frustration.

Moon glanced at Chime just in time to see him flinch, as if something had suddenly poked him. "Are you all right?" Moon asked, as they followed Jade down the ramp.

"Yes." Chime kept his voice low. "It's that . . . thing I told you about. It's worse here."

Chime meant he was sensing the leviathan again. Unlike Chime's flash of insight about the barrier over the door, Moon didn't see how an awareness of the leviathan could help them. It wasn't like they didn't know the creature was here. Though maybe Chime would be able to give them warning if it was about to move again.

"What thing?" Flower demanded from behind them.

"You didn't tell her?" Moon said, his attention on the corridor ahead. It still sloped down, curving back toward where the mortuary temple lay on the surface.

Chime protested, "I didn't have a chance—"

Then Jade said, "Quiet, there's light ahead." She handed the light-rock back to Stone, who tucked it away in his pack. After a moment, Moon's eyes adjusted, and he saw the dim white glow somewhere down the corridor.

Following it, they found the passage ended in a wide doorway that led to a much bigger space, scented of earth and cold water and more decay.

They stepped through and made their way down a crumbling set of steps into a cavernous chamber, the ceiling curving up out of sight. It was lit by fading mist-lights, their vapor heavy in the air. The lamps stood on metal stands only ten paces high and secured to the floor with clamps, leaving most of the chamber in heavy darkness. Dozens of thick, square pillars supported the ceiling, and every surface Moon could see, the walls, the pillars, was covered with plaques carved with unintelligible writing. It felt like a deep underground cavern, but they hadn't come down nearly far enough for this space to be completely below the surface. "We're under that dome," Moon said softly.

Her tail lashing, Jade turned to Balm, River, and Chime. "Scout this place."

River flicked his spines in annoyance, but he leapt to the nearest pillar, and scrambled up to jump to the next. Esom ducked nervously as River passed over his head. Balm and Chime bounded away in different directions. Moon tasted the air, but the stench of decay and the competing odor of the fermenting edilvine overlaid any more subtle scents.

Jade looked around again, thoughtful. "This carving—is it writing?"

"It's in the city's native language. I think it's names, the names of the dead." Esom stepped closer to the nearest column and squinted to see in the dim light. "The plaques must cover their burial vaults."

Moon wondered why the inhabitants of this place had chosen that method. He had seen groundling cities that stacked their dead in aboveground mortuary vaults, and it never seemed like a good idea to him. For a city on the back of a leviathan, it was worse. But it might be a holdover from their homeland of Emriat-terrene, an attempt to show their dominance over the leviathan by keeping the same customs they had practiced on solid ground.

Flower frowned. "So this is where the dead are supposed to be put, and instead they sell them to water travelers?"

"That's the rumor," Stone said, suspiciously studying the shadows overhead. "From the death-stink in that passage, I'd say the rumor's true."

Moon said, "They can't be selling all their dead." Surely the water travelers had to have some other food source besides dead groundlings from this city. "Maybe just the ones who can't pay for a place here." Or maybe there was no room left, all the space taken up with the ancient bones of turns and turns of dead.

Flower lifted a brow, dubious. "You have to pay for a place to be dead in?"

Moon shrugged. "Sometimes, in cities. It's a groundling thing."

Balm bounded back to Jade's side and reported, "There's a stairway and a passage, but it goes up, toward the doorway in the plaza that the groundlings were guarding."

"There has to be a trap at that entrance," Moon said. Ardan would be expecting them to come in that way, and had placed the barrier at the water traveler dock to keep them from using it as an escape route.

Scrabbling sounded overhead, and River's voice called out, "There's something here!"

They crossed the dark space, following River's progress back over the ceiling, Esom sprinting to keep up.

They were headed toward the center of the huge chamber, toward an open space ringed by more pillars. In the very center, standing on the paving, was a tall, domed structure made of stained, coppery metal. It stood forty paces high, and was at least that wide. Wrapped around the verdigrised metal was a figured sculpture of a sea serpent, coiled over the curve of the roof. Its triangular head hung over the top and glared sightlessly down at them.

"This is what you want," Esom said, breathing hard as he caught up to them. "This looks like part of another structure, much older than the mortuary."

As the others spread out to examine the structure, Moon stepped close to look at the surface. The metal showed pitting and discoloration that might be from harsh weather, as if it had been exposed to the elements for turns before the mortuary temple had been built atop it. He felt air move across the scales on his feet and looked down at the base of the dome. There was a gap there, too regular to be a crack, and it seemed to stretch all along the foot of the metal shell. "He's right—it's not sitting on the floor. The floor's built around it."

Jade had circled the dome and returned to stand next to Moon. "We're close; we have to be," she muttered. "Does anybody see a door?"

Chime arrived a moment later and dropped lightly down from the ceiling. "I found a small passage going off toward the east, but there were no lights, so I couldn't tell—" He stared at the dome, then threw an uncertain glance at Jade. "We think the seed is in there?"

"We think something's in there," Flower said in frustration, and flattened her hands against the discolored metal.

Then Balm leaned close to one of the metal coils of the serpent. "Wait, I think there's a seam under here. Someone come and—"

"Quiet." Flower turned suddenly and stared intently into the shadows past the pillars. The tension in her body made Moon turn to follow her gaze, but the shadows were empty. The air was undisturbed, not even by a drift of dust motes in the mist-light. The stillness made an uneasy prickle creep up under his spines. Then Flower said, "Something's coming."

The others stirred uneasily. Stone shifted, the sudden blur of dark mist making Esom flinch and stifle a yelp. Looming over them, Stone took in a breath with a hiss.

River shook his head, but watched the darkness warily. "There's nothing here. We searched."

Flower didn't even glance at him. Her voice had a grim edge. "It's coming through the air."

"The wardens," Moon said. They had known this place might be under their protection. "Ardan's guard creatures." But even as he said it, he felt a shiver across his scales as the air turned cold and dry, as if something was drawing the damp out of the stone surfaces. That hadn't happened when the wardens had appeared in Ardan's tower.

Impatient, Jade told Flower, "You look for a way to get into this damn thing while we kill these creatures."

Moon said, "Getting out of the temple is going to be the problem." The air grew tight, making it a little difficult to breathe. *Ardan could have put a hundred of the things down here.* "We don't know how many—"

"Getting out is not the problem," Flower said flatly. She shifted to her Arbora form, her scales white as bone, catching no gleam from the light. "*That's* the problem."

It formed out of the darkness just past the pillars, a shape so large its head brushed the lowest point of the ceiling's arch. Moon's spines flared and he snarled in astonishment as the diaphanous shape solidified into blue scales and massive clawed hands. He saw the fish-like tail with giant fins, stretched away between the pillars. It was the giant waterling that hung in Ardan's tower. From the sickening scent that wafted from it, it was still dead.

It went from insubstantial to solid faster than Moon could shout a warning. It lunged forward with a muffled roar, its unhinged jaw gaped. Stone flared his wings, leaping at its face.

The waterling roared, flung up an arm to push Stone away, but the distraction gave them all a chance to move. Jade snatched Flower out of the creature's path and fell back as the others scattered. Moon darted forward and dodged the giant hand that slammed down a pace from his tail. That too-close look told him it was only too true. The creature was still dead. Its scales were discolored. The flesh around its gnarled claws gray with putrefaction. He jumped over its hand, raked it with his feet claws in passing. It snarled, turned toward him and away from Chime, who had just grabbed Esom and bounded away. Stone hit the waterling's face again, and as it batted him away Moon ducked under its arm, bolted across the floor, and leapt up to the pillar where the others had taken cover.

They all clung to the far side, with Jade, Balm, and River peering around the corner at the waterling. Flower had pulled away from Jade and hooked her claws into the carving to support herself. Chime crouched above her, clutching a terrified Esom. Stone had retreated to the opposite side of the chamber. Hanging from a pillar, he lashed his tail and growled to keep the waterling's attention.

Moon climbed around River, who hissed, "What is that thing?"

"We can kill it." Balm clung to the pillar next to Jade, watching the creature with predatory speculation. "It's not as bad as a major kethel."

"But it's already dead," Moon told them. "It was hanging in Ardan's tower, stuffed."

"He's right," Esom seconded miserably from above them. "It's been reanimated, somehow, or this is a spirit-construction. I really have no idea how Ardan did this."

Jade and Balm stared at Moon and he said, "Me neither."

Flower said, grimly, "There's nothing I can do."

"Then how do we get past it?" Chime asked, frantic. "The serpent-dome—"

"We'll take care of this thing. You, Flower, and the groundling get the dome open," Jade snarled.

"How?" River demanded.

"Go for its face, distract it so Stone can attack." She tensed to spring off the pillar. "Now!"

Jade, Balm, and River took the direct route and sprang from pillar to pillar. Moon swarmed up to the ceiling, then jumped rapidly from carving to carving to drop down on the waterling's head just as the others hit it in the face and shoulders. It roared and flailed at them, then Stone hit it from behind, slamming into its back to dig his claws into its scales.

Its tail flipped up, slapped Stone, and sent him tumbling across the chamber. Moon caught a glancing blow from its hand and it flung him away to bounce off a pillar. He hit the floor and rolled to his feet, his head ringing. River was on the floor, struggling to stand, and Balm clung to a pillar, shaking out her wings. Jade had managed to hold on to the waterling and still tore determinedly at the creature's neck. *Oh, this is going to be a tough one,* Moon thought grimly. He saw Chime, Flower, and Esom had managed to get back over to the little dome, that they were crouched down to examine the gap in the floor. Moon took a deep breath and dove for the waterling again.

He struck at its face, twisted away to avoid its teeth as it snapped at him. The thing didn't react to pain like a living creature, and it didn't bleed, and that was going to be a problem. River struck at its lower body and opened a gash across its stomach, and the creature barely noticed.

As Moon bounced back to a pillar and braced himself for another strike, Jade got in a rip across its throat, just above the decaying gills. That should have opened an artery, but it only released a short burst of foul-smelling fluid. It clawed at the wound and reached for Jade, forcing her to scramble back over its shoulder.

Moon saw that Balm clung to the ceiling carving just above, caught her eye, and pointed emphatically toward the creature's head. Balm nodded, and Moon pushed off the pillar as she dropped from the ceiling. As Balm landed on the waterling's head, Moon darted at its face, distracting it. Then Balm stretched down and raked it across the right eye.

The waterling roared, flailed its arms, and Moon twisted away only to run smack into a giant blue palm.

It slapped him out of the air. Instinct made him snap his wings in to protect them. Moon hit the paving in an uncontrolled tumble, and bounced to a halt to land on his back. The breath knocked out of him, he looked up to see the waterling's big ugly face looming over him, one eye ripped open and leaking puss, the other filled with fury.

Then the waterling jerked back, roaring.

Moon shoved himself back and scrambled away, far enough to see Stone clamped to the creature's back, his teeth and claws sunk deep into its flesh just above its spine. Then Stone twisted his head.

There was a muffled crack and the waterling stiffened, its tail lifted and fell with a thump that Moon felt through the paving. Then it slumped sideways, its body going limp.

Stone released it, spat in disgust, and jumped down off the creature's back. The waterling was still alive, or at least animate. Its one working eye was still aware and furious, and its fingers twitched, though it couldn't seem to move its arms. Moon took a deep breath in relief. He didn't think they could have kept that up much longer. Jade and River glided down from the pillars to land at a safe distance, staring uneasily at the fallen creature.

Then from the dome, Chime shouted, "We've found a way in!"

Moon staggered upright. Chime had somehow managed to lift up the heavy figured metal of the sea serpent's coil, next to the seam Balm had found earlier. Flower leaned down and pried at something hidden under the coil, while Esom tried to peer over her shoulder without getting poked by her spines.

Moon reached them just as Jade arrived, River limping after her. Chime said breathlessly, "This metal piece is on a hinge, see? And there's a—"

"A place for a key." Flower had found a slot in the smooth metal under the coil. The slot was meant for something round, with oddly-shaped projections; it did look like a keyhole.

Esom said, "But we don't have the key. There might be some way to pick it."

Flower stepped back to look at the foot of the dome where it fit against the floor. She straightened up and tapped the edge of the seam. "Stone, push on this. I think this is a separate piece that slides sideways."

Stone leaned in, retracted his claws to plant his hands on the metal, and pushed. With a creak and a squeal of distressed metal, the whole section of the dome started to slide, slowly revealing a split at the seam that leaked dim white light.

They moved hastily back, and Jade pulled Flower away.

As the dome opened, they saw an empty room only half the size of the structure, lit by two hanging vapor-lights. The walls were covered with the now-familiar carvings of blue-pearl groundlings, discolored with age. In the center stood a broad waist-high plinth, the slanting surface set with polished crystals in various blues, greens, golds.

Flower stepped inside and moved toward the plinth. Esom hung back, telling her, "Careful. It could be dangerous."

Moon leaned inside the doorway for a better look at the plinth. Metal plates set beside the crystals were covered with incised writing and figures. *We didn't know it, but this was what we were looking for.* He said, "You know what that looks like?"

Chime nodded, almost bouncing with excitement. "The steering device of a flying boat."

Stone braced himself and gripped the sliding panel more tightly. Apparently the mechanism wouldn't allow it to stay open on its own. Jade stepped over the threshold, and said, "Steering? You mean this is where they control the leviathan?"

Flower frowned at the plinth and shifted back to her

groundling form as if she could see it better that way. "But there's no way to turn it, no way to steer."

Watching anxiously, Esom said, "It has to be some kind of control mechanism. We know the Magisters controlled the leviathan when the city was first built, but they lost the ability." He edged forward, trying to see better but still clearly wary about approaching the device. "Maybe they lost the knowledge to make this work."

At the moment, Moon didn't care. He stepped inside, moved close to the plinth, and tried to make some sense of the objects set into its surface. Only one was even vaguely familiar, a round brass plate protected by a glass cover. Inside was a sliver of metal on a pin, pointing south, that quivered and settled again when he tapped the glass. But Flower was right; unlike the steering column of the Golden Islanders' flying boats, there seemed to be no way to turn the plinth.

"Where's the seed?" River demanded from the doorway. "Is it in that thing?"

Flower shook her head, bared her teeth in an unconscious grimace. "I don't know, give me a moment. We'll have to search this room. There might be more hidden doors."

Jade glanced up, started to speak, then frowned. "Wait, where's Balm?"

Moon turned. Balm wasn't in the room, and wasn't outside with Stone. *Oh no,* he thought, and felt his heart sink. The last time he had seen her, she had been on the waterling's head, just before it had swatted Moon out of the air. She hadn't been there when Stone had hit the creature from behind.

Flower looked up from the plinth, her brow furrowed with worry. "What? Where is she?"

River and Chime turned away from the doorway and stepped back out into the mortuary chamber. "I don't see her," River said. "Unless she's . . ." He hesitated, and stared at the waterling where it lay sprawled across the floor.

Jade threw a worried look at Moon, and started after River.

Moon caught her wrist to stop her at the threshold. "Stay here and help Flower search for the seed. Let us look for Balm." If they had to dig Balm's crushed body out from under the waterling, he didn't want Jade to see it.

She hesitated, her spines flicking uncertainly. She clearly wanted to search for Balm herself, but they had to find the seed and get out of here, before Ardan sent anything else after them. After a moment, she nodded reluctantly and turned back to Flower.

Moon stepped out of the dome. Esom still hovered uncertainly by the doorway, nervously watching Stone. "Should I help them look for the seed?" he asked. "I know you don't trust me, and I don't want to . . ." He waved a hand helplessly. " . . . provoke someone to kill me, but we should hurry before—"

"Ask Flower," Moon told him, distracted. Chime and River moved around the still-twitching body of the waterling, looking for any sign that Balm was trapped under it. He wanted to get over there and help.

Esom drew breath to speak. Then Stone hissed a warning. With a loud plop, five of Ardan's warden-creatures appeared, barely paces away.

Four of them leapt for Stone's head, one came at Moon. Moon yelled a warning to the others, and slung Esom away from the claws that reached for him. Stone tried to hold onto the dome's panel, but the wardens hit him hard, knocked him off balance and away from the dome. The panel snapped shut.

Moon snarled in fury and slashed at the wide, fanged mouth of the warden bearing down on him. It slammed him to the floor, its weight crushed him down, and he sunk his claws into its jaw. He barely held it back from biting his head off.

Hot ichor washed over his hands. The warden jerked back and howled. Moon ripped it across the eyes and scrambled up in time to see more wardens pop into existence all over the chamber, as far as he could see.

Stone leapt for the nearest group and Moon lunged after him. Jade and Flower were trapped in the dome. *Unless there's a latch—there has to be a way to open it from—* Then the wardens charged him, and Moon had no time to think of anything but fighting.

Moon and Stone fell back across the big chamber, fighting warden after warden. Stone took them on directly. Moon darted in to slash at them, harried them into Stone's reach, or finished off the walking wounded. Moon was peripherally aware of Chime and River doing the same, protecting their flanks. He kept getting glimpses of Esom, as he scrambled to stay behind them and away from the wardens. They must have killed dozens of the creatures but more came. Ardan was throwing every resource he had against them.

Then River called out, "We're nearly to the wall! What now?"

Moon risked a look and saw they were nearly against the far wall of the chamber. There was a wide chased-metal gallery built across it, about thirty paces up, probably meant as an access to the tombs there. Unless Ardan had wardens who could fly, it would provide a needed respite. "Get up there!" he shouted to the others.

River bounced up to the gallery, and Chime snatched up Esom and followed. Stone pitched one last warden across the chamber and climbed after them, Moon close behind.

Panting, dripping with the creatures' bitter blood, Moon gripped the railing, looking over the chamber. He couldn't see the dome from here. It was lost in the shadows. He could see the scattered, bleeding bodies of the wardens. The dozen or so still on their feet edged forward. And past the first row of pillars stood a group of blue-pearl guards. They surrounded a single robed figure: Ardan.

"He's here," Moon said, glancing at the others. "The groundling magister."

Chime and River were breathing hard, their scales covered with claw marks, the nicks and scratches of near-misses. Esom was flattened back against the wall, his expression numb with fear. Stone curled around the railing, most of him resting on the delicately incised metal of the gallery floor, tail dangling and deceptively relaxed. He snorted derisively, making his opinion of Ardan clear.

The magister moved forward, to the last row of pillars, barely fifty paces from them. He called out, "Please, let me speak to you!"

"We can hear you," Moon said, pitching his voice to carry.

Ardan stepped forward again, and shaded his eyes against the glare of the nearest vapor-light. Squinting up at them, he said, "Surely we can come to some agreement."

Moon hesitated. He knew Ardan had a talent for sounding sincere, but it was hard to resist the appeal. Ardan must not know Jade and Flower were trapped in the dome. If they could just talk him into letting them get back over to it . . .

Esom whispered urgently, "Don't believe anything he says."

River hissed in contempt. "He only wants to talk because we're winning."

"We're not winning by that much," Chime said, keeping a nervous eye on the wardens.

Stone jerked his head, telling Moon to go ahead and talk.

Moon spread his wings and dropped down from the gallery to land lightly on the floor.

Ardan regarded him for a moment. He was breathing roughly too, as if he had been in a battle. It must have cost him an enormous effort to send all these creatures after them. It was a relief that it wasn't much easier to send them than to fight them. Ardan said, "I should have taken even more precautions, but I didn't realize Esom knew where the seed was." He hesitated, and looked up at the balcony again. "I didn't realize there were so many of you here, or that one was so . . . formidable. I don't see Rift. I assume he's unhurt?"

So all their speculation was right and the seed was here, hidden in the dome. *At least all this wasn't for nothing,* Moon thought. "Why do you care about Rift? Worried you missed a chance to have a Raksura stuffed and mounted?"

Ardan's voice tightened. "He's my friend. I don't want him injured. He's told me what he can expect from his own people. Your reaction to him was proof enough of that."

"He stole our seed. He knew what that would do to the tree," Moon said, and thought, *He thinks Rift is here. He wants him to hear this.* "Give it back, and we'll leave. That's all we want." It was worth a try.

"I'm afraid I can't." Ardan's voice was low and intense. "I persuaded Rift to help me take it from the forest because I had no other choice. It is a powerful artifact, and it means the survival of everyone in this city." He stepped forward, and his men spread out to either side of him, watching Moon nervously. "Over the turns, our own magic has waned. We have to use substitutes, objects that carry inherent power that can be transferred to the devices that keep the leviathan from sinking below the surface or thrashing until it destroys the city. When I brought the seed here, the other magisters were only days away from losing what little control over the creature we have." He spread his hands. "You must understand. Your people can find another place to live. Mine have no choice."

Moon said, "We both know that's not true."

Ardan's face went still, and a flush of heat darkened the blue skin of his cheeks and forehead.

Moon's spines twitched. He had meant the traders' ships, that the people here could leave the city if the magisters and the other wealthy residents bought the use of them for an evacuation. But that wasn't what Ardan had heard. *Jade was right.* It wasn't a coincidence that the leviathan had moved further out to sea. *Ardan is controlling it.*

Ardan said, thickly, "Then I'm glad we had this conversation."

Then the floor dissolved under Moon's feet, crumbling to dust. He dropped, shot his wings out to stop himself. Air rushed straight up from below and he caught it, played it across his wings to stay aloft. Several of Ardan's men weren't so lucky, and flailed as they tumbled down toward a great dark space below, along with fragments of the floor.

Moon couldn't see what was down there, where the wind came from. The thick stench of the leviathan filled the air.

Moon twisted enough to get a look behind him. The balcony had broken into a twisted mass of metal supports, and Stone clung to a post. River and Chime clung to him, and Esom clung to Chime. *I'd tell Esom he was right, but I think he already knows,* Moon thought, and looked back up at Ardan.

The Magister had gone to his knees, his face turned dull blue-gray by the terrible effort of destroying the floor.

The rush of air, the leviathan's breathing, Moon thought suddenly. That wind came from the leviathan itself. There was some opening just below them, and in a moment it would— Moon flapped, tried to get out of the draft, shouted, "Stone, get away—"

The air reversed with a terrible suction as the creature inhaled. It dragged Moon down, tangled his wings. The pressure was terrible, irresistible. It dragged the air out of his lungs and made the edges of his vision go black. He flipped over in time to see it yank River and Chime away from their grip on Stone. Stone made a wild grab for them. The suction jerked him off the remnants of the balcony, shattered metal hurtling down after him.

Moon swore helplessly and used every bit of his remaining strength to wrench his wings in. The force of it rolled his body over again, so at least he could see what they were plunging into. He had the terrible feeling he already knew.

All he could see was a great dark space, then his eyes adjusted. It was a crater, a giant black crater in the back of the leviathan, surrounded by a ridge of scaly skin. *An air hole,* Moon thought, sick with dread, as they dropped helplessly down into it.

CHAPTER FIFTEEN

They fell, dragged down by the powerful suction of the leviathan's breath. Moon couldn't even struggle, the pressure so intense he couldn't breathe. He thought his body would snap in half before he had a chance to smash into anything.

At first the darkness was complete. Then Moon caught flashes of blue light, just enough to show him that he was falling past a dark-gray surface ridged by scaly bone rings. He had a hard time believing this was really happening. He had always thought he would probably die by being eaten. Being inhaled by a leviathan wasn't a fate he had considered.

Then he slammed into something ropy and semi-porous, bounced off it with stunning force, and tumbled through an opening in the surface.

Knocked nearly out of his wits, it took Moon moments to realize he was falling free into a huge open space lit by an eerie blue glow, that the pressure was gone. He spread his wings and cupped them to slow his headlong plunge.

Thick webs stretched from all sides of the big chamber and formed a shadowy, complicated architecture, as if he were surrounded by the towers and galleries of a near-transparent city. The moving lights were small bundles of blue-tinged phosphorescence, suspended on long poles and somehow attached to the heads of creatures like giant slugs that crawled ponderously over the heavy cables of the webs. The light from those ambulatory bundles lit other shapes, big ones, small ones, that moved through the webs, hopped from strand to strand, or glided on ridged wings.

Oh, this is . . . different. Horrible and different. Moon's throat was too dry to swallow, but at least he could breathe. He looked up, saw Stone not far above him, and the smaller figures of Chime and River. Chime had, somehow, managed to hold on to Esom. Moon wasn't sure Esom was going to thank him for that; it might have been a kinder end to die in the fall down onto the leviathan's skin.

Moon looked down and spotted a solid mass below, some distance from the walls. It was an oblong shape, a couple of hundred paces long and wide, suspended near the center of the space. Moon aimed for it and landed on the rubbery surface, then pulled his wings in and dropped to a defensive crouch. River and Chime landed on either side of him, Esom still clinging tightly to Chime. Stone reached it a few moments later. He snapped his wings in and crouched low.

The bulk of Stone's body looming over them gave Moon what was probably a false sense of security. He peered into the dim blue light; nothing seemed to be coming for them, but that had to be just a matter of time. "What is this place?"

"Didn't we fall into the monster?" River said, a thread of panic in his voice. "Where are we?"

"Parasites." It was Esom who gasped it out. "Colonies of parasites . . ."

"He's right," Chime said, sounding near the edge of panic himself. "These creatures live inside the leviathan. They could be animals, or intelligent, I don't know."

Moon looked around again, his gorge rising, and wished he could unhear that.

"They carved out this space, out of its body? Wouldn't that hurt?" River said, clearly still dazed from horror.

"Apparently they don't care," Moon snapped. Next to him, Stone made a low, soft growl and nudged Moon with a claw. Moon turned, saw Stone was staring at a thin column about twenty paces away. Glinting faintly in the blue light, it stretched up out of a ridged aperture in the gray rubbery ground. Moon looked up, traced its path upward . . . to where it connected with a thick strand of web crossing the chamber. *Oh, no . . .* This mass wasn't suspended from the web; it was creating the web. "What are we standing on?"

Chime and River turned to look, just as the surface under them rippled. From the near end of the mass, an immense head suddenly loomed up. It had multiple glaring eyes and a round, fanged mouth. Spiked tentacles stretched up from its sides, as the whole creature started to curve up and inward toward them.

Stone surged over their heads and hit the creature's face claws first. Moon yelled, "Up and over, now!" and sprang into the air.

He couldn't tell if Chime and River understood his incoherent command or if they were just blindly following him. As they took flight, Moon saw a tentacle whip toward Chime, who was still burdened with Esom. Moon twisted toward it and slashed at the slick surface. It twitched at him, missing Chime, just as another tentacle slapped at Moon's leg and knocked him into a sideways tumble.

He rolled, frantically tried to get his wings under control, and saw the tentacle dive toward him. Then River swooped past and swiped at the tentacle with his foot claws. It flinched, hesitating just long enough for Moon to drop out of reach.

Still falling away, Moon looked up at the creature. From the bottom it had a beetle-like carapace, the edges bristling with tentacles. It roared as Stone whipped over its head and gave it one last swipe with his tail. Stone tore through the tentacles that reached for him and dropped out of its range.

There was movement all over the web as the big creature turned ponderously on its supporting strand to follow them. There was no place to go but down, and Moon dove.

He dropped until the passage narrowed again and the lighted webs were left behind. He had no idea where he was going, and the light was running out, when Chime shouted, "Wait, stop!"

Moon swerved in toward the wall and found a perch to cling to. Chime hit the wall next to him and gripped it tightly. River landed on the far side of Chime, and Stone slammed into a spot just above them.

"There!" Chime pointed urgently at something about ten paces below. "We'll be safe if we go that way!"

"Safe?" River growled. "We were standing on something's belly!"

"But we have to go that way!" Chime sounded frantically certain. "All right, it's not safe, but it's better than this!"

Moon had no intention of arguing. He swung down, scrabbled along the wall, and felt the edge of an opening. It was a rough-edged hole in the creature's flesh, about ten paces across. "This way, come on!"

Chime climbed down and slipped past him into the passage, as Esom gasped something in his own language. River hissed reluctantly as he followed. Stone's large form moved down, and hung onto the wall over the opening. "You're too big," Moon told him. "Shift, I'll catch you!"

For a long heartbeat he didn't think Stone would do it, from stubbornness or fear of being so vulnerable here or both. "Come on!" Moon yelled. "There's no other way!"

Then Stone shifted. Moon lunged forward and grabbed his arm; the sudden weight nearly jerked him off the wall. Stone managed to grip Moon's shoulder and dragged himself up. Moon heaved, lashed his tail, and hauled them both through the opening.

They tumbled down over a bumpy surface, into complete darkness, and landed hard with Stone on top. Moon felt Stone sit up, heard him fumble in his pack for their light. Esom's harsh breathing sounded from a few paces to Moon's left, and Chime and River were putting out such a fear-scent he could smell them even over the leviathan's stench. Stone managed to get the rock uncovered and the light glowed from between his fingers as he held it up.

They were in a passage maybe fifteen paces wide, the rough, lumpy walls and floor a sickly blue color. Stalactites covered the ceiling, leaking a chalky-colored ichor. Moon pushed away from Stone and shoved to his feet. The passage wound off into the creature's body and split into multiple tunnels, each disappearing into darkness. He could still hear, distant and muffled, the familiar rush-pause-rush of the leviathan's breath.

Chime and River crouched nearby, Esom huddled between them. "So where are we now?" River said. From his expression, he wasn't sure he really wanted to know.

Chime turned to the nearest wall and ran his hand over it. "I think these are teeth marks. I think something gnawed its way through here."

Moon looked down the dark tunnel again. Revulsion made his skin creep under his scales. "Another parasite?"

Chime nodded, his eyes wide and frightened. "Maybe more than one."

Stone pushed to his feet with a half-snarl. "We'll follow it. Maybe it got out." He paused and glanced at Moon, his expression opaque. "Thanks."

Moon flicked his spines in a half-shrug, avoiding his gaze. "We need to move."

River started forward and hissed in disgust as his frills brushed against a dripping stalactite. Chime followed, but Esom still huddled on the floor. Moon reached down, caught him by the shoulders, and pulled him to his feet.

Esom stared blankly. The right lens of his spectacles was cracked and his eyes were shocky. "Esom, you have to stay with us." Moon couldn't think of anything reassuring to say. They were trapped inside a leviathan, standing in a tunnel gnawed out by giant parasites. Going blank with terror was a perfectly rational way to react, especially for a groundling.

Esom blinked, took a gasping breath. "I— Yes, of course." Awareness came back into his eyes, and he nodded sharply. "I'm fine, I'm really fine. I just had a moment there."

If they ever got out of this, Moon was going to have a moment of his own. A long one. Tugging Esom along, he moved after the others.

They picked their way cautiously along, the light making shadows leap across the weird shapes of the stalactites. The tunnels formed a honeycomb, split off, then rejoined again. Whatever had chewed out all this, it hadn't needed to make an even surface to walk on, and they had to clamber over lumps and broken chunks. Esom had the most difficulty, stumbling and breathing harshly. Stone, hampered by his groundling form, couldn't move fast either.

The quiet wore on Moon's nerves, and he couldn't stop thinking about Jade, and Flower. And poor Balm. And it was his fault they were down here. He said, "Ardan did this because he thought I knew he'd been lying all this time. He can do more than just keep the leviathan from sinking, he's steering it, telling it where to move and when and how far."

Chime said, "It's not your fault. He was going to get rid of us anyway. He was just making sure Rift wasn't with us." He glanced at Moon. "He must really like Rift. That's very creepy."

Esom said, slowly, "He wouldn't be afraid of the people. He's too powerful." He sounded better, calmer, though his voice was still shaky. "It's the other magisters, like Lethen. They must not realize he can send the leviathan anywhere he wants. He's doing it to keep control of the traders, moving it so the ones who don't pay him off can't find it."

Too bad we can't tell them about it, Moon thought bitterly. The resulting battle would be interesting to watch, but not much help to them. The other magisters wouldn't want to give the seed back, either.

Then Stone said, "Chime, how did you know this passage was here? Did you feel it?"

"Yes. As we got closer, I just knew it was there in the wall. It hurt, like a—" Chime waved a hand beside his head. "I can't describe it."

"I thought you weren't a mentor anymore," River said, making it sound like an accusation. "That's what you told Pearl."

"I know what I told Pearl. I'm not a mentor anymore." Chime's spines flicked in irritation. "This is different. It's not augury, it's . . . flashes of insight."

Stone said, "Can you tell if that big spider thing is coming down here after us?"

"The one we landed on?" Chime shook his spines uneasily. "No, I can't tell."

"But it's too big to get into these passages," Esom protested, stumbling after them.

Moon wasn't going to explain, but River said, darkly, "It could eat its way through here, just like the things that made this tunnel."

Esom didn't reply for a moment. Then he said, bleakly, "Of course it could."

It was hard to judge the passage of time, but Moon didn't think they had traveled much of a distance when Stone said, "Here we go." He stopped and held the light high. It fell on an irregular hole in the top of the passage that led upward. "That could go all the way to the outer skin."

"It's worth a try," Moon said in relief. It might be the way this particular set of parasites had gotten down here in the first place. Even if it didn't go all the way through the outer skin, if there was room for Stone to shift, he might be able to tear an opening for them to slip through.

"Wait." Esom's expression was pained and reluctant. "As much as I want to get out of here . . . there's a magical source that way." He pointed down the bigger tunnel that wound off through the leviathan's flesh. "If it's your seed, I don't know how or why it would be down here, but—"

No, Moon wanted to say, *we need to get out now, we need to go after Jade and Flower.* "Are you sure?"

Esom winced in resignation. "Unfortunately, yes. Believe me, I'd rather go up."

Stone turned to Chime. "Is he right? Can you feel it?"

Chime's spines ruffled again. "No. I'm not a mentor anymore."

Stone eyed him deliberately. "You knew there was a barrier over the outer door."

A muscle worked in Chime's jaw. He said, flatly, "I can't do magic like Esom does."

"How do you know you can't?" Esom challenged. "Did you ever try?"

Chime hissed at him, and Esom drew back, affronted.

"I hate trusting the groundling, but we have to look." River faced Stone. "We can't come all this way and—"

"We know," Moon snapped. He looked at Stone. "We'll take the other tunnel."

Stone gave him a grim nod.

They followed the bigger tunnel, passing two more passages that led directly upward. Moon gritted his back teeth and resisted the urge to alter their course.

Moon sensed the change ahead before he saw or heard anything. He halted abruptly. The others froze in place behind him, but Esom stumbled. It didn't matter. Moon had the feeling that whatever blocked the airflow ahead already knew they were here. Nothing came at them, but after a moment he heard movement, scraping, a low grunt.

Moon eased forward. As the tunnel curved, he saw another narrow passage that intersected with it at a sharp angle. A group of beings climbed up it toward them.

They had mottled gray-white bodies, heavily muscled, with oblong heads, eyes protected by heavy folds, and wide mouths. Their skin was made up of tough armor plates, overlapping like scales. Moon realized these were the same pallid creatures he had seen in the space below the city, that bore a superficial resemblance to the big tree frogs from the suspended forest. *So the tunnels that lead upward probably do go all the way out,* he thought. Several pushed forward to block the main tunnel, the creatures in the back jostling each other for a look at the Raksura.

"What do they want?" Chime whispered nervously.

He had spoken in Kedaic, which everyone except River had been speaking for Esom's benefit. It was a surprise when the creature in the lead rasped in the same language, "These tunnels belong to the Thluth. What do you want here?"

"We need to get past," Moon said, his voice tight with tension. "That's all."

"You use our tunnels?" The leader's mouth split in a wide, fanged grin. It had the largest, sharpest teeth Moon had ever seen in something groundling-sized, well-suited for gnawing through leviathan hide. It nodded toward Esom, who stood frozen behind Chime. "We let you—if you give us something to eat. One of them will do."

Moon heard Chime's and River's spines rattle in reflex, and Stone made a derisive hiss. The skin under Moon's claws started to itch. He said, "That better be a joke." He had had a bad day, and this was about all he could take.

The leader surged forward aggressively and grinned, its hot, foul breath washing over him. It said, "No joke. Give us food."

Moon slashed it across the throat, his claws sliding between the armor plates to sink into the thin line of vulnerable white skin. Hot blood splashed on his scales as the creature gurgled and staggered back. The other Thluth caught it as it sunk to the ground. Moon said, "You want any more, or is that going to be enough for you?"

The other Thluth drew away, watching him warily, and some prudently scrambled back down the side passage. Moon stayed where he was, flexing his claws, as Stone prodded Chime and Esom past. River eased by after them. Moon followed, watching as the Thluth dragged their leader's body away.

They continued up the tunnel. After a moment, Esom said shakily, "Thank you for not feeding me to them. I appreciate—"

"Later," Stone told him, and flicked a look back at Moon. "Don't talk right now."

They didn't pass any other intersecting passages. The tunnel itself began to get smaller, rougher, and they had to duck under the stalactites. Moon set his jaw, and suppressed the urge to go back and kill a few more Thluth. They had demanded tribute for passage to a dead end.

But as the tunnel narrowed to a point where Moon thought they would have to turn around, they came to a large hole chewed out of the wall.

Stone stopped in the entrance and tasted the air as he held up the light, though all Moon could smell was rotting leviathan.

"This could be something," Stone muttered, and stepped through the opening.

Moon followed with the others, and climbed through into a round chamber. It stretched upward, far beyond their light, the ceiling lost in darkness. A round column in the center plunged down into the leviathan's flesh.

Moon paced impatiently around the chamber to make certain it was a dead end. He didn't know why the Thluth had chewed this space out, but there was nothing here for them. "This isn't it. We need to keep moving."

"No, we're in the right place," Esom said. He had stepped to the edge of the center shaft to examine the column. "I don't think this is the source, but arcane emanations are echoing through it." He glanced at them. "I meant the source of the magical power—"

Teeth gritted, Chime said, "They understood you."

"—must be in contact with it," Esom finished stubbornly.

Stone tilted his head, staring hard at the column. "He's right. That's metal under there."

"What?" Moon came back to his side and squinted to see. He had thought it was just another part of the leviathan's flesh. Looking more closely, he saw verdigrised metal glinting between calcified lumps and dried ooze.

Chime went to the wall of the chamber and ran his hand over the surface. "I don't see any teeth marks. I don't think the parasites made this chamber. Maybe the groundlings cut it out so they could put that thing here."

Moon turned back to the column. Maybe they had found something after all. "So this is anchoring part of the city to the leviathan?"

"Maybe," Esom said, "But it must be in contact with something magical—"

"Up there somewhere?" River demanded, looking up into the space above them.

Stone held the light up, but all they could see was the column stretching up into darkness. Stone said, "River, take the light, climb up there. Not the column, go up the wall."

River took the light-rock, clutched it in his teeth, and started up the chamber's wall. It was the first time Moon had ever seen him do anything without a bad attitude. They watched his progress, the light growing smaller, until they stood in heavy darkness. Moon estimated River had gone about a hundred paces up the wall when he stopped. Moon hissed out a curse. River's light shone on the roof of the chamber, where the leviathan's flesh had grown back to enclose the column and close off any passage or opening. "If there was anything up there, we can't get to it," he said, frustrated.

Then Chime said, "Look, look at this!"

Moon turned around. It was too dark to see Chime, but it was obvious what he was pointing at: a faintly glowing shape outlined against the column. It was round, like a panel in the metal, with something behind it giving off a faint illumination.

Moon stepped close, stumbled on Chime's tail, and moved him out of the way. He ran his hands over the panel to feel for seams under the encrustations. "Careful," Esom said anxiously. "An arcane power source could be very dangerous."

"The seed wouldn't glow, would it?" Chime said, sounding doubtful. "Unless they did something drastic to it."

Stone growled in frustration. "Get it open."

Moon growled back at him and dug his claws into the crusted ooze to strip it off the old metal. River climbed back down the wall, bringing the light-rock. The glow from behind the panel faded as the chamber grew brighter, but Moon found the seams. He worked his claws in and yanked on the panel. It gave way so abruptly he stumbled backward.

River pushed off the wall, landed beside Moon, and held out the light-rock. Behind the panel was a small compartment, and mounted in it was a discolored metal plaque set with rough crystals, about the size of Moon's palm.

Esom said, "That's it, that's the arcane source I've been sensing!"

Moon paced away, too angry to speak. *That's not it. Jade and Flower are still trapped up there, Balm could be dead, and we don't even have the damn seed to bargain with.*

Behind him, Stone hissed with bitter disappointment. "It's not the seed," River said, pointedly speaking in Kedaic so Esom could understand him.

"I never said it was your seed," Esom said, exasperated. "I said—"

"What is it doing to the leviathan?" Stone asked him, cutting across the budding argument. "It has to be doing something, or it wouldn't be down here."

"I don't know." Esom lifted his hands helplessly. "It could be helping to control the creature—"

"It has to be," Chime broke in, his spines shaking with excitement. "Think about where we are. We went a long way down, but we're not that far from where we started."

"Maybe five hundred paces, give or take." Moon tilted his head, and found that place inside himself that always knew where south was. "We're below the mortuary temple, just in the center—"

Chime finished, "We're under that dome, under that steering device." He thumped the column. "This thing could be part of it."

"Huh." Stone looked up the column again.

"But we can't get out that way," River said impatiently. "There's no opening. The flesh closes in around the top of this pillar-thing."

"Yes, but . . ." Moon stepped back to the column, reached into the compartment and touched the crystal thing gingerly.

"I still think you should be careful," Esom persisted.

Moon nudged the device a little. It wiggled back and forth, but didn't seem to do anything. "Could this be how they control the leviathan?"

They all looked at Esom, who wiped his forehead wearily. "I don't know. Our ship the *Klodifore* works by arcane power, using the metora stone as fuel. But it still has a wheel, a steering mechanism. There wasn't anything like that on the device we saw. Not that I could tell, anyway."

"But it's not a ship, it's a creature." Chime eased forward and leaned close to the compartment. "Maybe the device controls a spell that lets the groundlings communicate with it."

Esom nodded, preoccupied. "Oh, that's a thought. Yes, I think that's likely."

If they were right . . . it didn't matter how many seeds Ardan stole, they were all useless without this. This could be the whole key to Ardan's power, the power of all the magisters. Moon reached for the crystal-studded metal piece, gripped it, and twisted it free.

As it snapped loose he felt the ground underfoot tremble. The rhythmic rush of the leviathan's breath halted mid-inhale, the silence sudden and absolute. Stone cocked his head thoughtfully, listening. Esom and Chime were wide-eyed in alarm, while River's spines twitched nervously. The moment stretched, then the creature's breath whooshed out in a long sigh.

As the breathing resumed, Chime said, "It felt that. I don't know what happened, exactly, but it felt that."

Moon weighed the metal piece in his hand. "Good. Maybe Ardan felt it too."

☾

They went back down the Thluth tunnel, and took one of the vertical passages upward. The Thluth didn't appear to demand tribute again.

The passage worked its way up through the leviathan's hide along a narrow and twisty path. After a short distance it turned into a vertical shaft, too steep for Esom or for Stone in his groundling form.

Esom groaned but didn't otherwise protest being carried by Chime again. River hesitated, looking dubiously at Stone. Stone hissed in annoyance and turned to Moon.

Moon supposed that if Stone had to be carried, he would rather it be by another consort, no matter how awkward. So they started up with Stone's warm weight hanging on to Moon's neck, and it was just as awkward as Moon could possibly have imagined.

The pocked surface was slick and pieces chipped off under their claws, but the leviathan's breathing grew steadily louder, a welcome sign that they were nearing an opening to the surface. River, unencumbered, got a little ahead.

They climbed in silence for a while, until Stone muttered, "I remember why the Arbora hate this."

"It's not like we have a choice," Moon answered, concentrating on feeling for the next good claw-hold.

There was another long silence, broken only by whispers from somewhere below, where Esom seemed to be interrogating Chime about mentor abilities. Chime's answers were tinged with irritation. Then Stone said, "I don't kill solitaries just because they're solitaries. And I would never have killed you."

It was so unexpected, Moon's claws almost slipped off the wall. Stone waited until he recovered, then continued, "If I'd decided you were crazy, or lying to me, I would have left you behind. I wanted you with me at Sky Copper so I could watch your reaction, make sure you'd never seen a court before. But by the time we got there, I'd already made my decision." He added, "You little idiot."

Moon hissed reflexively. After a moment, he said, "Sorry." Deeply reluctant, he admitted, "I'm still not . . . good at this."

"You'll get over it," Stone told him.

Above them, River hissed to get Moon's attention. He looked up and realized they were very near the top. The space above them was dark, and the hole through the last layer of hide was small. A little ahead of Moon, River stopped just below the opening. He pointed to himself, then up. He was saying he should go first, since he was the only one not carrying someone. *I hate it when he's right.* Moon nodded for him to go ahead.

River climbed to the lip of the opening, stopped to peer out, then scrambled over the edge.

After a tense moment, he leaned back down to whisper, "Come up."

Moon gave Stone a boost, then followed him. As he climbed out, he knew where he was by scent and sound before his eyes adjusted to the dim green glow from the phosphorescent molds. They were in the underground space below the city, the stone of its foundations high above, supported by giant pillars and columns. The foundations were much lower here than in the area below Ardan's tower, which was closer to the midpoint of the leviathan. The highest supporting arch was barely fifty paces above their heads.

Esom scrambled out with Chime right behind him. Chime stood and looked around, his spines flicking uneasily. Esom collapsed on the lumpy leviathan hide and said in relief, "I never thought I'd be glad to see this place again. Now it looks homey and welcoming."

"I wouldn't go that far," Moon said. He turned to Stone and pointed north, toward the leviathan's head. "The mortuary temple is back that way."

Stone's mouth twisted in an ironic grimace. He said, "Let's hope Ardan's not expecting us." Then he shifted.

Stone's larger body flowed into being so fast that Esom yelped and bumped into Chime as he flinched away. "Sorry," he muttered. "I'm just not used to it when he does that."

CHAPTER SIXTEEN

Moon led the way across the dark space, finding the way back toward the mortuary temple. They moved in long bounds, and Chime carried Esom. That had to be rough on Esom, though Chime had partially extended his wings so he could make each landing a fairly light one. Esom didn't complain, but kept a grimly tight grip on Chime's collar flanges. There wasn't another choice. They had to move fast and they couldn't leave Esom behind down here.

The foundations and heavy buttresses above them dropped even lower, the columns grew wider. Then Stone came to an abrupt halt, head cocked as he listened. They all stopped and froze into place. Moon tasted the air, but all he could scent was rot and leviathan. It was hard to hear over the rush of the leviathan's breath, but he was certain there was a voice from somewhere to the east, not far away. An oddly familiar voice. Incredulous, Chime whispered, "Is that Root?"

Before Moon could answer, River interposed, "Of course it is. He's the only one who can't shut up."

"He's not the only one," Moon told him. Stone growled low in his throat and bounded away to follow the thread of sound.

The supporting pillars were closer together through this area, blocking the view, but as they traveled Moon started to make out some movement in the hazy light ahead. At least it was no mystery how the others had gotten down here. Vine and Drift would have seen Ardan's men enter the mortuary from the main entrance, and had gone back to the tower-camp for help. Now they must be trying to find the underground entrance to the temple, which was what Moon would have done in their place.

Ahead, dim light glittered off scales and Moon spotted the Raksura, gathered with their backs to a pillar. He couldn't tell what threat they faced . . . Then his eyes adjusted and he thought in disgust, *Oh, that's typical.* The Raksura confronted a large group of the pale armored Thluth.

Moon shot ahead of Stone, River, and Chime. Coming up behind the Thluth, he swarmed up the nearest pillar, hopped to the next to get above them. In the group of Raksura he saw Vine, Floret, Song, Root, Drift . . . *And Balm!* She was leading the others, and faced the Thluth leader, her spines bristling. Relief was sharp and almost painful. Balm was alive; he just wished he could tell Jade.

And there was one extra Raksura: Rift was here, too.

Moon saw enough to tell the confrontation with the Thluth was angry. The Thluth seemed to be demanding tribute and Balm and the others weren't taking it much better than Moon had. The Thluth leader spoke, pushed forward aggressively. Balm lunged to swipe him back.

Then Stone slammed between the pillars and sent the Thluth scrambling frantically away. Moon leapt down behind the leader.

He wasn't certain if this was the same tribe of Thluth, but apparently it didn't matter. The leader spun around, saw Moon, and bellowed a wordless warning. It wasn't needed, since the other Thluth were already loping rapidly into the shadows. The leader bolted away, desperate to catch up with the others.

Chime and River arrived, and Esom staggered away as soon as Chime set him on his feet. Then Karsis darted out from behind the pillar and flung herself at Esom. They hugged each other, speaking rapidly in their own language, Karsis laughing with relief. Moon tried not to be envious.

"Balm!" Chime shouted. He grabbed her in a hug, and released her immediately when she gasped, "Ow!"

"Are you all right?" Chime asked her worriedly, holding onto her arm to steady her. "We couldn't find you. We thought you were dead!"

"No, I'm fine," Balm insisted. At close range, she didn't look fine. She had scratches and dark patches in her golden scales, and her left wing-join had a dark, livid scrape. She asked, "But what happened? I thought you were trapped."

"We got out the hard way," Chime told her. "It was horrible, but it worked."

Drift greeted River enthusiastically, Root bounced around trying to greet everybody, and the others gathered around, excited, relieved, and demanding immediate answers. Only Rift hung back, watching them uneasily. "We thought the groundling sorcerer had you," Floret said to Moon. "Balm saw—"

Balm frowned suddenly. "Wait, where's Jade and Flower?"

Moon said it quickly, to get it over with. "They didn't get out. They were trapped in that dome we found. We opened it, but then the warden-creatures attacked, and the door slid shut."

That put an end to all the relieved excitement. Balm hissed in dismay, and looked from Moon to Stone. "Are they all right? Can the sorcerer get to them?"

"We don't know." Moon didn't want to think about that right now. "How did you get away?"

Balm's spines flicked in agitation, but she let her question go. "The waterling threw me back toward the other side of the chamber, and I hit the wall and fell to the floor. I must have been knocked out for a time. The next thing I knew, some groundlings ran right past me. When I managed to stand, those warden-creatures swarmed me and I flew up the first passage I found. It was the one that went outside to the plaza, where the guards were. They shot darts at me, but I got past them." Her expression was bleak. "I found Vine and Drift, and we tried to get back in through the entrance in the flooded area, but the magical barrier was still there. So we went to the tower to get the others, and we decided to come down here to look for an underground passage into the temple."

"That's where we're headed now," Chime told her.

"You brought the solitary and the groundling woman?" River demanded, with an angry gesture at Rift. "What was the sense of that?"

"I told her not to do it," Drift said. He sounded self-righteous about it, despite the fact that he had a fist-sized swelling around his left eye and another one low on his jaw. Moon hadn't seen any of the Thluth land a blow, so it had to have happened earlier.

Rift, who had been hovering in the back to listen, twitched uneasily and looked away. Unexpectedly, it was Floret who rattled her spines and said, "The groundling woman showed us where the entrance to this place was, the one above the leviathan's tail."

Her voice flat and angry, Balm added, "We couldn't leave them there. Rift would run away, and if we were all killed, Karsis would be stuck up in that tower unable to get out. I was going to just let her go, but she said she wanted to come along to find her brother."

Moon flicked his spines at River, and told Balm, "No, you did right." Stone touched her frills lightly with one claw tip, sympathy and reassurance combined. Moon looked around at the others. "We need to go."

Balm nodded. "We think it's this way."

As the others moved away, Moon stopped her with a hand on her arm. He asked quietly, "What happened to Drift?" If Rift had tried to escape and Drift had gotten hurt stopping him, Moon needed to know.

Balm's spines twitched at the memory. "He tried to take over the group, so I had to fight him. I didn't trust him to do the right thing, and I knew we had to get back to Jade fast." She hesitated, then in a mix of pride and relief said, "When I won, I was still afraid the others wouldn't follow me, but they did."

Moon thought that was the important part. Balm had to know that she could physically beat Drift. It was the fact that the others had not only stood by and let her, but supported her over him afterward, tacitly acknowledging Balm's status in the court, even over one of Pearl's favorites. He said, "Good."

☾

It was better hidden than Moon had anticipated, and they found it only because Stone was able to follow the stench of the fermenting edilvine and rot, buried in with the leviathan's pervasive scent.

The tunnel entrance was in the deeper shadow up near the city's foundation, in a buttress that joined two pillars, about fifty paces above the leviathan's skin. When Moon climbed up to investigate, he found a broad walkway along the buttress, with the tunnel just above it, opening into a dark passage up through the layers of rock and metal.

Moon made the others stay below and climbed up with Chime and Floret, Chime in front to sense any magical barriers. The city's foundation was much thinner here than it had been under Ardan's tower. Barely twenty paces up, Chime hissed for them to stop, then climbed back down to report, "There's a tunnel up there, pretty narrow. It stinks of those vines. It's coming from the direction of the mortuary, going off toward the east."

River hovered impatiently under the passage opening. "Come on, let's go," he said. "We have to find out what the sorcerer did with Jade and Flower."

Moon, who hadn't been able to think of anything else except what the sorcerer might be doing to Jade and Flower, managed not to give in to the impulse to drop back down and tear River's head off. He said, "No, we scout first." He didn't intend to make any mistakes, or to let them all rush up there and find themselves running right into Ardan. "Floret, follow the tunnel back toward the mortuary, as far as you can without being seen. See if there's anyone guarding it. Take Chime, to check for barriers."

Floret flicked her spines in acknowledgement and started to climb. Chime, nervous but determined, followed her.

Moon dropped back out of the passage to wait, as River stomped away to sulk with Drift. But no one questioned the decision.

Stone settled under the opening to wait and Moon paced uneasily. It didn't help that the others were all sitting or standing there staring at him, even Karsis and Esom. This was much easier when Jade was here to take all the responsibility, and all Moon had to do was have the crazy ideas. It had been easier having responsibility only for himself.

Rift hovered a little apart from the others, his whole body suggesting reluctance to be anywhere near them, though he hadn't tried to run away. Seeing him again made Moon realize just how confused his feelings were. He felt sorry for Rift, he was deeply suspicious of him, he wanted to help him, he just wanted him to go away. Rift was a miserable reminder that there were pitfalls to living with the Raksuran courts that Moon hadn't even stumbled into yet. None of it was going to matter if they didn't get the seed back and get off this damn leviathan, but he couldn't stop his thoughts from drifting in that direction.

Balm looked up at the passage, worried and preoccupied. She said, "You think the sorcerer knows Jade and Flower are trapped in the dome?"

"He has to." Moon thought it was dangerous to assume anything else. "He would have wanted to open it to see if the seed was still there."

"Maybe they can fight him off," Song said. "There's two of them, and Flower's still pretty strong." She flicked her spines nervously, a young and deceptively delicate predator.

"Your friends might have been able to lock the door from the inside," Esom pointed out. "Or dismantle the mechanism that opens it, if it's not too complicated." Karsis elbowed him and he blinked and added, "Not that I think they wouldn't be able to figure out something complicated—"

"It's all right," Moon cut him off before he made it any worse. "We know what you mean."

Karsis cleared her throat. Obviously trying to distract everyone from Esom's gaffe, she asked Moon, "Is Jade your wife?"

In groundling terms, it was close enough. "Yes."

With bitter emphasis, Rift said, "He's a consort. It's not like he had a choice. It's not like anyone in a Raksuran court has a choice."

And having Rift speak for him didn't decrease Moon's irritation. Moon said, pointedly, "I had a choice."

Rift threw a glance at him, half-angry, half-wary. "To compete for a queen or to be a useless burden to the court?"

If Stone had heard that, he ignored it. Balm hissed and Song and Vine bristled angrily. Glaring at Rift in annoyance, Karsis said, "You know, I don't think anyone here cares for your opinion. I know I never have."

Rift barred his teeth at her. Then Root, seething with indignation, said, "Moon was a solitary, too, and he stays with Jade because he wants to."

Rift stared at Moon, so incredulous his spines flattened. Vine thumped Root in the side of the head, and hissed, "No more talking. Ever."

Moon set his jaw. Rift had always had a hold on him; now he would know what it was. Rift said, "That's . . . Consorts don't leave their courts . . ."

"Tell him the story," Moon said. He walked away and circled around Stone to take up a position under the passage. Stone, proving that he had been listening, heaved a deeply annoyed sigh.

There was a long moment of awkward silence from the other side of the walkway, then Moon heard Balm speak quietly to Vine. Vine gestured and Rift, still badly shocked, followed him down the walkway to talk. Song shook her head grimly at Root, whose spines drooped with embarrassment.

Time seemed to drag. Standing still, without immediate danger as a distraction, Moon could feel every cut and slash that had penetrated his scales, the exhaustion dragging at him like a net, making his wings feel like they were iron weights. It had been a long time since he had shifted to groundling, but if he did it now he might fall down and not be able to get up again.

As they waited, everyone showed signs of fatigue: Balm's spines were drooping, Root had trouble keeping his eyes open, and River leaned against a pillar, trying to pretend it wasn't holding him up. There was only so much more of this they could take without a chance to eat and rest. He hoped Ardan was tired too, and feeling the strain of doing so much magic at once. But Moon was willing to bet Ardan had had time to stop for a meal, and they hadn't.

There was a scrabbling in the passage above them, then Floret and Chime dropped out.

The others bounded over to gather around, Esom and Karsis hurrying after them. Floret reported, "We got all the way up to this room full of stinking vines in barrels. There were two blue groundlings in the corridor just past it. Chime said they belonged to the sorcerer."

"I didn't feel any barriers," Chime added. "I bet Ardan doesn't know about this way out."

Moon nodded, thinking it over. Ardan must believe that the people who were trading with the water travelers only used that doorway to the flooded street. "If the guards are there, then Ardan is still in the mortuary. Maybe he didn't get the dome open yet." And everyone on the leviathan must have felt the jolt when Moon had removed the crystal piece. Maybe Ardan had more to deal with at the moment than just the Raksura.

"But he must be trying to get it open," Chime said. "Even if we can get past the guards and get into the mortuary, he'll be right there."

"So how do we get past him?" Balm said, frustrated.

Moon shook his head. "We can't. We have to talk to him."

River snarled skeptically. "What, so he can feed us to the leviathan again?" Drift hissed agreement.

Moon didn't bother to argue that. The trick was going to be to make Ardan want to talk more than he wanted to get rid of them. He looked at Esom. "That spell you did, the one that made it so no one could see you and Karsis when you were trying to get out of the tower. Can you do that again?"

Esom straightened his cracked spectacles, and nodded.

"Yes. You want me to use it so we can get back into the mortuary without anyone knowing we're there?"

"Will that work? Can you get past Ardan?"

"I . . . think so. I know I can hide myself and one other person, reliably." Esom hesitated, his expression uncertain. He admitted, "Ardan was always distracted when I tried the spell inside his tower."

"I can distract him," Rift said. He bristled his spines uneasily as everyone turned to stare at him. "He'll listen to me." He looked at Moon. "You know he will."

Behind them, Stone shifted to groundling. Esom flinched and cursed, Karsis just stared in fascination. Stone folded his arms and regarded Rift thoughtfully.

Rift threw him a frightened look but held his ground. Still focusing on Moon, he said, "You know it's true. He wants me back, doesn't he? He'll talk to me."

Moon let out his breath. Yes, Ardan wanted Rift back. Moon just wasn't sure what Rift wanted. "If you tell him about Esom's spell, what we're planning—"

"You'll kill me, I know." Rift glanced around at the others, spines lowered. "I didn't mean to hurt your court. I thought the colony tree was abandoned forever. If I'd known you were coming back—"

"That's not the point." Stone's voice cut across Rift's, silencing him immediately. It was the first time Stone had spoken directly to him. "That colony tree is our court."

Rift flattened his spines but said, "A court is Aeriat and Arbora, not the empty shell of a tree. For all I knew, your court had died out and I was doing the tree a favor, letting it die so it wouldn't live forever alone."

Stone grimaced, equal parts irritation and disgust, probably because Rift had given him an answer that was hard to argue with.

Moon asked Rift, "What do you want in return?"

If Rift said "Nothing," Moon wasn't going to believe him. Rift wasn't the self-sacrificing type, even if he did feel sorry about the colony tree. But Rift said, "When you find a way to leave the leviathan, take me with you. I want to go back to the forest Reaches. Ardan may want me back, but he'll never trust me again, and I can't trust him." His scales rippled uneasily. "And I'm sick of this place."

Moon thought it rang true, but he didn't quite trust his own judgment when it came to this. The others watched Rift with varying degrees of skepticism, doubt, and even a little sympathy. Moon looked at Balm. She studied Rift carefully, her eyes narrowed. She caught Moon's gaze, and gave him a grimace of doubt and a slow reluctant nod.

That summed up Moon's feelings accurately. He told Rift, "All right, we have a deal. Don't make me regret it."

☾

Moon and Rift crept up the tunnel, climbed through a doorway that had been knocked out of the wall and into the edilvine chamber. Making their way silently past the stinking barrels, Moon saw there were now three blue-pearl guards in the passage. Most of their attention was on the upper part of the passage, as if they were expecting someone to try to come in through the smugglers' entrance. Which made it easy when Moon and Rift barreled in among them and knocked them flat.

Moon kicked a dart gun away from the one that was sprawled on the ground but still conscious, and told him, "Go tell Ardan that Moon and Rift want to talk. We have something he wants. Say that to him."

The man scrambled back, shoved to his feet, and ran.

Then they waited, Moon still and Rift pacing and lashing his tail. "What if he doesn't—" Rift began, and Moon hissed at him to be quiet. If Ardan didn't take the bait, he had no idea what they were going to do.

He heard the groundlings coming back, at least six of them. They approached cautiously up the passage, one carrying a small vapor-lamp. Another craned his neck, trying to see the two men still lying unconscious in the shadows. Moon said, "They're alive."

The guard stared, startled. Either by the fact that the Raksura hadn't killed and eaten the men as a matter of course, or that Moon had thought the other guards would care. The one in the lead said, stiffly, "The Magister will speak with you."

The others moved back against the walls. Moon walked past them and Rift followed. Moon caught a whiff of fear-sweat, but no one pulled out a dart gun at the last instant. As he and Rift went toward the passage into the mortuary, he heard the guards move to collect the unconscious men.

Esom and Stone would be waiting down in the edilvine tunnel, and would follow them under the concealment of the spell. Esom could only make the spell big enough to conceal Stone in his groundling form, but Moon hadn't thought there would be any possibility of Stone sliding the dome's door open without Ardan noticing. But if Ardan tried to turn on them, Stone would be there. And Moon wasn't leaving without Jade and Flower.

They reached the doorway, where more nervous guards waited, and went past them, down the steps into the huge chamber. Moon had asked Rift if Ardan would have been able to make more warden-creatures by this time. Rift had said that even if he could, he wouldn't be able to let the creatures run loose with his guards here. Moon hoped he wasn't lying.

Shadows still clung to the upper half of the room, concealing the vaulted ceiling and the tops of the huge pillars, but more vapor-lamps had been lit. Moon spotted Ardan immediately. He waited under a lamp stand, about fifty paces from the doorway, with a large group of his guards spread out behind him. Beside Moon, Rift twitched uneasily.

Moon couldn't see the dome from here. It was somewhere past the shadowy outline of the undead waterling's tail. He couldn't see the spot on the far side of the chamber where Ardan had made the floor dissolve, either.

He started across the wide expanse of pavement toward Ardan, and tried not to look as if he was thinking about it disappearing under him at any moment. He and Rift stopped ten paces away from the sorcerer.

Ardan said, easily, "Rift, it's good to see you well. I hope they haven't treated you badly."

Rift twitched again, uncomfortable. He couldn't seem to meet Ardan's gaze. "No. Not . . . No."

Ardan turned to Moon and assessed him cautiously. "I didn't expect to see you alive."

It was nice of Ardan to admit it. "We're hard to kill," Moon said. "But it turned out for the best."

Ardan's mouth tightened. Moon thought, *he guessed we were responsible for the jolt, but he was hoping he was wrong.* Ardan said, "I felt the leviathan's distress. I take it that was something you did?"

"I don't think the leviathan was distressed. I think it was relieved." Moon hoped they were right about what the crystal piece did. If Ardan laughed in his face at this point, they were going to be in a lot of trouble. "The thing that was telling it what to do is gone."

Ardan's self-control wasn't quite perfect, and Moon could hear the tension in his voice. "What thing?"

"The metal piece with the crystals. The one down there, in the pillar that cuts through the leviathan's hide. The one that lets you use the power in the seed to send the leviathan all over the sea, anywhere you want."

There was an uneasy ripple among the guards, but no one seemed surprised or appalled—as if they suspected Ardan had been lying to the whole city but didn't like to hear it mentioned aloud.

Ardan's expression hardened into annoyance. He glanced at the guards, and said, "You're wrong, of course, no one can steer the leviathan. But that device, the leviathan's bridle, is almost a legend. I've seen drawings, but . . ." With grim urgency, he said, "This creature could decide to sink at any moment. You could kill us all."

Yes, that's the point, Moon thought. He said, "Then give us the seed. It's useless to you without the bridle, isn't it? You've got a choice: lose all of your control over the leviathan, or just part of it."

Ardan took a deep breath and watched him appraisingly. "You don't have it with you."

Moon flicked his spines, though Ardan couldn't read that as a gesture of dismissal. "Of course not."

"The others have it," Rift said suddenly. "I've seen it."

Ardan gave Rift a slight nod of thanks. Still thoughtful, he said to Moon, "As you must have guessed, I wasn't able to open the sanctum. There is a wheel on the inside that operates the door, and whoever is in there was clever enough to find a way to jam it."

Moon was fairly certain that a queen and a mentor working together had had absolutely no difficulty finding a way to jam the mechanism. Especially since they would have felt no need to be careful with whatever materials were available inside the dome. He just said, "They'll open it for me."

Ardan lifted a brow. "And would your companions trade both the seed and the bridle for you?"

Moon showed all his teeth. "If you try that, they'll smash your bridle and scatter the pieces in the sea."

"Why should I believe you?" Ardan smiled thinly. "Perhaps you're too valuable to them. You are a consort. I know what that means."

Rift said, "No. He's like me, he was a solitary. His queen is the only one who wants him and she's trapped in the sanctum. They won't trade for him."

Moon flinched. It wasn't true; it was just Rift trying to help, melding truth with lies, which was apparently what he did best. It was just an accident that he had hit so close to the bone.

Ardan's brow furrowed. His sharp gaze hadn't missed Moon's reaction. He said, "You're certain?"

Rift had nothing in his voice but complete conviction. "They would never have sent a consort they cared about into your tower. Not even to save a colony tree seed."

Moon set his jaw, and tried to ignore the sinking sensation in his stomach. *They didn't send me, I sent myself.* Jade would never have agreed to the plan if she had been there to object. Somehow knowing that didn't help.

Ardan hesitated, his face hard. *He doesn't want to make the trade, but he can't see another way out,* Moon thought. *You hope he can't see another way out.*

Then a guard approached from out of the shadows in the direction of the mortuary's main entrance. He moved forward cautiously, saluted Ardan with a half bow, and said, "Magister, please."

Ardan said, through gritted teeth, "Excuse me a moment." He turned and moved back to the line of guards to talk to the man. They faced away, speaking in whispers, and not in Kedaic.

Quietly, in Raksuran, Moon asked Rift, "Can you understand them?"

Rift glanced down. "Yes, they're speaking Ilisai, a trader's language. He said Magister Lethen is at the gate with Magisters Giron and Soleden. They have all their guards with them, and they say they have firepowder."

"What's that?"

"A weapon. It makes a big burst of fire. The fishermen use it to keep the giant waterlings away." Rift listened a moment more. "The guard says that the people are gathering in this area, too. When they felt the leviathan jolt, someone ordered the traders to cast off and the fishing boats to be secured for a move, so everyone knows something is wrong."

"Good." Moon rippled his spines, trying to release the tension in his back. That explained why the guards had been in the passage. Ardan had known the other magisters would be trying to get inside, and if any of them knew about the smuggler's entrance, they might have enough magic of their own to get through his barrier.

Ardan turned away from the messenger. From his expression, none of this was welcome news. He said to Moon, "Very well. I'll return the seed in exchange for the bridle. If Rift will be good enough to go and get it now."

That hadn't been in Moon's plans. "After you let us go with the seed."

Ardan's expression was derisive. "I'm not a fool. Then you'd have both."

Moon bared his fangs. "I don't want both."

Ardan held out for a long moment, then took a sharp impatient breath. "Send Rift for the bridle. You and I will go and get the seed. We'll make the exchange here."

Moon controlled a frustrated hiss. He could continue to argue, but he didn't want the other magisters to break this up anymore than Ardan did. He told Rift, "Go and get it."

Rift flicked his spines in assent, threw an opaque look at Ardan, and bounded away toward the doorway to the tunnel.

Ardan started toward the dome and the guards hastily moved out of his way. Moon followed him, forcing himself not to twitch under the suspicious regard of a large group of hostile groundlings.

He took in a quiet breath and tasted the air. There was no hint of Stone or Esom, but then the air was thick with rot, the leviathan's stench, and decaying preserved waterling. Using Esom's concealment spell, the two of them should be working their way around the outer perimeter of the big chamber, as far away from the guardsmen and Ardan as possible.

Once they were past the bulk of the dead waterling, Moon could see the dome. Ardan hadn't lied; it looked undisturbed, except for some new scratches and scuffs at the door seam where the guards must have tried to pry it open.

As they reached the dome, Ardan said easily, "Continue to speak in Kedaic, please. I wouldn't want reason to doubt our arrangement."

Moon didn't argue. He stepped up to the door and tapped on it. "Jade, it's me." He couldn't hear anything from inside, but after a long, fraught moment, something creaked in the wall and the door began to slide open. It stopped, leaving a gap only a pace or so wide. Jade stepped into the opening.

Moon realized that until that moment he hadn't been certain that she and Flower were really still inside the dome, that this hadn't been an elaborate ruse by Ardan. She was still in her winged form, her spines bristling. Moon heard muted exclamations from some of Ardan's men. They sounded startled and uneasy, as if Jade was more formidable than they had expected. Jade kept her expression neutral, though her gaze flicked over Moon briefly, possibly looking for open wounds. Then, with a slight narrowing of her eyes, she regarded Ardan.

He said, "I had never expected to see a Raksuran queen in the flesh."

Jade tilted her head inquiringly. "Have you seen many dead ones?"

Ardan smiled, acknowledging the hit. "I've seen the wall carvings."

Moon said, "We're giving him the thing that he needs to keep the leviathan from sinking, and he's going to let us leave with the seed."

"Is he." Jade sounded unconvinced, but she lifted a hand.

Flower stepped into view behind Jade, and she held something tucked under her arm. It was a light brown object the size of a melon, with a ribbed outer shell. Flower said, "It was in a holder in the altar, or whatever it is, in here." She peered past Jade at Ardan. "That's him, is it?"

Ardan frowned at Flower. "I'm sorry. You're not a Raksura, surely?" Apparently he couldn't contain his curiosity even under these circumstances.

Flower's brows quirked. This was probably not a question she had ever been asked before. "I'm an Arbora."

Ardan didn't look convinced. "You don't resemble the carvings."

That was possibly an attempt at a polite way of saying that the carvings showed Arbora to be stocky and heavily muscled, and not raw-boned thin and fragile. Flower said, dryly, "I'm old."

Jade took Flower's shoulder and moved her away from Ardan, putting Flower between herself and Moon. Ardan gave her a polite nod. He stepped back, and said, "Very well. We'll go and make the exchange."

Jade lifted a brow at Moon, but didn't object. Ardan wasn't stupid by any stretch of the imagination, but he was desperate, and Moon was fairly sure he would try something to keep the seed. He might believe now that the other Raksura wouldn't trade the seed and the bridle for Moon, but that wouldn't stop him from trying to make them trade for Jade's release. But that wouldn't happen until Ardan had his hands on the bridle. They started to follow the sorcerer back toward the tunnel entrance, where Rift would be waiting.

As they walked, Ardan said, "I was told that your consort is not accepted by your people, that he has the same disadvantage as Rift."

Flower looked up, startled. Jade's spines were already bristling and didn't betray her reaction. She flicked a look at Moon, who couldn't afford to do anything but stare back at her. He hoped she just played along and agreed, but some traitor part of him wanted her to argue with Ardan even if it did wreck their plan. She said to Ardan, "I think it's laughable to expect a groundling to understand our customs."

Ardan wasn't willing to let her avoid the issue. "I think anyone of feeling can recognize a despicable custom. And if you support it, why make an exception for your consort?"

Flower hissed quietly to herself. Jade's spines rippled. She said, "You have your own share of despicable customs."

Unperturbed, Ardan said, "I've offered Rift a refuge here. Your consort would be welcome as well."

Jade's claws flexed. Flower gave Moon a look of pure consternation, but Jade only said, "I think your refuge comes with a price."

Then they were past the bulk of the dead waterling, and Ardan abruptly lost interest in the argument. He stopped, and said, grimly, "Speaking of Rift, it seems he has returned with company."

Three Raksura waited on the steps below the tunnel entrance. From the colors of their scales, it was Rift, Balm, and Chime. Moon hoped the others waited past the doorway, just out of sight, and the men that Ardan had stationed there had been chased away down the tunnel.

"They don't trust him," Moon said. There were so many things that could still go wrong, he couldn't count them. "Just like you don't trust us."

"True." Ardan hesitated, his expression still, and Moon could practically see him turning over the decision whether to betray them or not. He didn't let himself tense. They had the seed and a mostly clear shot to the tunnel entrance, and Stone and Esom should be nearby. His only worry was if Ardan could do some sort of magic before they all reached the tunnel. Then Ardan said, "Tell Rift to bring it—"

An explosion shook the chamber, sent a tremor through the paving. A shower of dust and rock chips rained down from above. Jade half-flared her wings. Moon ducked instinctively and threw a protective arm around Flower. She shifted to Arbora under his hand, crouching to shield the seed.

Someone shouted, "Magister, they're coming, they broke through the wall—"

The firepowder, Moon realized. *The waterling weapon.* Ardan staggered to his feet, shouted at the guards. Moon looked back, trying to see through the dust, and spotted Esom stumbling barely thirty paces away. Stone, still in groundling form, tackled him down, and rolled them both out of sight behind a pillar. Moon grimaced, stricken. The shock of the explosion must have made Esom lose control over his spell. The guards were going to see them any moment. He told Jade, "Go for the tunnel, go now! We'll distract him—"

Jade hissed agreement, grabbed Flower, and leapt for the tunnel.

Then suddenly the ground underfoot dipped and turned, threw Moon sideways as the paving lifted under them. He thought it was Ardan opening a passage down to the leviathan again, and snarled in fury. But Ardan staggered as the floor tilted, trying to stay on his feet. Water rushed in through the tunnel entrance, down the stairs, and bowled over Ardan's guards. Jade changed her direction in mid-leap and flared her wings. She whipped around to land on the nearest pillar, Flower and the seed still tucked under one arm. Chime, Balm, and Rift jumped up through the spray as the wave rolled across the floor.

The water had to be coming up the flooded street, obviously not hampered by the magical barrier over the door.

But the floor still tilted down at a sharp incline. *The levia-than is lowering its head,* Moon realized in horror, *getting ready to go under . . .*

As the wave hit, Moon lunged forward, grabbed Ardan around the waist, and jumped down the incline to the side of the nearest pillar. Water washed over him, stale at first and then fresh. Moon shook Ardan and shouted, "What are you doing?"

"It's not me!" Ardan gritted out, his hands digging into Moon's arm. "It's the leviathan! Those fools, when they used the firepowder so close to its head, they must have woken it. Without the bridle it's free to do whatever it wants."

It sounded horribly likely. The leviathan had lowered its head immediately after the explosion. "Can you stop it?"

"I can try. Get me the bridle, take me to the sanctum, and I'll try!"

Moon looked around. Balm and Chime had joined Jade, perched on a pillar about a hundred paces away. They all stared this way, doubtless wondering what Moon was do-ing with Ardan. He couldn't see Rift . . . No, there he was, holding on to the corbelled ceiling high overhead. Moon bellowed, "Rift, come here!"

Rift hesitated, long enough for Moon to think about where he would have to put Ardan while he flew up to drag Rift out of the ceiling, to wonder where Stone and Esom were. Water poured continuously in from the tun-nel entrance, roared down the slope of the floor. Then Rift dropped down to the pillar and cupped his wings to land on it a few paces above Moon.

"Give him the bridle," Moon said. "I've got to take him to the sanctum to try to stop this."

Rift handed the bridle to Ardan, and said, "Good luck."

Rift ducked away as Moon flared his wings and leapt for the next pillar. The sloped stone surface made for a difficult landing, and his claws slipped. He slid down a few paces be-fore he caught hold of the carving. Ardan grunted in alarm, but didn't struggle or panic. Moon pushed off again, more carefully this time, and crossed the room in long bounds.

Halfway across, Chime caught up and landed above him on a slanting pillar. He said breathlessly, "Jade says to hurry up and do whatever it is you're doing."

Moon didn't need to be told that. He leapt into the air again.

He finally splashed down beside the sanctum's open doorway. A moment later Chime landed atop the dome. Water poured down the slope of the floor, most of it flowing past the angled doorway, so the sanctum wasn't flooded yet. He set Ardan on his feet. The Magister staggered, caught the wall to steady himself, and said, "Thank you. You can send your friend for the seed."

Moon wasn't buying that. "You said you could do it with the bridle. It's a little late to change your story." The man was as bad as Rift.

Another wave washed down and sloshed partly into the sanctum. Ardan smiled tightly. "It was worth a try." He pulled himself inside and staggered across to the plinth.

Moon climbed the side of the dome, up to where Chime crouched. The big room was even darker; the vapor-light stands in the lower part of the chamber had been swamped. Though it didn't douse them, they didn't put out much light under water. "Did you see Stone and Esom?"

Chime watched the swirling water below. A drowned groundling floated by, one of the blue-pearl guards. Chime grimaced. "No, where were they?"

"Behind a pillar, not far from the tunnel entrance." Moon squinted to see through the shadows. "Esom lost the spell when the firepowder went off. They should have—"

A high-pitched roar echoed across the chamber. "Uh oh," Chime said, nervously. "Now what?"

It came from the direction of the hole in the floor, the one Ardan had made above the leviathan's blowhole. Moon had a bad feeling about that. "I hope that's not what I think it is. Come on." Moon jumped off the dome and headed toward the sound.

As they made their way from pillar to pillar, Moon saw Stone first, in the big dark shape of his Raksuran form. He was at the edge of the jagged opening in the floor, and struggled with something. Then they reached a pillar overlooking it, and the scene made Chime gasp in horror. "I thought we were done with these things!"

Big beetle-like parasites climbed up through the opening from below. The creatures had armor, spines around their mouths, big fangs. They must be coming up out of the area around the leviathan's blowhole, driven by the water. Stone dodged around, slapped them back down into the opening.

"How long can he keep that up?" Chime wondered.

Not long enough, Moon thought, sick. At least Stone didn't have to fight in water; it was all pooling down towards the other end of the chamber. The only other advantage seemed to be that the creatures only came up on one side of the opening, the side that was mostly in shadow, the side furthest away from the nearest vapor-light.

"I've got an idea. Light, they must hate light—"

Chime caught on immediately. "We get the lights, dump them down the opening—"

"Come on!"

They went back, unhooked the metal vapor-light chambers from the tops of the nearest poles, carried them to the opening, and flung them down into it. The parasites shied away from the light, shrieking in dismay, and proving the theory correct.

Fortunately, the big chamber had a lot of vapor-lights, and Ardan's men must have lit more when they arrived. Moon's world narrowed down to finding, carrying, passing Chime, throwing, and dodging the flailing claws of the parasites. Balm came to help, and Moon saw Rift at one point, carrying a lamp. He was glad Jade had stayed to guard Flower, and almost wished Balm had remained with her. He wasn't counting Ardan out of this game yet.

The tide of parasites slowed, then stopped, and Stone clung panting to the sloping floor. Then abruptly the entire chamber rolled.

The pillar Moon had perched on suddenly changed from a slanted surface to a vertical one, and he slipped off and landed badly. A foul-smelling wave washed over him as the water that had collected at the other end of the chamber flowed back this way.

Nearby, Stone abruptly shifted back to groundling. Still sprawled on the floor, he demanded, "What was that?"

"The leviathan lifted its head," Moon explained. Air thundered through the blowhole again as the creature expelled a breath, and they all hastily retreated from the edge of the opening.

"The floor's still moving," Balm said, stumbling a little as she joined them. "No, wait, the whole thing is moving."

"Ardan must be sending the leviathan somewhere," Moon said. "I gave him the bridle so he could stop it from going underwater."

"I thought he couldn't tell it where to go without the seed," Chime said.

They all stared at each other, stricken. Stone dropped his head into his hands, and muttered, "Not again."

"No, it can't be." Moon shook his head and dismissed the momentary fear. "He couldn't have gotten back across the mortuary on his own, let alone gotten the seed from Flower and Jade."

Stone said grimly, "I'll make sure. And I've got to get Esom. I left him around here somewhere." He jerked his head at Moon. "You three find out where Ardan's sent this thing."

Moon turned back for the sanctum with Balm and Chime, making slower progress through the big chamber now that it was in almost complete darkness. Most of the vapor-lights were down below on the leviathan's skin, lighting the area around the blowhole.

The sanctum's door was still open, and light shone out of it. They dropped silently to the floor about twenty paces away. Moon motioned for Balm and Chime to hang back. He went forward slowly, and eased up to the doorway to look inside.

Moon hissed, startled. *Wasn't expecting this.*

Ardan lay curled on the floor near the plinth. His eyes stared in blank surprise, and he still held the bridle in one hand, his fingers clutched around it. Moon stepped closer and knelt, touched the body lightly, then moved the head. Blood pooled on the floor beneath it. He thought Ardan had been hit from behind, cracked with force on the lower part of the skull, below the protective crown of bone and pearl. The angle was wrong for a fall. He might have somehow struck the edge of the plinth, but he had died facing it.

Worry about it later, Moon thought. On impulse he took the bridle, gently freeing it from Ardan's nerveless fingers, and then fled the sanctum.

Chapter Seventeen

With the leviathan mostly level again, the water had drained out of the tunnel, so they were able to escape the mortuary that way. But the passage out to the flooded street was now completely under water. They would have to make their way out through the underground.

They found the others waiting for them on the buttress below the edilvine tunnel opening, wet but otherwise unhurt. There was some water below on the leviathan's hide, but not much, and it rapidly drained away.

There was a general expression of relief as Jade and then Flower dropped out of the tunnel. Then River, his spines and wings still dripping from the flood, demanded, "Did you get the—"

Flower held up the seed. That shut everyone up. They all gathered around and studied it reverently.

"It's not hurt?" Vine asked, and elbowed Root aside to get a better look. "The groundlings didn't ruin it?"

Flower tucked it securely under her arm and patted it fondly. "It's fine."

"But now what?" Still worried, Floret looked at Jade. "Is the sorcerer going to come after us for it? How do we get away from here?"

"Ardan's dead," Moon said. He had told the others briefly on the way out, but he hadn't gone into detail. He had his suspicions, he just wasn't sure what to do about them yet.

There were murmurs of relief. Esom must have already told Karsis, because the two groundlings stood further down the buttress, talking excitedly in their own language. Jade said, "We still need a way off the leviathan." Watching Esom and Karsis carefully, she stepped past the others to ask them, "You have a boat. Would you be willing to share it with us?"

Esom said, "If we go back to Ardan's tower first." His clothes and hair dripped from the flood, and he had taken off his cracked spectacles. "Our people are still trapped there. With Ardan and his guards gone, we can free them. But only if we hurry and get there before the other magisters try to take it over."

"If you help us, we can all get away," Karsis added anxiously. "Our ship can take you all the way back to the forest coast, if you need it to."

Jade lifted a brow at Moon. In Raksuran, she said, "It's a fair offer."

He nodded, and answered her in the same language, "They've helped us so far. And realistically, I don't know if we could figure out how their ship works without their help." And he didn't want to strand them here. From what they had said, an ordinary boat wouldn't be able to get them back through the dangerous waters surrounding their homeland. He switched to Kedaic to ask Esom, "What about Ardan's spells, the warden-creatures, the barrier?"

"Those would have died with him," Esom said. Then he grimaced uncertainly and added, "That's how it generally works."

Jade looked at Flower, who shrugged, then at Rift. She asked him, "Is that true?"

Rift seemed startled to be consulted. He said, "I don't know."

Moon watched Esom, who looked tired and earnest. He could be lying but . . . *But it would be stupid to lie about this,* Moon thought. And he had never had the image of Esom as a very good liar, despite the fact that he had concealed his abilities from Ardan. He exchanged a look with Jade, who hissed out a breath. She said, "Then we'll go to the tower."

☾

They traveled through the dimly-lit underground, back to the well in the city foundations that led up into the lower level of Ardan's tower. Moon led them up through the lichen-illuminated passage, back to the panel that opened into the first floor of the exhibit hall. It had been sealed again, and Esom stepped forward to whisper, "Wait, let me make sure . . ."

"I thought he said the magics would all be gone," Root muttered in the back.

Moon snarled absently. If Esom was wrong about the tower being undefended, he didn't know how they were going to free Negal and the other groundlings. Esom frowned, touched the door lightly, then ran his hand over it. Relieved, he said, "There was something here, I can feel the resonance, but it's gone now." He turned to Moon. "Ardan must have been hoping to catch us if we tried to come back this way."

"Good." Moon stepped past him to push on the door and felt it move just a little, enough to tell him there had been no attempt made to block it off from the other side.

"Wait." Jade turned to face the others. Stone had had to shift back to groundling to fit through the last part of the passage. Everyone looked exhausted, wet, and worried, including the groundlings. She said, "Don't kill anyone. We don't want a war with these people."

"They keep trying to kill us," Drift protested.

"Because Ardan ordered them to," Moon said impatiently. "He's dead, and we can't fight every groundling in this city. If they think we're out to slaughter them, they'll all band together against us."

"And because I said so," Jade added, and cuffed Drift in the head. She clearly wasn't in any mood to put up with an argument. She nodded to Moon, and he and Vine pushed the panel out and lifted it away, letting in a spill of brighter light from the corridor. Moon was the first one out.

Moon took a deep breath of air only lightly tinged with the leviathan's stench. After the underground and the mortuary, the polished floors and bright vapor-lights were a relief.

He led the way around and out from under the stairwell, to the main room. It seemed even bigger without the giant waterling, with the chains that had supported it hanging empty. The outer door was securely locked and barred, but there were no guards and no sound of movement anywhere. Most if not all of them must have gone with Ardan. Presumably the survivors would be looking for new jobs and wouldn't be returning here.

"It feels empty," Rift said, his voice hushed. "But the servants must still be here."

Moon tasted the air. He caught only the scents of decay from the upper exhibit hall and the traces left behind of the giant waterling. "Somebody would have had to open the doors for Ardan and the others when they came back."

Jade ordered, "Search the place, chase out any of Ardan's people left behind, and find the prisoners."

Leaving Jade and Chime behind to guard Flower and the seed, and Stone to watch the outside door, they all spread out to search the place floor by floor.

Moon followed the stairs up through the tower and opened every door he came to, breaking the locks if necessary. Vine flushed out the first frightened servant, and they quickly organized a system for chasing them out to the stairwell where Song or Root waited to make sure they ran all the way down and out the front door, where Stone made certain they left. They didn't run into anyone who was armed; Ardan must have taken all his guards with him to the mortuary.

They were all hungry and drooping with exhaustion. The younger warriors were having difficulty keeping up, and Karsis had to tow Esom up the stairs. On the third floor above the exhibit halls they passed a foyer with a running fountain. Moon stepped into it just long enough to put his head under the spray and wash the last residue of the leviathan off his scales. It helped revive him a little. It had been a long time without sleep or real food, and he didn't know how much longer he and the others could last.

They were in the upper levels of the tower, where the public rooms were, exploring a servants' area near a second set of kitchens, when Balm stumbled on a heavily locked door that seemed to lead to a separate section of the level. They forced open the door to find a corridor with doors not unlike the guest quarters—except these doors had no open transoms to allow in light and air, and all had locks on the outside. "This could be it," Esom breathed. He ran to the first door and pounded on it, shouting, "Negal? Orlis?"

Karsis took the other side of the corridor, pounding on each door. Midway down, someone inside shouted an incomprehensible answer and pounded back.

"It's them!" Karsis fumbled at the lock as Esom ran to join her.

Balm glanced at Moon, got a nod, and went to help them. She broke the lock off the handle and ripped the door open.

Negal stepped out first, then stopped, astonished. He stared from Esom to Balm, Moon, and past them at Vine, who looked in from the foyer. Orlis and six other men crowded behind him. They were all a similar type of groundling, with dark hair and brown skin, dressed in worn clothes, with the thin, pinched look of people who had been away from the sun and fresh air for a long time. Smiling with relief, Negal said to Esom, "I take it the situation has changed drastically?"

Esom explained, "Ardan is dead, and we have an alliance with them, now." He gestured vaguely toward Moon and the others. "Of course, most of the population of the island probably wants to kill us—"

Karsis cried, "But we're alive and finally free!" She hugged Negal, overcome with emotion, and Moon and Balm hastily withdrew to the foyer. "Stay with them. Keep an eye on them," Moon told Balm, speaking in Raksuran to avoid any awkwardness. "Make sure the others are as willing to be friendly as Karsis and Esom. And keep Rift away from them."

Balm nodded understanding, and glanced back at the groundlings. "I will. Especially the part about Rift."

Moon left her with them, took Vine, and continued the search.

In a stairwell foyer two levels up, they ran back into Floret and Song.

"I found some groundlings hiding in these rooms," Floret said. "A woman, and some baby groundlings. The babies screamed when they saw me. When I shifted, they just screamed again." Looking embarrassed, she admitted, "It's a little upsetting. I don't want to scare them anymore."

She, Song, and Vine all stared expectantly at Moon. Song said, encouragingly, "You know how to talk to groundlings."

Moon sighed. Warriors weren't fertile and presumably had little experience with children. Except to play with them occasionally, and hand them back to the teachers when the babies got tired or hungry. "Wait out here. Stay back away from the door."

Moon went into the anteroom. The statues carved into the walls were female, the first ones he could remember seeing here, draped with graceful swaths of fabric and, unlike the male statues, smiling faintly. He shifted to groundling, and staggered, nearly going to his knees. Every cut and bruise, every sore and strained muscle, was suddenly magnified a hundredfold. He groaned, managed to straighten up, and walked into the suite.

It was furnished even more finely than the other private rooms Moon had seen, with thick carpets and heavy hangings on the walls in patterns of soft colors. The wooden furniture was elegantly carved and set with polished mother-of-pearl, the vapor-lamps shaped into fanciful fish and seabirds. It smelled of the perfumes the wealthy groundlings here wore, cloying false-flowery scents, combined with a musk of fear.

Moon heard muffled weeping and followed it back through the rooms to a bedchamber. A young blue-pearl woman wrapped in a rich robe was huddled on the floor between the heavily draped bed and a carved chest, with four blue-pearl children of varying ages, all sniffling in terror. There was an elderly blue-pearl man and a woman huddled in with them, both dressed like servants.

Moon said to the young woman, "You have to leave now. Do you have somewhere to go? Your family's house, maybe?"

She stared at him in confusion, the light blue skin around her eyes bruised with weeping. But some of the panic in her face subsided. If she had met Rift, she had to know Raksura could look like groundlings, but maybe she was only seeing Moon as a slender young man in dark clothing, and not a potential monster. Or maybe what he had said was so far from her worst fear that it had shocked her back to her senses. She said, hesitantly, "May I take anything?"

"Sure." Moon figured she would probably need money. She glanced at the chest and Moon saw jewelry spilled across the top, silver chains with polished gemstones. He said, "Take all that."

Moon waited while the woman and the two servants hurriedly swept the jewelry into a bag and collected clothing and a few other possessions. The activity seemed to calm them down, and he ended up helping one of the children extract a cloth doll from under the bed. He led them out to the foyer, where the woman flinched at the sight of the lurking Raksura, who all fled up the stairwell when Moon grimaced at them.

He shepherded the groundlings down the stairs, through the lower exhibit hall. Stone, in his groundling form, was standing beside the passage to the outer doors. The adults avoided looking at him, as if they were afraid to see some outward sign of what he was. But the children stared curiously, and Stone quirked a smile at them as they passed.

Moon pushed the outside door open for them. The sun was shining, the miasma that usually hung over the leviathan torn away when the creature had jolted into motion. The plaza and the surrounding walkways were empty, though somewhat protected from the rush of wind. The woman blinked at the daylight as if she had never expected to see it again. Moon said, "Will you be all right?"

"It's not far," she said, automatically. Then she focused on him, her eyes intent. "Thank you."

He shrugged uneasily. "It wasn't your fault."

She nodded tightly, then turned away. He watched the little group walk away across the plaza and take a path toward the nearest cluster of towers.

Moon went back inside, and helped Stone pull the door shut and lever the locks and bars into place again.

As they came back out into the exhibit hall, Jade leapt down from the gallery. She caught Moon by the shoulders, her expression worried and preoccupied. "Moon, you should rest. We'll need you when the groundlings are ready to talk. We can't try to get to the harbor until after nightfall, anyway."

That was true. They needed to make a plan to reach the harbor and steal back Negal's flying boat. Moon considered it, wavering back and forth, then thought, *Why not?* He might as well give in to his consort's privilege to rest while everybody else was working. "All right."

Jade pointed him toward the back corridor of the tower. "Go back there. Flower is resting and Chime's watching over her."

Moon found his way toward the back of the first floor of the tower, to what must be the servants' and guards' quarters. A short stair led up to a big common room. There were thin rugs, not nearly as nice as the ones upstairs, padded benches, and a few stray floor cushions. A couple of narrow corridors and several small rooms opened off it. He looked into the first room to see Flower lying on the bed with Chime sitting beside her. She was in groundling form, curled around a pillow with the seed tucked under her arm; she looked tiny and almost withered. "Is she all right?" Moon whispered. She looked terrible.

Chime glanced up, his expression uneasy. "I don't know. She's just so tired. Rift is showing Root where the food is kept. I was going to try to get her to eat."

Without moving, Flower hissed, "Both of you, hush."

Moon hastily backed away. He went to one of the padded benches in the common room and sat down, then lay down for a moment to rest his eyes.

He wasn't aware of falling asleep, though he was dimly aware of the others coming and going through the room, or lying down to sleep on the floor. He smelled dried fish at one point, but was too tired to wake and look for his share. Then he woke abruptly, with Song leaning over him. She was in her groundling form, and her expression was anxious and a little frightened. "Moon. Flower says it's time."

Moon blinked, having trouble dragging himself out of sleep. "Time for what?"

Song seemed startled to be asked. "She's dying."

That jolted him fully awake. He sat up, pushed to his feet, and followed Song into the bed chamber.

Flower still lay on the bed, propped up on some cushions. Her eyes were closed, and her skin looked almost translucent under the vapor-light. Jade sat beside her, in her Arbora form, her spines twitching anxiously. Stone stood nearby, the seed absently tucked under one arm. Chime sat on the floor by the head of the bed, hunched in misery. The other warriors were gathered around in groundling form, all grim and sad.

Jade glanced up as Moon came in. Keeping her voice low, she said, "Sorry. I would have sent for you sooner, but she wasn't sure until just now." She looked around, taking stock of who was here. "Root, Vine is guarding the outer door. Go take his place so he can have a chance to see her. Hurry."

As Root darted out of the room, Stone sat down on the bed. He touched Flower's limp hand, but she didn't stir.

"What's wrong?" Moon asked. Nobody seemed to be doing anything. "What happened to her?"

Balm said softly, "Nothing. It's her age, it's caught up with her."

Moon couldn't believe that they were just standing here. It had to be some stupid Raksuran custom, maybe because there was no other mentor to help her. Chime might have an ability to sense things about the leviathan and Ardan's magic, but he couldn't use mentor skills to heal anymore. Moon said, "Karsis is a healer. Let me get her."

With a trace of impatience, Jade said, "Moon, it's no use. It's Flower's time."

Moon bit back his first angry response. He had to convince them that a groundling healer would be better than nothing, and losing his temper wouldn't help. "It doesn't have to be."

Flower spoke, her voice a bare whisper, "Moon doesn't know."

Jade frowned and shook her head slightly, not understanding. Chime looked up at Moon then, blinking, startled. The other warriors stared at him, confused. Stone winced, but didn't look away from Flower. Frustrated, Moon said, "Know what?"

Chime said, slowly, "She's been dying. We've known for most of the turn. Since before you came."

Stunned, Moon looked around at the others. It was in all their expressions. This hadn't been a surprise to anyone but him. He sank down on the end of the bed. "How did you know?"

"When her skin and her scales lost all their color, it's the sign. It means your time is coming . . ." Jade said, then hissed in realization. "But you didn't know that."

Moon couldn't answer. Of course he hadn't known. Before Indigo Cloud, all the Raksura he had known had died by being torn apart by Tath, not from old age.

Nobody else said anything, not even River or Drift, as if the subject was too sensitive. Chime twitched restlessly, folded his arms. He said, "She should have died at home."

Stone made a softly derisive sound. "If she hadn't come with us, we wouldn't have a home."

In a dry rasp, still without opening her eyes, Flower added, "And don't you forget it. Now, each of you come and talk to me."

Everyone took turns to sit by Flower and speak to her one last time. When Stone prodded Moon to take his turn, he held her hand, the skin and bones as dry and delicate as old parchment. She said, "Don't give up. Promise me you won't give up on us."

He wasn't sure if she was having an augury, or if she had just noticed his uncertainty, or both. He said automatically, "I promise."

It didn't take long after that, as if she had only been holding on long enough to say goodbye. Vine left, to go back to guarding the first floor. Moon and the others stayed, as Flower's breathing grew softer and slower and more shallow, until finally, it stopped altogether.

Moon turned away, went blindly through the common room, out into the corridor. He couldn't watch the others' grief; it felt private. They had known Flower all their lives, she had held them when they were fledglings. In Stone's case, he must have watched her grow up. Moon's feelings couldn't compare to that.

When he walked into the exhibit hall, he saw Negal and Esom at the bottom of the stairs with three other groundlings from their crew. Esom looked bleary and half-awake, as if he had been dragged out to talk to the dangerous Raksura when he would rather be sleeping. He called, "Moon, what's going on? Is there a plan yet for how we're going to—"

"Flower died," Moon said.

Taken aback, Esom stared. "Oh. I'm— I'm sorry. I didn't realize she was injured."

Moon shook his head; he couldn't explain now. "Just give us a little time." Without waiting for an answer, he shifted and leapt up to the gallery, ignoring the startled exclamations from the other groundlings.

He paced the hall there, past the decaying Tath and the other creatures, half-listening as Esom persuaded Negal and the others to go back upstairs to wait. It was hard to believe that it had really happened, that Flower was really gone. He had never seen anyone die from old age before. It had been so quiet.

Moon ended up standing in the cubby with the dead sea kingdom woman. He wondered what would happen to her when someone else took over the tower, what they would do with her body, if there were any other imprisoned spirits here like the waterling, or if Ardan's death had released them. After a time he heard movement and looked up to see Jade, moving slowly down the hall, looking at Ardan's collection. She was in her Arbora form, her spines flattened in dejection.

When she reached the cubby, he shifted back to groundling, and said, "Are you all right?"

"Yes, just . . ." Jade rubbed her temple and frowned down at the sealing's body. "I have to get used to the idea that she's gone." She looked up at him, wincing apologetically. "Moon, I'm sorry. I never thought that you didn't know."

He shook his head. He didn't want her to apologize to him for something that wasn't anyone's fault. "She didn't tell me." Moon had asked Flower if Raksura were born live or in eggs; she had to have realized he didn't know how they died of old age, either.

"Maybe she wanted someone to talk to who didn't know." Jade touched a curl of the sealing's hair, then drew her hand back, as if she had just realized it was a real body and not a very realistic statue. "When the change first happens to someone, it's a shock. After a while, you get used to it. No one talks about it, but you don't forget."

No one had talked about it at Emerald Twilight, but they had seen Flower and surely realized she was dying. Moon wondered if that was why Ice had been inclined to let the mentors help them, for Flower's sake. *Ice,* he thought suddenly. *Her scales are nearly white.* Queens lived longer than Arbora, but she must be nearing the end of her life. He wondered who would replace her, if it would be Tempest or someone else, if Shadow would retain his influence or be just another older consort. He would have to ask Jade and Stone. Their alliance with Emerald Twilight might be even more tenuous than it had seemed. *Worry about that later,* he told himself. *We have to get back home first.*

Moon suddenly didn't want to stand here with the dead any more. He took Jade's wrist, absently rubbed his thumb over the softer scales on the back of her hand. "We need to talk to Negal about their ship, how we can get to it."

Jade took a deep breath. "You're right. We'll do that now."

☾

They went back to the servants' common room. Balm, Chime, and Stone were still in the bedchamber with Flower, but the others sat around on the floor and the couches. Everyone looked weary and sad. Rift was back against the far wall, separated from the others, still wary. Floret made an effort to perk up, and said, "What are we doing now?"

"We're going to get off this damn leviathan." Jade settled on one of the cushioned benches and pulled Moon down next to her. She told Song, "Go find the groundlings. Ask them to come here."

Song hurried away, and a short time later they heard the groundlings in the corridor. Drift shifted to Raksura. River hissed at him before Jade or Moon could, and Drift immediately shifted back. He said, "Sorry, I was startled." He actually sounded sorry. Moon suspected the good behavior was only going to last until the shock over Flower's death faded.

Song came in, followed by Esom, Karsis, Negal, and Orlis, then one of the men who had been imprisoned in the tower. He was about Negal's size, but his brown skin was more lined around the eyes, his hair more sprinkled with gray. Orlis smelled of nervous fear, and the new man looked as grim as if he was already resigned to some kind of betrayal. His expression tightened even more when he saw Rift.

Karsis stepped forward, cleared her throat, and said, "I believe you don't know our leader, Negal, our second assistant deviser Orlis, and Captain Damison. This is Jade, sister queen of the Indigo Cloud Court, and her consort Moon."

Moon caught Song giving Karsis a slight nod of approval. Taking her diplomatic duties as a female warrior seriously, she must have quickly informed Karsis of the proper way to greet Jade.

Negal inclined his head politely. "I'm sorry to have to make your acquaintance under such unpleasant circumstances. And I wish to apologize to you for our part in the theft of your property. Our assistance to Magister Ardan was involuntary, but I know it has put your court in a dangerous position."

It was the right thing to say. Moon could feel Jade's tension uncoiling. She said, "I'm willing to believe that. Karsis and Esom have said that you want an alliance with us, that together we can use your flying ship to escape this place. Do they speak for you?"

Negal glanced at Esom and Karsis, and smiled slightly. "In this case, yes."

Song pushed a couple of stools forward and indicated that the groundlings should sit down. Negal and the others moved to take seats, but Captain Damison said, "What about him? Rift."

Behind them, Rift stirred, started to stand. Moon turned his head enough to pin him with a look. Rift froze, and sunk back to the floor. Jade didn't even bother to flick a spine in Rift's direction. Her eyes on Damison, she said, "He isn't your concern."

"That problem appears to be sorted," Esom said to Damison. He pushed a stool at him and said pointedly, "Now sit down."

Damison hesitated, still watching Rift with deadly intensity. Then Stone came out of the back room. He stopped, glanced over the groundlings noncommittally, then came around to sit on the floor near Jade's feet. He said, in Raksuran, "Chime is taking it hard."

Moon started to get up. Jade caught his arm and gently stopped him. "Balm is with him."

Moon settled back, reluctantly. Esom looked from Stone to Jade. "Is Chime all right?" he asked, concern evident in his voice. Chime's name would have been the only word he could understand in the Raksuran exchange.

Karsis added, "If he's injured, perhaps I could help?"

Jade shook her head. "He was close to Flower; she taught him, when he was a mentor."

"Oh, I see. Of course," Esom said, though it was clear he didn't really understand, except that Chime had been Flower's student. Esom sat back, but the moment seemed to ease the tension. Damison glanced around uncomfortably, then finally took a seat.

Negal leaned forward and clasped his hands on his knee. "As you proposed, the best way to escape this city is on our ship, the *Klodifore*. If we cooperate, we should be able to reach the harbor and secure it. As long as the city authorities don't realize that we're working together, they shouldn't suspect that retrieving the ship is our goal." He spread his hands. "Then we can take you east, all the way to the forest coast if need be, before we head back to our own home."

Jade asked, "Can you launch the ship while the leviathan is still moving?"

Esom exchanged a look with Orlis. "It won't be easy, but I'm certainly willing to try."

"If I never see this creature again it will be too soon," Orlis agreed. "I'll risk anything to get off it."

Then Root ducked into the doorway, so abruptly the groundlings flinched. He said, "A groundling banged on the outside door and said Magister Lethen wants to talk!"

Jade frowned and asked Moon, "Do you know who that is?"

"Yes." He pushed himself upright. "He was outside the mortuary with the other magisters. I don't think he and Ardan were friends."

"They weren't," Negal said, frowning. "They were bitter rivals."

Jade tapped her claws on the couch cushion, thinking. "How strong is his magic?"

"He certainly couldn't seem to do anything about Ardan," Negal told her. "I think he would have if he could." He hesitated. "Will you speak to him?"

Jade nodded reluctantly. "We'd better. Just to stall him, if nothing else." She told Negal, "You come to the hall and listen, but don't let him see you."

☾

Out in the exhibit hall, Jade had Negal stand just out of sight to one side of the entrance passage, so he could listen to the conversation. Stone stood just out of sight to the other side, in case it wasn't a conversation that Lethen had in mind. Vine, Floret, River, and Drift were also clinging to the wall above the passage. The others, with Negal's crew, were poised to retreat into the underground if they had to.

Jade put her hand on the door bar and said, "Ready?"

"Probably," Moon told her. If Lethen had magic like Ardan's, all their preparations meant nothing. But if Lethen had magic like Ardan's, Moon was betting he wouldn't have had to use the firepowder to get into the mortuary.

Jade lifted the bar and pulled the door open.

Lethen stood just outside. He was as Moon remembered him from the evening in the tower: a richly-dressed, ruinously old blue-pearl man. His gaze went to Jade first. He stared at her with guarded curiosity. Then he looked at Moon and frowned, startled. "You. The trader." His expression turned saturnine. "You're one of them. Did Ardan know?"

There was no reason not to admit it now. "Yes."

Lethen swore. "The fool."

Jade said sharply, "He attacked us. He came to our colony while we were gone and stole from us."

"I'm not disputing that." Lethen folded his gnarled hands over the head of his cane. "He claimed to need artifacts of arcane power to keep the leviathan from sinking. Since we're all still alive, I assume that wasn't true."

Moon didn't see any reason not to admit that, too. "No. All he needed was the bridle."

"Then I'm a fool as well, for I believed him." Lethen eyed them a moment. "Do you know where this creature is taking us?"

"No."

Lethen said, "I do. We're headed northeast, toward Emriat-terrene."

Jade flicked a look at Moon. He said, "It's going home." That was the place in the story Rith had told them, the home of the sorcerers who had originally built the city atop the leviathan.

"A logical assumption," Lethen admitted. "It's returning to its original position." He added, "I'm a very old man. Unlike Ardan, I have all the wealth and temporal power I'm likely to ever need, and I have no wish to live on something that moves, either at someone's direction or its own random whim."

Moon said, "You want the bridle."

Lethen inclined his head. "The question is, what do you want?"

Moon exchanged a look with Jade. She said, "We want the flying boat."

Lethen frowned. "The what?"

"The metal ship in the harbor, the one that Ardan stole from the foreign explorers." Jade hesitated. "It's still there, isn't it?"

"I believe so. The harbormaster was charged with lifting it out of the water with the fishing fleet. I assume he still did his job." Lethen regarded her with open skepticism. "That's all you want?"

"Yes," Moon told him. "We'll give you the bridle, if you let us leave, with the explorers, on that boat."

Jade said, "That's not all. In Ardan's collection, there's a wooden container, an urn—"

Lethen waved that away. "My dear, take anything from this tower that you want. You can strip the place down to the foundations if you like. I've spoken with Ardan's wife. She makes no claim on his property." His sharp gaze switched back to Moon. "She told me that you allowed her to leave with her children and personal servants. It was the reason I thought it might be possible to negotiate with you."

"We don't kill unless we're provoked," Jade said. It wasn't quite a threat.

Lethen's expression was sardonic. "I'll keep that in mind. I don't supposed you'd like to give me the bridle now."

Hardly, Moon thought. "At the harbor, by the boat."

"I'll be waiting." He gave them an ironic nod and turned away. They watched him hobble briskly across the square.

As they closed the door behind him, Jade said, "Do you think we can trust him?"

"No. But I think he wants the bridle, and he doesn't care about us."

Negal stepped into the passage. "I agree. And I think we should leave, now, before he changes his mind."

Nobody wanted to argue with that.

CHAPTER EIGHTEEN

Moon stepped into the room where Flower had died. The vapor-lights were dimming, issuing only a little glowing mist, and the room was thick with shadows. Her body still lay on the bed, wrapped in silky sheets. It made an absurdly small bundle. He made himself look away, to the corner where Balm and Chime sat.

Chime huddled half in Balm's lap, and she stroked his hair. Moon went to kneel beside them and put a hand on Chime's back. "We have to leave. We're going to the flying ship in the harbor."

Balm lifted her brows. "Now? Isn't it still daylight?"

"We have a deal with the magister who's taking Ardan's place." At her expression, he added, "I know, but we're hoping this one works out better."

Chime took a sharp breath and sat up. He looked sick, exhausted. "What about her body? Do we have to leave her here? We should hide her, so they don't—"

"No, we're going to take her." Jade had decided to take the queen's funerary urn from Ardan's collection for the purpose. It was big enough to hold a small Arbora body, once the current occupant was removed. Moon was going to let Stone handle that part.

"Oh." Chime nodded, swallowed, and made to get up.

The groundlings hadn't had many personal possessions with them, just clothing and a few things Ardan had allowed them to bring from their ship. They went up to quickly gather what they needed, and the Raksura spent the time raiding the tower's kitchens and food stores, taking everything that could be easily transported and stuffed into bags. "There's no meat," Drift complained at one point as he turned out the contents of a cabinet.

"You'll eat bread and dried fish and like it," Balm told him, in the tone of someone on her last nerve.

Once that was done, both groups assembled in the exhibit hall, in the passage to the outer door. Moon had wondered if Negal's people would take the opportunity to loot Ardan's belongings, as compensation for their imprisonment. It didn't look like they had; the packs they carried were all stuffed with bags from the tower's dry food stores. Maybe they didn't want any reminders, or maybe their isolated land valued different things. All Negal had was a shoulder bag stuffed with paper, perhaps writing done while he was trapped here.

"You haven't changed your mind?" Jade asked Negal. She had the seed, carefully wrapped in Flower's old pack, securely fastened between her wing join and her shoulder. Vine, the largest male warrior, had shouldered the big pack that contained the urn. It was a heavy burden, more than four paces tall and two wide, but Stone was going to be too occupied to carry it.

Negal glanced back at the others. All of them except Karsis and Esom watched the Raksura with suspicion. They kept looking at Rift and then looking away. Negal had said they wouldn't want to be carried through the air, an attitude that Moon could understand given their experiences with Rift. But that wasn't going to make getting to the port any safer. "Unfortunately not," Negal said, a little wryly. "Though we are certain it would be a unique experience."

"I hope your walk to the harbor doesn't turn out to be a unique experience," Jade said, and nodded for Stone to go ahead.

Stone pushed open the doors and stepped out into the daylight. He shifted and his dark form blocked the doorway for a heartbeat. There was a chorus of gasps and startled flinches from the groundlings who hadn't seen him before. Then he sprang into the air so fast he seemed to vanish.

Moon followed Jade to the doorway, the warriors behind them. The plaza looked empty from here, but Stone circled overhead to scan for ambushes or hidden traps. He tipped a wing to show it was clear.

Turning back to Negal, Jade said, "Follow us. We'll make certain your route is safe."

Negal gripped his bag and said, "We will."

Jade stepped out and leapt into flight; Moon and the warriors followed her. As soon as they were above the surrounding buildings, the wind hit them like a hammer. The warriors dropped back low over the rooftops, but Moon fought it, tried to ride it without being slammed into anything, until he caught Jade's signal. Then he angled off and made for the harbor.

Jade and the others would stay with the groundlings, following them roof to roof to make sure they weren't attacked on the way through the city. They had decided that Moon and Stone would fly ahead to the ship to see if there were guards or magisters lurking aboard.

Buffeted by the wind, Moon saw mostly empty streets below, with only a few moving figures. He had to circle around to hit the harbor, but saw it was almost deserted too, the big slips for the trading vessels empty, the small fishing boats swinging in their raised cradles. The *Klodifore* was still there, tied to its pier, suspended several paces above the water. The leviathan's motion was causing the water in the harbor to churn, kicking up huge fountains of spray along the piers.

Stone circled overhead, and as Moon dropped down for a landing on the roof of the ship's top steering cabin, he turned and dipped down toward the water, abruptly vanishing behind the fishing fleet's cradles. *I hope he knows what he's doing,* Moon thought.

He crouched on the edge of the cabin roof, the wind tearing at his frills. A door on the lowest deck opened and three groundlings hurriedly exited to climb carefully down the narrow ramp that connected the ship to the pier. Those must be Ardan's men, the ones who had been taught to make the ship lift itself out of the water when the leviathan moved. Moon glanced across to the docks. A small group of groundlings waited in the shelter of one of the rickety buildings, as far away from the churning water as possible. One was Magister Lethen.

So far so good. Moon climbed down to the deck just below, found a door, and stepped inside.

To be out of the wet wind was a relief. He flicked his spines, shaking off the spray, and tasted the air. He caught a scent of nervous groundling, but it was fading fast, probably from the men who had just left.

Still, he searched the ship quickly, looking into every room and cubby, but found no one hiding aboard. He came back out onto the main deck in time to see Jade and the warriors above the harbor, about to make the difficult aerial approach to the boat. Negal, Karsis, Esom, and the other groundlings were just coming down the steps onto the dock.

Lethen and his men moved out from the shelter to meet them. Moon jumped down to the pier. From this angle he could see the bottom of the *Klodifore,* its hull hovering a few paces above the swirling water. Waves rushed continuously over the pier and made the walk along it wet and dangerous. Moon reached the dock just as Negal and the others reached Lethen.

"You have it?" Lethen demanded, raising his voice to a bellow to be heard over the wind and water. The men with him weren't all armed guards, and they weren't all blue-pearls; a few members of the other two dominant groundling races were present, the golden-skinned and dark-skinned people. Some were dressed richly enough to be other magisters or prominent traders. A few wore working clothes.

Negal looked at Moon, who shifted to groundling, to startled exclamations from Lethen's companions. He took the bridle out of his pack and said, "Let them go to the ship, and I'll give it to you."

Lethen glared, frowned suspiciously at the bridle, then said, "Very well."

Negal threw Moon a guarded look and led his people past. This was their most vulnerable moment, but somehow Moon didn't think even a magister would have brought this diverse group out to see him betray the Raksura.

Moon waited until the groundlings had made the uneasy trek down the pier and were crossing the little walkway up to the ship. Jade and the warriors had already landed on the upper deck and were watching intently. Then he handed the bridle to Lethen.

The Magister turned it over, examined it carefully, rubbed at the crystals with his thumb. Then he grunted, and asked Moon, "Will you need assistance casting off?"

In other words, *go away and don't come back.* That suited Moon. He said, "No, thank you."

He turned his back on them and went to the edge of the dock, then shifted and reached the *Klodifore's* lower deck in two long bounds.

The groundlings were all aboard, gathered on the deck. "Thank you," Negal said to Moon. His voice shook a little, though he kept his expression calm. He looked back at the city, the towers rising on the leviathan's flanks. "I never thought we would leave this place."

"We're not gone yet." Captain Damison was still grim. "We'll need help to cast off. They've still got us tied to the—"

The deck jerked as the forward cable snapped. Moon said, "It's all right."

With a tremendous splash, Stone slung his big body up onto the pier, making the wood groan. He snapped the stern cable between his claws, then shifted to groundling. Rolling to his feet, he wrung out his shirt and crossed the walkway onto the deck.

Damison shouted orders in his own language and strode away toward the nearest hatch. Two men scrambled to cut the walkway loose, while the others bolted along the deck. Negal followed Damison, and Esom and Orlis hurried inside to clatter down the first stairwell into the bowels of the ship. Karsis stood with Moon and Stone.

Drifting loose, the ship was already moving over the pier. Or the pier was moving under the ship as the leviathan pushed forward. Moon felt a tremor through the metal deck underfoot, and there was an answering rumble from somewhere deep in the hull. Then the ship rose a little higher and jolted into motion.

Moon swayed and Karsis caught the rail to steady herself as the *Klodifore* pulled rapidly away and turned to head for open water. As they came about, Stone muttered, "Uh oh." They were nearing the giant ridge of the leviathan's leg, which pumped rhythmically as the creature swam, water swirling in a dangerous whirlpool around it.

That could be a problem, Moon thought, glancing up to where Jade and the other Raksura climbed down from the top deck. If the ship was struck, the Raksura could get into the air, but the ship would be sucked under before they could get the groundlings out. And then the Raksura would be trapped out here. As aware of the danger as he was, Karsis leaned forward on the railing and said grimly, "We can make it. I know we can make it."

The big chimneys atop the ship belched white smoke, then it suddenly surged forward. The thrashing leg fell behind them and they angled sharply away. The city passed them rapidly, the creature's mountainous body moving forward with powerful strokes of its legs and tail.

Moon let out his breath in relief and shifted to groundling. They were going to miss the tail by a good distance. The wind fell away with the sound of the churning water. The sun was moving toward evening and then there was only the ship chugging along, a few paces above the gentle waves.

Karsis slumped, and her expression revealed relief and all the raw emotion she had been holding in check for all the months of her captivity. "I didn't think we'd ever get away."

"I didn't either, and we were only there for four days," Stone told her.

"It was a long four days," Moon admitted. Jade swung under the railing on the deck above and dropped down next to him. The others were all lined up there, watching the mountainous leviathan grow slowly smaller in the distance. The ship turned and Moon could feel they were heading east, as promised, back to the coast of the forest Reaches.

Karsis pushed her hair back, her voice thick, as she got herself under control again. "If there's anything else we can do for you . . ."

"Show us a place where we can sleep," Jade said.

☽

Karsis showed them to two small cabins, side by side, on the first deck above the water. Moon suspected they might have belonged to her and Esom, but he was too tired to care where the groundlings were going to sleep. Jade claimed the narrow bed in the first room, then divided the warriors up and made certain they would take turns on watch, just in case any groundlings decided to kill them. Moon was only dimly aware of most of that, since Jade had claimed the bed by dumping him in it, and as soon as his body was horizontal he had started to fall asleep.

He woke much later, with Jade in her Arbora form warm and heavy on top of him, her head pillowed on his chest, a knee pushed between his thighs. The room smelled of Raksura in groundling form who needed to bathe and wash their clothes. He was aware that the sun was now rising over the sea, that they had slept from the late afternoon through the night. *Flower's dead,* he remembered suddenly, with a spark of pain that brought him fully alert.

He could feel the ship still heading east, pulling a little toward the south, but that was probably the wind. The *Klodifore* vibrated in a way that the *Valendera* hadn't, but it wasn't entirely unpleasant. Soon they would be close enough to the coast to fly the rest of the way. There was something he needed to take care of first.

He nudged Jade gently, and she tightened her hold on him. "I have to get up," he whispered, and tugged on one of her head frills. She hummed low in her throat and rolled onto her side without really waking. He sat up and then had to spend a moment just looking at her. *You're lucky,* he told himself. He didn't think there were many young sister queens who would have willingly shouldered this responsibility, or who would have let their consorts take the risks he had. *I hope we're done with that now.* He was more than willing to get back to the colony and try living the normal Raksuran way.

Moon climbed out of the bunk and picked his way across the floor, where Chime, Balm, Song, and Vine were curled up on the spare cushions and blankets they had found in a cabinet. He opened the door quietly and stepped out into the corridor.

Floret sat on a cushion on the floor, leaning back against the wall. "Are you hungry?" she asked, keeping her voice low. "We saved you some food."

"Not yet." Moon sat on his heels and glanced through the partly open doorway of the other room. Stone was sprawled in the bed, with River, Drift, and Root in a comfortable pile on one side of the room, and Rift on the other. "Has Rift tried to leave?"

"No. Everyone's been quiet." Floret sat forward, stretching her back. "Most of us woke up in the middle of the night to eat. The dried fish wasn't as bad as Drift said it was. Karsis and the older one, the leader, came by once to see if we needed anything, but that's it."

"Good." Moon pushed to his feet. "I'll be back."

The ship was quiet, but Moon could smell cooking odors, some kind of grain porridge. He followed the scent down a corridor and then a set of stairs, to a sitting area. There were couches against the walls, and Esom sat on one reading a leather-bound book. He was dressed in fresh clothes, and had replaced his broken spectacles with a different set. In the far wall was an open doorway leading to the room with the big metal stove and the storage for dishes and food supplies. A couple of crewmen were in there, eating at the table.

Esom looked up, blinking, startled out of deep concentration. "Oh, hello, Moon."

Moon pulled a padded stool closer and sat down, facing Esom. "Can I talk to you?"

"Yes. Is something wrong?"

Moon couldn't think of any way to ease up on the subject. He asked, "Did you kill Ardan?"

"What? No. What?" Startled, Esom closed the book and sat up. "I thought you said he fell and hit his head when the leviathan moved?"

"He might have. But the way he fell, it would make more sense if someone hit him from behind." The men at the table in the next room had stopped eating, and watched them with a mix of suspicion and curiosity. They were a little too far away to hear the conversation.

"It wasn't me." Esom seemed earnest and baffled. "Stone left me on the west side of the chamber. I was trying to work my way over to the door to the tunnel, but with the water and the angle of the floor, it was slow going. I kept sliding down and ramming into the pillars. I'd just gotten within sight of the door when Stone came back for me."

That sounded true, unfortunately. "I was hoping it was you." Esom had plenty of reason to hate Ardan, and his friends had still been trapped back in the tower; he might have seen it as the best opportunity to free them.

"Sorry to disappoint you, but I see what you mean." Esom looked thoughtful. "If not me, then who? Do you think it was one of his own men? I don't think most of them knew he was in control of the leviathan. They may have suspected it, but . . ."

"But it doesn't make much sense."

"No," Esom admitted. He leaned forward, struck by a sudden thought. "Unless one of them secretly worked for Magister Lethen."

"Maybe," Moon said, and let Esom talk about it until he could pretend to be convinced. He was fairly certain he knew who had killed Ardan, but he didn't want to be on this ship when he confronted the guilty party.

☾

Since they were getting along with the groundlings, they spent another day and a night resting on the *Klodifore*. Moon slept through most of it, though he made sure someone was always watching Rift. River and Drift became unwilling allies in this, since they distrusted Rift far more than they disliked Moon, and never hesitated to take a turn guarding him.

Moon hadn't spoken about his suspicions to anyone but Esom.

The weather was good, windy but clear. The ship stopped at one point and settled down in the water to fill its tanks directly from the freshwater sea. It was a far more convenient system than having to fill jars or buckets and haul them up the side, the way the Golden Islanders did on their boats. It meant there was plenty of bathing water, which they all took advantage of. The basins were small, but capable of producing hot water, which made up for a lot.

The rest of Negal's crew had adjusted reluctantly to the presence of the Raksura, though they were still obviously wary. They stared at them, and asked Karsis and Esom questions, most of which they had to pass along to Moon or Chime. Or to Floret, who had spent a while talking with Karsis while waiting at the camp in the abandoned tower. The crew was especially nervous of Stone at first, but he used his uncanny ability to disarm groundling fears, which to the untrained eye involved hanging around in their cooking room and asking about their food. By the evening they were so used to him that none of them seemed to mind when he fell asleep in front of the stove in their main sitting area. Esom tried hard to talk to Chime about groundling magic, and Chime resorted to hiding in their cabin, clinging to the ceiling above the doorway where no one could see him from the corridor.

Moon didn't think these groundlings would ever be entirely comfortable with the presence of shifters, but maybe that was for the best. He hoped that the next time they left their isolated land, they would explore in a different direction.

☾

On the morning of the second day aboard, Stone judged they were more than close enough for the warriors to make the flight to land. Moon stood on the highest deck with Chime. It was a sunny morning, and the groundlings had brought the ship to a hovering halt to make it easier for them to take off. On the deck just below, Jade spoke with Negal, formally taking their leave. The other warriors were still inside, with Balm tasked to make sure they were all prepared for the long flight.

Chime squinted toward the east, though they were a little too far out to see the shore. After the two days of rest, Chime was at least able to pretend to be like his usual self. He still hadn't talked about Flower yet, the way the others did, sharing good memories, but Moon thought he just needed more time. Moon nudged him with a shoulder. "Ready to get home?"

"Of course," Chime said, but he didn't sound ready. It might just be the flight to shore. Moon didn't think any of the warriors were looking forward to that.

"This is going to be interesting," Stone muttered, and leaned over the rail to gauge the distance down. His size made launching from the boat problematic.

"I could carry you up in the air and drop you," Moon offered, and dodged the resulting slap at his head.

Jade leapt up from below and swung over the railing. Balm and the other warriors clattered out of the hatch behind them, already shifted and ready to go. The groundlings came out onto the deck below to watch.

"Ready?" Jade asked, rippling her spines to test the wind. "The weather's perfect."

"It's not the weather we're waiting for," Moon told her.

Stone growled. "Hold on." He took a deep breath, and climbed up onto the railing. Then he flung himself forward. He shifted in mid-fall, eliciting gasps and cries of excitement from the groundlings. He flapped hard, wingtips brushing the water before he got enough lift to rise. Then he caught the wind and soared upward.

Moon and the others followed him over the rail. Karsis and Esom waved and called goodbyes, and Moon waved back.

It was an easier flight toward the shore than away from it, and they were able to ride the wind the whole way. Moon kept an eye on Rift, making sure he didn't drop behind and turn back while the *Klodifore* was still in range.

☾

It was late evening when they landed on the shore, about midway between the Kek city and the point where they had originally camped.

It was a grass-covered beach on the edge of the great forest, perfect for a night's camp. Stone climbed up a mountain-tree sapling to sleep on one of its big branches, while the warriors stretched and got ready to go hunting. Back on the *Klodifore*, they had decided to send Stone ahead with the seed and the urn. The Emerald Twilight mentors had given them instructions for trying to re-attach the seed, and the process sounded like it would take at least a few days. His ordinary pace was twice as fast as even Moon and Jade could fly, and he could get the seed back to the colony tree much faster alone. They were all going to have a big meal and sleep here tonight, then take off at dawn.

As the warriors broke up into hunting parties, Vine jerked his head toward Rift. "Do we still need to watch him? I mean, aren't we going to just let him go?" He looked from Jade to Moon, a little worried. "Or were we going to let him stay with us?" Rift was out of earshot, standing in the shadow of the trees, looking into the forest.

Jade lifted a brow at Moon, who said, "We're going to let him go. I'll take care of it."

Jade cocked her head, a little surprised. "You weren't—" She had clearly assumed Moon would want to at least ask Rift to stay. "Are you sure?"

"Yes. It's all right." He touched her hand in reassurance, and walked across the soft grass, into the forest shadow where Rift waited.

Rift glanced at Moon, and flattened his spines in deference. He said, "It's good to be back."

Moon didn't see any reason to waste time. He said, "Why did you kill Ardan?"

Rift's spines flicked, and he turned to face Moon. He shook his head, as if flustered. "Why do you think it was me? You said he was hit on the head. That's the way a groundling kills, not the way we do it."

Moon thought, *So he did do it.* He had been nearly certain, though there had been a slight chance that Esom's spy theory was true. But Rift had formulated that objection too fast for an innocent person, as if he had already thought about what he would say if he was accused. "Esom was the only groundling nearby, and he says it wasn't him. It could have been one of Ardan's men, who managed not to get washed away by the flood, but I don't think so." He watched Rift thoughtfully. "He was hit on the head so whoever found him would think a groundling did it."

Rift showed his teeth briefly. "And none of your friends are smart enough to think of that?"

"None of my friends would have bothered to hide it." All the Indigo Cloud Raksura could have killed Ardan to protect the seed, but none of them would have thought of concealing the act. Moon shook his head. "Ardan helped you. He took care of you. You could have left when he took you back to the Reaches to look for the seed. He could have chained you up, put spells on you, but he didn't. He didn't need to. He'd made you his friend, and that was the only chain he thought he needed. But he didn't really know you, did he?"

"You're wrong. He would never have let me leave." Rift leaned forward urgently. "He would have made me take him to steal another seed."

"Maybe." But something about his expression told Moon that Rift had just thought of that convenient excuse. "He wasn't afraid of you. He had his back to you."

Rift hissed, glaring at him. "So you've never killed anyone by stealth? You've never had to, to survive?"

Moon snorted. It was almost funny. "I killed a Fell ruler by stealth. But that was a Fell." It had made him a target and eventually brought the Fell to Indigo Cloud, but that was beside the point. "What's it like to kill someone who trusts you?"

Rift snarled silently and looked away, but there was something false about the emotion behind it. Moon realized at that moment what had bothered him all along about Rift. Rift had been playing a part for him, just like the groundlings who acted out plays for the festival crowds in Kish. Just like Moon had pretended to be a groundling for all those turns. *You saw through him, because he's not any better at it than you are.* That story that Rift had told, about being thrown out of his court because of a fight with another warrior, had been calculated to engender sympathy. Moon hadn't believed it at the time, and it seemed less and less likely the more he spoke to Rift.

Groundlings had always been wary of Moon because somehow they had sensed he was lying to them, even if they weren't sure why or what about. Now he knew just what that elusive sense of wrongness felt like.

For Moon, Rift had been playing the part of a poor lonely solitary who needed help, probably just a variation on the part he had played for Ardan, but more geared toward Raksuran sensibilities. The part he had played for the guards and the crew of the *Klodifore*, the groundlings he had been free to terrorize, was probably a lot closer to the real Rift. With considerably less patience, Moon said, "Just tell me why you did it."

"I've told you why. He wouldn't let me go." Rift sounded more sulky than angry.

"After you told him I was a solitary, he offered to let me stay on the leviathan, if I didn't want to go back with the court," Moon said. "What did you tell him, about why you left your court?"

Rift tensed up again, his spines trembling. "I didn't tell him anything."

"If you'd lied to him to make him feel sorry for you, that wouldn't have mattered. I lived with groundlings; everything I did and said was a lie. But what if you told him the truth, and you couldn't take the chance that he'd tell us." It was a guess, but Moon saw Rift's whole body go rigid.

Rift bared his fangs. "You're assuming I was planning to beg to join your court. From what I've heard, it's so close to dying off, they had to take a solitary as a consort."

Moon didn't take the bait, but it made him more certain he was on the right trail. "No, I'm assuming you want to find another group of Raksura to get close to, because you're tired of killing groundlings."

Rift's expression was more amused than anything else. He said, "They're just groundlings."

"Arbora are just groundlings who can shift. Is that who you killed at your old court, until they figured it out?"

Rift shook his head, still amused, then lunged for Moon. Moon had been waiting for that. He ducked away from Rift's clawed swipe, and punched him in the face hard enough to stun him. Then he caught his throat and slammed him down on his back. Low and close to his ear, Moon said, "Better stick with helpless groundlings, and leave feral consorts alone."

Rift whimpered, such a patently false manipulation that Moon almost tore his throat out right there. Rift said, "I'll go. You'll never see me again."

"If I do, you're dead." Moon dragged him upright and tossed him away, further into the forest. Rift tumbled into a crouch, threw one last look back, then bolted away into the trees.

Moon turned back toward the others, only just now realizing they were all gathered on the grassy beach, watching him. Even Stone had dropped back out of the tree and stood there in groundling form.

Root said, "I'm confused. I thought Rift was a nice solitary, like Moon."

Song clapped a hand over her eyes in embarrassment. Vine told Root, "Remember how I told you you weren't allowed to talk anymore?"

Root hissed at him, but Moon ignored all the byplay. Jade seemed concerned, and he doubted it was because of the aborted fight. She said, "Should I ask?"

Moon shrugged, rippled his spines to take the tension out of his back. "Balm was right."

Jade looked at Balm, who shrugged too. She said, "I just said that that solitary was not like him."

Jade flicked her spines in acknowledgement, and smiled at her. "Good." She turned to the others. "Go now, if you want to get back before dark."

The group reluctantly broke up. Balm took Chime's wrist and led him away, saying, "We'll build a fire and make tea." Moon could see River struggling with the urge to make a comment, and the knowledge that Jade would probably not react well to it and that he was still several days away from Pearl's protection. He finally looped an arm around Drift's neck and hauled him away.

"Are you going to say 'I told you so'?" Moon asked Stone. Stone rolled his eyes and turned to go back to his tree.

Jade stepped up to Moon. As he shifted to groundling, she put an arm around his waist and pulled him against her. Keeping her voice low, she said, "I know that was hard."

He leaned his forehead against hers. It had been hard, even knowing what Rift was really like. "He wasn't who I hoped he was."

CHAPTER NINETEEN

Moon and Jade saw Stone off at dawn the next morning, while the warriors slept in a little longer. From the wide branch of the mountain tree, they could see the rising sun reflecting rose and gold off the wispy clouds. It would be another good day for flying.

Stone stretched extravagantly, yawned, and told Jade, "Don't think I don't know why you're sending me ahead."

Jade nodded. "So Pearl can take it out on you instead of us."

Moon knew they were right, but he couldn't help saying, "We got the seed back. What kind of sense does that make?"

"Sense doesn't enter into it where queens are concerned," Stone told him. He jerked his head at Jade. "Get used to it."

Jade folded her arms, regarding him deliberately. "Please. Coming from you, that's funny." She hesitated, her gaze on the pack that held the urn and the carefully bundled seed. "Don't let Pearl hold Flower's farewell until we get there."

Stone shouldered the bulky pack without apparent effort, though with the urn it was almost four paces tall. He said, "I won't." With that, he walked to where the branch sloped down, and jumped off. He shifted in mid-fall, snapped his wings out to catch the air and flapped to stay aloft, hard wingbeats taking him away through the forest.

Watching him vanish in the green shadows, Moon realized he didn't even know what Raksura did with their dead. He knew from what the others had said that the bodies at the old colony had been burned inside the ruin, with the Fell dragged out and left for predators along the river bank, but he didn't know what the normal practice was. He said, "What's going to happen at Flower's farewell?"

He hadn't phrased the question particularly well, but Jade understood what he meant. "At the old colony, we buried our dead in the gardens. But here . . . The histories said that there's a place down in the roots of the tree for burials of Arbora and warriors. They used to put the royal Aeriat inside the wood itself, somehow, and made the tree grow over them. I don't think we know how to make that happen anymore."

Stone had said something about that, when they had found the urn in Ardan's collection. That thought made Moon remember just how much he wanted to return to the tree. "I don't care how crazy Pearl is going to be, I can't wait to get back."

Jade smiled at him. "Then wake the warriors and let's go."

☾

They still took it easy on the warriors, finding a place to camp before dark and sleeping past dawn. One evening, they stopped on a mountain-tree platform to rest and hunt the herd of furry grasseaters grazing on one of the stretches of open meadow. They weren't too hungry, so Jade told Balm, River, and Floret to only take three kills, while the others got a camp ready.

Moon flew up to a branch to keep watch over them, so had a good view of it when River tried to slam Balm out of the way and take the buck she was stooping on. Balm, who had either been expecting something like this or just had lightning-fast reflexes, rolled up and away from the blow, twisted to come down on top of River, and flung him out of her way. River righted himself with a couple of wild flaps, Balm took her kill, and Floret circled away to make it clear she wasn't involved.

When the warriors returned to the camp, no one mentioned the incident. Moon just smiled to himself. Balm obviously had no intention of allowing River to push her around anymore.

They traveled steadily for six days with no trouble, then ran into a heavy rain that lasted a day and a night. It was too heavy to fly through, so they took shelter in a hollow in an ancient, dying mountain-tree. The tree was crumbling and the hollow had leaks, something they didn't discover until it was raining hard enough that no one wanted to venture out to look for a better shelter.

It didn't make for a good night's sleep, and they all emerged early the next morning wet and cranky. To make up for it, Jade decided they would make camp on a small forest platform nearby, with the idea that full stomachs would make up for the lack of sleep.

Jade, Balm, and Song stayed at the campsite, and the others broke up into groups for hunting. Moon went with Chime, with Root tagging along, and they flew some distance from the camp before they found a platform big enough for a grasseater herd.

They took a big buck, and Moon bled the carcass by draping it over the branch, while Chime and Root kept a lookout for predators. "You think Stone's had time to get there yet?" Chime asked. He sat nearby, and Root was above them, exploring the knobs and hollows on an upper branch.

Moon thought about it, gauging time and distance and Stone's superior speed. "No, not yet." They were taking the direct route from the coast to Indigo Cloud, but Stone had planned to stop at Emerald Twilight. He should have reached it two or three days ago, and he would have stayed the night at least, both for the meal and the chance to sleep. He would have also told them about the seed and how they had gotten it back, in order to make sure Emerald Twilight knew Indigo Cloud was no longer a weak court at the verge of disaster. Jade had thought this would make for a better chance of good future relations between the two courts. "It'll probably take him another day or so."

"The others will be so relieved that we got the seed back." Chime frowned. "Until he tells them about Flower." He shook his head. "At least by the time we get there . . ."

Moon hesitated, but Root was still on the branch above them, occupied with poking a stick into a hole, and wasn't listening. He said, "It's still going to be hard. They're all going to want to talk to you about her."

"I know." Chime shrugged his spines uneasily. "It's not that I don't want to talk about her, but it's just . . . hard right now. We knew she was dying for so long, and yet it still feels like it happened so quickly. I guess I was too good at putting it out of my mind, pretending she was going to be fine if she just got more rest."

Moon nudged the carcass over, and sat back on his heels, hooking his disemboweling claws into the wood to steady himself. "Did you have a chance to talk to her about what happened inside the leviathan? How you kept getting—" He waved a hand beside his head. "Visions from it?"

"No. I wish I had." Chime looked up at Moon, the scales on his brow furrowed with worry. "Esom kept wanting to talk about it. He seemed to think I'm going to be able to sense things like he can. I told him I wasn't like a groundling sorcerer, and I wasn't going to be like one, no matter what."

"Would it be so bad if you were?"

Chime glared at him. "Yes." He glanced back around, toward the west. "The others are coming this way."

Moon stood and leaned over the steaming carcass to see if it was ready to move. Then Chime said, "Wait. Who's that with—" His voice sharpened. "That's not them."

"What?" Moon looked, straightening up. Four warriors . . . no, five warriors came toward them through the trees. The colors and sizes were all wrong; these were strangers. "We're about a day's flight from Emerald Twilight." He looked down at the carcass, belatedly wondering if they were trespassing. "Are we hunting in their territory?"

"Yes, but we're just passing through. Nobody cares about that." Chime pushed to his feet, watching the warriors approach.

There were two big males with copper-red scales, a smaller blue male, and two females, one green and one dull yellow. It was obvious they were heading this way. Maybe nobody cared about poaching back in the territory the old Indigo Cloud colony had occupied, but things might be different here in the Reaches. Moon said, "Root, come down here."

Root dropped from the branch above to land next to Moon. "What do they want?" he asked, sounding a little nervous.

"We don't know." Moon wondered what the penalty for poaching was, if they would have to fight, and how many warriors he could take out on his own. Chime wasn't the best fighter, and Root was still on the small side. Chime's spines flicked uneasily and he whispered, "This isn't good. I don't know everything about being a warrior, but I don't think they should be approaching a strange consort like this."

Moon flicked his spines back. "If they're from Emerald Twilight, they know who we are. We're not strangers."

"Still . . ." Chime muttered.

The warriors banked in, then split up at the last moment so that three landed on the branch above and two came down on this branch, about ten paces from Moon, Chime, and Root. There was something about them that made Moon's spines itch. He didn't recognize any of them from Emerald Twilight, but there had been a lot of warriors and he hadn't been paying much attention to the ones clustered around the younger queens.

The green female had landed on their branch, and now she said, "What court are you from?"

She didn't sound angry or aggressive, and Root and Chime both lowered their ruffled spines. Chime said, "We're on our way back to Indigo Cloud. Are you from—"

Something hit Moon in the face, a wet membrane filled with liquid, thrown by one of the warriors above them. He staggered back a step, startled more than hurt, and snarled in surprised fury. Root growled, astonished, and crouched to leap upward. But Chime grabbed for Moon, shouting, "No, don't breathe, don't breathe!"

But the heavy sweet fumes of the splattered liquid filled his lungs, his head. Another membrane hit Chime in the side of the head and he jerked away. Moon stumbled sideways, darkness closing in around him rapidly, falling . . .

☾

Moon drifted awake slowly, weighed down by a heavy lassitude. He felt oddly reluctant to move. He made himself turn his head, and felt leaves and branches creak and rustle beneath him, smelled the pungent scent of crushed foliage. *Leaves?* he thought, and remembered falling. He opened his eyes.

He was lying on a woven surface of leafy branches, more branches arching over him, latticed with big broad fern fronds. Chime lay beside him, sprawled on his back with one arm over his eyes. They were both in their groundling forms. The reason for the shelter was obvious; rain pattered gently on it. The light coming through the leaves was much darker, and it felt close to early evening. Moon rubbed his forehead, frowning. *I don't remember . . .* anything. How they had gotten here, building the shelter, where here was.

Something stirred behind him; there was someone else in here with them. He managed to roll to his side and shove himself up on one arm.

A young warrior in groundling form sat near the mouth of the makeshift shelter. He was heavily built, with light copper skin and red-brown hair, and wore a faded gold vest and pants, and copper armbands with polished grey-white stones. Moon stared, trying unsuccessfully to recognize him.

Then the warrior smiled complacently and said, "Don't be afraid."

"What?" Instinctively, Moon tried to shift. But he felt the pressure, the constriction that halted the change, that meant there was a queen nearby deliberately preventing him from shifting. *That doesn't make sense . . . wait.* Memory returned. The strange warriors. *They drugged me.* The liquid the warrior had thrown at him had been a simple to cause sleep. Moon snarled, lunged forward, and slammed the heel of his hand into the warrior's face.

Moon had moved too quickly for the warrior to shift. He reeled back with a yelp and clutched his bloody nose. Moon shoved him aside, scrambled out of the shelter, and pushed to his feet.

They were on a platform high in the suspended forest, in a small camp in a clearing surrounded by fern tree saplings. The mountain-tree supporting the platform arched and twisted above them, the giant branches deflecting most of the rain, so it fell on them only as a light drizzle. There were two other shelters, just lean-tos, with warriors scattered around, all staring at Moon. He counted at least seven, all still in their winged forms. It looked like a semi-permanent camp. They had dug a small firepit in the center, and there was an embossed metal kettle on the coals. Then a queen stepped out from the shadow of one of the shelters.

Moon had been half-expecting Ash, young, arrogant, foolishly persistent Ash. But it wasn't her.

For a moment he thought it was Tempest. Her scales were the same light blue, the webbed overlay the same tint of gold. But this queen's build was a little slighter, her features sharper. Moon tried to shift again, just on the off chance she would let him, but the pressure preventing him was still there.

She eyed the warrior with the bloody nose, who stumbled to his feet, then cocked her head speculatively at Moon. She said, "So that rumor about you being a fighter wasn't all talk."

Chime crawled out of the shelter, tried to stand, and sat down hard. He focused on Moon, and said, worried and wary, "What happened?"

Moon shook his head to show he had no idea. He asked the queen, "Who are you?" She hadn't been introduced with the other queens at Emerald Twilight; he would have remembered her. *Unless that was her out on the balcony when Ash fought Jade, and not Tempest.* At that distance, it would have been hard to tell them apart. "You were with Ash, at Emerald Twilight?"

She inclined her head. "I'm surprised you noticed me. I'm Halcyon."

Halcyon. From her appearance, and her name . . . "You're Tempest's clutchmate?"

"Yes. And I'm afraid I'm the one who provoked Ash to challenge your queen. It was her own impulse to confront you in the greeting hall, but I decided to make use of the opportunity. Ash has always been easily led." Halcyon stepped toward him, casually rippling her spines to shed the rainwater. "And she'll be blamed, when word of your disappearance is carried to Emerald Twilight."

Moon's head was beginning to clear, enough to realize just how much trouble they were in. Chime said, incredulously, "You've been out here all this time, waiting for us?"

"No, only for the past three days, since your line-grandfather stopped at Emerald Twilight," Halcyon tilted her head, still studying Moon. "All we had to do was search the direct routes from the coast to Indigo Cloud." She added, "You were easy to find, but we won't be. We're a half a day's travel away from where my warriors found you, not in the direction of Emerald Twilight."

They wouldn't have caught us, if we hadn't stopped for the rain. Moon bet Halcyon had forced her warriors to fly through it. "Why? What do you get out of this?" He couldn't believe that besting Indigo Cloud, small and struggling as it was, would be any kind of triumph for an Emerald Twilight queen. And he couldn't believe that an ex-feral consort from an unknown bloodline was that big a prize.

Halcyon took another step toward him. "Ice is nearing the end of her reign, and the last thing she wants is trouble from another court. She'll have to punish Ash, and Tempest will step forward to shield her, and be disgraced."

Moon exchanged a look with Chime, who grimaced in dismay. Moon turned back to Halcyon. "And that will leave you as sister queen? What about all the others?"

Halcyon flicked her spines, this time in a shrug. "Ice knows I'm the only one who could replace Tempest. I'm not worried about the others."

I'm worried about us, Moon thought. This plan wouldn't work with a live consort or warrior around to explain that Ash wasn't the guilty party. He wasn't sure why they were both still alive now. *Wait, we weren't alone.* He looked around and didn't see any sign of a third prisoner. He demanded, "What did you do to Root?"

"The young warrior who was with you?" Halcyon glanced at one of her warriors, the big green-scaled woman.

The warrior snorted with contempt. "Nothing. He ran away."

Chime hissed at her. "He wouldn't run away, he's too stupid. You hurt him."

"We didn't," the warrior said, and her spines ruffled angrily. She repeated with emphasis, "He ran away."

Moon didn't believe it either. *Root might be dead.* But if he had run back to the others, all he could tell them was that strange warriors, possibly from Emerald Twilight, had taken Moon and Chime away. Which would suit Halcyon's purpose completely.

Maybe she had planned to kill them, but when it came down to it, found it hard to take that final step. Especially with a consort. Maybe she just wasn't certain if her warriors would go that far. Moon didn't think pretending he didn't understand that would do any good. "When are you going to kill us?"

Chime made a faint noise. Either he hadn't realized this inevitable component to Halcyon's plan, or he just didn't want Moon to mention it aloud.

The warriors stirred a little uneasily, but Halcyon hissed with amusement. She stepped close, close enough for Moon to feel her breath. Every muscle tensed and the back of

Moon's neck prickled, but he didn't step back, didn't drop his gaze.

She said, with dry amusement, "I didn't say I'd kill you."

"Then what did you plan to do with me?"

"That's up to you. You could cooperate." Halcyon trailed the back of her claws against his cheek, sending a shivering pulse down Moon's spine.

"What do you mean?" Moon was fairly certain he knew exactly what she meant, but he wanted to stall. It had to take extra concentration to keep Moon and Chime from shifting without affecting her own warriors. All they needed was a chance to escape. Moon thought he could outfly a queen, especially a queen who hadn't been doing much of anything but sitting around Emerald Twilight plotting against her clutchmate. It was Chime he was worried about; with all the long distance flying they had been doing lately, Chime might have an advantage over the other warriors. But a queen could catch a warrior easily. Which was probably why they had bothered to drug Chime and bring him along, as a hostage for Moon's good behavior.

As if in idle speculation, Halcyon said, "I could say I took you from Ash. Your queen wouldn't want you after that. You could stay with me."

Moon hoped she couldn't hear how hard his heart was pounding. "I think you're underestimating my queen."

She laughed. "They said you knew very little of our ways. I see they were right."

"What about your consort?" Presumably he was back at Emerald Twilight, enjoying the respite from his queen.

Her lip curled. "He does what I tell him to do." Her hand dropped and she ran sheathed claws down Moon's throat. "A change would be interesting."

"No," Moon said, reacting before his brain caught up to him. *Keep stalling,* he thought. Keeping himself and Chime alive was all that mattered. "It wouldn't—"

A sound high above them made everyone look up. It was a warrior, flying down from the upper branches. *Not flying,* Moon realized. He was falling. One of the others leapt up to catch him, breaking his fall. But the others stared at what hurtled down after him.

A flash of vivid blue and silver-gray resolved into Jade, wings spread and spines furled, as she dropped down on them like vengeance itself.

With a startled growl, Halcyon jerked Moon around, his back to her, her claws pressed against his throat. She yelled at the warriors and they sprang into the air to attack.

Jade flared her wings to meet them. She slapped three Emerald Twilight warriors out of the air without a pause for breath, then closed with a big male and tossed him aside in a spray of blood.

Root appeared out of nowhere, leapt on a smaller warrior, and wrestled him off a branch, but Moon didn't see any of the others. Not that Jade needed them, apparently. Moon couldn't do anything but stare, Halcyon's claws pricking his skin. He had seen Jade fight Fell, but never seen her take on other Raksura, not when she was really angry. The fight with Ash had been nothing; these warriors had no chance against her.

Halcyon must have realized it too. She shrieked, "Stop! I'll rip his throat out!"

The remaining warriors broke off and veered away from Jade. Three were gone, either fallen to the forest floor or caught on the branches and platforms somewhere below them. Some of the others flapped unsteadily to nearby branches, badly wounded. Root dropped to land on the platform near Chime, who crouched uneasily.

Jade snapped her wings in and landed ten paces away from Moon and Halcyon. Flexing her bloody claws, she bared her fangs. She radiated fury like a furnace. Her scales were slick with rain but unmarked. None of the warriors had been able to land a claw on her. She took in Halcyon's position, how she was using Moon as a shield, and sneered. "Coward."

Halcyon snarled, her voice rising in rage. "Bitch."

Jade hissed an unpleasant laugh. "Dead woman."

Halcyon tossed Moon aside and leapt for her. Moon hit the wet grass with a thump and rolled, then scrambled up. Jade and Halcyon slammed into each other, tumbled across the platform, and broke apart. Their scales were already streaked with scratches and blood. They circled each other, moving fast, then Halcyon darted in and nearly caught a slash across the face.

Moon tried to shift to his winged form and hissed with relief when the change flowed over him. Halcyon was obviously too distracted to maintain control over him. But unlike Ash, Halcyon was closer to an even match for Jade. And after that brief conversation, Moon doubted either of them were in any state to think about consequences or negotiate. He stepped over to the firepit and grabbed the kettle. It was a heavy one, with an iron bottom meant to hold warming stones. As Halcyon ducked away from a slash, Moon lunged in and slammed her in the head with it, putting all his weight behind the blow.

Halcyon jolted forward, right into a blow from Jade that rocked her head back. Between that and the kettle, she dropped like a rock.

Jade stood over her, breathing hard. She stared at Moon, incredulous, offended, and still wild-eyed. "What was that?" she demanded, her voice gravelly with rage.

"You can't kill her," Moon said deliberately. He dropped the kettle beside the firepit and shifted back to groundling, hoping that would calm Jade down. Halcyon's head was cut and bleeding, some of her spines broken and crushed, but he saw her furled wings tremble, showing she was still breathing. "We have to take her back to Emerald Twilight and make her tell what she tried to do." If Jade killed her, the warriors could lie about what had happened, claim they were attacked. Emerald Twilight might choose to believe them just to avoid the disgrace.

Jade didn't think much of that idea. A growl thickening her voice, she said, "She won't tell them. She'll lie."

"Her warriors won't, if you threaten them. Tell them you'll kill her unless they tell the truth." The survivors had all fled the tree, but Jade could still catch one if she hurried.

Jade shook her spines and hissed in pure fury. Root shifted to groundling and dropped to a crouch, prudently not taking sides. But in a small voice, Chime contributed, "You can ask for a mentor as witness when you get to Emerald Twilight. That will involve the Arbora, and the other queens can't pretend it didn't happen. They'll be forced to deal with her."

Jade shook her spines and grimaced with contempt. "We'll never get her there without killing her, so I might as well do it now."

Moon countered, "They have simples that make you sleep. It worked on me. It'll probably work on a queen."

Jade's shout of thwarted rage was so loud it hurt Moon's ears. He winced, and Chime and Root both flattened themselves down in the grass and covered their heads. She stalked back and forth, then stopped and flung her hands in the air. "You're right! I'll go get a damn warrior. If that piece of excrement moves—" She growled again and flung herself into the air.

"Get the green female!" Moon yelled after her. She had seemed like the leader of the warriors, and was probably the one most attached to Halcyon.

Root sat up to watch Jade speed away. "She carried me here, so I could show her the way," he confided to Moon. "I've never flown so fast!"

Chime pushed to his feet. Shaking a little, he wiped the sweat off his forehead. "I'll go look for the simple. It's probably in one of these shelters." He went to the first one and ducked down to look through the entrance.

"Hurry." Moon sat down the grass, keeping a wary eye on Halcyon. The simple had given him a headache and a dry throat. His neck was bleeding a little from Halcyon's claws, but not enough to worry about. It felt like the end of a very long day, though so far he had only been conscious for a small part of it. "Where are the others?" he asked Root.

"On their way here, following Jade's markers. We were going to wait until they caught up, and attack in the middle of the night, but—" Root waved a hand, indicating the disturbed camp. "Jade changed her mind."

"This is it." Chime came out of the shelter, holding a lizardskin bag, intricately tooled and dyed. He sat down to rummage in it and pulled out various cloth packets and a couple of stoppered bottles. "I'll have to mix another batch, but it won't take long. You don't have to be a mentor to make it work, which is probably why they picked this one."

Moon reached over to ruffle Root's hair. "So you just pretended to run away?"

Root nodded, fairly pleased with himself. "Right, until they stopped chasing me. Then I followed them from a distance, until they got to this camp. Then I flew back to find Jade. We left the others, so we could get back here by dark."

Chime glanced up from the herb packets. "That was smart."

"I know." Then Root popped up and cuffed Chime in the head. "Ow!" Chime protested in outrage, reeling back.

"I heard what you said earlier. I'm not stupid," Root said, coming back to sit next to Moon. "I have a big mouth, but I'm not stupid. There's a difference. A big difference."

"Hey, no hitting," Moon said belatedly. Though he figured Root probably did owe Chime that one.

"I'm sorry." Chime subsided, looking abashed.

"Jade's back," Moon said, and got to his feet.

Jade dropped down to the platform and flung the dazed warrior to the ground. She was in groundling form, a tall woman with light bronze skin and reddish hair. Her shirtsleeves were torn, and there were scratch marks on her arms, and a few rapidly darkening marks on her face about the size of Jade's fist. "Are you happy?" Jade shouted at Moon.

"Yes," he told her. "But I'm easy to please right now."

Oddly enough, Jade didn't appreciate the joke.

While she paced, fumed, and made certain that any of Halcyon's warriors still lurking in the area knew that a rescue attempt would end in a bloodbath, Root tied up the female warrior and Chime made the simple. Halcyon was groaning and starting to wake by the time he finished, but once it was administered she settled into a deep sleep. While searching the packs left behind for rope, Moon found a cake of very good tea, so he built up the fire again, filled the dented kettle from a waterskin, and made some. Chime and Root went to scout for injured warriors, and found three dead, victims of the first clash with Jade. They found a few blood trails, but the survivors must have retrieved all their wounded.

Darkness had fallen and it was well into the night before the Indigo Cloud warriors arrived. It was good timing, because it had taken about that long for Jade to calm down.

While Chime and Root greeted them and answered questions and traded various congratulations and re-criminations, Moon stood up and stretched his back. His headache had gone, but he had spent most of the time sitting by the fire, watching Jade stare grimly at Halcyon's unconscious body, braced to intervene if she suddenly changed her mind about leaving the other queen alive.

Moon circled around the fire to the shadows where Jade stood. "I'm sorry," he said. "I know you wanted to rescue me, again."

"I did rescue you," she pointed out, though she sounded more huffy than angry. Her sigh was too weary to be a hiss. "Did you have to hit her with the kettle?"

"It had a handle. It was easier than a rock." Moon felt some of the tension melt out of his spine. As impressive as she was while enraged and defending her consort, he still liked her normal self better.

"It's not going to make a very good story, in the annals of my time as sister queen." She quoted dryly, "'Then her consort jumped up and knocked the foreign queen unconscious with a kettle.'"

"If Cloud had been fast with a kettle, then you wouldn't be here," Moon admitted.

"That is hardly fair to Indigo. Indigo was nothing like—" She waved a hand back toward the camp. "That."

Before she could get worked up again, he took her wrist. "Come on, the others can keep watch. Let's go to bed."

"Sometimes you have good ideas," she said grudgingly, and let him tow her over to the shelter.

(

The trip to Emerald Twilight took a day and a half, with Jade and Balm taking turns carrying the unconscious Halcyon, and Vine carrying the woman warrior, whose name turned out to be Torrent. During the awkward and desultory conversation around the camp at night, she admitted that she was from a queen's clutch, sister to Tempest and Halcyon. She seemed to feel bad enough, so Moon managed not to ask her if there were any sisters besides Tempest from that clutch who weren't crazy.

They knew Halcyon's surviving warriors followed them at a distance, but none of them ventured any closer, or tried to talk to them. Balm said, "I bet they would have tried to stop us if we were heading toward Indigo Cloud. But they know we must be taking her back to Emerald Twilight. They're probably going to quietly slip back into the colony, and hope Ice is too distracted by dealing with Halcyon to worry about who was with her."

Once they arrived at the court, Jade didn't waste any time. She dropped the still limp Halcyon on the landing platform outside the greeting hall, and Vine set the woman warrior down. At first the warriors and Arbora who hurried out seemed to think that they had found Halcyon and Torrent injured in the forest, and brought them back here for help. It was reassuring evidence that only Halcyon's group of warriors had been involved in the plot, and that most of the court had known nothing about it. But it made Moon feel even worse for those about to hear the truth. Then Jade demanded a mentor be called as witness, and the whole colony had seemed to go still.

One of the older mentors who had helped Flower came out, and Tempest, Ash, and three of the other sister queens, and every warrior and Arbora who could get outside in time. They all listened in shocked silence to Torrent's guilty recital. Tempest kept her expression under control, though her spines trembled with the effort. Ash kept alternately flaring hers and flattening them, looking from Jade to Tempest to the other queens, incredulous and horrified.

Afterward, Tempest stiffly offered Jade hospitality, seemed relieved when Jade refused it, and they left. Ice and Shadow hadn't appeared, and Moon was glad for it, because the whole thing had been deeply embarrassing. He made a resolution to ask Stone if he had ever fathered any clutches who tried to kill each other and what to do if they did.

It was a relief to be shed of Halcyon and Torrent, and they made good time back to Indigo Cloud, reaching it during the late afternoon five days later.

As they approached the colony tree, Moon could see already that the Arbora had made progress while they were gone.

Several of the garden platforms had neat planting beds built, others had plots that had been stripped of grass and were now covered with turned earth. The weeds and moss that had choked the main runoff pools were gone, the deadfall cleared away from some of the old orchards. There were Arbora out on the platforms too, digging in the gardens, weeding, moving baskets of dirt. The two flying boats were still anchored in place, with a few Arbora climbing over them, sanding claw-damaged wood and making other repairs.

Warrior lookouts had already spotted them and carried the word to the tree. More warriors flew out to meet them, and swooped around and called out greetings. Moon and Jade and the others landed in the knothole and were almost swept through the passage into the greeting hall by a happy swarm of Arbora.

The well rapidly filled up with Raksura, coming up the stairs from the level below or dropping down from above.

All the shell-lights were lit, and caught reflections off the polished wood and the rich carving, the slim pillars along the criss-crossed stairs, the overhanging balconies. The waterfall across from the entrance ran clear and fresh, streaming down the wall to the pool in the floor, which now boasted floating flowers.

Heart pushed her way through the growing crowd to hug Jade impulsively, and tell her, "We were so worried! We expected you days ago!"

"We were delayed unexpectedly. I have to tell Pearl about it first." Jade released Heart and asked anxiously, "What about the seed? Is it all right?"

Heart admitted, "We're not sure yet. The instructions the Emerald Twilight mentors sent said it had to be coated in mud from below the roots and then soaked in heartwater." Before Moon could ask, she said, "That's the water drawn up through the roots. We had to get it just as it came out of the wood, through the spring in the top of the tree. But first we had to find the spring. That took most of a day. Stone thought he knew where it was, but apparently it moves around when the tree grows. Or that's what Stone said, anyway. Now we're just waiting to see if it will show the signs that it's ready to be placed in the tree."

"I see." Jade exchanged a worried look with Moon. It had been a big unspoken fear that all Ardan's meddling with the seed might have damaged it somehow. Moon had been hoping that fear would be banished by the time they arrived. It wasn't good to hear that they would still have to wait and see.

Heart turned to Chime, and they looked at each other a long moment. They had been Flower's last students, and Chime couldn't act on her teaching anymore. Heart stepped forward and Chime caught her in his arms, burying his face against her shoulder.

Stone wandered up out of the crowd, stopped and eyed Moon for a moment, then nudged his shoulder. "You all right?"

"Yes." Suddenly that was all Moon could trust himself to say. He felt like he had never really come home before, not to a permanent home, not to a place where everyone knew the real him. He couldn't even trust himself to shift to his groundling form, even though it was technically rude to stay like this while Stone was a groundling. What he really wanted to do was run away and hide in a corner, and enjoy this intense, unaccustomed feeling privately.

Then Pearl dropped down from the levels above. Arbora and warriors scattered to make way for her. River impulsively started toward her, and remembered just in time to stop and wait with the others, while she greeted Jade. Moon was so emotional at the moment he even felt a spark of pity. River might sleep in Pearl's bower, but he would never be her consort, anymore than Chime could ever be an Arbora again.

"You're late," Pearl said, and frowned at Jade. "Stone was ready to go out looking for you." Then her gaze hardened. She had obviously spotted the recent scratches on Jade's scales, though they had faded over the past few days. Knowing Pearl, she might even be able to tell they had been made by another queen. Her spines started to lift in agitation. "What happened?"

Jade set her jaw and braced herself. "Halcyon, a sister queen from Emerald Twilight, tried to steal Moon."

Moon had half-expected Pearl to express disappointment that Halcyon hadn't succeeded. But Pearl's eyes went black with fury. Her spines stiffened, until they flared out around her head.

Stone lifted his brows and gave Moon an incredulous look. Moon shrugged helplessly. Pearl ignored them. Her voice flat, she said to Jade, "Did you kill her?"

Jade's spines lifted in response, but she kept her temper. She said, "No." Her voice heavy with irony, she said, "I was persuaded not to."

Moon belatedly shifted to groundling. The last thing he wanted at the moment was Pearl's attention. But Pearl stayed focused on Jade. She tilted her head, her gaze hard-

ened to ice. "Why not?" The words dropped into a near perfect silence. No one in the hall breathed. Moon could hear
the breeze rustling leaves outside.

Jade flicked her spines. "I didn't want to start a war. We
took her back to Emerald Twilight with one of her warriors,
and made the warrior speak before a mentor." She paused,
and added deliberately, "They owe us a great debt now."

Pearl was silent for so long there were probably warriors in
the hall starting to suffer from lack of air. Then she said, "I'm
surprised you thought of that, in the heat of the moment."

Moon tried not to react in any way. He wondered if he
had made things worse by talking Jade out of immediate
vengeance. But Jade was calm and didn't take Pearl's bait.
She said, "It seemed the best course."

Pearl held her gaze a moment more, then said, "We'll see."

She turned away, and the whole hall took a collective
breath of relief. Out of the corner of his eye, Moon saw
Chime's knees buckle, and Heart and Balm reach hastily to
steady him.

As the crowd parted for Pearl, she lifted one hand in a
signal to River. He hurried after her. Moon regretted the
sympathetic impulse. Keeping his voice low, he said, "He'll
tell her everything that happened."

"So he will." Jade wasn't worried. The long flight here
from Emerald Twilight had evidently given her a much
more sanguine perspective on the situation. "She'll see the
advantages."

"Somebody needs to tell me everything that happened,"
Stone pointed out. "But you need to do it on the way to the
nurseries, because Frost accused me of leaving you somewhere for dead, and she's managed to convince the rest of
the clutches that she's right."

Moon winced. When he had left, he had been afraid of
something like that happening, but there hadn't been any
real choice.

Jade took his wrist and pulled him with her as she followed Stone. She said, wryly, "We'll both go. I think I need
to spend more time with Frost."

Moon thought that was probably the best thing they could do.

☾

They held the farewell for Flower later that evening, after Jade and Moon and the warriors had had a chance to sleep and rest. The Arbora had found a niche in one of the walls up in the unused Aeriat levels, which Stone said was one of the old grave niches for royal urns. Heart and the other mentors didn't know how to make the wood grow to seal the niche yet, but it would still make a good resting place.

The whole court sang for Flower. Moon didn't contribute, but he made himself sit still for the whole uncomfortable performance. It wasn't as eerie this time, though it still felt alien to him.

Afterward, Moon ended up sitting outside with Chime on a ledge above the waterfall. They watched the tiny flying lizards chase lightbugs in the spray, while the sun set somewhere past the mountain-trees and the green twilight deepened toward darkness. The whole court felt tense and uneasy. From what Moon understood, either the seed would show that it was ready to be reattached to the tree within the next day or so, or it wouldn't. There was nothing to do now but wait.

Chime said suddenly, "They're choosing a new chief mentor tonight."

That was an uncomfortable thought. The balance of power in the court was already delicate. Moon asked, "Who is it going to be?"

"Probably Heart."

That was an uncomfortable thought for a different reason. After the fight to escape the Dwei hive, Heart hadn't been able to put Moon into a healing trance. "But she's so young."

"That's not actually a problem," Chime said, though he still sounded depressed. "You want someone young, to grow into it. And she still has all the other mentors to help her. Heart is reasonable, and good at settling differences, and Pearl and Jade both trust her. She was Flower's second . . . first choice as a successor."

"The first choice after you," Moon said, then realized a moment later that he should have withheld that thought.

"But I'm not a choice anymore," Chime said, sounding less depressed but more exasperated.

"Sorry."

Chime shook his head. "It's all right. It's just . . . I wish I could help with the seed."

Moon wished Chime could help, too. He tried to imagine packing the two flying boats again and heading off for some new destination, and it felt like a little stab in the heart. He wanted to stay here.

Stone had been right from the beginning. The court belonged here. And Moon meant to belong here, too.

☾

Late that night, when Moon and Jade were asleep in their bower on the teachers' level, someone banged loudly on the hanging bed. Moon, closest to the bottom, started awake and Jade rolled off him with a growl. They both leaned over the edge to see Blossom looking up at them expectantly. She said, "It's the seed! It's ready!"

Moon realized he could hear a lot of movement and voices out in the passage. Jade gasped, vaulted out of the bed, and bolted out of the room with Blossom. Still half-asleep, Moon climbed out, got his clothes on, and joined the trickle of Arbora moving toward the nearest stairs. Moon passed Niran, half-dressed and bleary with sleep, his long hair wrapped up in a scarf for the night. "What is it?" Niran asked.

"They think the seed's ready," Moon said as he passed by. "They're going to try to attach it to the tree."

"Ahh! Good luck!" Niran called after him.

Moon followed the others all the way down to the lower level where the seed's chamber lay. The corridors leading to it were already packed with Arbora and warriors, everyone whispering anxiously. Some had shifted and clung to vantage points on the low ceiling, though Moon didn't think they would have much of a view up there, either. He was standing on tiptoes, trying to get an idea of what was happening, when Balm elbowed her way through the crowd, grabbed him by the wrist, and unceremoniously hauled him back with her through the passage and up to the door of the seed chamber.

Jade was there in a little group with Pearl, Stone, and Chime, and the leaders of the Arbora, Bone, Bell, and Knell. River and Pearl's other warriors crammed into the corridor behind Pearl. Balm deposited Moon at Jade's side, and Jade whispered, "What were you doing back there?"

"I didn't know I was supposed to be up here."

Pearl hissed at them to be quiet and Moon gave up on an explanation.

The door was open and the seed chamber softly lit. From here Moon could see the mentors all in the small room, standing back against the walls. Even Copper, the young mentor-to-be, had been brought from the nurseries. He stood next to Merit and clung to the older mentor's leg. Heart knelt in the center of the room, holding the seed.

It was easy to see how they had known the seed was ready. The hard outer husk had softened and was now covered with soft white petals. Another female mentor crouched beside Heart, holding a sketch that they compared the seed to. "It looks right," the other mentor muttered. "It should be sprouting."

"I think I feel tendrils," Heart said, gently lifting one of the petals. She looked back at Stone. "Should we try?"

Stone shrugged, not helpfully. Pearl said, "Just go ahead."

Heart took a deep breath and set the seed carefully into the cradle in the center of the web of dried and broken tendrils. Moon realized he was holding his breath along with everyone else.

Heart said, "I think now we just have to wait. It's bound to take time to— Everyone, out!"

As the mentors scrambled to get out of the room, Moon fell back with Jade and the others to make space for them in the foyer. As the last mentor hopped out of the chamber, Moon saw that the seed had sprouted new white tendrils. They snaked out and twined around the crumbling remnants of the dead tendrils to follow their path into the heartwood. The tension ran out of Moon's body and he leaned back against the wall, letting his breath out. *That's it,* he thought. The seed was alive and well and back in its place.

"It worked," Chime said, his voice trembling, and the word passed through the crowded passages, a growing murmur of relief.

Stone pushed the chamber door closed, and said, "Well, we're home now."

☽

APPENDIX I

AERIAT

Queens

> Pearl—Reigning Queen
> Jade—Sister Queen
> Amber—former Sister Queen, now dead
> Azure—the queen who took Stone, now dead
> Frost—a fledgling queen of the court of Sky Copper, now adopt-
> ed by Indigo Cloud

Consorts

> Stone—line-grandfather
> Rain—Pearl's last consort, now dead
> Moon—Jade's consort
> Thorn and Bitter—fledgling consorts of Sky Copper, now adopt-
> ed by Indigo Cloud

Warriors

> River—leader of Pearl's faction of warriors. A product of
> one of Amber's royal clutches.
> Drift—River's clutchmate
> Branch—River and Drift's clutchmate, killed in a Fell ambush
> Root—young warrior from an Arbora clutch, a member of Jade's
> faction
> Song—young female warrior, a member of Jade's faction
> Spring—fledgling female, one of only two survivors from Am-
> ber's last clutch of warriors
> Snow—fledgling male, Spring's clutchmate
> Balm—female warrior, and Jade's clutchmate. Jade's stron-
> gest supporter and leader of her faction.
> Chime—former Arbora mentor, now a warrior, a member of
> Jade's faction
> Vine and Coil—male warriors of Pearl's faction, though they

chafe under River's authority
Floret—female warrior of Pearl's faction
Sand—a young male warrior of Jade's faction
Sorrow—female warrior who took care of Moon as a fledgling, killed by Tath

ARBORA

Mentors

Flower—leader of the Mentor Caste
Heart—young female mentor, one of the Arbora rescued from the Dwei Hive by Moon
Merit—young male mentor, rescued with Heart
Copper—a young male mentor, still in the nurseries

Teachers

Petal—former leader of the Teachers' Caste, killed in the Fell attack on the old Indigo Cloud colony
Bell—new leader of the Teachers' Caste, and clutchmate to Chime
Blossom—an older female, one of only two teachers to escape during the Fell attack on the colony. Later learned to pilot a Golden Isles Wind-ship.
Bead—a young female, she escaped the colony with Blossom
Rill, Bark, and Weave—female teachers
Gift, Needle, and Dream—young female teachers, rescued from the Dwei Hive by Moon
Snap—young male teacher, also rescued from the Dwei Hive

Hunters

Bone—leader of the Hunters' Caste
Braid, Salt, Spice, Knife—male hunters
Bramble—a female hunter
Strike—a very young male hunter, who volunteered to test the Fell poison

Soldiers

Knell—leader of Soldiers' Caste, and clutchmate to Chime

APPENDIX II

EXCERPT FROM *OBSERVATIONS OF THE RAKSURA:*
VOLUME THIRTY-SEVEN OF A NATURAL HISTORY
BY SCHOLAR-PREEMINENT
DELIN-EVRAN-LINDEL

The Two Breeds of the Raksura

ARBORA: Arbora have no wings but are agile climbers, and their scales appear in a variety of colors. They have long tails, sharp retractable claws, and manes of flexible spines and soft "frills," characteristics that are common to all Raksura. They are expert artisans and are dexterous and creative in the arts they pursue for the court's greater good. In their alternate form they are shorter than Aeriat Raksura and have stocky, powerful builds. Both male and female Arbora are fertile, and sometimes may have clutches that include warrior fledglings. This is attributed to queens and consorts blending their bloodlines with Arbora over many generations.

The four castes of the Arbora are:

Teachers—They supervise the nurseries and train the young of the court. They are also the primary artisans of the court, and tend the gardens that will be seen around any Raksuran colony.

Hunters—They take primary responsibility for providing food for the court. This includes hunting for game and gathering wild plants.

Soldiers—They guard the ground and protect the colony and the surrounding area.

Mentors—They are Arbora born with arcane powers, who have skill in healing and augury. They also act as historians and record-keepers for the court, and usually advise the queens.

AERIAT: The winged Raksura. Like the Arbora, they have long tails, sharp retractable claws, and manes of flexible spines and soft frills.

Warriors—They act as scouts and guardians, and defend the colony from threats from the air, such as the Fell. Warriors are sterile and cannot breed, though they appear as male and female forms. Their scales are in any number of bright colors. Female warriors are usually somewhat stronger than male warriors. In their alternate form, they are always tall and slender. They are not as long-lived generally as queens, consorts, and Arbora.

Consorts—Consorts are fertile males, and their scales are always black, though there may be a tint or undersheen of gold, bronze, or blood red. At maturity they are stronger than warriors, and may be the longest lived of any Raksura. They are also the fastest and most powerful flyers, and this ability increases as they grow older. There is some evidence to suggest that consorts of great age may grow as large or larger than the major kethel of the Fell.

Queens—Queens are fertile females, and are the most powerful and deadly fighters of all the Aeriat. Their scales have two brilliant colors, the second in a pattern over the first. The queens' alternate form resembles an Arbora, with no wings, but retaining the tail, and an abbreviated mane of spines and the softer frills. Queens mate with consorts to produce royal clutches, composed of queens, consorts, and warriors.

Appendix III

Excerpt from
Additions to the List of Predatory Species
by scholar-eminent-posthumous
Venar-Inram-Alil.

Fell are migratory and prey on other intelligent species.

The Known Classes of Fell

Major kethel—The largest of the Fell, sometimes called harbingers, major kethel are often the first sign that a Fell flight is approaching. Their scales are black, like that of all Fell, and they have an array of horns around their heads. They have a low level of intelligence and are believed to be always under the control of the rulers.

Minor dakti—The dakti are small, with armor plates on the back and shoulders, and webbed wings. They are somewhat cunning, but not much more intelligent than kethel, and fight in large swarms.

Rulers—Rulers are intelligent creatures that are believed to have some arcane powers of entrancement over other species. Rulers related by blood are also believed to share memories and experiences through some mental bond. They have complete control of the lesser Fell in their flights, and at times can speak through dakti and see through their eyes. (*Addendum by scholar-preeminent Delin-Evran-lindel: Fell rulers in their winged form bear an unfortunate and superficial resemblance to Raksuran Consorts.*)
There is believed to be a fourth class, or possibly a female variant of the Rulers, called the *Progenitors*.

Common lore holds that if a Fell ruler is killed, its head must be removed and stored in a cask of salt or yellow mud and buried on land in order to prevent drawing other Fell rulers to the site of its death. It is possible that only removing the head from the corpse may be enough to prevent this, but burying it is held to be the safest course.

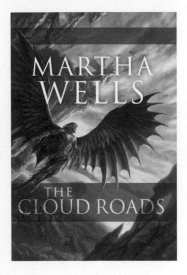

THE CLOUD ROADS:
VOLUME ONE OF THE BOOKS
OF THE RAKSURA
978-1-59780-216-1
TRADE PAPERBACK / $14.99
(AVAILABLE NOW)
978-1-949102-18-5
MASS MARKET PAPERBACK /
$7.99 (AVAILABLE NOW)

Moon has spent his life hiding what he is: a shape-shifter able to transform himself into a winged creature of flight.

An orphan with only vague memories of his own kind, Moon tries to fit in among the tribes of his river valley, with mixed success. Just as he is once again cast out by his adopted tribe, he discovers a shape-shifter like himself— someone who seems to know exactly what he is, who promises that Moon will be welcomed into the shape-shifter community.

What this stranger doesn't tell Moon is that his presence will tip the balance of power, that his extraordinary lineage is crucial to the colony's survival, and that his people face extinction at the hands of the dreaded Fell! Now Moon must overcome a lifetime of conditioning in order to save himself . . . and his newfound kin.

AVAILABLE FROM NIGHT SHADE BOOKS
WWW.NIGHTSHADEBOOKS.COM

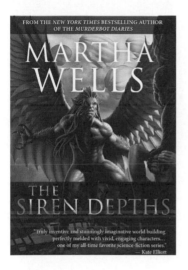

THE SIREN DEPTHS: VOLUME THREE OF THE BOOKS OF THE RAKSURA
978-1-59780-440-0
TRADE PAPERBACK / $14.99 (AVAILABLE NOW)
978-1-949102-30-7
MASS MARKET PAPERBACK / $7.99 (COMING FEBRUARY 2020)

All his life, Moon roamed the Three Worlds, a solitary wanderer forced to hide his true nature — until he was reunited with his own kind, the Raksura, and found a new life as consort to Jade, sister queen of the Indigo Cloud court.

But now a rival court has laid claim to him, and Jade may or may not be willing to fight for him. Beset by doubts, Moon must travel in the company of strangers to a distant realm where he will finally face the forgotten secrets of his past, even as an old enemy returns with a vengeance. The Fell, a vicious race of shape-shifting predators, menaces groundlings and Raksura alike.

Determined to crossbreed with the Raksura for arcane purposes, they are driven by an ancient voice that cries out from . . . the siren depths.

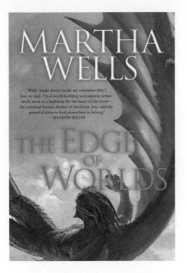

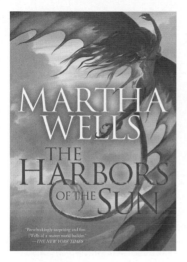

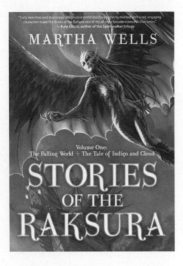

STORIES OF THE RAKSURA, VOLUME ONE: THE FALL-ING WORLD & THE TALE OF INDIGO AND CLOUD
978-1-59780-535-3
Trade paperback / $15.99
(available now)

In "The Falling World," Jade, sister queen of the Indigo Cloud Court, has traveled with Chime and Balm to another Raksuran court. When she fails to return, her consort, Moon, along with Stone and a party of warriors and hunters, must track them down. Finding them turns out to be the easy part. . . .

"The Tale of Indigo and Cloud" explores the history of the Indigo Cloud Court, long before Moon was born. In the distant past, Indigo stole Cloud from Emerald Twilight. But in doing so, the reigning Queen Cerise and Indigo are now poised for a conflict that could spark war throughout all the courts of the Reaches.

AVAILABLE FROM NIGHT SHADE BOOKS
WWW.NIGHTSHADEBOOKS.COM

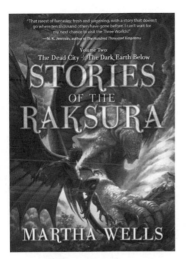

STORIES OF THE RAKSURA,
VOLUME TWO: THE DEAD
CITY & THE DARK EARTH
BELOW
978-1-59780-537-7
TRADE PAPERBACK / $15.99
(AVAILABLE NOW)

"The Dead City" is a tale of Moon before he came to the Indigo Court. As Moon is fleeing the ruins of Saraseil, a groundling city destroyed by the Fell, he flies right into another potential disaster when a friendly caravanserai finds itself under attack by a strange force.

In "The Dark Earth Below," Moon and Jade face their biggest adventure yet; their first clutch. But even as Moon tries to prepare for impending fatherhood, members of the Kek village in the colony tree's roots go missing, and searching for them only leads to more mysteries as the court is stalked by an unknown enemy.

ABOUT THE AUTHOR

Martha Wells has written many fantasy novels, including The Books of the Raksura series (beginning with *The Cloud Roads*), the Ile-Rien series (including *The Death of the Necromancer*) as well as YA fantasy novels, short stories, media tie-ins (for Star Wars and Stargate: Atlantis), and non-fiction. Her most recent fantasy novel is *The Harbors of the Sun* in 2017, the final novel in The Books of the Raksura series. She has a new series of SF novellas, The Murderbot Diaries, published by Tor.com in 2017 and 2018. She was also the lead writer for the story team of Magic: the Gathering's Dominaria expansion in 2018. She has won a Nebula Award, a Hugo Award, an ALA/YALSA Alex Award, a Locus Award, and her work has appeared on the Philip K. Dick Award ballot, the USA Today Bestseller List, and the *New York Times* Bestseller List. Her books have been published in eleven languages.